Twenty years ago Kylie Chan married a Hong Kong national in a traditional Chinese wedding ceremony in Eastern China. She and her husband lived in Australia for eight years, then in Hong Kong for ten years. She has seen a great deal of Chinese culture and come to appreciate the customs and way of life.

Two years ago she closed down her successful IT consultancy company in Hong Kong and moved back to Australia. She decided to use her knowledge of Chinese mythology, culture, and martial arts to weave a story that would appeal to a wide audience.

Since returning to Australia, Kylie has studied kung fu (Wing Chun and Southern Chow Clan styles) as well as tai chi and is now a senior belt in both forms. She has also made an intensive study of Buddhist and Taoist philosophy and has brought all of these together into her storytelling.

Kylie is a mother of two who lives in Brisbane.

WHITE TIGER

DARK HEAVENS: BOOK ONE

KYLIE CHAN

HARPER
Voyager

HarperVoyager
An imprint of HarperCollinsPublishers
77–85 Fulham Palace Road,
Hammersmith, London W6 8JB

www.harpercollins.co.uk

This paperback edition 2011
1

First published in Australia by
Voyager 2006

A catalogue record for this book is
available from the British Library

ISBN: 978 0 00 734979 1

Set in Sabon 9.5/12 by Helen Beard, ECJ Australia Pty Ltd

Printed and bound in Great Britain by
Clays Ltd, St Ives plc

MIX
Paper from
responsible sources

FSC
www.fsc.org

FSC® C007454

For my sister, Fiona,
my best friend, Alana,
and most of all my fantastic kids,
William and Madeleine.

At the bottom of the
Mariana Trench, where
the water is freezing and dark,
a great black Serpent
sleeps in the mud.

CHAPTER ONE

'Emma, this is your final warning. If you do not wear a suit to my kindergarten, I will dock your pay.' Miss Kwok glared at me over her expensive reading glasses. 'Jeans are not acceptable at any of my kindergartens. More smartly dressed. Remember.'

I didn't say anything. I just wanted to be out of her office and up to Mr Chen's place.

'Your hair is unacceptable as well. You should come with me to the salon. Your hair is messy, you don't wear make-up — really, Emma, your whole appearance is just not good enough. You should work harder to make yourself more presentable.'

A flood of words hit the back of my throat. I swallowed them all.

'I have had some complaints from the parents.' She shuffled the papers on the desk. Her face suggested she was in her early forties — the work of an excellent plastic surgeon — but her hands showed her true age. 'The parents say you are spending too much time talking with the children and not enough time teaching them the ABC's.'

'Talking is the best way to learn English,' I said.

'Well, make sure they learn their ABC's. They need

3

to be able to recite the alphabet and spell some words to pass the examinations for first grade. They're here to cram for the best schools, you know that.'

I tried to control my expression as I thought about what I'd like to do to a school that had examinations for entry into first grade.

'Well?'

I shrugged. 'It's your school, Miss Kwok. I'll do more ABC's.'

'I do not like your attitude sometimes, Emma.' She became more fierce. 'Oh, and stop wasting the drawing materials. I only budget for one set a year and they're using them too much.'

I glanced at my watch. 'Is that all? I'm supposed to be at Mr Chen's in less than an hour.'

'How is the work going with Mr Chen?'

'He's taken every private spot I have. He's my only private client now.'

This caught her attention. 'He is the only client you have outside the kindergarten?'

I nodded.

'But I gave your number to quite a few people I know. Don't tell me you're so lazy you have stopped working for them. You should work until 11 p.m., you make good money. Don't waste your evenings doing nothing.'

'As people left Hong Kong and private teaching slots freed up, he took the times. I think he even negotiated with some of the parents to release me so I could look after Simone. Which suits me just fine, really, because she's the most delightful child I've ever worked with.'

She studied me intently. 'Do you like working for him?'

'Sure. He's very nice.'

'How would you like to earn a little more money?'

'You already pay me very well, Miss Kwok.'

4

Her eyes rested heavily on mine. 'If you tell me about some of his business dealings, the names of the people who go in and out of his house while you're working there, you could earn even more.'

I stared at her.

'I could make it very good for you.'

'No.'

She lifted her head slightly. 'You will do this for me, Emma.'

'No,' I said. 'I resign.'

'You can't resign. You will stay with me.'

'I'll have a resignation letter on your desk tomorrow morning.'

She grimaced with exasperation.

I met her eyes and held them. 'I resign.'

'Nobody in Hong Kong will pay you as well as I do.'

'I don't care,' I said. 'I'll find something.'

'You have to give me two weeks' notice,' she said. 'You have to continue to work for me for two weeks, Emma.'

'I feel a sudden bout of the flu coming on,' I said, then rose and went out without looking back.

My friend, April, was sitting at the computer outside Miss Kwok's office, with her fiancé, Andy, hovering behind her. April was a lovely Australian-born Chinese who worked as a systems programmer in a bank, but occasionally came in to help with the computers at the kindergarten. She had a soft, kind face framed by shoulder-length hair dyed a rich russet brown.

'Hi, April, bye, April. Gotta run, I'm late for Mr Chen,' I said as I hurried past.

'We going for Thai Saturday?' April called after me.

I stopped. 'Yeah. Wan Chai.'

Andy, a slim, well-dressed Chinese guy, glanced unsmiling over the top of April's head at me. 'I can't come,' he said. 'I have to be in China. Don't stay out too late.'

I didn't like the way Andy looked at me. 'Oh, that's too bad,' I said, trying to sound disappointed.

'Saturday, then,' April said, and turned back to the screen. 'We should do another backup.'

'As long as we don't lose any of the data. It's very important,' Andy said.

I leaned against the divider in the MTR carriage and mused. Done it again. But I was thoroughly sick of being bullied by Miss Kwok; no amount of money she paid me would compensate.

I shook my head as the carriage swayed through the darkness of the Cross-Harbour Tunnel. I couldn't believe her nerve, asking me to tell her about Mr Chen's activities. I knew she had more business interests than just the chain of kindergartens; she was one of the wealthiest women in Hong Kong. People called her the Merry Widow, the Social Godmother. But asking me to spy on my private clients was way over the line.

I sighed. I had a tidy nest egg saved: the combination of Miss Kwok's excellent salary with the fat cheques I'd received from private clients over the last four years. It'd keep me going for a while. I wasn't ready to return to Australia and a mundane life in suburbia. At only twenty-eight I felt no great rush to settle into anything boring.

I tried to tidy my hair — as usual my short brown ponytail had come out everywhere. Nobody took any notice of me; I was just an uninteresting Westerner, the only one on the train. Medium height, about five six; slightly overweight. Plain clothes, plain face, plain brown shoulder-length hair. Nothing special at all. But my skills as an English teacher were highly sought after in Hong Kong. I wouldn't have any trouble finding something new.

Or maybe Singapore. Gifted English teachers were always welcome in Singapore, and the correspondence course I was halfway through could be taken from anywhere in the world.

The train stopped at Admiralty station and I joined the rush onto the platform. I rode the escalator up to ground level and the terminal where I could take a bus to Mr Chen's apartment on the Peak.

The traffic noise and polluted air hit me like a physical force as I walked out of the station. Chinese New Year had just finished — the Year of the Horse in 2002 had begun. The late February weather was cool, but there was a hint of humidity in the breeze that suggested the presence of the stifling summer just around the corner.

Maybe Singapore.

'And then the Dark King kissed the Dark Queen and the baby Princess goodbye,' four-year-old Simone said, moving the Lego figures around on the cream carpet.

'Why is he the Dark King?' I said.

'Because he is, silly Emma.' Simone leaned forward as she moved the Lego, and her tawny hair fell over her shoulders. Her mother had been European, giving her flawless porcelain skin and light brown eyes. 'The bad people came, and scared the Dark Queen, and she ran away.'

She made the Queen figure run, until another block — obviously the bad people — smacked into her and she fell. She picked up a white block and flew it over the figures. 'The White Tiger came to help, but the Dark Queen was already gone. The Dark King came back ...' she returned the Dark King figure '... but the Dark Queen was gone, and the King and Princess cried together, and hugged, and promised to look after each other forever and ever.'

7

'That's a really sad story, Simone,' I said. 'Let's bring the Queen back, maybe?'

She shrugged, and appeared to be about to say something, then froze. Her face went blank, then she lit up. 'Daddy's home!'

The complicated gears on the metal gate outside the front door clashed, then the lock on the door rattled. Simone leapt to her feet and dashed through the living room. '*Daddy*!'

Mr Chen came in. Simone's father was in his mid-forties, and tall for a Chinese, at more than six feet. He wore an old-fashioned Chinese cotton jacket and pants, all in black, and moved with restrained power that hinted at hard muscle. He had very long hair, well past his waist, and as usual it had come out from its tie and fallen over his shoulder. He ignored it as he kicked off his shoes.

When he saw Simone, he bent and held a hand out to her. She raced to him with her arms up and he hoisted her easily with one hand, and with the other snapped the sword he'd been carrying into its clips on the wall.

Simone threw her little arms around his neck and kissed him loudly on the cheek. He smiled at her, his dark eyes sparkling, then saw me over her shoulder and nodded, more serious. 'Miss Donahoe.'

I rose and nodded back to him; I was always careful to treat Chinese employers with respect. Employer. He was the only one left now.

'And what have you been doing?' he asked Simone.

'Ngoh tong Emma —' Simone began.

'English, Simone,' he said with mock ire.

Simone giggled and started again. 'Me and Emma are playing Lego. We're having fun.'

'Good.' He lowered her carefully. 'Go and play with Miss Donahoe.' He turned to the door in the hallway behind him. 'Monica!'

Monica, the Filipina domestic helper, opened the kitchen door part-way and poked her head out. She saw Mr Chen, threw the door open, and came into the hallway, wiping her hands on a towel. She was short, round and middle-aged, with a kind face. 'Sorry, sir, didn't know you were home.' She saw the Lego strewn on the living room carpet. 'Sorry about the mess, sir, I'll clean it up.'

'Don't worry about that,' he said. 'Make me some noodles while I take a shower. Ho fan, soup, choy sum. Not too much, I may go out again later.' He stopped and a look of concentration passed across his face. 'Why is Leo downstairs?'

'He's washing the car,' Monica said. 'It was very dirty, sir.'

'Call him on his mobile and tell him to come back up right now,' Mr Chen said.

Monica disappeared into the kitchen.

Mr Chen turned back to me. 'How long do you think you can stay, Miss Donahoe?'

'As long as you like, Mr Chen,' I said. 'I resigned from the kindergarten this afternoon, so I don't need to be in early tomorrow.'

'You've found a new job? You'll be leaving us?' he said, concerned.

'Don't go, Emma!' Simone cried.

'I won't go, I was just tired of working for Kitty Kwok. I'll find something else, but don't worry, I won't leave you.'

'Good,' Simone said, and returned to the Lego.

'So how long will you need me?' I said.

He smiled gently. 'About fifteen years. How about coming here full-time?' He raised his hand. 'Wait, don't answer, let me shower and change first, and then we can talk about it.' He strode down the hall towards his room.

'You can stay *forever*?' Simone said, wide-eyed with delight.

'I don't know, Simone,' I said. 'I'll need to think about it.'

Her little face screwed up with hope. 'Please say yes.'

The gate and the front door opened and Leo, Mr Chen's driver, came in. He was a black American, nearly six and a half feet tall and a wall of muscle. He had a spectacularly ugly face, the centrepiece of which was an artistically broken nose, but he had a kind smile and adored Simone.

'Hi, Leo,' Simone said.

'Hi, Simone, Emma.' Leo kicked off his shoes at the front door then poked his nose into the living room. 'Where is he?'

'Having a shower,' I said.

He nodded.

Simone jumped up from her Lego. 'Guess what, Leo?'

His small brown eyes sparkled at her. 'What?'

'Emma's going to stay *forever*.'

Leo glanced sharply at me. 'Is that right?'

'No, no,' I said. 'He just asked me to go full-time. But I have to think about it.'

Leo came into the living room and towered over us. He crossed his massive arms over his chest. 'Actually, Emma, it would be a good idea if you came full-time. You're the best teacher Simone's ever had.'

'Thanks, Leo, that means a lot to me.' I glanced down at Simone's hope-filled face. 'I'll think about it.'

Mr Chen came down the hallway barefoot, towelling his damp hair. He always wore incredibly scruffy clothes at home, and this evening was no exception. His black T-shirt was faded and frayed, and his black cotton pants had a large shredded hole in one knee.

He had unusually dark eyes, nearly black, and the

sculpted face of a Southern Chinese, with prominent cheekbones and a strong chin. He pulled the towel from his hair and threw it over one shoulder, then ran one hand through his long hair, tossed it back, and smiled into my eyes.

Suddenly Singapore didn't seem so good.

Then Mr Chen saw Leo and scowled. 'You. In here. Now.' He turned and went into the dining room across the hall without looking back.

Leo bowed his bald head and skulked into the dining room after Mr Chen.

'Leo's in big trouble,' Simone confided to me. 'My dad's going to yell at him *a lot*.'

'Why? He just washed the car. That's what a driver does.'

'He's not supposed to leave us alone,' Simone said, deadly serious. 'We could get hurt.'

'Hurt? Who by?'

She leaned closer and whispered, '*Bad people*.'

Good god, Leo wasn't a driver; he was a bodyguard. Kidnapping didn't happen often, but it did happen; all children of rich families in Hong Kong were targets. *Of course* Leo was a bodyguard, it was obvious. No wonder Mr Chen was so upset about him leaving us in the apartment alone.

Simone's eyes were wide. 'That's why Daddy carries his sword everywhere. Bad people.'

'Sword?' I said.

She pointed towards the sword on its clips next to the front door.

I jerked back with shock. What was he doing running around with a sword in his hand? *And why the hell hadn't I paid the sword any attention before?* I had been working part-time there for six months, and I hadn't thought to question why my employer needed to carry around a *sword*.

'Why does he need a sword, Simone?' I said. 'Does he work with the movie studios? Or teach martial arts?'

'Arts.' Simone shrugged. 'Stuff. Daddy's stuff.'

I suddenly realised that I had no idea how Mr Chen made his money, and he was obviously extremely wealthy. He could be involved in organised crime. He didn't seem like that sort of person to me, but I had to wonder.

'What kind of stuff does Daddy do?'

Before Simone could answer, the dining room door opened and Leo came out, looking cowed and miserable. He gestured with his thumb over his shoulder. 'Your turn, Emma. Simone can go to Monica for a bath.'

'I want Emma to bath me!' Simone yelled.

'I have to go and talk to your daddy about working full-time, remember?'

'Ooh, yes.' She pushed me towards the dining room. 'Go and talk to him.'

Mr Chen had tied back his long hair and was checking the mail as he ate a bowl of noodles.

'Sit, Miss Donahoe.' He pushed his ho fan noodles aside.

'Eat,' I said. 'You look starving.'

He smiled and his eyes wrinkled up. 'No, no, it can wait. Full-time. Yes or no?'

'You haven't said how much you'll pay me or what hours I'll be working, Mr Chen. I can't decide until you tell me.'

'Yes, you're quite right. How about six days a week, live-in, full-time? Sunday off — that's Monica's and Leo's day off. I can probably give you a few extra days off a month as well. Five thousand US a month.'

I fell back slightly. '*Five thousand US?*'

He nodded. 'I think it's a generous offer. Room and board as well. Is that acceptable?'

Sixty thousand US a year to be a nanny? I studied him. He seemed genuine. I'd worked for him for six months and he'd been perfectly honourable in his dealings. There was just one question I needed answered.

'Mr Chen,' I said, then finished the question in a rush, 'are you involved in anything illegal?'

He stared at me, his expression completely blank.

'I mean, is the ICAC likely to burst in with guns and drag you away?'

He stared at me a little longer, then snapped out of it. 'Nothing I am involved in is illegal. The ICAC could not possibly be interested in me. All of my activities are perfectly legal. I would never put Simone's happiness in danger.'

'Why do you have a bodyguard then?'

He watched me silently for a while, then said, 'Leo protects Simone.'

'Are there people after you?'

His eyes were very intense. 'I am powerful. That makes me a target. You don't need to worry — you will never be in danger if you work for me.'

'Is that why you carry a sword around? Don't the police stop you?'

'I never carry the sword in the street. It stays in the car when I go out.'

I leaned over the dining table. 'What do you do for a living, Mr Chen?'

His dark eyes looked straight into mine. 'I will tell you after you've worked here for a while. If you decide to stay.'

'Why wouldn't I decide to stay?'

He smoothly avoided the question. 'Will you take the job, Miss Donahoe?'

I hesitated. Sixty thousand US dollars a year, a delightful little girl and a handsome mystery man. How could I say no? 'Yes.'

He smiled, full of warmth and good humour. 'When can you start?'

'I could start tomorrow, but I'd need to sort out my rent first. Oh,' I said as I remembered, 'I have to give Miss Kwok two weeks' notice.'

He waved it away. 'I know Kitty Kwok. She gave me your number in the first place. I'll sort it out with her, and I'll fix it up with your flatmate. You can move in tomorrow if you like. You can live in?'

'Sure.'

He rose and held out his hand, and I shook it. He had surprisingly cool hands, with hard calluses on his fingers. 'Leo will help you move your belongings tomorrow,' he said. 'Welcome aboard.'

I shook my head as I went down the hall to say goodnight to Simone. Done it again. Two snap decisions in one day. That was a new record, even for me.

CHAPTER TWO

It took me more than an hour on crowded MTR and KCR trains to make it home to Sha Tin. I stopped at the shopping mall under our apartment block to grab some takeout, and when I was home I sat at our tiny four-seater table and pulled the foam box out of the plastic bag.

'Louise, come and sit down,' I called. 'I have news.'

Louise poked her head around the doorway from our minuscule kitchen. 'Wait till the water boils.'

'Okay.' I used the plastic cutlery provided by the fast-food place to attack the baked pork chop on its bed of rice.

Louise came out of the kitchen with a mug of coffee and sat across from me. Her blue eyes sparkled under her short, spiky blonde hair. She was about the same height as me, and Australian like me, but the resemblance ended there. She was thin, blonde, bony and covered in freckles; I was soft and round and not nearly as good-looking. People noticed her and ignored me, and that suited me just fine.

She gestured towards the takeaway box. 'Where's mine?'

'You starve,' I said. 'Where's my tea?'

'You die of thirst,' she said. 'What's up?'

'I'm moving in with Mr Chen,' I said. 'I'll be full-time —'

I didn't have a chance to finish because she flew to her feet and yelled with delight. 'Way to go, Emma!'

I stared at her.

'That hunky guy on the Peak? The Chinese widower? The really rich one? What a catch!'

I sighed with exasperation. 'Full-time, live-in nanny.'

'Yeah, yeah,' she said suggestively. 'I know what you mean.'

'That's all it is, Louise. Nanny. That's all.'

She sat down again. 'Geez, Emma, can't you do better than that? You have a freaking degree, girl. Go out and work for a bank or something.'

'What, like you?'

'Yeah, like me. I meet heaps of guys in the bank. Lots of traders from Europe. Really cute. What about Miss Kwok?'

'I already resigned from the kindergarten.'

'You could do a lot better than being a nanny, Emma. I'm on nearly twenty thousand a month.'

'I'll be on five thousand US a month. That's nearly forty thousand Hong Kong.'

Her mouth dropped open.

'I'll be moving out tomorrow,' I went on.

She shook her head. 'Okay. Tell me all about it. Will it be just you and him? There is *some* hope for you, isn't there?'

'Me, the bodyguard, Monica the domestic helper, and of course Simone, his daughter.'

'Bodyguard? Is he cute?'

'God, Louise, is that all you think about? Leo's a big black American, lovely guy. But I don't think he's into chicks.'

Her eyebrows creased. 'Wait a minute. Leo, you said? Big American guy? Black?'

'You know him?'

'Not personally, but I've seen him at the Last Hurrah. Really popular. Knows everybody.'

'What the hell were you doing at the Hurrah?' I demanded. 'You won't find a date there, *none* of them are into chicks.'

She shrugged. 'Sometimes it's nice to have a quiet drink in a place you won't be hit on. Scenery's always good, too.'

'That sounds like fun. Let me know next time you're going.'

'We'll still go out on the town together, right?' She was sounding concerned. 'I mean, we're going for that Thai meal with April tomorrow night. We can still go out, can't we?'

'I don't think Mr Chen will stop me,' I said. 'If he tries to he'll get a piece of my mind.'

'I believe it.' She leaned back. 'You'll need to keep paying your half of the rent until I find a new flatmate. But on your salary that won't be a problem.'

'I'll make sure you don't lose out,' I said. 'He said he'll look after you anyway.'

'He'd better,' she growled. Then her face lit up. 'Way to *go*, Emma. What a catch.'

'Nothing there.'

'Yeah, right. You haven't stopped talking about this gorgeous man with the long hair since you started working for him.'

I sighed. 'Yeah, I know, but he's the employer. Not going to happen. I'm more professional than that.'

'Geez, you're cold-blooded.'

'I wish you people would stop saying that.'

The next morning I sat in the front of the car alongside Leo, who drove me and my stuff up to the Peak in Mr Chen's monstrous black Mercedes.

'How long have you worked for Mr Chen?' I said, making conversation.

'About six years,' Leo said, 'but I worked for Mrs Chen before that.'

'You always been a bodyguard?'

He glanced at me, then turned back to the road. 'Done some other things.'

'Like what?'

He sighed. Then he obviously decided to tell me. 'In the Navy for a while. Bouncer for a while, but that was really tough, I didn't like it. Sorta fell into the bodyguard business by accident.'

'That was nice, what Mr Chen did for Louise. He didn't need to pay her out for the rest of the year like that.'

'It was the least we could do, hiring you and having you move out so quickly.'

'*We*? You and Mr Chen?'

He glanced away from the road to me. Then grinned as he looked back at the road. 'Absolutely not.'

I stared incredulously at him and his grin widened.

'*Absolutely not*,' he emphasised, without looking away from the road. 'Not Mr Chen.' He glanced at me again, then turned back to the road. '*Not* Mr Chen.'

'Okay, okay.' All right, not Mr Chen.

He was still grinning as he shook his head. He deliberately changed the subject. 'How long have you been an English teacher?'

'About four years. I just sorta fell into it when I arrived in Hong Kong,' I said, intentionally echoing him. 'Very lucrative, easy work, hours aren't very long.'

He nodded. 'Seems to be the way with most people here. Just find themselves doing something after they arrive. Where you from originally?'

'Australia.'

'Oh. I hear it's nice there.'

'Nice does not begin to describe it,' I said with feeling. 'You have no idea. You've obviously never been there.'

'Nope.'

'What does Mr Chen do for a living?'

Leo watched the road silently.

'Leo, what does Mr Chen do for a living?'

He grinned at the road. 'You'll have to ask him that. I'm just the driver.'

'Yeah, and I'm the Queen of Sheba.'

The minute I had Mr Chen pinned down I would ask him. I spent a few quiet moments enjoying the delightful concept of having Mr John Chen pinned down. And then I pulled myself together. Keep it professional, Emma.

Leo froze and his eyes glazed over. He continued to drive, but appeared not to be paying any attention to the road.

'Are you okay, Leo?'

He raised one hand to stop me, still with his eyes unfocused. Then he snapped back and quickly poked the hands-free earpiece for his mobile phone into his ear.

The phone rang and he pressed the button and spoke without hesitation. 'We'll be coming into the tunnel very soon, we're in Kowloon City. I think it'll be about another thirty, forty minutes, then you can have it, sir. Is that all right? Should I hurry?'

He nodded, listening, then said 'Sir,' and hung up.

'Mr Chen wants the car?' I said.

Leo glanced at me. 'Yes. But he'll wait, no great rush.'

'So he only has one car?'

'Yeah, we only need one. There's only four of us: him, me, Simone and Monica. Most of his staff make their own way. I drive Simone out for her lessons and I take Monica to the market.' He glanced away from the road and became more serious. 'After you've moved your stuff up there, we'll go through Simone's routine. She has lessons outside, and quite a few at home as well, and you'll be in charge of making sure she gets to them on time.'

'You'll need to show me where everything is, as well,' I said. 'And make sure you give me a set of keys.'

Leo nodded. 'Sure. Forgot about that. Tell me if I miss anything, okay?'

'Okay, Leo.'

Mr Chen's apartment building was very high on the Peak, much higher than the Peak Tower. When Leo reached the gates at the end of the overgrown drive they swung open and the security guards waved him in.

The building was eleven floors, with two enormous flats to a floor. It wasn't new, and pollution had turned the light brown tiles dingy grey with patches of mould from the damp. Hong Kong's clouds come down very low sometimes, swathing the Peak in moisture that makes everything dripping wet both summer and winter.

The view from the building was spectacular. One side overlooked Hong Kong Harbour, which was packed with highrises on both the Hong Kong Island and Kowloon sides. The other side of the building faced south, with a view over the crammed boats in Aberdeen Typhoon Shelter to the ocean stretching beyond.

An open car park surrounded the entrance lobby on the ground floor. Parked cars covered most of the land around the building. Every second one was a huge Mercedes; there were a couple of monstrous Rolls-Royce and a few exotic, extremely expensive European sports cars.

Leo parked the car, and helped me carry my boxes up in the lift to Mr Chen's apartment.

'How many square feet is this apartment, anyway?' I said when we reached the front door.

'Big enough.'

The front door was a standard wooden one, but as usual in Hong Kong it had a large steel gate in front of it. Leo entered the code for the security gate into the pad next to the wall and opened it outwards. He unlocked the deadbolt on the wooden door and held it open for me.

We kicked off our shoes at the entrance, then Leo led me down the main hall and turned right. He passed the first door and opened the second on the left. 'This is your room.'

I went in and stopped dead. It wasn't a room, it was a suite. The huge rectangular space had been divided in two: the first part was a living room with a comfortable leather couch, a small television and a desk with a computer. Further in, the bedroom had a trim modern double bed and a door on each side.

Leo lowered the box he was carrying. He opened one of the doors. 'This connects with Simone's room.' He closed the door and went to the other one. 'Your bathroom.'

'I get my own bathroom?'

'Yep. Anything you need, tell me.'

I looked around. 'This is terrific. I wasn't expecting anything as good as this.' The large picture window overlooked Hong Kong Harbour and the highrises of Kowloon beyond. 'What a view.'

'Let me show you around,' Leo said, 'and then we'll get the rest of the boxes.'

'Thanks.'

He took me out to the hallway, which ran the full width of the apartment, and pointed to the doors on the same side as my room. 'Mr Chen's bedroom. Mine. Simone's. You.'

I nodded.

'All of ours are the same size; Mr Chen's is slightly larger,' he said. He opened the door opposite. 'This is the music room.' The room had a piano, a table holding a Chinese musical instrument called a guzheng, which was something like a zither, and a black electric guitar in one corner. 'Next to the music room, the TV room. The surround sound is really good. You can use it if nobody else is.'

He stopped at the door next to my bedroom and hesitated.

'What's in there?' I said.

'You might as well know, you'll be living here. Here goes.' He opened the door.

At first I thought it was a dance studio. Soft white mats completely covered the floor. One wall was mirrors from the floor to the ceiling.

And then I saw the other wall. A fearsome array of martial arts weapons sat on racks on the floor and hung off hooks on the wall. Swords, staves, chucks, knives, axes, everything.

'Holy shit,' I said softly.

Leo crossed his arms in front of his chest. 'Use language like that in front of Mr Chen and you'll be out the door before you know it.'

I wandered closer to the weapons. I bent to lift a sword from the rack but Leo put his hand on my wrist to stop me. 'Don't touch anything. All of these are extremely sharp and you could easily get hurt. Don't come in here if the door is closed, or you could be seriously injured,' he said. 'Stay out. Okay?'

I nodded. 'Whatever you say.'

He took my elbow and gently led me out, closing the door behind us. He gestured towards the end of the hall. 'Mr Chen sometimes has ...' He hesitated, searching for the right word. '... *people* come here to learn from him. They stay in two rooms at the end of the hall there. Don't try to talk to them, they are here to ... ah, learn and not socialise. So don't talk to them, okay?'

I shrugged. 'Whatever.'

He glowered down at me. 'I mean it.'

'I won't talk to them.'

'Good.'

He led me back up the hall to the main corridor. 'Linen closet and powder room on the corner.' He gestured to the doors on the left, across the hall from the large living room with its twin cream couches and picture windows overlooking the spectacular South side of Hong Kong Island. 'Mr Chen's ...' He hesitated again. 'Study.'

'Disaster area,' I said, looking through the open door. He made a soft sound of amusement. 'I've seen some messy offices, Leo, but his absolutely has to win first prize.'

'I'll tell him you said that. Dining room next, then the kitchen.' He took me into the kitchen, past Monica who was cutting up some vegetables on the counter. He led me to the back. 'Monica's room's in the back here. Next to it, the storeroom.'

I went into the storeroom and looked around. Most of the stuff seemed to be poles covered in cloth. An enormous glass jar, easily up to my waist, sat in the corner. It appeared to be full of large black beads, like olives, and had a complicated metal seal. I bent to study it, curious.

'Don't touch that!' Leo grabbed my arm and pulled me away. 'Don't ever go near that. If you open it, it could kill you.' He released my arm. 'Don't ever go anywhere near that.'

'What the hell's it doing here if it's toxic?' I said. 'Simone could get into it.'

'She knows better, and now so do you,' he said. 'Stay away.'

'What is it? It looks like preserved fruit.'

'I think you've seen enough.' He closed the door behind us after we went out of the storeroom. 'We'll bring up the rest of your boxes, and then, if you don't mind, we'll go through Simone's schedule. She's a very busy little girl.'

'Sure.'

After dropping the boxes in my room, Leo led me into the dining room. It had a round rosewood twelve-seater table and a rosewood side table. A couple of fluid ink paintings adorned the walls.

He went out and came back with a large folder bulging with coloured paper. He thumped it onto the table between us. 'Thank God you're handling this now — this schedule is enough to drive anybody crazy.'

He opened the folder and handed me the papers one at a time. 'Chinese lessons. Violin. Piano.' He put one paper aside. 'Not singing any more. You're here full-time, so no English either.' He raised a pink piece of paper and studied it, expressionless. 'Ballet. Damn.'

'What?'

He put the paper on the table, then ran his hand over his bald head, finally dropping his hand onto the table with a slap. 'Please don't be too freaked out by this, Emma.'

'Freaked out?'

'Ballet is in Central. You've worked out that I'm a bodyguard. Okay. I'll take you down in the car and wait. You are *not* to take her *anywhere* without either me or Mr Chen along. It's because of who her dad is.'

'Who is he?'

Leo smiled slightly. 'Don't take her on public transport. She must be driven by me or Mr Chen, and one of us must be with her at all times to guard her. I know it sounds strange, but her safety is paramount.'

'Who's after her?'

Leo pushed the papers over to me. 'And that's all. Oh,' he said, suddenly remembering, 'she goes out to Lo Wu on Saturday mornings to ride a pony. Any questions?'

I studied the huge stack of papers on the table. 'I thought he was paying me well. Now I think he's not paying me enough.'

'Don't worry, as long as one of us is with you, you'll be perfectly safe.'

'Tell me, Leo.'

'Right now, just settle in, get the feel for the job. I'll tell you more later.'

'Promise?'

He smiled. 'Promise. Mr Chen teaches her Wu shu as well — he'll tell you when they have a session. Drop her off in the training room, come back half an hour later ... easy.'

'What's Wu shu?'

'Martial arts. Kung fu. Ask her to show you; she's really cute.'

'It's normal for children to learn off their parents, isn't it?'

'If there's a family tradition, then it's absolutely expected. He teaches me too.'

'Mr Chen learnt from his father?'

'What an interesting idea,' he said. 'But I don't think so.'

'Leo?' I tapped on his bedroom door.

'Come on in, Emma.'

Leo sat at his desk reading a website on his computer.

I raised the pile of books. 'Someone left these on the desk in my room.'

'Oh.' He spun in his chair to face me. 'The last nanny must have left them there. You can have them if you want.'

'This one looks valuable,' I said, indicating the large illustrated compendium of Chinese gods.

He shrugged. 'Keep 'em.'

I shrugged as well. 'Okay. I'm interested in Chinese mythology, anyway. I go with my friend April when she has festival stuff to do, it's really interesting.'

That caught his attention. 'You're interested in the Chinese gods?'

'Yeah.' I raised the books again. 'This is a good collection. I borrowed some of these from the library before.'

He turned back to his computer. 'Definitely keep them then. They'll be useful.'

'How come all the furniture's new? Even though there was someone there before?'

'Just is,' Leo said.

I shrugged again. 'Whatever.'

When I returned to my room I put the books on the desk and did an internet search on John Chen. It was a very common name and produced more than a million hits. When I narrowed it with his address, 'One Black Road, Peak', I found a news story in the English newspaper, a translation of an article in one of the Chinese tabloids. Apparently Mr Chen's building was widely considered to be haunted because many people had seen dragons flying around the top floor. The reporter had asked the opinion of a number of local experts in the supernatural. Three said it was because the building was cursed; two said it was because the building had exceptionally good luck; and one said it was the spirit of a dragon that had died when the building was constructed.

I shrugged, and opened the large compendium of Chinese gods. It was a good one; the introduction explained how Chinese mythology was a mishmash of Confucian precepts, Taoist alchemy and Buddhist philosophy. All three religions existed side by side in Chinese society (although Confucianism was widely regarded as a set of social rules rather than a true religion). Confucianism had sets of gods that were rather like saints: deified humans. Buddhism taught reincarnation and karma, and the eternal search for freedom of the soul and attainment of Nirvana; but there were also Buddhist gods who returned to Earth to help people attain Nirvana themselves.

I found Taoism the most interesting. Taoism's basic principle was similar to Buddhism, in the search for the Tao, or the Way, and attainment of Immortality, something similar to Nirvana. But Taoism also taught a variety of ways to gain Immortality, including physical and elemental alchemy and magic.

I put the book down and returned to unpacking the last of my stuff from the boxes. I didn't really have much to show for my four years in Hong Kong; I'd never had space to store very much in any of the places I'd lived. But it looked as though my life had taken a turn for the better: a tremendously attractive employer and his daughter, who was a delight to be with.

CHAPTER THREE

Later in the afternoon the door slammed and Simone yelled, '*Is Emma here?*'

I went out to find them taking their shoes off at the front door, Simone and Mr Chen together. He hadn't taken his sword, he'd left it on its hooks near the front door. Simone carefully put her little shoes in the shoe cupboard, then did the same for her father. He watched her with delight, then smiled at me. He looked right into my eyes, and for a split second those gorgeous dark eyes hypnotised me; then Simone charged to tackle me, nearly knocking me over.

'Hello, Emma!' she yelled. 'Are you here all the time now?'

I bent and picked her up, warm with pleasure at the thought of being full-time with her. 'Yes, sweetheart, I'm all yours.'

She threw her little arms around my neck and kissed me on the cheek. Then she rested her forehead against mine and looked seriously into my eyes. 'Good.'

She wriggled out of my arms and took my hand. 'Have you seen everything?'

'Yes I have, Simone. Leo showed me around.'

She screwed up her face. 'I'm *hungry*.'

'Dinner will be soon, Simone, don't ruin your appetite,' Mr Chen said from the doorway where he was watching us with amusement. 'Did Leo tell you about meals, Miss Donahoe?'

'No, sir.'

'When I am home at dinner time, we'll have a family dinner together — me and Simone, you and Leo. We can discuss what we've done during the day. Is that acceptable?'

'Sure,' I said. 'Will I be able to go out occasionally? I'm supposed to be having dinner with some friends this evening. I usually go out on Saturday night.'

'Of course. We don't want to impinge too much on your private life. If you want to have dinner with someone outside, of course, go.'

Louise didn't bring a guy along for me for a change. She seemed to know every unattached male in Hong Kong and constantly set me up. Sometimes it worked and I would spend a few months in a pleasant casual relationship; sometimes it didn't and I was left to my own devices. Either way suited me just fine. I couldn't keep a relationship in Hong Kong for long anyway; people were always coming and going.

We all drank far too much and stayed well past our welcome in the Thai restaurant in Wan Chai, but we continued to order food so the staff tolerated us.

'You should go and see Miss Kwok,' April said. 'You should have talked to me if you were unhappy there. She's very upset that you left.'

'Of course she's upset.' I sipped my beer. 'She'll lose half the kids without me working there.'

Louise's blue eyes sparkled. 'Don't go back to working for that bitch, Emma. You can do better.'

April was offended. 'Don't be mean. Miss Kwok is a nice person. She's very rich; you should respect her.'

'You're just saying that because your fiancé's related to her,' Louise said. 'She doesn't even pay you to fix the computers at the kindergarten.'

'How is Andy anyway?' I said, attempting to change the subject.

'The wedding's all planned — we'll have it with my family in Sydney.' April was obviously happy. 'I'm looking forward to it. My family is so pleased. Andy's family are very wealthy. Very prestigious.'

'God,' Louise said under her breath.

'When is it?' I tried to appear interested, but I agreed with Louise. Andy was always perfectly polite to us but there was something about him that I just didn't like.

'Next month.' April leaned back and smiled with satisfaction. 'It was easy to get a ceremony on a good day in Australia. The date will be very auspicious.'

'God,' Louise whispered again.

April didn't seem to hear her. 'I'm going to the temple tomorrow to get the . . .' she hesitated, searching for the English word, 'blessing from the ancestors.'

'Which temple?' I said, interested.

'The one in Pokfulam.'

'The one in the cemetery?' Louise said.

April nodded.

'Can I come along and have a look?' I said.

April shrugged. 'Sure. Not much to see, though, just tablets. Ancestors and stuff.'

'What time?'

'After yum cha. About twelve, one.'

'Can I meet you there?'

April nodded, then leaned forward and rapped her fingertips on the table. 'You should go back to Miss Kwok, Emma. She says she needs you at the kindergarten. Go ask the fortune sticks. They'll tell you that you should stay with her.'

'I already have a new job.'

'But you only resigned yesterday,' April said.

'She moved out today,' Louise said. 'Fastest damn thing I've ever seen.'

'You'll be live-in?' April said.

'Yep,' I said. 'Live-in nanny.'

'You can do better than that, Emma. Go back to Miss Kwok.'

'You kidding?' Louise said. 'Nearly forty thousand a month, living with this gorgeous rich dude? I'd do it in a second.'

'Strictly professional.'

'Yeah, right.'

'Forty thousand a month?' April said, shocked.

'Yep,' Louise said.

April scowled. 'Everybody will think that you are more than nanny if he pays you that much.'

'I don't care,' I said.

'Geez, you're definitely the most cold-blooded chick I've ever met, Emma,' Louise said. 'Don't even care.'

'Don't be mean,' April said. 'Emma is a lovely person.'

I raised my beer. 'Oh, no, April, I think I'm the most cold-blooded chick I've ever met too.'

Louise snorted with amusement. 'Sure you are. Look at how you adore his little girl. You have a soft spot for kids, Emma, don't deny it.'

'This one is special,' I said, studying my beer. 'She always worries about everybody else. She was really concerned that other children were missing out because I was spending all my time with her. She felt guilty about hogging me.'

'Yeah, she's a perfect little angel.'

'In this case, I think she really is.'

It was very late when I arrived back at the apartment building on the Peak. I hopped out of the taxi and it reversed away down the drive. I walked up to the gates, waved to the security guards and they opened the pedestrian gate for me.

I saw the lights and turned. Another taxi pulled up. A smart-looking young European stepped out of the car, and Leo came out the other side. Leo stopped when he saw me, then walked up the drive to the gates.

I held the gate open for them. Leo didn't say anything, just nodded to me and went through.

'Hi, I'm Emma, a friend of Leo's,' I said to the young man.

'Hello.' He held his hand out and I shook it. He was quite good-looking, tall, blond and slender. Looked to be in his mid-thirties, about the same age as Leo. He had a definite American accent. 'Rob.'

Leo walked in front of us and opened the ground-floor door to the lift lobby.

We all entered the lift together.

'You live here too?' Rob said.

'Yep, I'm the nanny.'

Leo gazed at the numbers above the lift door without saying a word.

'It's really humid,' Rob said.

'Yeah. Summer's here, all right.'

'You been in Hong Kong long?' Rob said.

'About four years,' I said. 'But I never get used to the humidity in the summer.'

'Are you English?'

'No, Australian.'

The lift doors opened and the three of us entered the lobby of the eleventh floor. Leo unlocked the gate and opened the front door for us. We went in and removed our shoes at the front entrance, then walked together down the hall towards the bedrooms.

I stopped at my bedroom door. 'Nice to meet you, Rob. 'Night, Leo.'

Rob nodded and smiled, and followed Leo to his room. Leo still didn't say a word.

I went into my room, carefully closed the door, and collapsed onto my bed laughing.

'Emma?'

I stopped laughing. I'd woken Simone.

I opened the door between our bedrooms a crack. 'Sorry, sweetheart. I woke you up.'

Simone sat up in her bed, her face swollen with sleep and her honey-coloured hair tangled around her head. 'Oh. Okay. Can you sit with me while I go back to sleep?'

I slipped in and sat next to her on the bed. 'Did you have a nightmare?'

Simone slid under the covers and rolled onto her side. 'Leo brought his boyfriend home again,' she said. 'He's funny.'

I rubbed her back under the covers.

'I'm glad he has someone to love,' she said, her voice sleepy. 'It makes him happy.'

'I'm glad too,' I said softly.

'Bad people take away the people you love.' She curled up into a ball. 'I hate the bad people.'

'I'm here,' I said softly, at a loss. I wondered what had happened to her mother. All I knew was that she had died. I opened my mouth to ask and closed it again.

Simone sighed under the covers. 'Wouldn't it be nice if there were no bad people? If nobody had to be scared of them any more? If Daddy didn't have to stay here and get hurt all the time to look after me, if he could go back to his Mountain and be happy, like he used to? Before —' She choked it off, then her voice dropped to a whisper. 'Before the bad people came. We had a lot of fun. He did lots of secret stuff all the time, and we laughed.'

'What secret stuff?'

'You have to ask Daddy. I'm not allowed to tell you.' Her voice filled with her cheeky smile. 'Both Leo and Daddy said I'm not allowed to tell you, so you have to ask. Ask them about the secret stuff, it's really fun.' Then her voice saddened again. 'I just wish we could have the secret stuff, and all of us together again, and no more bad people ... and ...'

She sighed and curled up tighter. 'Ask Daddy. I'll be okay now, Emma, you go to sleep. I'm sorry I made you come in. Go to sleep, and we'll have fun tomorrow, you and me. I'm glad you came to look after me. We'll have fun.'

'Yes, we will,' I said, still stroking the covers. 'I can stay here until you fall asleep.'

'Ask Daddy,' she said, almost a whisper, then her breathing softened and deepened into sleep.

A taxi pulled into the lay-by outside the temple the next afternoon and April stepped out holding a large plastic shopping bag. She saw me and waved.

'What's in the bag?' I said.

'Stuff for the ancestors. So they bless my marriage and make it good. I'll put it in front of the tablets.'

'The ancestral tablets?'

She nodded a reply.

I stopped at the front gate to the temple and grinned. The wrought-iron fence and gate had swastikas worked into the metalwork. They were the reverse direction from the Nazi swastika, but still recognisable, picked out in red paint against the black fence.

I pointed at one. 'In the West, that's a symbol of Nazi Germany and sort of ...' I searched for the word. 'Bad.'

April looked at the fence, bewildered. 'What is?'

I outlined the swastika on the gate with my finger. 'This symbol.'

She shook her head. 'It's just good luck.'

'Do you know anything about the Nazi regime in Germany? Hitler?'

She hesitated, thinking, then said, 'Hitler was a great European General, right? He conquered most of Europe.'

I suppressed the laugh. 'That's one way of describing him. He tried to kill a whole race of people.'

She shrugged. 'I don't know anything about that. We didn't do much European history in school.'

'Didn't you go to school in Australia?'

'No, I went to Australia to study IT at university, then got citizenship, then took my parents out there after Tiananmen.'

She pressed the intercom button next to the gate and it unlocked for us. We went inside.

The temple sat on top of the Pokfulam hill, overlooking the steeply terraced cemetery that led down to the sea below us. A few highrises were scattered at the base of the hill, mostly inhabited by expatriates who didn't care about the bad fung shui of living near the cemetery.

April led me past the main hall and towards the steps down to the tablet rooms.

'What's in the main hall?' I said, pointing towards three huge statues inside.

'The Three Big Gods,' April said. 'You know, the gods in charge of everything.'

'This is a Taoist temple, right?'

She hesitated for a moment, then said, 'Just a temple.'

'But the Three Big Gods are Taoist?'

'I don't know,' April said. 'They're just the big Gods, but they're different from the Buddha, so I suppose they are.' She moved closer and whispered, 'It's all just old people's superstition anyway, but it's important to worship the ancestors, otherwise they get mad at you and you get bad luck. And I want good luck for my marriage.'

We went down the steep steps to the tablet rooms at the back of the temple. Dark green and brown mosaic tiles covered the floor and walls, with a bare painted concrete ceiling. A family sat on grimy vinyl couches to one side, folding squares of gold paper into the shape of ancient gold bars and stuffing them into paper sacks.

'Funeral,' April whispered, and passed the people without glancing at them again.

The rest of the offerings were ready for the funeral in the main hall of the tablet rooms. A house stood in the middle of the hall, about two metres high, made of flimsy bamboo bracing and covered with paper. It had three storeys, with tiny air conditioners in the windows and a mah jong table in one room. A male and a female servant and a guard dog stood in the front garden. Next to the house was a Mercedes, with a driver made of paper, and stacked next to the car was a variety of day-to-day necessities, all made out of paper: a portable stereo, a mobile phone, clothes, a television, a tea set with a vacuum flask for the hot water, and more servants. The whole lot was waiting for the main funeral ceremony, when it would be thrown into the furnace in the garden next to the tablet rooms and burned. The essence would travel to heaven for the use of the dead relative.

April moved to the next room. The walls were lined with glass-fronted cabinets, with rows upon rows of ancestral tablets inside, rising all the way to the ceiling. There must have been a thousand of them. One wall had larger tablets for the more wealthy, but April's ancestors inhabited one side cabinet and were smaller. The tablets were each about ten centimetres high and five wide, made of red plastic. The name of the ancestor was in raised lettering picked out in gold.

A large laminated dining table sat in front of the tablets, with an incense burner holding a stick of incense and a red plastic plate of oranges on it. The room smelled strongly of incense, and the ceiling was black with smoke.

While April fiddled around placing plates of oranges, apples and roast pork and chicken on the table, I wandered around the temple, carefully avoiding the grieving family and their paper-folding.

Another table with a cabinet above it stood next to one of the temple's peeling mouldy walls, under a heavily barred window. The table and cabinet were packed full of statues of gods, many of them an identical statue of a woman in flowing robes carrying an urn.

A small elderly man, one of the temple attendants, approached me, grinning broadly. They obviously didn't get many Westerners in this temple, it wasn't on the main tourist route.

'Who is this?' I said, pointing at the goddess statue.

He shook his head, still grinning. No English. I asked in Cantonese, 'Nidi hai binguo?' and he nodded. 'Kwan Yin.'

'Ah, m'goi,' I thanked him. Kwan Yin, the Goddess of Mercy, a Bodhisattva of the Buddhist faith who had attained Nirvana and then returned to Earth to help others achieve the same goal. The book in my room was good: its picture of Kwan Yin was almost identical to the statue.

The attendant pointed to a fierce-looking, red-faced god holding a halberd, a broadsword blade on the end of a pole. 'Gwun Gong.'

I nodded, recognising the statue. The God of Justice was worshipped throughout Hong Kong, with altars in shops and restaurants as a protector against demons and bad luck.

Then I saw a statue in the corner whose image resonated with me, making me shiver. It was a small statue of a middle-aged man with long wild hair and black robes. He held a sword in his hand, ready for battle, and his bare feet rested on a snake and a turtle. 'Nidi binguo?'

The attendant nodded wisely. 'Pak Tai.'

'On Cheung Chau?' I asked, naming the outlying island that had a temple devoted to Pak Tai and was a popular tourist destination.

He nodded, grinning widely.

'M'goi sai.'

'M'hai,' he said, and wandered off.

I studied the statue for a while, wondering why it made me feel a prickle at the back of my neck. It was simply decorated in black, unlike many of the Kwan Yin statues which were awkwardly splashed with a variety of garish colours and picked out in gold. I shrugged. I'd look him up in the book later.

When I returned to April she had finished kneeling on the cushion provided and bowing to her ancestors with the incense in her hands, and was putting the food back into her bag.

'Do you know anything about Pak Tai?' I said.

'He has a temple on Cheung Chau,' she said.

'What else?'

She shrugged. 'I think he has something to do with water, or rain, or something. Not sure. Let's go to Central for afternoon tea.'

'Sure.'

As we walked back through the temple's courtyard I noticed a small concave mirror above the main entrance, with the eight Pa Kua symbols around it in a red octagonal frame. Demons couldn't stand to see their own reflection, so the mirror was a barrier to them approaching the temple. The large screen just inside the door of the temple was another demon barrier: demons were well known to be unable to turn corners and could only move in straight lines.

'Kwan Yin is a Buddhist icon. Why's she in a Taoist temple?' I asked April as we waited at the taxi rank for a passing cab.

'She looks after people. If you buy a statue of her and donate it to the temple, you get good luck,' April said.

'Old people's superstition?' I said playfully, teasing.

She shrugged again. 'Can't hurt to get a little extra good luck.'

After dinner, back in my room I checked the Chinese gods compendium for Pak Tai and was referred to H'suantian Shangdi. Pak Tai was his name in Cantonese, the dialect spoken in Hong Kong and Southern China. In Northern China and in the standard Mainland dialect of Putonghua, he was called Xuan Tian Shang Di, the Supreme Emperor of the Dark Northern Heavens. There were a variety of legends about him, many of them conflicting, but he was credited with controlling weather and destroying demons, and he was also the Supreme Warrior and God of Martial Arts.

A fascinating deity. The book described his exploits at length; apparently one of the Chinese classics of literature was his story, how he had lived through more than a hundred incarnations before achieving Nirvana and being promoted to Heavenly Emperor.

I could see why he resonated with me now. The similarities between him and Mr Chen were obvious. Both in black, both with long hair, both involved with martial arts. Mr Chen probably took Xuan Tian as a role model to the point of making his appearance similar. I wondered if I should be concerned about this obvious piece of eccentricity, but Mr Chen was too delightful a person to let it worry me too much. He was as generous and caring as his daughter, and both of them were great fun to be with.

Simone squealed and water splashed in her bathroom next to my room. I closed the book. I hadn't even heard them come back. I wanted to go in and see them, maybe help with Simone's bath and putting her to bed. They were in there together, father and daughter, both of them adorable.

Then I shook my head. Keep it professional, Emma, and besides, it's Sunday, the only day they can have some private time together without the rest of us hanging around.

I opened the book again to find out more about Xuan Tian Shang Di. Maybe there was information about him on the net as well.

CHAPTER FOUR

Simone was still sleeping when I headed to the kitchen for breakfast on Monday morning. Monica was busily frying eggs for Leo as he sat at the small kitchen table nursing his coffee. He didn't look up from his coffee as I walked in, but the expression on his face was priceless.

I found a mug in the cupboard and poured myself a cup of tea from the urn on the kitchen bench.

'Can I make you anything, Miss Donahoe?' Monica said.

'Just Emma, Monica, and I can make my own toast, thanks. Does Mr Chen have peanut butter?'

'Yeah, in the pantry,' Leo mumbled into his coffee. 'But no bread, nobody eats bread here. Monica will have to buy it for you.'

'I'll buy you bread, Emma,' Monica said. 'Milk bread?'

'No, wholemeal if you can get it, please.'

Monica nodded. 'I'll see if I can find it in the Western supermarket when I buy food for Leo.'

'Yeah, Leo has exotic tastes,' I said, then sat at the table next to him and grinned. He looked as if he'd like to climb into his coffee cup. 'Does Mr Chen know about your nocturnal activities?' I asked.

He studied his coffee carefully. 'He's caught me too.'

'And he's okay with it?' Sometimes Chinese tradition wasn't very accepting.

'Yeah, he's okay.' He smiled up at me. 'Actually, he's great.'

'Does Rob have a brother?'

Leo shoved me playfully. Then he became more serious. 'He's okay with you bringing people home, but you have to check with me first. Call me on my cell phone and I'll clear them before they come in.'

I stared at him.

'I have to, you know?'

I shrugged. 'Yeah, okay. But the way my social life is right now, I'd be lucky to bring home a stray dog.'

'That is *way* too much information.'

I leaned over the table. 'So tell me, what's the big secret?'

He looked piercingly at me for a moment, then down at his coffee again. 'Can we wait a while before we talk about it? Until you've decided that you really want to stay?'

'Okay. So what does Mr Chen do for a living?'

He turned the coffee cup in his hands, then nodded thanks to Monica as she put a huge plate of greasy eggs and ham in front of him. 'That's part of the "later" thing too.'

'What's the thing he has with Xuan Tian Shang Di?'

Monica dropped the frying pan into the sink and froze completely.

Leo looked sharply at me and opened his mouth to say something, then relaxed when Simone came in. She was still in her little Hello Kitty pink nightshirt, her hair mussed from sleep. She hugged Leo and kissed him on the cheek, and he wrapped one huge arm around her and kissed her back.

She came to me and kissed me too. 'Good morning, Emma.'

'Good morning, sweetheart.'

'What are we going to do today?'

'Well, yesterday I bought some paints and paper and scissors and glue and stuff, so I thought we might make things today.'

Simone lit up as she pulled herself onto her chair. 'Really? We can make things? And paint?'

I nodded. 'And then if Leo doesn't have to go anywhere, we're going to teach him how to play snap.'

Simone squealed with delight. 'Are you going anywhere today, Leo?'

'I'm taking Monica to the market this morning, but after that I can play while Mr Chen goes out to a meeting,' Leo said, his deep voice warm with pleasure.

'Mr Chen's going to a meeting?' I said.

Leo nodded. 'He'll be back after that and he'll spend the afternoon in the training room.'

'Guarding his energy?' Simone said.

Leo frowned and shook his head.

Simone's little face fell. 'Sorry.'

Leo took her hand and squeezed it. 'Yes. Then he'll teach you at three o'clock, and Emma can take a break.'

Simone lit up again, and turned to me with a broad smile. 'It's going to be *so fun* having you here, Emma.'

'I think so too, sweetheart,' I said.

'Gin,' Simone said triumphantly and placed her cards on the table.

Leo threw his cards down. 'Not fair, you keep beating me.'

'Leo.' Simone bent forward, her little face intense. 'Please stop letting me win, it's not fair. It's not fair on you and it's not fair on me. I don't want to win all the time, and it makes you sad when you lose.'

Leo grinned broadly. 'You know what, Simone?'

'What?'

He bent to look mischievously at her. 'I'm not letting you win at all.'

Her little eyes unfocused for a second, then went wide. 'You're telling the truth!'

He leaned back, still grinning. 'That's right. You're winning fair and square.'

Simone giggled and patted his arm. 'Then I have to let *you* win sometimes, silly Leo.'

I gathered the cards together. 'Didn't you just say that it's not fair to let someone win, Simone?'

Simone's eyes unfocused again for a moment. 'Miss Lee is here.'

I checked my watch. 'No, she isn't due for another ten minutes or so.'

Monica tapped on the door and opened it. 'Piano teacher's here, Emma. She's in the music room waiting for Simone.'

Simone sighed. 'I'd rather play with you and Leo.'

I looked at her. 'Remember what I said, Simone. If you ever want to give up piano or violin because it's not fun any more, you just say so. Your dad doesn't want you doing anything you don't enjoy.'

Simone pulled herself to her feet. 'No, I like playing the piano, it's fun. It's just that the practice gets a bit boring sometimes.'

'I have a session with Mr Chen in the training room,' Leo said, and rose to tower above me.

Simone's eyes unfocused again. 'Yep, he's waiting for you, doing katas.'

'Wait.' I raised one hand. 'You know where your dad is without looking, Simone? And you knew Miss Lee had arrived?'

'I have to go to piano lesson, Emma,' Simone said cheekily. 'Ask Leo.'

Leo moved to the doorway. 'Ask me about it later, Emma.'

I snorted with exasperation. 'When later?'

'Oh ...' He waved one hand airily. 'In about three weeks?' He turned and went out, still grinning.

I slapped my forehead with the deck of cards and put them back into the box.

After I'd tidied the rest of Simone's toys I went up the hall to the kitchen to get a cup of tea.

The door to the training room was ajar and I stopped to peer in without being seen. Leo and Mr Chen were there together. Only glimpses of them were visible as they moved around the room, but their reflections appeared in the mirrored wall as well.

Leo had a sword, and he fiercely attacked Mr Chen with it. Mr Chen was unarmed and I felt a jolt of concern for him, then saw with relief after a couple of minutes that he had no difficulty at all evading Leo's attacks; he even managed to strike Leo a few times.

Leo moved with the grace of a cat. He was extremely fast and flexible for such a big guy.

But Mr Chen would have made a cat look clumsy. He was magnificent. He moved so fast he was a blur. His long hair flew behind him as he spun and kicked Leo in the abdomen, knocking him flat and spinning the sword out of his hand.

Leo pulled himself to his feet. 'What level would that have been equivalent to?'

'Forty,' Mr Chen said.

'Damn.' Leo retrieved the sword. 'I need to be able to take at least up to sixty. What if a Mother comes after her?'

'You are human, Leo,' Mr Chen said. 'You have human limitations.' He saw me watching through the gap in the doorway and his face went rigid. He came to the door and closed it with a click.

I wandered back towards my room, deep in thought. Leo was *human*?

About two weeks later, two teenagers turned up to learn from Mr Chen. They were about sixteen years old, a Chinese boy and a European girl. I didn't see them arrive; it was as if they'd always been there. I couldn't get a single word out of either of them when I tried to talk to them; they both pointedly ignored me.

After they'd been there a couple of days, sharing meals with us and still not talking to me, Leo pulled me aside. 'Stop talking to them.'

'I was just being friendly.'

He grimaced. 'They've given up a lot to learn off Mr Chen. It's the most important thing in the world for them. And they've been told that if they talk to you, they're out.'

'What?'

'They're here to learn, Emma. Leave them alone. If either of them says a single word to you, they'll lose it all.'

'That's not fair.'

'That's the way it is. Stop trying to talk to them; you'll only get them into trouble. Okay?'

I shrugged. 'I don't think it's very fair, but okay, if that's what everybody wants.'

'It is.'

'Going to tell me how they fit into the big secret?'

'Nope,' he said, and gestured down the hallway. 'Simone's waiting for you to bath her and read her a story.'

I poked him in the chest with my finger. 'You *will* tell me what's going on here, Mr Alexander.'

'Yes, I will, Miss Donahoe, but not right now.'

I snorted with exasperation and stomped off to Simone's room.

'Can you tell me *anything at all* about what your dad does, Simone?' I said as I tucked her in and pulled out her favourite storybook. 'When he's at home, he's either locked in the training room or in his office. I hardly see him to ask him. And Leo won't tell me.'

'I promised them I wouldn't,' Simone said, snuggling further under the quilt. 'You have to ask them.'

I sighed. 'I want to know what's going on.'

'I want you to know too. None of the aunties and uncles can come over 'cause you don't know about them. I miss Uncle Bai. We can't do any of the special fun stuff. Daddy even had a big argument with Leo about getting the students in 'cause Leo said they'd do something special and you'd see it.'

'What sort of special stuff can they do?'

She shook her head with a small smile. 'I promised.'

When Simone was sleeping I went up the hallway to the kitchen and stopped. The door to the training room was glowing; a golden light leaked around it.

Mr Chen charged out of the dining room, threw open the door of the training room and slammed it shut behind him.

The light blinked off and I heard excited voices inside, but couldn't understand what they were saying.

Mr Chen came back out, and stopped when he saw me. 'Is Simone all right, Miss Donahoe?'

'I just put her to bed. I was going to the kitchen for a cup of tea.'

He nodded and continued up the hall towards the dining room.

The two teenagers came out of the training room. The girl was helping the boy; he was leaning heavily on her. His face was ashen. They moved away from me, not noticing my presence behind them.

'Go and rest,' she said.

'I can't believe I did it,' he said. 'After trying for so long. Finally.'

'You must recentre it.' She helped him to the end of the hall. 'Don't want to kill yourself now that you've finally gained the skill.'

'Did you hear what the Dark Lord said?'

'Which part?' She was obviously amused. 'The part about trying it alone again and he'll throw you out, or the part about being one of the best energy students he's had in a while?'

They turned to go into the student rooms, saw me and clammed up completely.

I stood speechless, wondering. She'd called him the Dark Lord. One of the titles for Xuan Tian Shang Di was the Dark Lord of the Northern Heavens.

I returned to my room and flipped open the book. I referred to another one. Yep, definitely Dark Lord.

No *way*.

CHAPTER FIVE

Over the next few months the weather grew hotter and the Hong Kong summer arrived. I had to keep my air conditioner on day and night to stay comfortable. Monica replaced my traditional silk bed quilt with a lighter polyester-filled 'air-con' quilt.

I was still enjoying Mr Chen's and Simone's company, although I didn't see as much of him as I would have liked. Leo's promise of telling me about Mr Chen's 'secret' in three weeks had stretched into a vague 'later', and eventually I gave up.

I didn't really mind not knowing. Simone was a delight to be with — creative and good-natured. And Mr Chen was a caring and considerate employer, always concerned that I spent too much time with Simone and didn't take enough breaks. Eventually I had to explain to him that I didn't consider being with Simone as work.

His dark eyes wrinkled up when he smiled, and sparkled with intelligence and good humour. He was always interesting to talk to over the dinner table, and I occasionally skipped dinner with the girls to spend time with him.

I often found myself wondering what it would be like to have his strong arms around me, but he was older than me and he was my employer. Not going to happen, I was way too professional for that.

But he really did have very lovely eyes.

By the middle of August I was sick to death of staying inside in the air conditioning. Most of the time it was too hot and humid to go out, but the continued confinement wore me down and eventually I gave up.

'Can someone escort us to the beach tomorrow?' I asked over the dinner table.

'I'll do it,' Leo said.

'I'll come too,' Mr Chen said. 'Some time beside the sea would be good.'

Simone jiggled with happiness so much that she fell off her chair and took her apple juice with her.

'"Did a Simone",' Leo said.

Simone's face popped up over the edge of the table. 'I'm okay. Can you dry it up, Daddy?'

'Not here, sweetheart, you know that.'

'All right.' Simone went into the kitchen and returned with Monica, who wiped the spill up for her.

'If she keeps doing this, the carpet will be ruined. Take it out,' Leo said.

'No,' Mr Chen said. 'She'll grow out of it.'

'It's not too bad,' Monica said. She rose and smiled around the table. 'Are you finished?'

'Thank you, Monica,' Mr Chen said, and Monica cleared the dishes. 'Which beach would you like to go to, Miss Donahoe?'

'How about Repulse Bay? We can look at the statues.'

Leo's head snapped around and he studied me carefully.

Mr Chen smiled. 'Do you know anything about the statues? Some of the Chinese deities are very interesting.'

Leo looked from me to Mr Chen and back to me.

'Absolutely nothing at all,' I said. 'You'll have to tell us all about them.'

His smile widened and his eyes wrinkled up. Delightful. 'It would be my pleasure,' he said.

Leo parked the car and we all piled out. The minute we were on the sand Mr Chen pulled his shoes off. He wore a pair of tatty black shorts and a faded black T-shirt. Simone raced towards the water with her bucket and spade.

It was a weekday, so the beach wasn't too busy. On the weekend it was often so packed that the sand was hardly visible.

Leo followed Simone down to the water and watched her as she fell into the sand and dug a hole, spraying sand everywhere. He shook it off his smart polo shirt and moved away slightly.

I unfolded the bamboo beach mat and lay it on the sand. Mr Chen and I sat on the mat together.

Simone jumped up, took her bucket to the water and filled it. The bay had no waves at all; the water was completely flat. A line of buoys marked the swimming area and the location of the shark net.

I looked back towards the hills behind the bay. Luxurious low- and highrise apartment buildings clung to the hillside. This was one of the most exclusive residential areas in Hong Kong. And then I realised: I lived in one of the other exclusive areas, up on the Peak. It felt strange.

Mr Chen stretched his long legs out in front of him and leaned back on his hands. His legs were much whiter than his arms; he obviously spent most of his time in long pants.

He saw me watching him and smiled.

'You know, I've been working full-time for you for nearly six months now,' I said.

He seemed surprised. 'Is it that long already?'

'Yes. I started at the beginning of the year, right after Chinese New Year.'

He sat up, pulled his hair from its tie and shook it. I watched, fascinated, as the shining black curtain flew around him. He tied it back and leaned on his hands again.

'So you can tell me what you do for a living now,' I said.

'I suppose I should.'

'Well?'

He moved to sit cross-legged, put his elbow on his knee and his chin in his hand. He appeared to think about it. 'You've seen the students come in, and you've seen me teaching Leo.'

'I don't know how you can afford your lifestyle just by teaching martial arts.'

He smiled sideways at me. 'That's just a small part of my job.'

'What *is* your job?'

He put both elbows on his knees and looked down. 'I do government work. Some administration, some management. Occasionally fieldwork, but not since Simone was born.'

I stared at him. What an idiot I'd been, thinking the secret was something supernatural, that he might be more than human. He was a secret agent. That explained everything: I worked for a spy.

And then I couldn't control my huge grin. I worked for a *spy*.

'Which government? China or Hong Kong?'

'Same thing now. Truth is, neither. A much higher government than both.'

An agent for the UN! 'Wicked! Tell me more.'

He glanced sharply at me. 'No. That's all I can say about it.'

'Oh, come on. I'm in the household, I need to know.'

'Maybe later I'll tell you more. Now is not the time.'

'Later? You'll tell me all about it?'

'Later. I promise. I will.'

'So teaching martial arts is a part of it?'

'Yes. A very large part. I go out to teach as well.'

So that was what he did. He went out to give international spies their basic training in martial arts. How cool was *this*. 'Can you teach me?'

He studied me carefully. 'You want to learn?'

'Yes!'

He watched me silently for a while. Then he turned away. 'No. I won't teach you.'

I opened my mouth to object.

He spoke before I had a chance to. 'I won't teach you. Don't bother asking again, because the answer will always be no.'

'Why on earth not? Is it because I'm a woman?'

'Here they come. They're both soaked.'

He was right. Simone was full of smiles, but Leo was miserable. He gestured at the bottom of his smart designer slacks. 'Ruined.'

'I'm all wet too,' Simone said. She pulled at her T-shirt. 'Leo hates it, Daddy, can you fix it for him?'

'Simone . . .' Leo said, warning.

Mr Chen rose. 'Could you fold up the mat for us please, Miss Donahoe?'

'Sure.'

When I'd finished folding the mat, both Simone and Leo were perfectly dry. Mr Chen took Simone's hand and led her down the beach towards the statues. Leo followed. I brought up the rear, holding the mat and wondering.

The government had concreted the little peninsula at the end of the beach, and local rich people had donated statues of the various deities to be placed there. Most of them were life-sized, but some were enormous.

The two largest statues were of goddesses: one stood wearing flowing white robes and holding an urn; the other sat on a throne, wearing brightly coloured robes.

'Is that Kwan Yin?' I asked Mr Chen, pointing at the standing goddess.

'Yes, it is,' Mr Chen said.

'I've heard about her, and seen her on temple tours.' Everybody who'd spent any amount of time in Asia quickly learned to recognise Kwan Yin. People put statues and images of her everywhere, from small roadside altars to the front panels of taxis. The Goddess that Hears the Cries of the World. She was depicted in both Buddhist and Taoist temples, and was the only deity that the temple guides would talk about in detail. Everybody loved her; she was the spirit of mercy. She even had her own type of tea.

'Who's the other one?' I said.

'That's Tin Hau, Goddess of the Sea.'

'The same one as the MTR station?'

'Yes. The station is called "Tin Hau" because there's a temple nearby. Tin Hau has many temples in Hong Kong; the people here are traditionally seafarers, and she cares for them. Both of these ladies care for the sailors.'

'What about the god in the temple on Cheung Chau island? He's supposed to be a water god as well.'

'Pak Tai? He's very boring,' Mr Chen said. He raised his voice to call to Simone. 'Don't go too far, sweetheart.' He grinned at me. 'You said you didn't know anything about the deities.'

'I thought I didn't,' I said.

'Look at the dragon, Daddy,' Simone called from a statue a short distance away. 'It's *blue*! Dragons are supposed to be *green*!'

'Dragons can be any colour they like, darling,' he said.

I stopped to look at a statue of an old man smiling with his arms raised. He wasn't in the book they'd so conveniently left in my room. 'Who's this?'

'That's the Old Man Under the Moon,' Mr Chen said. 'Yuexia Laoren in Putonghua. He makes sure everybody finds the right partner. Bang on the rock next to him and ask him to find you a good man.'

I just grinned at him. We moved further on.

'Why does this one have a rabbit? And what's the rabbit doing?' The woman wore flowing brilliantly coloured robes, and the rabbit next to her seemed to be pounding something in a mortar and pestle. This goddess wasn't in the book either.

'You never stop asking questions, do you?' Mr Chen said with amusement. He raised his hand to stop me before I could apologise. 'This lady is very interesting. Her husband fought a great battle and was rewarded with the Elixir of Immortality. She stole it and drank it. Her husband was furious and she ran from him, to the moon. She's lived on the moon ever since, cold and alone.'

'That's really sad. But what does the rabbit have to do with it?'

'When we look at the full moon we see a rabbit pounding beans to fill rice cakes. If you know what to look for, it's quite obvious.'

'We see the face of a man.' Then my mouth flopped open as I realised: 'Oh my God. Sailor Moon. She has long hair like rabbit ears, and her English name in the manga is Bunny.'

'I bought some of those videos for Simone.' He turned to walk on. 'Now she pesters me all the time to buy her the complete set.'

'I know. I'll have to introduce her to some other good anime. I think she'll love Cardcaptors.'

'Having you as a nanny becomes more and more expensive all the time,' he said, smiling. 'How many books did you order from that online bookstore anyway? The bill was enormous.'

'Hey, I checked with you first. And you know there isn't a great selection of English books here.'

He stopped and gazed into my eyes. 'I appreciate what you're doing for her. I don't know what I'd do without you.'

I smiled up at him. 'It is absolutely my pleasure. I've never enjoyed working with anyone as much as I've enjoyed working with you and Simone.'

Suddenly he stiffened and his eyes turned inward. He snapped back and looked around. 'Leo! We need to move. Get Simone.'

'What's the matter?' I said, but he was distracted.

Leo picked Simone up and came quickly over.

'What's happening, Daddy?' Simone said from Leo's arms.

'Bad people, Simone, we have to move.'

'Where?' I said, but he ignored me. I looked around. Everything seemed perfectly normal. A couple of families with children wandered around the statues. A Taiwanese tour group piled off a bus nearby, talking loudly to each other in Putonghua.

'Where, sir?' Leo said. 'Which direction?'

'Hold.' Mr Chen was still looking around.

'My Lord, we should move,' Leo said quietly.

'I'm not sure which direction. Hold, Leo.'

I silently watched them both. This was way weirder than any spy stuff.

'You should see Ms Kwan, my Lord,' Leo hissed under his breath. 'You're leaving it very late. You're very weak. You can't even tell where they're coming from.'

'Wait, Leo. They are a good distance away. I will be able to pick the direction soon ... There.' Mr Chen turned to look up the beach, away from the tourists. 'The young couple halfway up the beach. Let's go.'

The young couple looked perfectly normal to me.

'I was having fun, Daddy,' Simone said.

'You know we have to go, sweetheart,' Mr Chen said sadly. 'There are bad people here.'

Simone kicked her legs into Leo with frustration.

'*Chen See Mun*!' Mr Chen barked softly. 'Discipline.'

Simone subsided and made a face.

'Let's go, Leo.' Mr Chen was unruffled. 'Walk right past them. Ignore them. They will not go for us, this place is too public. They were probably hoping to catch us in the shelter of the statues.'

'My Lord.' Leo turned and walked up the beach. Mr Chen gestured for me to follow.

'What's going on, Mr Chen?'

'I'll tell you later, Emma. Right now we need to go home.'

As we approached, the young couple saw us and moved to intercept us. Leo and Mr Chen both tried to walk around them, but they stopped in front of us, blocking our way.

Leo took my arm and pulled me behind him. He lowered Simone and pushed her behind him as well. 'Hold Simone there, Emma.'

I took Simone's hand and held her next to me. I wasn't afraid of the two people; whoever they were, they were probably no match for the men in front of me.

Leo readied himself in front of Simone and me.

Mr Chen stood quietly, apparently relaxed. 'What do you want?'

The couple were an ordinary-looking pair of Chinese in their early twenties, wearing jeans and plain T-shirts.

'We're not here to hurt anybody,' the young man said.

Mr Chen didn't say anything, he just waited.

'What's the little girl's name?' the young woman said. 'She's very pretty.'

Leo hissed under his breath and shifted slightly.

'Hold, Leo,' Mr Chen said without moving. 'Is there a point to this?'

'There is a price on your head,' the young man said. 'A very rich prize.'

Mr Chen went completely still. He even seemed to stop breathing. 'I know they are after me. What is the prize?'

'To be Number One.'

'Why are you telling me this?'

The young man saluted Mr Chen Chinese-style, holding his closed fist in his open palm and shaking his hands in front of his chest. 'Protect us.'

The woman saluted as well.

'Leo,' Mr Chen said without moving, 'take Simone and Miss Donahoe back to the car.'

'No more than these, sir?' Leo said.

Mr Chen concentrated. 'No others. Just these. Go back to the car.'

'Come on, Emma,' Leo said, hoisting Simone into his arms again. 'Let's go.'

I glanced back to see Mr Chen as we walked to the car. The young couple had knelt in front of him. When I reached the car, I looked back again. They were gone. The entire beach was deserted, except for Mr Chen's lone dark figure walking back to us.

No way could the couple have walked off the beach in the time between my glances. But I couldn't see them anywhere. They'd disappeared completely.

I didn't ask about them in the car on the way home; I didn't want to frighten Simone. Leo and Mr Chen were quiet and subdued; Simone was wide-eyed and silent.

* * *

Later that evening, after I'd bathed Simone and put her to bed, I went to Mr Chen's office to ask him what was going on. He and Leo were talking inside his office, and Leo's voice was so loud it made the door rattle.

'They know exactly how weak you are!' he shouted.

I had to strain to hear Mr Chen's voice. 'Those have been tamed. They won't be back.'

'You need to see Ms Kwan *now*!'

Mr Chen said something, but I didn't hear it.

'I don't know why you keep delaying it!' Leo yelled. 'You let yourself run down and you can't protect her! They're moving in!'

'Leo.' Mr Chen spoke louder now, irritated. 'I can only do this a limited number of times. I will only last a maximum of four, five years. Then I'm gone.'

Leo's voice softened. 'What?'

'Even with Mercy's help, eventually I will not be able to hold it together any longer and I will be gone.'

'*Why didn't you tell me?*' Leo bellowed. His voice softened. 'Oh my God.'

'I must delay as long as possible between each feed.'

Leo's voice broke. 'You're going to leave Simone.'

'Hopefully she will be able to defend herself by then. She should be able to handle almost anything by the time I go.'

'Oh, that's very reassuring,' Leo said sarcastically. His voice became louder again. 'You still need to see Ms Kwan *now*.'

'I am making the arrangements, Leo.' Mr Chen sounded tired. 'I was planning to tell you over dinner tomorrow.'

'Well, it's about time.' Leo threw the office door open so hard that it almost hit me. 'Sorry, Emma.'

'What the hell is going on?' I glanced into the office; Mr Chen sat behind his desk, stricken.

'I'll tell you tomorrow,' Mr Chen said. 'Right now, I have people to call.'

'Just leave him, Emma.' Leo closed the door behind him. 'He has things he needs to do.'

'Tell me what's going on!'

'Later.' Leo sighed with exasperation and headed back to his room, shaking his head. 'God, he drives me completely crazy sometimes.'

'Both of you drive *me* crazy!' I shouted. 'Why the hell don't you just tell me what's going on? What's the big secret?'

'I'll tell you all about it real soon, Emma, I promise. We need to make some arrangements now, and it's late.'

'Stop avoiding telling me!'

Simone squealed. We'd woken her up. I rushed to her room to comfort her. Damn.

CHAPTER SIX

The next day Leo avoided me until he had to take Simone and me to lunch with my friends. Simone had wanted to come, and Leo was grudgingly forced to drive us so decided he might eat with us as well.

We walked across the cracked pavement next to Queen's Pier and Simone stopped. 'Look, Leo, the Star Ferry!'

The green and white oval-shaped Star Ferry that carried passengers the short hop between Central on Hong Kong Island and Tsim Sha Tsui in Kowloon pulled into the pier nearby.

'Don't know why they don't just build a bridge,' Leo said. 'With all the reclamation, it's not so far across.'

'They can't,' I said. 'Fung shui. The harbour is the money flowing through Hong Kong. If they build a bridge, it'll interrupt the flow.'

'How much fung shui do you know?'

'Absolutely none at all. My friend April told me that.'

Simone jiggled. 'Daddy's shui!'

I took her hand to lead her into City Hall. 'Daddy's water?'

'Yep.' She shook my hand free and ran ahead, then tripped over her feet and fell.

I caught up with her and helped her up. 'You "did a Simone" already. Now we have to wash your hands.'

'You always wash my hands before we eat anyway, Emma.'

'Don't complain,' Leo said. 'If you wash your hands before you eat, you'll never catch a nasty disease.'

'Don't be silly, Leo,' she said. 'You know we never get sick.'

'Emma!' Louise was standing at the top of the stairs and gesturing for us to hurry. 'We have a table. Move!'

We raced up the stairs to take the table before the receptionist called the next number in the queue. She led us into the enormous hall with its huge floor-to-ceiling picture windows overlooking the harbour and sat us at the round six-seater table.

'Louise, April, this is Simone, and Leo, her bodyguard.'

'I'm the *driver*, Emma,' Leo said, quietly exasperated.

'Yeah, sure you are,' Louise said, eyeing him up and down. 'Nice outfit, Leo.'

As usual, Leo was dressed very well in a made-to-measure dark business suit. He stared at Louise in disbelief.

'Don't mind her — she's Australian, like me,' I said.

'Is that supposed to make a difference?' Leo said, sceptical.

'All the difference in the world, mate, get used to it,' Louise said. 'Hello, Simone. How old are you?'

'Four and a half.'

'Only four? You look older than that,' Louise said.

Simone nodded, eyes wide and serious. 'Everybody says that. I think it's because Daddy's so special.'

'He's special, is he?' Louise said, then grinned knowingly at me.

The white-jacketed waiter threw the bowls, spoons and chopsticks onto the table with a loud rattle.

'What tea would you like?' April said.

'Sow mei,' Louise and I said together.

'You happy with that, Leo?' I said.

'I'm not here. Ignore me,' Leo said, looking around at the other diners.

'You're too big to ignore, mate,' Louise said before I could. 'You're here to eat too. If you want a beer or something, just say so.'

'Not on the job,' Leo said.

April was distracted. 'No trolleys anywhere,' she complained.

The waiter returned with a pot of tea and an extra pot of hot water.

Louise reached into her handbag for a notebook. 'Who paid last time?'

'I did, and I'm winning this time,' I said. I pulled out my own notebook. 'I've collected some really good ones. Wait 'til you hear them.'

Louise and I flipped the notebooks open.

'Apple,' she said.

'Had that one before, it's not new,' I said. 'Winsome.'

'Buxom,' she retorted.

'Good one. Did she know what it meant?' Louise shook her head. 'Alien. Sha Tin McDonald's,' I went on.

'Coffee.'

'Girl, Ivan. Pronounced Yvonne.'

'Winky,' Louise said.

'Ringo,' I snapped back.

'Had that before. Freedom,' Louise said triumphantly. 'At the university.'

'Heman,' I said. 'A girl.'

'Yugo,' she said. 'Also a girl.'

'Yellow.'

63

'Honda.'

'Napoleon.'

'*Hitler*,' Louise said defiantly.

I was losing. I played my trump card. 'Satan!'

Louise glanced up from her notes. 'No way.'

'Absolutely. In the bank on the Peak.'

'I don't believe you.'

'Leo,' I said, 'what's Satan's last name?'

'The kid in the bank? Chow, I think,' Leo said.

Louise snapped her notebook shut. 'No way I can beat that. I'm paying.'

'What the hell was all that about?' Leo demanded. 'What's Satan Chow got to do with anything?'

'We collect Hong Kong English names. Some people seem to choose them out of a hat, whatever takes their fancy. We have a competition. Whoever can come up with the weirdest name they've heard since last time wins. The other one has to pay.' I smiled with satisfaction. 'I win.'

April seemed bewildered by the whole exchange.

'How's married life, April? Do you have photos of the wedding?' Louise said.

April's face lit up and she pulled a few small photo albums out of her briefcase.

'This is in Sydney, where we had the wedding,' she said, passing me some of the books.

I flipped through the first one, and handed it to Louise.

'Can I see?' Simone said.

'Sure.' I handed her one of the books, and Leo looked through it with her.

Louise raised the album she was looking at. 'How many dresses did you have for this?'

'Five,' April said. 'One white one for the wedding, one white one for the formal photos. They're not back yet. One traditional red one for the reception, another white one for the reception. And a going-away dress.'

I leaned over the table to speak closely to her. 'You know, we usually only have one wedding dress.'

April looked horrified. 'Only one dress?'

Louise and I both nodded.

'Your Chinese dress is very pretty,' Simone said. 'Is that gold and silver?'

'Yes,' April said. 'Red silk, gold and silver embroidery. Boring traditional style. My grandmother wanted to see me in one.'

Simone suddenly squeaked, clambered out of her chair and pulled herself into Leo's lap, facing him. He looked around.

'What?' I said.

Simone put her hand on Leo's shoulder and whispered urgently into his ear. He listened carefully, then moved her so that she sat facing the table and wrapped his huge arms around her.

'We're okay,' Simone said, eyes wide.

Three teenage boys walked past our table. They seemed perfectly ordinary, wearing baggy denim jeans and black T-shirts. Simone and Leo didn't shift their eyes from them as they went between our table and the next one.

One of the boys leered at Simone, and Leo held her tighter and whispered something in her ear. She nodded, her eyes still wide. The boys went out of the restaurant. Leo and Simone visibly relaxed.

'Are you guys okay?' I said.

'What was all that about?' Louise said.

'Where the hell are the trolleys?' Leo said. 'What sort of yum cha is this without any food?'

'Here's one,' April said. The waitress stopped the trolley next to our table. April read the signs on the front. 'Har gow, siu mai, cha siu bow, sticky rice, tripes.' She smiled around the table. 'Who wants?'

'Cha siu bow, please, Emma!' Simone said, and climbed off Leo's lap and sat in her own chair. 'Siu mai too. I'm *hungry*!'

'Okay now?' Leo said.

'Yes.' Simone grinned broadly.

'Sticky rice,' Leo said.

'So you and Andy have your own place now?' Louise asked April after the steamers had been set on the table.

'Yes. Andy spends most of his time in China for his work, so I see him once every six weeks or so.'

Louise stared at her. 'You only see your husband once every six weeks?'

April nodded through the dim sum. 'We've decided to go and live in Australia. He wants to get Australian citizenship. I'll go first, do the papers, find us a place to live. He'll come later.'

'You're leaving Hong Kong?' I said. 'When?'

'In about a month, I think,' April said. 'September, October.'

'I'll miss you.'

'I'll be back all the time,' she said. 'To visit. And go shopping.'

Another trolley rolled up beside us. Instead of the little bamboo steamers, it had four square pots with lids and ladles. 'Who wants pig's blood?' April said. 'Congee, mixed beef guts. Anybody?'

Everybody shook their heads. April ordered some pig's blood anyway: dark red jelly-like cubes in clear broth. She passed the card to the waitress who stamped it with a tiny circular stamp held on a string around her neck.

April stirred the blood. 'Emma, you have to go and see Aunty Kitty.'

'Aunty who?' Louise said.

'Aunty Kitty.'

'Kitty Kwok?' I said.

'Yes. She wants to see you.'

'What for?'

'Don't go, Emma, she just wants to bully you into working there again,' Louise said. 'Business has really gone downhill at the kindergarten since you left.'

'You have to go and see her,' April said again.

'No, I don't.'

'Call her then,' April said. 'She wants to talk to you.'

I rose and went to the ladies' room without saying another word. Louise followed me. As soon as we were out of earshot, she was onto me. 'Quick, tell me all.'

'About what? Kitty Kwok?'

'No, silly,' she hissed with a grin. 'Your new job.'

'Nothing much to tell,' I said. 'I work as a nanny, I look after Simone, end of story.'

'What about her dad?' she said. 'What's he like? Are he and Leo ...' She nodded back towards the dining room. 'You know?'

I smiled. 'He's absolutely gorgeous. A total gentleman. And him and Leo? No.'

'Really?'

'I'm sure of it. Leo brings guys home all the time. Real man-about-town. Leo even told me himself: not Mr Chen.'

'But what about Mr Chen? What's he *do*?'

'I have no idea,' I said. 'I think he's a spy. He teaches martial arts to kids, but he says that he works for the government.'

Louise stared incredulously at me. I nodded, reinforcing the point.

'Can you invite me up?' she said as we went through the doors. 'I'd love to check him out, Emma. Sounds unreal.'

'You have no idea.' I lowered my voice. 'You know he only ever wears black? Everything. Sometimes he even wears a black shirt with his suits.'

'You have to get me up there,' Louise whispered. 'I have to see. *Please*, Emma.'

'I'll see what I can do.'

She reached out and squeezed my arm. '*Please*.'

We walked out from City Hall and back along the waterfront.

'Can we go to the shops in Central before we go home, Emma?' Simone said.

'Is that okay, Leo?'

'Yeah, no problem.'

We walked towards the pedestrian underpass that would take us across the road to the shops. The concrete walls were black from car exhaust fumes. Advertising billboards blanketed the underpass, and a beggar crouched under one of the columns, displaying his withered limbs.

On the other side of the underpass we stopped at the kerb to cross Chater Road. The pedestrian light turned green, and I went to lead Simone across the road, but she wouldn't move.

'Leo!' she called loudly.

Leo had taken a few steps to cross the road, but quickly returned to us. He bent to Simone. 'What, sweetheart?'

Simone cast around, her eyes unseeing. 'Take me home, Leo, *now*.'

Leo scooped her up and hurried back to the underpass. 'Come on, Emma,' he called.

'Hurry, Leo,' Simone said.

Leo strode down the underpass, pushing through the crowd. 'How many, sweetheart?'

I struggled to keep up with him.

'I don't know, Leo. *Hurry*,' she said, desperate. 'It's the *same ones*!'

'Where? *Where*?'

'I don't know!' she wailed.

We raced out of the underpass, into the Star Ferry car park, and stopped at the Shroff Office to pay the parking ticket. Leo gently lowered Simone and she clung to his massive leg.

'You know how far away?' he said as he pushed the ticket to the cashier.

Simone's eyes were still unfocused. 'Close, Leo, hurry.'

I looked around. Three teenagers were approaching us from the Star Ferry terminal.

'If it's the same guys as in the restaurant, they're over there,' I said, pointing.

'For God's sake don't point at them!' Leo hissed. He grabbed the parking ticket and the change, hoisted Simone into his arms, and took off towards the stairs. 'Quick, Emma!'

He raced up the stairs to the car and I trailed behind him.

I looked back. The teenagers were running towards us. One of them held out his hand and a Chinese cooking chopper appeared in it. No, not possible. I turned and ran after Leo.

Simone squealed. Leo had reached the top of the stairs and pelted towards the car. I sprinted to keep up with him, my handbag flapping.

He unlocked the car with the remote and gently dropped Simone into the back seat. 'Buckle her up, Emma. We need to get out of here.' He pulled himself into the driver's seat and started the engine before I had my door closed. I slammed it shut as he took off.

Leo drove out of the car park dangerously fast, the tyres of the Mercedes squealing as he took the corners. He had to slow to ease the car down the ramp, then put the paid ticket into the machine and charged straight out of the car park lane into the street, ignoring the other furious drivers who sounded their horns and yelled at him. He ran an amber light and turned into Connaught Road, five lanes wide with concrete dividers on both sides. The traffic flowed smoothly and he raced up the hill towards the Peak.

'Okay, Leo, you can slow down now,' Simone said.

Leo slowed the car and relaxed, breathing a sigh of relief.

'What the hell was all that about?' I demanded loudly.

'Bad people,' Simone said. 'I need to go home and tell Daddy. He'll be really sad.'

'What's going on, Leo?'

'I recognised one of them. They've tried to kidnap her before. Good thing I saw them.'

'*I* saw them, silly Leo,' Simone said. 'You can't even tell the difference most of the time.'

'What difference?' I said.

'Between normal people and bad people,' Simone said patiently. 'Only Daddy and me, and special people like Jade and Gold, can tell the difference.'

'Who are Jade and Gold?'

'We'll be home soon, sweetheart, and then you can tell Daddy all about it,' Leo said gently. 'Until we get there it's not a good idea to talk about it.'

'You have to explain for Emma,' Simone said.

'Yeah, explain for me,' I echoed.

'Not right now. Maybe later.'

'Tell me!'

'No.'

I crossed my arms over my chest and glowered at him. I shouldn't be kept in the dark like this. I could handle any spy business they threw at me.

Leo and Simone went into Mr Chen's office and spoke to him for a long time. They all emerged grim-faced, even Simone. I waited for them in the hallway.

'Are you people going to tell me what's going on?' I demanded.

'Come into my office, Emma,' Mr Chen said.

I sat down across from him. He pulled up his chair and leaned on the papers strewn all over his desk.

'You know that Simone is a kidnapping target?'

'I know,' I said impatiently. 'But what was all that about in Central?'

'Leo spotted some criminals who would be interested in her —'

'No, he didn't,' I said quickly. 'Simone saw them. Leo didn't see anything.'

He remained silent, carefully studying my face.

'Tell me!' I snapped.

He took a deep breath, still calm. 'Simone had seen one of those people before. They have tried to take her in the past. She warned Leo.'

I waited for more, but it wasn't forthcoming. He just sat watching me.

'If you don't tell me what is going on very soon, I will resign.'

He studied me closely, then shook his head. 'You're really not frightened at all, are you?'

I glared defiantly at him. 'Of course not. And I *will* find out what is going on here.'

He leaned back. 'We'll explain it all soon. But right now, Simone's Chinese teacher is here. Go and let her in.'

The doorbell rang and I jumped. 'How do you know it's Simone's Chinese teacher?'

He just watched me.

'I'm not finished yet,' I warned, and opened the door to go out.

'I sincerely hope not,' he said softly behind me.

Monica was ahead of me and had already let the Chinese teacher in. I sighed with exasperation and went into my room. I lay on the bed and opened one of the books on Chinese gods. I was certain now that they'd been left there for me.

That couple on the beach had disappeared completely. The kid today had made a chopper magically appear in his hand. Both Simone and Mr Chen could tell who was in the house without seeing them.

I did another internet search on Xuan Tian Shang Di and was referred to a page about Xuan Wu. I clicked the link and the screen filled with information about the Dark Lord of the North, Xuan Wu. Something to do with snakes and turtles — he either defeated them or he *was* one or even both of them. Controlled water; brought rain.

Xuan Wu, also called the Dark Emperor Zhen Wu, and Chen Wu and Pak Tai in Southern China. Pak Tai, who had a temple on Cheung Chau devoted to him. Boring Pak Tai.

God of Martial Arts, Emperor of the Northern Heavens. Always in black; dishevelled hair, bare feet. Destroyer of demons.

Could it be a codename?

But spy things wouldn't explain all the weird stuff in the Chen household ...

I stared at the screen with disbelief. Dark Lord Xuan Wu? No *way*.

CHAPTER SEVEN

We had the usual Chinese vegetarian meal that evening. Simone chatted about the yum cha and the wedding photos, but didn't mention our mad rush home.

'I have arranged a trip for us to Paris,' Mr Chen said.

Leo let out his breath in a long hiss, but didn't say anything.

'Can we see Aunty Kwan?' Simone said.

'That's why we're going — I need to meet with Aunty Kwan.'

'I wanna go to the Eiffel Tower!'

'You always want to go to the Eiffel Tower,' he said, smiling indulgently.

Simone screwed up her face. 'I like it. Can I go to the Science Museum as well?'

'You want to go to London too?'

Simone nodded, wide-eyed. 'Yes, please, Daddy. I want to see James and Charlie.'

He sighed. 'All right. But only for a couple of days. I can't stay away for too long, you know that.'

'Okay, Daddy.'

'Leo, ask Monica to take Simone and we'll discuss the details.'

After Monica had taken Simone out of the dining room, Mr Chen became much more businesslike. I listened carefully; this would be my first trip overseas with them and I didn't want to screw up.

'Out of Macau as usual, Leo,' he said. 'We'll stay with Ms Kwan in Paris, and in the house in Kensington in London.'

'Understood, sir,' Leo said.

'Have you ever been to Europe, Miss Donahoe?' Mr Chen said. 'Do you speak French?'

'No. Australia and Asia only.' I grimaced with embarrassment. 'My French is pathetic.'

'Not a problem. Leo's French is perfect, and he will escort you and Simone while I meet with Ms Kwan.'

'How long will you meet with her, sir?' Leo said.

'Five days.'

Leo nodded.

'Then three days in London, and back here. Guard them well, Leo, we will be a long way from the Mountain.'

'Sir.'

Mr Chen turned to me and put his palms firmly on the table. 'Any questions, Emma?' He saw my face. 'What?'

'You called me Emma. You usually call me Miss Donahoe.'

'Oh,' he said. 'Sorry.'

'No, no.' I waved my hands in front of me. 'Please. Emma. Call me Emma. Miss Donahoe is so formal.'

He smiled and his eyes wrinkled up. 'Very well ... Emma.'

'Don't even think about it, girlie, you don't have a chance,' Leo growled as we walked together down the hallway.

'Don't worry, Leo, he's far too old for me,' I said, still thinking about those eyes.

'You're not wrong there.'

'How old is he anyway? He looks mid-forties, but sometimes he seems older, sometimes younger — he's hard to pick.'

'You're in your late twenties, right?'

I nodded.

'Well then, let's just say that he's a hell of a lot older than you and you really don't have a chance. So just forget it.'

'Jealous?'

Leo stopped. 'Mr Chen's wife was a truly wonderful human being. I knew her for a long time before she met him, and I loved her like a sister. His heart is still broken, Emma. He'll never love anybody again the way that he loved her.'

'What happened to her?'

'She died.'

'I know she died, Leo,' I said gently. 'What happened?'

'None of your goddamn business.' He stomped into his room and slammed the door.

We travelled to Macau in a fifteen-metre Chinese-style junk. It had an air-conditioned central lounge with a large-screen TV. Simone and I sat in deckchairs on the open-air back of the boat and watched the scenery go past.

It was fascinating to see the sudden change as we left Hong Kong Harbour. We moved from the densely packed highrises on Hong Kong Island and Kowloon to the sparsely populated Outlying Islands. We went in close past Lantau Island, its rocky crags extending right to the edge of the water. Most of Lantau was deserted, its steep hillside covered in scrub and wild azaleas. The new airport was on the other side of the island.

'Why do we have to go to Macau?' I shouted to Mr Chen, who sat in the lounge reading a Chinese book.

'Private jets aren't allowed in Chek Lap Kok, it's too busy.'

I was thrilled. I quickly rose and went into the cabin to speak to him. 'We're going in a *private jet*?'

He nodded and returned to his book.

I sat down. 'Why didn't you tell me?'

He shrugged without looking up from his book.

'Hey,' I said sharply, and he glanced up at me. 'You need to tell me what's going on, Mr Chen.'

Leo snorted with amusement from the other side of the cabin and I rounded on him. 'You too. Tell me what's going on!'

Mr Chen opened his mouth to say something, then obviously changed his mind and smiled. 'Very well. We will take my jet from Macau airport to Paris. We will stay in Paris for five days, then fly to London. London for three days, where I have a house in Kensington. Then we'll take the jet back here. Is that acceptable, Miss Donahoe?'

I bobbed my head and spoke with mock appreciation. 'Thank you for explaining, Mr Chen.'

He smiled over the top of his book. 'You are most welcome.'

'Do you own this boat?'

'Yes. I need to buy a bigger one. It's very slow; it takes nearly two hours to travel to Macau.'

'Hey, it's fun to go slow. There's a lot to see.'

'It's not safe,' Leo said.

'We'll be fine,' Mr Chen said.

'We shouldn't leave Simone in the back by herself like that! It's not safe!'

Mr Chen sighed with exasperation. 'Leo, we're on the *water*.'

'Oh,' Leo said. 'Sorry.' He went to the back of the boat and sat with Simone anyway.

Mr Chen smiled over the top of his book, as if to say: he worries too much.

I smiled back: yes, he does.

The jet was ready for us when we arrived at Macau.

Simone behaved perfectly through all of the customs and immigration procedures. She seemed experienced in the rush-and-wait of the airport paperwork. Fortunately Macau airport wasn't terribly busy and we reached the customs checkpoint reasonably quickly.

Leo nodded to Mr Chen as he lifted the large carry-on bag onto the conveyor belt for the safety inspection. As the bag went through the X-ray machine, the two security staff shot to their feet and stared at the monitor. Mr Chen went rigid and concentrated on them. They waved us through.

I glared at Leo as we walked towards the plane and he pointedly ignored me. Mr Chen seemed oblivious, and Simone chatted about visiting Aunty Kwan. It was as if nothing had happened.

I held Simone's hand as we walked up the small staircase into the jet. It was about the size of a bus, with large comfortable seats inside and a couch against one wall. Leo almost had to crouch to go through the door.

We sat in the seats and buckled up. The ground staff closed the door and rapped on the side. Mr Chen went up to the cockpit to talk to the pilots.

'Been on a private jet before?' Leo said.

'No,' I said. 'Pretty cool.'

'Yeah. Mr Chen had this one specially fitted. Behind the kitchen there's a little bunk for Simone.'

'He owns this plane outright?'

Leo hesitated, then, 'Yes.'

'How much money does he have anyway?'

'Let's just say that if he wanted his own 747, he could buy one tomorrow.'

'But I've never seen his name on the Richest Men list.'

'That's because he doesn't want to be,' Leo snapped, and turned away.

Mr Chen returned from the cockpit. 'Brian says we should have smooth flying most of the way.'

After we'd taken off, Mr Chen rose and touched Simone's shoulder. 'Are you tired, darling?'

'No, Daddy, I'd like to draw.'

'Leo, show Emma where everything is. I'll go up the back and rest. If anything happens, call me immediately.'

'Yes, sir.'

'Make sure Simone drinks plenty of water, please, Emma.'

'Sure, Mr Chen.'

He nodded and went towards the back of the plane.

Leo pointed at the back wall. 'There's a little kitchen in there. Behind that is the bunk room. Anything you need, it's in the kitchen.'

'Can you turn on the video for me, Leo?' Simone said.

'Sure, sweetheart.' Leo went to the television which was set into the wall. 'There's a few videos in the cupboard here, Emma — just put something on for her, it's a long flight.' He showed me where the videos were, turned on the unit, then went into the galley and returned with a soda for himself and an apple juice for Simone.

Simone watched some of the videos then fell asleep in my lap. I must have fallen asleep as well, because the sound of their quiet voices woke me. I heard my name mentioned so stayed still to listen.

'You should tell her, my Lord. She won't stop pestering both of us until we do. And if we don't tell

78

her soon, she's going to resign. You'll have to tell her, and prove it.'

Mr Chen's voice was full of pain. 'I can't do anything to prove it, Leo. I am too weak.'

'It's really that bad?'

Mr Chen didn't reply.

'Damn,' Leo said softly. 'You left it too long. But you still have to tell her, otherwise she's going to lose her goddamn temper again and leave us anyway.'

'I don't want to lose her,' Mr Chen said, wistful. 'If we tell her the truth, she may be scared away.'

'She won't be scared away. She doesn't seem to be frightened by anything.'

'You're quite right, she's remarkable.'

'You should tell her.'

'I know.' Mr Chen groaned. 'She keeps pushing me to tell her, she knows something's going on. We'll do it in Paris. I was planning to tell her there anyway, with Mercy present. No, I have a better idea. You do it. Mercy can help you if she takes it badly.'

'As long as *somebody* tells her,' Leo said. 'She's been working here for months without knowing who you really are.'

'I've had staff who worked for me for years without knowing who I was,' Mr Chen said. 'Look at Monica.'

'Monica knows all about it. She just ignores it because it freaks her out.'

'I don't want to lose her,' Mr Chen said. 'I'd love to teach her. She moves with natural grace and would probably be a formidable warrior.'

'Teach her then. She wants to learn.'

'She's agile and fearless. She's intelligent too, it sparkles in her eyes.' His voice became wistful again. 'She has wonderful eyes.'

'Well then, teach her.'

Mr Chen dropped his voice. 'I will discuss the possibility with Mercy, but I don't think it would be a good idea for me to spend so much time in close physical contact with Emma.'

Leo was silent for a moment. Then he spoke again, his voice a soft growl. 'No way. I do not believe this. No *way*.'

Mr Chen was silent.

'Tell me it's not true,' Leo said.

Mr Chen sighed loudly.

'This is all we need,' Leo said. 'You should dismiss her now, my Lord. Don't even think about starting something you can't finish.'

'Simone adores her.'

'And you?'

Mr Chen was silent for a moment. Then, 'I don't want to lose her. I love being with her, having her around.' His voice softened. 'I wish things could be different.'

My heart leapt.

'Well, they can't, so both of you will just have to get over it,' Leo said. 'If you really feel that way then you should let her go.'

They fell silent again. I was about to make a display of waking when Mr Chen spoke. 'There are some interesting weather patterns over the Mediterranean.'

'Mess with the weather and Ms Kwan will rip your shell off,' Leo growled. 'How long before they'll come after us? They know how weak you are.'

'It is only a matter of time. Mercy can tell us more. We should be safe now that we are far from their Centre. They are weak.'

'So are you. You shouldn't have waited this long to see her.'

'I'll be fine.'

'You shouldn't take risks like this!' Leo hissed. 'Think of what's at stake here!'

'I am very well aware of what's at stake here!' Mr Chen whispered ferociously.

Leo threw himself out of his chair and went out. Something crashed in the galley and Simone shot upright with a squeak.

Charade over.

'It's okay, sweetheart,' I said, and pulled her to me.

She freed herself from my arms and scurried to her father, then clambered into his lap and curled up. He smiled down at her and stroked her hair.

I yawned, stretching. Leo came out of the galley with a soda and flung himself into one of the chairs, which protested under his weight. 'You snore.'

'I do not!'

'Leave her alone, Leo.'

Leo grunted and turned his chair away from us.

'Leo, you are very tired and you have lost your edge. Go and rest.'

Leo didn't move.

'That's an order, Leo.'

Leo glared at Mr Chen and stomped towards the back of the plane.

Mr Chen and I shared a smile. 'Sleep well?' he said.

'How long was I out?'

He checked his watch. 'Only a couple of hours.'

We sat quietly together. He stroked Simone's hair.

I shifted and he glanced at me. I opened my mouth to say 'Mr Chen, are you a god?' and then closed it again, feeling ridiculous. I decided to make a sideways attack on the issue.

'Mr Chen, what's your real name?'

He looked straight into my eyes and I nearly became lost in them. 'Why do you ask?'

'Because on the letters that come in, you have six different first names.'

'You've been in my study?'

'No, of course not, I respect your privacy. But I've seen the letters.'

'I'll have to tell Leo and Monica that; they're always trying to tidy my study.' He didn't seem fazed. 'Six names would be about right.'

'So which one is the right one?'

He smiled slightly. 'They all are.'

'Oh, come on,' I said. 'What's your real name?'

'Right now, my real name is John Chen Wu. That is me.' He smiled into my eyes. 'You can call me John if you like.' His gaze became intense and he dropped his voice. 'Call me John.'

I looked back at him and spoke softly. 'I don't think that would be appropriate.'

'As you wish.' He leaned back and stroked Simone's hair. 'We'll be there soon.'

Loud snores floated from the back of the plane and we both smiled.

CHAPTER EIGHT

Once again Mr Chen did something to the airport staff and they didn't notice the bag as it went through the x-ray machine.

A van with a driver was waiting for us at the airport and took us into the city of Paris. Simone stared out the window, delighted, as we drove past the elegant, old-fashioned buildings. We pulled into a side street on the edge of Montmartre, around the corner from the Moulin Rouge. Five-storey townhouses stood either side of the tree-lined street, with curved facades and elaborate windows.

The driver parked the van outside what appeared to be an apartment building. Inside, it was a house. The large entry had sweeping Art Nouveau stairs and a glittering chandelier.

A slender, middle-aged Chinese lady came down the stairs to meet us. She wore a flowing pantsuit of white silk, and had an enormous amount of hair piled on her head. She moved with the grace of a princess and her smooth oval face was angelic.

Simone ran to her and clutched her around the legs. 'Aunty Kwan!'

Ms Kwan crouched and pushed a stray lock of hair out of Simone's eyes. 'Simone, Simone. You are more beautiful every day, and more and more like your mother.'

Simone kissed her loudly on the cheek.

Ms Kwan rose and went to Mr Chen. She put one slender manicured hand on his shoulder and leaned up to kiss him on the cheek.

I'd never seen him blush before. It was charming.

'Hello, old Wu,' she said. 'Keeping well?'

'All the better for seeing you, my Lady.'

'You have left it a long time, my friend.'

'I know.'

'Jade and Gold?'

'Coping.'

She sighed. 'Next time I will come to you.'

He shook his head.

'Fine then, be stubborn.' She saw me. 'Who is this?' Her eyes widened. 'I don't believe it. Haven't you learnt your lesson?'

'No, no, this is Simone's nanny. Miss Emma Donahoe.' He looked into her eyes. They concentrated on each other, then both snapped out of it.

'I see.' Ms Kwan glanced down at Simone. 'And is Miss Donahoe a good nanny?'

'Emma's great,' Simone said. 'She's fun.'

'Then Emma is a welcome guest. Welcome to Paris, Emma.'

I had the irrational feeling that I wanted her for my mother. 'Thank you.'

Ms Kwan patted Leo's arm. 'Make sure he comes sooner next time, Leo.'

'That's very easy for you to say, Ms Kwan.'

Ms Kwan raised her arms in welcome. 'Shall I show you to your rooms?' She took Simone's hand, then linked her other arm in mine. 'Come, let me show you where you will stay, Emma. Tomorrow Leo will take you and Simone to see beautiful Paris while I talk to Ah Wu. And then you, Leo and I will have a little chat.'

I was too awestruck by her graceful presence to say a word.

Simone adored the Eiffel Tower. There was a long queue for the lifts, but she was happy to wait, hopping from one leg to the other with excitement until she fell over.

'Try to stay on your feet, Simone,' I said with mock exasperation.

'I know, I keep "doing a Simone",' she said. 'I can't help it.'

Leo studied the crowd around us carefully.

'What?'

He shook his head.

I moved closer to him and spoke more softly. 'We're a long way from home, Leo. I don't think anybody around here even knows who she is.'

'You can never be too careful,' he said.

When we reached the top of the Tower we had to run to keep up with Simone. She raced from one side to another, showing me all the landmarks: the Louvre, Notre Dame, the Arc de Triomphe.

'How come you know Paris so well?'

'Because I come here all the time, silly Emma. We used to come here a lot before. Now we don't come as much.'

'Before what?'

She ran away.

'Is Ms Kwan Mr Chen's sister?' I asked Leo.

'Nope.'

'But they're related, then?'

Leo turned to follow Simone without answering me.

It was already dusk by the time Simone had finished with the Tower. By then Leo and I were thoroughly sick of it.

'Wait until the Science Museum,' Leo said. 'She likes it even more than this.'

Leo called the driver to collect us from one of the side streets bordering the Tower gardens. As we walked through the darkening city, he put his mouth next to my ear. 'Don't stop, keep walking, don't look back.'

I did as he said. We walked on a few metres without him, then Simone stopped dead. I pulled her hand, but she refused to move. She shook my hand free and ran back. I hurried to follow her, but she had stopped.

Leo was facing off against three young Chinese men. All of them appeared strong and muscular and they were concentrating on Leo.

'Move back, Emma,' Leo said without looking at me. 'Take Simone back out of the way.'

I did as he said. I thought about running, but I didn't know how many more of them might be waiting for us in the shadows.

In martial arts movies, the villains take on the hero one at a time and he defeats them individually. All three of these guys threw themselves at Leo at once.

Leo grabbed one and lifted him easily, then pushed him into the other two, knocking them backwards. Then he raised the man he held with one hand and smashed him into the ground.

The young man hit the pavement with a crack, then exploded into black streamers that dissipated quickly.

'Bad people,' Simone whispered. I pulled her closer to me.

Leo straightened. The other two guys held back, watching him. He gestured a come-on.

They both threw themselves at him. He caught the first one's hands and crossed them over his chest, pinning them, then turned him to block the other guy. He smashed his fist through the first guy's face. This one also dissipated into feathery streamers.

The last guy held back, smiling at Leo. Leo lunged forward, grabbed him, and hoisted him by the scruff of the neck with one hand. The young man struggled, then went still. Leo carried him to us.

'Check if this is one as well, sweetheart,' Leo said. 'I want to be sure.'

'Okay, Leo.' Simone shook my hand free and went to him. I tried to stop her, but Leo raised his free hand.

'It's okay. Let her.'

Simone touched the young man's arm. He screamed and his arm went black. When Simone moved her hand away, his arm returned to normal.

'Thanks, sweetheart,' Leo said. 'I just wanted to be sure. Next time, tell me if any are nearby, okay? I'm not as good as you.'

'Okay, Leo,' Simone said. 'You'd better take it to Daddy, he'll want to see.'

'I know. That's why I didn't destroy it.'

Simone came back to me, took my hand and smiled up at me. 'Leo's really good, isn't he?'

I was speechless with shock.

'You okay, Emma?' Leo said.

I recovered my voice. 'What the hell is going on?'

'I'll explain when we get back to Ms Kwan's house.'

I opened my mouth to protest and he raised his hand to stop me. 'I promise. I'll tell you all about it when we get back. Right now,' he glanced at the young man hanging limply in his hand, 'we need to take this one back to Mr Chen.'

It was an uncomfortable ride back to Montmartre. Leo put me in the front passenger seat and the young man in the middle seat in the back, between himself and

Simone. Leo's trouser legs were covered in black sticky foul-smelling goo, from when he'd destroyed the other two men.

At Ms Kwan's house, Leo hoisted the young man out of the van and carried him into the house. The driver didn't seem to notice.

Leo stopped in the entry hall. 'Mr Chen!' he called.

Mr Chen hurried out from the back of the house. He stopped dead when he saw the young man. He sighed. 'What happened?'

'Three of them attacked us. I thought I'd better bring this one back here for you to question,' Leo said.

Mr Chen glanced at me.

'Yes, I saw a great deal of very strange stuff,' I said, 'and if you don't tell me *right now* what's going on, I'm out of here.'

Mr Chen and Leo shared a look.

Ms Kwan came out of the back of the house. 'Is there a problem, Ah Wu? Why is there a —' She saw Leo holding the young man and sighed. 'Dear Leo, you are such an idiot sometimes.'

The young man struggled and freed himself from Leo's grasp. He threw himself to lie at Ms Kwan's feet. 'Protect me, Merciful Lady!'

'Shit,' Mr Chen said under his breath.

'Chen Wu!' Ms Kwan scolded.

'Protect me,' the young man said again, watching Mr Chen like a rabbit caught in headlights.

'Leo, you have broken every seal in this house and ensured that we will gain no information,' Mr Chen said. He gestured towards the young man. 'The Lady's nature is mercy to any creature that requests it. Even one of these.'

'Uh-oh,' Simone said.

'Oh no, *damn*!' Leo said. He ran his hand over his bald head and turned away. 'I am so sorry.'

'What's done is done,' Mr Chen said, still watching the young man cowering at Ms Kwan's feet. He glanced sharply at Leo. 'You destroyed the other two?'

'Yes, sir. This is the only one left.'

'But I must release it, Ah Wu,' Ms Kwan said. 'It will return and report, and there is nothing we can do about it.'

'Damn,' Leo said again, softly.

'Emma, please take Simone upstairs to wash for dinner,' Mr Chen said.

I opened my mouth to protest.

'Just do it, Emma,' Leo said gently. 'I'll tell you everything after dinner. I promise.'

I glared at him. 'I'll hold you to that.'

I took Simone's hand and led her up the stairs. We looked at one another quickly, then crouched at the top of the stairs to watch the little drama below.

Leo brightened. 'How about you let it go and I nab it again?'

'That is not possible, Leo,' Ms Kwan said stiffly. 'He has asked. I must give.'

'Thank you, thank you, Merciful Lady,' the young man said, still not shifting his eyes from Mr Chen.

'Go,' Ms Kwan said. 'The Dark Lord will not follow, neither will his Retainer. Go far, go fast, they will not follow. I will not tolerate you, I detest your kind.' She raised her hand towards the front door. 'Go.'

The young man turned, flung open the door and ran through it.

Ms Kwan closed the door as if nothing had happened, then linked her arm in Mr Chen's. 'Dinner time. I have employed a wonderful French chef to prepare something special for us.'

'Western food?' Mr Chen said suspiciously.

'Oh, come, Ah Wu, French food is very good. You may learn to like it.'

She smiled over her shoulder at Leo. 'Go and change, dear Leo. Once again your clothes are ruined.'

Leo frowned down at his goo-covered slacks. 'Yeah.'

'And you two ladies had better wash for dinner as well,' Ms Kwan called up to Simone and me. 'Hurry, or it will be cold when you come down.'

'She's right, Emma,' Simone whispered. She pulled me to my feet. 'I need to wash my hands after touching that thing.'

I followed her into the elegant bathroom. 'What was special about that man, Simone?'

Simone carefully washed her hands. 'That was a bad person.'

'The kind that can hurt you, like you said?'

'Yes.'

'Did his arm really go black when you touched him?'

'Yes.' She grinned. 'It hurts them when I touch them — that was cool.' She wiped her hands on one of the towels.

'It's not cool to hurt things, Simone,' I said automatically.

'It's okay to hurt *them*. You have to destroy them, otherwise they'll hurt me, and you, and a lot of other people besides.' Simone opened her mouth to continue, then gave up. 'I think you need to talk to my dad about it.'

'I think I do as well.'

Leo had already changed his slacks and was waiting for us at the bottom of the stairs. Simone ran ahead to find her father. I stopped in front of Leo and glared up at him. 'Well?'

'Dinner isn't the time to be discussing this, Emma. After dinner, I'll tell you the whole story.'

'Promise?'

He smiled slightly. 'Cross my heart.'

'Good.' I stormed past him into the dining room.

CHAPTER NINE

The dining room was as elegantly furnished as the rest of the house. I sat at the table; Leo followed me and sat as well.

Ms Kwan smiled compassionately. 'Dear Emma, I know you have no idea what is happening, but we will tell you all.'

'My Lady,' Mr Chen began, but she waved him down.

'Don't worry, Ah Wu. Emma, after dinner Leo will explain everything for you. Now ...' She raised her hands. 'Let's see what Jean has prepared for us.'

The meal was everything that Ms Kwan had promised, but I was bursting with so much curiosity that I could barely touch the food.

As we ate Simone prattled about the Eiffel Tower and Ms Kwan listened indulgently, asking questions to keep her talking. Ms Kwan also questioned me about myself: where I had come from and what I did in Hong Kong. She seemed genuinely interested in what I had to say. Mr Chen and Leo were quiet and morose.

When Simone had finished her ice-cream, Ms Kwan gently led her out of the dining room, with Mr Chen following. The maid brought a pot of coffee for Leo and me.

The minute she was out of the room I exploded. 'What the hell is going on, Leo?'

Leo smiled slightly as he poured the coffee. 'Yeah, I was wondering how long it would be before you worked out that things aren't completely ...' He put the coffee pot back on the table '... *normal* in the Chen household.'

'That's the understatement of the century.'

He turned the coffee cup in his hands. 'Let me work out where to start.'

'How about you start at the beginning and tell me everything?'

'Yeah, if you want to be here all night.'

'Just tell me!' I hissed.

He put the cup down and pushed it aside, then took my hand in both of his and looked into my eyes. 'Before I tell you anything, I want you to understand ... Staying with us may be dangerous.'

I jerked back.

'Don't worry. As long as you're with Mr Chen or me, you're safe. You're not involved in this; it's us they want. But if you feel at all worried, then go. Go now, before I tell you anything.' He gazed into my eyes. 'We'll put you on the next flight back to Hong Kong. You can forget about all of this, you can go back to the kindergarten, you can go home.'

I stared at him for a split second, then pulled my hand away. 'No way!'

'What?'

'I'm staying here with Simone,' I said fiercely. 'Now tell me what this is all about.'

He sat straighter and drank some coffee. 'Okay,' he finally said. 'You remember when we went to Repulse Bay and you saw the statue of Kwan Yin, Goddess of Mercy?'

I nodded.

'That's her. That's Ms Kwan, the lady we're staying with. She's a goddess.'

I stopped and stared at him, then put some pieces together. 'Oh my God, that's why he calls her Mercy.'

'Yes. It's not her name, it's what she *is*.'

I decided to give him some rope and see where the story went. 'Okay, so she's a goddess. And he thinks he's Xuan Tian Shang Di.'

Leo nearly dropped his coffee. '*What*?'

'Dark Lord of the Northern Heavens,' I said. 'Zhen Wu, Chen Wu, Xuan Wu. God of Martial Arts. Always wears black. Controls water. The Cheung Chau Bun Festival is held for him. Pak Tai.'

Leo was obviously astonished. 'How the hell do you know all that?'

'Oh, come *on*, Leo, both of you deliberately left those books in my room. And I got curious and did some research. It's obvious that he thinks he's a god.'

'No thinking about it. He really is a god, Emma. Believe me.'

I leaned forward and spoke fiercely. 'Why should I?'

He snorted. 'Don't think I didn't believe it either when I first joined them. Didn't take him long to prove it to me though; he just showed me his True Form and then did some unbelievable things with water and ...' He hesitated, searching for the words. 'Some of the stuff he can do is like magic.'

'His True Form?'

'This form, the human form, is only temporary. He has a True Form that he'd prefer to use most of the time. But back to the topic. If I could prove it to you, would you believe me?'

'Sure, go for it. Let's see something truly godly,' I said, my voice thick with derision.

He rose and went out without saying another word.

Before I had a chance to react, he was back with Ms Kwan, who sat next to me. Leo sat on the other side.

'How to prove to Emma?' Ms Kwan said. 'How did he prove to Michelle?'

'He showed her his True Form,' Leo said. 'Animal, not Celestial. It completely freaked her out and she hid in her room for two hours, crying. I had to go in and console her, she was nearly hysterical. She made him promise not to do it again.'

'He always was one for making foolish promises,' Ms Kwan said.

'Animal?' I said, and hesitated. Then, 'You think he's an *animal*? What the hell sort of animal is he?'

'Trust me,' Leo said. 'You really do not want to know.'

'It wasn't that bad, was it, Leo?' Ms Kwan said. 'He didn't even have the Serpent then.'

'*Serpent*?'

Leo ignored me. 'It was pretty bad, Ms Kwan. Freaked me out too. To tell the truth, I'm glad he can't do it now.'

'So I must,' Ms Kwan said. She rose and moved to the end of the room. She gazed compassionately at me. 'Do not be afraid. I will not harm you.'

I opened my mouth to say something sarcastic and stopped. She was *glowing*. A gentle white light was emanating from her. Then she grew. She spread and rose and her pantsuit turned into flowing white robes, with a hood over her shining mass of hair. She was nearly ten feet tall. Her face changed into a beatific mask of serenity. She was the image of the statue at Repulse Bay.

No way; had to be an illusion.

No illusion, she said straight into my ear, her beautiful face not moving. *Approach, Emma Donahoe.*

I rose and walked towards her. As I moved nearer, a warm feeling of comfort filled me.

'You're not frightened, Emma?' Leo said behind me.

'No,' I said, turning to look at him. 'Should I be?'

Leo didn't say anything so I turned back to her. She held her hand out and I took it in mine. The feeling of comfort spread and filled me until I thought I would overflow. She was vast and wide and wonderful; compassion and help and mercy.

I sighed with bliss.

'It's real,' Leo whispered behind me. 'She's Kwan Yin.'

'It could just be an illusion,' I said. 'Or you could have hypnotised me.'

She shrank and pulled inwards and the glow disappeared. My eyes went blurry and she became an ordinary graceful Chinese woman again. She held both her hands out, palms up, and a glowing ball of pure silvery energy appeared above them, about the size of a volleyball. The energy floated towards me and I inhaled sharply and backed away.

'Do not fear it. It will help you,' she said.

It took all my courage to stand still while the ball of glowing energy approached me. As it neared I felt her consciousness inside it and relaxed. It was as wonderful as she was. I reached out tentatively to touch it, then looked to Ms Kwan for confirmation.

'Touch it,' she said.

I moved my hand carefully towards it. When my fingertips brushed the energy, the charge jumped across to me. It was a wave of pure joy at being alive, as if nothing bad could ever happen to me. It was uplifting and euphoric. The energy drifted away from me and I reached to keep contact.

'Let it go,' she said softly.

I dropped my hand, disappointed.

The energy drifted towards the doorway where Mr Chen stood leaning with one shoulder against the doorframe. I hadn't seen him come in. He raised one hand and the energy drifted towards him, then entered his hand and disappeared into him. He nodded to her, his dark eyes full of amusement, and she nodded back.

'You are very brave, Emma,' Ms Kwan said.

'Yes, you are,' Mr Chen said. 'So now you know. I'd appreciate it if you didn't tell anybody.'

I opened my mouth to say that it could all be an illusion, then closed it again. Yes, it *could* all be an illusion. But the guys that attacked us had exploded into black stuff. Simone had touched the one Leo had captured and his arm had gone black.

I had an important decision to make. Either they were insane and delusional, all of them, or Mr Chen was a god. Either way I could stay or go.

I couldn't leave. I was much too fond of Simone to leave her. And I could bring a degree of normality into the poor child's life. I made the snap decision to play along with them for the sake of Simone, regardless of whether he was a god or not. I'd watch and wait and see what happened, and I'd look after Simone. The rest was detail.

'She is not fully convinced, but she will stay for Simone's sake,' Ms Kwan said.

I stared at her, speechless.

'We don't expect you to believe it at this early stage, Emma,' Mr Chen said. 'As long as you stay and care for Simone, that's all that matters.'

'Let us tell you more about it and you can make up your own mind,' Leo said. He turned and nodded to Mr Chen. 'I can handle the rest.'

'Good. I'll tell Simone.' Mr Chen went out and closed the door softly behind him.

I pulled my chair out and sat at the table. Leo poured me some coffee. I nodded my thanks and took a sip without really tasting it. It was possible that I was working for a god. I truly wanted to believe it; I still trembled from the euphoric experience of touching the ball of energy.

'What you have just experienced is a rare gift among mortals, Emma,' Ms Kwan said. 'It is not normally an energy we Celestials share.'

'You've been touched by the gods,' Leo said.

'Okay, Leo, so tell me the whole story, and this time don't leave anything out. I want to know everything.'

'Tell her, Leo,' Ms Kwan said. 'She is still unsure and looking for reasons to believe us.'

'Okay, here's the whole story,' Leo said. 'Xuan Wu is Emperor of the Northern Heavens, ruler of a quarter of the sky; he also owns a complete Mountain in Heaven, on the Celestial Plane. He has palaces, servants, the whole King thing. He gave it all away because his wife asked him to stay on Earth with her.'

'And that was Simone's mother,' I said. 'Good Lord, Simone's half *god*?'

'Half Shen,' Ms Kwan said. 'Ah Wu is a Shen. We are residents of the Celestial, Immortals. If a human being lives a life of purity and compassion they are Raised to the Celestial and become Immortal. That is what happened to me. He is older and stranger, though.' She smiled at the door.

'But his wife died,' I said.

'The demons got her,' Leo said. He dropped his head in misery. 'I failed. I worked for Michelle before she met him, when she was an opera singer touring the US. I was her bodyguard. This demon stuff was all still new when they attacked her. They got her.' His voice became very soft. 'I failed.'

'So now she's gone, he can go back to Heaven or wherever, can't he?' I was looking for gaps in the story. 'Why doesn't he?'

'He promised Michelle that he would not take True Form, and he kept his word,' Ms Kwan said. 'But it is a tremendous drain on his energy to stay in human form for so long, and he took it too far. He cannot return to his True Form now without staying in that form for a very long time. Maybe more than a lifetime. So he must stay here in human form and care for Simone, even though it makes him weaker than he has ever been in his history. The demons are after Simone and he must stay close to protect her, despite his weakness.'

'Those men earlier — they're demons?' I said, incredulous. 'And they're after Simone? Why?'

'If they have her, he must obey them,' Ms Kwan said. 'It would be dishonourable to harm her, but that would not stop them from taking her and using her as a hostage. He drove them from the face of the Earth a long time ago, and they would dearly like to return to its surface to terrorise humanity again. If they had Simone, he would be forced to let them.'

'If they have Simone,' Leo said, 'he would let them do anything they liked. And he's the one that protects everybody from them.'

'He is sworn to destroy them all,' Ms Kwan said.

Leo sighed. 'And he can't hold it together forever. He's like a battery, losing his charge all the time, getting weaker and weaker. He could charge himself up if he took True Form, but he's so far gone now that if he did that he'd be stuck in True Form for a long time. They know that and that's why they've targeted Simone. They think he's so weak he can't protect her, so they keep coming after her. He'll lose it eventually anyway, run out of energy and be gone.'

'That's what you were talking about in his office,' I said. 'After we went to Repulse Bay. He hadn't told you before that he only has a maximum of four or five years.'

Leo smiled sadly. 'He drives me completely crazy sometimes.'

'And you believe all of this?' I said.

'After a couple of weeks I think you will too, Emma,' Leo said. 'It's hard not to, because it really is true.'

I sat straighter; I'd found a hole in the story. 'Why's he in Hong Kong, not Northern China? He's the God of the North.'

'More opportunities for Simone. She's still in China, but she can learn about the West,' Leo said.

That made sense. I took a breath. 'So he really will leave her in four or five years? If people are really after her, what will happen then? She'll only be eight or nine years old.'

Leo spoke very softly. 'I'll guard her for as long as I can. And she's inherited some skills from him. Hopefully she'll be able to take any of them by the time he goes.'

'*Hopefully?*'

Leo's smile was full of misery.

'Okay,' I said. 'I don't completely believe you, but that's beside the point. The point is that there are people out there who want to kidnap this delightful little girl and we saw some of them this evening. There are people after her and she needs someone to care for her.' I swiped my hand through the air. 'All of this god stuff doesn't matter. Simone's safety and happiness is the most important thing.'

Leo and Ms Kwan shared a look. 'Impressive,' Ms Kwan said softly.

'He was worried you'd resign after this evening, like all the others did. And then Simone would be heartbroken,' Leo said.

'No way will I ever leave Simone as long as she needs me.' Then I heard what he'd said. 'Others? How many others?'

'At least fifteen in the twelve months before you arrived,' Leo said. 'He'd just about given up when you came on part-time. When the others saw the weapons they were scared away. You're the first to find out who he really is.'

'Leo, do you think he'll teach me? I'd really like to learn the martial arts.'

'I dunno, Emma, it's up to him. But I think it's a good idea. The more of us who are trained, the better we can defend Simone. You should ask him.'

'I did,' I said. 'He said no, definitely not, and never to ask again.'

Leo glanced sharply at Ms Kwan.

'Leave it for now then,' Ms Kwan said. 'I will talk to him.'

'Any questions?' Leo said.

'A million, but right now I think I'll just wait and see. I'm not completely convinced, but I'm willing to stay on for Simone's sake.'

'Let's go and tell him then,' Leo said. 'He'll be delighted.'

Mr Chen was sitting on one of the sofas with some Chinese tea on a side table next to him. Simone was busily drawing pictures of the Eiffel Tower, her drawing equipment spread all over the floor.

'Will you stay, Emma?' Mr Chen said.

'Yes, I will.'

'Thank you. You're very brave.'

I shook my head. 'No. I'm completely crazy.'

He made a soft sound of amusement, then nodded towards Simone. 'Simone's bedtime now, please.'

I stopped in front of Mr Chen. He was dressed all in black as usual, a scruffy T-shirt and a pair of torn cotton pants. His feet were comfortably bare and his long hair had already come out of its tie.

He saw the way I was looking at him. 'Don't worry,' he said. 'I'm not going to grow three heads any time soon.'

Ms Kwan sat in the armchair next to him and he poured her some tea. 'Four heads, a hundred arms and a thousand eyes,' she said.

'Maybe only two heads,' he said. 'I keep forgetting. It's been a very long time now.'

'Two heads again soon, I am sure, Ah Wu.'

'Not too soon,' he said, and they laughed quietly together.

'I am going to do some research on Xuan Wu the minute we're back in Hong Kong,' I said defiantly.

He seemed surprised, then grinned broadly. 'Go right ahead.' He crossed his arms over his chest and stretched his long legs in front of him. 'Seventy-five per cent of what's out there about me is wrong anyway.' He gestured with his teacup towards Simone. 'Bedtime, Simone.'

'Come on, Simone,' I said.

'I don't wanna go to bed. I wanna draw with Aunty Kwan.'

'You have to go to bed now if you want us to take you to Tuileries tomorrow,' Leo said from the dining room door.

Simone leapt up and grabbed my hand. 'Hurry up, Emma.'

I could feel Mr Chen's eyes on my back as I led Simone out. I turned. He *was* watching me, intently. When he saw me looking, he smiled and met my eyes. Something leapt inside me and I slapped it down, *hard*.

CHAPTER TEN

We walked over the Pont Neuf towards Notre Dame. Simone still had boundless energy and skipped beside us.

The forecourt of the cathedral was packed with tourists from all over the world and there was a long queue curling out from the main entrance.

'Do you want to go inside?' I asked Simone. 'There's a lot of people waiting.'

'Notre Dame's *boring*,' she said, and slowed to grab Leo's hand. 'Come on, Leo.' She dragged him across the road towards some three-storey stone buildings around a gated forecourt. Wigged and gowned lawyers walked up and down the stairs. I checked my mini map of Paris: the Justice Building.

'What are we doing here?' I said, but they ignored me and I had to hurry to keep up with them.

We went around the corner to where a tiny, dingy chapel nestled under the walls of the office buildings. I checked my map again: Saint Chapelle.

The queue wasn't as long as the one for Notre Dame. Simone stopped jiggling and stood quietly while we paid the entry fees.

Inside, it wasn't very impressive. The ceiling was

quite low, and there was only a small amount of stained glass.

'The rose windows are nice,' I said. 'Do you want to take a photo?'

'No,' Simone said and pulled Leo to the back of the chapel. A curving set of very narrow stairs led upwards. As Simone dragged Leo up the stairs his broad shoulders brushed against the walls, adding to the sheen of many bodies that had been there before.

When we reached the upper chapel the beauty of the interior took my breath away. The ceiling towered above us, with narrow stained-glass windows between the even narrower stone buttresses. The windows extended from ceiling to floor in a glittering dazzle of colours. They were like insubstantial glowing curtains between the fragile stonework of the walls.

A horseshoe of benches had been set up in the centre of the chapel to allow visitors a good view of the stained glass. Simone released Leo's hand, sat herself on one of the benches and spent ten minutes silently staring at the windows.

A group of young tourists walked past us and Leo watched them carefully. I caught his attention and raised my eyebrows. He shook his head slightly.

Simone hopped off the bench and dragged us down the stairs again.

'We have to be back at Ms Kwan's soon,' I said. 'Anywhere else you want to go before we leave for London?'

'Do I have time to go to Boulevard Haussmann and buy some stuff?' Simone said. 'I like the shops there.'

'Sure,' I said, stretching my feet.

'Sore?' Leo said.

'No,' I said. 'Completely killing me.'

He bent to talk quietly to me. 'Me too.' He straightened. 'Not finished yet. Boulevard Haussmann. Okay, I'll call the driver.'

Simone pointed to the entrance to the Metro station. 'I wanna take the train. Why can't we take the train?'

'Don't be silly,' I said. 'It's a long way down to the station and a long way up again. It's much easier to take the van, and we can get to the shops faster.'

'Okay,' Simone said. 'Hurry up, Leo. Can we go to the Eiffel Tower one more time before we leave?'

I sagged. 'Simone, you've been there three times already.'

She grinned up at me. 'But I like it.'

Leo pulled out his phone. 'You don't say.'

After a last lunch with Ms Kwan, we went out into the narrow leafy street where our van waited.

'I had fun with Aunty Kwan,' Simone said. 'She's my favourite.'

Leo opened the door of the van for us. Simone raced back to Ms Kwan for one last hug and kissed her on the cheek.

'Look after your father for me,' Ms Kwan said.

'Come and visit us in Hong Kong,' Simone said.

Ms Kwan nodded, smiling.

Leo took Simone and buckled her into the van.

I approached Ms Kwan and spoke softly. 'I hope it's all true, Ms Kwan.'

'Don't worry, dear Emma,' she said, smiling gently. 'Bring him back to me in about eight months; his energy will not last longer than ten. But it is best if I come to him.' She took my hands and clasped them, and again I felt the warm sensation of comfort. 'Look after our little Simone. She is very precious.'

'Don't worry, I will.'

I looked down at my hands where she held them. I wanted to tell her how much it meant to meet her, what it felt like to talk to her, how special she was. I wanted to thank her. But I couldn't find the words. I looked up at her in desperation, to find her smiling at me.

'It's all right,' she said, 'I understand.'

I climbed into the van and sat next to Simone.

Mr Chen came out of the house, stood in front of Ms Kwan, and smiled down at her.

'Let me know if you see any more of them,' she said.

'I will. Go back to your garden, Lady.'

'I certainly will. All of this is much too elaborate for me.' She raised her arms and sighed theatrically. 'Ah, the sacrifices I make for you, Ah Wu.'

He stayed perfectly still, watching her. Then he fell to one knee before her and held his hands clasped in front of his chest in the Chinese salute.

Leo gasped.

Ms Kwan stamped her foot. 'Ah Wu! If you ever do that to me again I will not speak to you for a hundred years.'

He rose and saluted her again.

Her voice trembled as she wiped her eyes with her sleeve. 'You are a silly old man.'

'I know. I will see you in eight months.' He climbed into the van and closed the door. 'Let's go.'

I glanced back through the rear window of the van as we pulled away. She was gone.

It was a short hop from Paris to the UK. A driver with a stretch limousine waited for us at Gatwick.

Leo and I sat facing the rear, and Mr Chen and Simone sat across from us, facing the driver. It was a crush with Mr Chen's long legs and Leo's huge mass and I understood why Mr Chen usually ordered a van.

Simone slept in the car, but Mr Chen seemed full of energy. He looked ten years younger after seeing Ms Kwan, nearly the same age as me. Whatever it was that she'd done to him, it had worked.

'Leo, do you think you will be all right without me tomorrow?' he said. 'If you and Emma take Simone to the Science Museum?'

'Should be okay, Mr Chen. There'll be plenty of people around everywhere we go,' Leo said.

'They only come after you when there aren't people around?' I said.

Both Leo and Mr Chen nodded.

'Okay,' I said. 'Good.'

They stared at me.

'Why good?' Leo said.

'Because if we always make sure there are plenty of people around, Simone will be safe,' I said. 'Obvious.'

Leo and Mr Chen shared a look.

'Where are you planning to go, Mr Chen?' I went on. Leo dug me in the ribs and I yelped. I rounded on him. 'What?'

'You ask too many questions,' Leo said.

'The hell I do. You're always keeping me in the dark. I need to know what's going on.' I gestured towards Simone, who was sleeping on Mr Chen's lap. 'For example, now I know that she's safer with more people around, I can make sure we're always in busy places.'

Leo chuckled and shook his head.

'I want to go to Cambridge and meet up with some of my old postgrad colleagues,' Mr Chen said. 'It's been a long time.'

'You studied at Cambridge?' I said, and yelped when Leo dug me in the ribs again. I slapped his arm. 'Cut it out!'

'Leo, I think I am capable of telling Miss Donahoe if I do not wish to answer her questions,' Mr Chen said, his eyes sparkling with amusement. 'I have a PhD from Cambridge. I did it about ...' He paused, thinking. 'Thirty years ago, I think. I had to rewrite the thesis six times before they'd accept it. I nearly gave up.'

'Thirty years ago? How old were you when you did it?'

His face shifted until he seemed younger, in his mid-twenties. 'I was about twenty-five when I studied there.' He changed again, until he appeared in his mid-fifties. 'I will be about fifty-five when I go back.' He changed back to his mid-thirties.

Dear Lord, it was real. I was working for a god!

'My Lord, that was an unnecessary waste of your energy,' Leo said, irritated.

'What?' I said, glancing from Leo to Mr Chen.

Leo thrust his hand palm-up towards Mr Chen. 'Throws his energy away all the time.'

I turned my attention back to Mr Chen. 'Please don't waste your energy on small things.'

'Oh come on,' Mr Chen said. 'You should have seen the look on your face.' He smiled at me and his eyes wrinkled up. I felt a rush of affection for him, then pushed it away. Only around for a limited time, and not even human. No chance.

'What was your PhD in?' I said.

'Comparative literature. I compared the stories surrounding the English King Arthur with the stories surrounding me. It was fascinating to draw the parallels — the stories become more embroidered and elaborate as time passes. My supervisor had never even heard of me, he hadn't done much Chinese literature. He said I was very interesting.'

I choked back the laugh. 'I'd love to read it.'

'It's in my study somewhere.'

'Oh geez, I'll never see it then.' I rounded on Leo before he could dig me in the ribs again and shoved him. 'Cut it out!'

Mr Chen chuckled. 'You have family here in England, don't you?'

'Yes, a big sister. Moved to England with her husband about ten years ago. I haven't seen her in ages.'

'If you would like to take some time to visit her, you can,' Mr Chen said.

'No, thanks.'

'You should see your family, Emma.'

'Maybe next time.'

'Very well, but next time you *will* see them.'

I sighed. 'Okay.'

'What's the matter — problems with your family?' Leo said.

'None of your business.'

'Suit yourself.' He looked away. 'At least I know when not to ask questions.'

'Bastard,' I said under my breath.

'I heard that,' he said, a low rumble.

Simone woke as we were passing Hyde Park in Kensington and watched the scenery with delight.

The limousine stopped in a quiet leafy side street outside a white four-storey townhouse with towering ground-floor windows.

A caricature of an English butler waited at the front door: mid-fifties, bow tie, the whole works. The driver opened the door for us and Simone ran to the butler and threw herself into his arms. She kissed him quickly, then pulled herself free and ran into the house.

'Help the others with the bags, James,' Mr Chen said, walking up the stairs to the entry.

James came down the stairs to the boot of the car.

Leo stopped in front of him. 'I don't need your help, Mr O'Brien.'

'Orders, Mr Alexander,' James snapped back.

They stood and glared at each other. I decided to go inside the house without getting involved.

I followed Mr Chen into the entry hall. Old-fashioned black and white tiles covered the floor, and the ceiling stretched away forever. Curved stairs led to the next floor up, with more stairs to higher levels. What appeared to be expensive European art hung on the walls.

Simone was hugging and giggling with a grandmotherly English woman wearing a pale blue maid's uniform.

'I missed you, Charlie!' Simone cried.

'I missed you too, little Princess,' Charlie said, lifting Simone and squeezing her. She lowered Simone to look at her properly. 'You are growing so fast, you're already a proper little lady.'

'That's what Aunty Kwan said.' Simone screwed up her face. 'I'm *hungry*.'

Charlie smiled at me. She had a soft, round face with cheerful sparkling blue eyes. Her greying brown hair was tied in a loose bun.

'Hi,' I said. 'I'm Emma, Simone's nanny.'

'Pleased to meet you.' She smiled down at Simone. 'Let's go and find you something to eat.' She patted my arm. 'Would you like something, Emma?'

'A cup of tea would be lovely, Charlie,' I said.

'Me too, Charlie, in the study,' Mr Chen said from where he was checking some documents on a rosewood hall table.

Leo and James came in with the bags, still glowering at each other.

Mr Chen saw them. 'Will you two let it go!'

Leo and James dropped their heads, apologetic.

'Put Miss Donahoe's bags in the room next to Simone's, James,' Mr Chen said. 'And as soon as you two are finished with the bags I want to see both of you in my study.'

Charlie spoke conspiratorially to Simone and me. 'Come on, girls, let's leave these silly men to their own business.'

Mr Chen glanced up at us, eyes sparkling, from the other side of the entry, but didn't say anything.

Charlie sat us at the kitchen table and gave Simone some warm scones with lashings of jam and cream. Simone messily buried her face in them, and slurped on some milk.

'What's the problem between James and Leo?' I asked.

'James will never forgive Leo,' Charlie said. 'He blames him for ...' She hesitated, and glanced at Simone. 'You know. What happened.'

'I don't think it was Leo's fault,' I said. 'He's very good.'

'It wasn't Leo's fault at all, dear,' Charlie said, 'but I think James has to blame somebody.'

Charlie and I were firm friends by the time James came in.

'I've put your bags in your room, Emma,' he said, and I nodded my thanks. He didn't lose his crisp London accent, and I began to suspect that the old-fashioned butler thing wasn't an act. He bent over Simone to kiss the top of her head. 'Hello, sweetie.'

'Hello, James,' Simone said through a crumbly mouthful of scone.

James pulled a cup and saucer from a cupboard and sat at the table with us. Charlie poured him some tea.

'So, Emma,' he said, 'how long have you worked for Mr Chen?'

'Full-time, about six months,' I said. 'But I'd been caring for Simone part-time for another six months before that.'

'And Simone is happy?' James said.

Simone nodded through her food.

'Good. Where are you from, Emma?'

'Australia. Queensland.'

'Don't know anyone there,' James said.

'How long have you worked for Mr Chen?'

James hesitated, probably working out something suitable in his head.

'It's okay, I know,' I said.

'What, already?' Charlie said.

Simone piped up. 'We were followed by some demons in Paris. Leo caught one, but Aunty Kwan let it go. So Leo had to tell Emma about Daddy and everything.'

The English staff shared a look. 'A demon, eh, Simone?' James said.

'Yes,' Simone said with confidence. 'That's the right word, isn't it?' she added, unsure.

'Yes, pet, that's the right word,' Charlie said kindly. She stiffened and spoke more sternly, 'I'll have none of that here.'

'Not much we can do about it, is there?' James said.

'Daddy and Leo will look after us,' Simone said, full of confidence.

'They had better,' James said.

'So, James,' I said, trying to turn the conversation away from a topic that might frighten Simone, 'how long have you worked here?'

'My family's been in Mr Chen's employ for five generations,' James said. 'I hope my nephew will take up the mantle when I retire, he's majoring in hospitality.'

'My family's been looking after him for three generations,' Charlie said. She smiled indulgently at Simone. 'If only my grandmother could see you, dear.'

'Mr Chen's owned this house for about a hundred and fifty years,' James said. 'Keeps it very well maintained.'

'A hundred and fifty years? He's been coming to the UK for that long?'

'Longer than that,' Charlie said. 'Apparently he's very unusual in being able to do it, most of them can't. The records say he stayed away during the Wars, but he's spent a lot of time here otherwise — diplomatic and trading things.'

'Wars? World Wars?'

'Opium Wars,' James said. 'Bad times. Don't even think he was in China. Probably went to the top of the Mountain in disgust. Very unhappy about the whole thing.'

'He wasn't involved?'

'Of course not,' Charlie said, genuinely shocked. 'He is an honourable man.'

'Played cricket for Cambridge when he studied there,' James said proudly. 'Best bowler in the team. Brutal fast ball. Broke the lights in the front hall practising.'

'Twice,' Charlie said.

I had to laugh; but I could see it.

'But we haven't seen nearly as much of him as we'd like, with things the way they are. He spends most of his time in Hong Kong now,' Charlie said. 'Poor dear can't even go to his Mountain. It's very hard for him.'

'When Daddy goes, I'm going with him,' Simone said. 'We'll go and live on his Mountain together.'

We all shared a silent look.

Charlie wrapped her arm around Simone's shoulders and gave her an affectionate squeeze. 'We'll just have to see what happens, dear.' She smiled at me without releasing Simone. 'Go and unpack, Emma. Simone and I will be fine here, we have a lot of catching up to do.'

'I'll show you the way,' James said, rising.

'Thanks.'

* * *

I lifted the suitcase onto my bed, then fell to sit beside it. He'd owned the house for a hundred and fifty years. They'd been working for him for generations. He'd studied in Cambridge thirty years ago.

A little knot of excitement tightened inside me. He *was* a god!

Mr Chen appeared in the doorway. 'Everything all right in here, Emma?'

'Yes, sir. This room is lovely.'

The room had been decorated in a delightful relaxed cottage style with a fluffy white double bed. The large window overlooked the leafy street.

'If you need anything, just ask Charlie or James,' he said.

'You've really had this house for more than a hundred and fifty years?'

He came in, leaned on the wall and crossed his arms over his chest. 'Something like that. One of my newer acquisitions.'

I shook my head with disbelief.

'You're handling this remarkably well, Emma.'

'I think the shock of the whole thing will catch up with me soon.'

'I do only have a limited time, Emma. And once I'm gone, I don't know how long it will take me to come back. I'm glad Simone has you now; she adores you.'

'She thinks you're going back to the Mountain and taking her with you, doesn't she?'

He dropped his head. 'That's right.'

'Why can't you go back to your Mountain?'

'When she was newly born I could,' he said. 'The Mountain is on the Celestial Plane, and a child can travel there under the protection of its mother. The three of us would go there regularly, and I could rebuild my energy there. The Mountain is a part of me, a part of my essence.'

'But now her mother's gone, Simone can't go?'

'That's right. And I can't leave her here alone while I travel to the Mountain; the demons would try for her immediately. I must stay here to defend her.'

'So you're stuck here like this.'

'Yes,' he said. 'I am so weakened now that I cannot even take myself to the Mountain without major risk.'

'What about taking True Form? Does that help you build your energy back?'

'Yes, but if I were to take True Form now I would not have the strength to return to human form. I would be stuck in True Form for a very long time. And that would mean leaving Simone unprotected.'

My heart went out to him: he was suffering for Simone; but, even worse, he would soon leave her.

I snapped myself out of it and changed the subject. 'You've really employed Charlie's and James's families for generations?'

He shrugged. 'Charlie's grandmother was an extraordinary woman. She taught me that Westerners expect to be treated differently, and the relationship they have with their Lord is different from what I was accustomed to. Frankly, I much prefer less formality; the Western way of doing things is very refreshing.'

'How old are you, Mr Chen?'

He smiled slightly. 'I have no idea. I don't remember being born, or gaining consciousness. I do know that I am more than four thousand years old.'

Far too old for me.

'Does your True Form really have two heads?'

He hesitated, studying me. Then he obviously decided to risk it. 'Yes. I am widely regarded as the ugliest creature in creation.'

Tall, dark, magnificent, the ugliest creature in creation ... It didn't matter.

'It's the inside that counts,' I said softly. 'The outside doesn't matter at all.'

'You are quite correct,' he said, gazing into my eyes. 'The inside is the only thing that is important.'

'Will we be attacked by demons while we're here? Or will they wait until we're back home?'

'I honestly don't know,' he said. 'They found my weakness when my wife was killed. They are beginning to move in. They definitely won't attack when I am at Simone's side; even weakened like this I am capable of taking any of them.' He sighed. 'I would understand if you chose to leave now. They will not come after you if you leave my service.'

'No!'

I said. 'I am staying with Simone!'

'You really do love her, don't you,' he said softly, his face intense.

The words came out before I even thought about them. 'More than anything in the world.' And it was true. Simone was very special to me.

We shared a thought: both of us loved her more than anything in the world.

He turned to leave. 'I think that Simone and I are very lucky to have you, Emma,' he said without looking back.

I watched him go, feeling that I was the one who was privileged.

CHAPTER ELEVEN

Simone and Charlie sat giggling together over breakfast. When Mr Chen came in he sat at the kitchen table next to Simone. He put his arm around her shoulders and kissed her on the cheek, and she kissed him messily back.

Charlie quickly rose to serve him some congee. 'I'll put this in the dining room for you, sir.'

'No need, I'll eat here with the ladies.'

Charlie stood stiffly next to the table, holding the bowl of congee. 'That's not fitting, sir, you should eat in the dining room.'

He waved her down. 'Here. With Simone.' He smiled into my eyes. 'And Emma.'

Simone giggled. Charlie sighed with exasperation and placed the congee in front of him. She collected some bowls of pickled vegetables from the kitchen bench and put them in the centre of the table.

'Sit, Charlie,' Mr Chen said. 'Finish your tea.'

Charlie looked uncomfortable, then sat down.

'Did you make the congee?' I said. 'Hold on, you cooked the Chinese meal we had last night?'

'Of course I did,' Charlie said. 'My mother taught me.'

'And you're nearly as good as she was,' Mr Chen said, reaching for some pickled vegetables with his chopsticks. He raised the pickles. 'These are very good.'

'Why, thank you, sir,' Charlie said with pleasure. 'I should come to Hong Kong and brush up.'

'That's a good idea. I'll arrange it for you.' Mr Chen stopped. 'Is the car fit to drive?'

'Of course it is; it's in the basement waiting for you. James has been taking it out for regular runs.'

'You had the rollbar fitted?'

'Yes, sir.'

'Good,' Mr Chen said. 'I'll drive it myself to Cambridge.' He bent his head to speak to Simone. 'Do you want to come for a drive with me before I leave?'

'Not in *that* funny old car,' Simone said without looking at him.

He moved his face closer to hers. 'You love my funny old car.'

She glared into his eyes. 'It's a silly old car.'

'Well, I'm a silly old man,' he said, and they both collapsed laughing.

Leo came in, and stopped when he saw them.

'Daddy's going to drive his silly car, Leo,' Simone said through her giggles.

Leo pulled a coffee mug out of the cupboard. 'It's not silly; actually it's a very nice car.'

'It's *silly*,' Simone said with scorn. She glared at her father. 'And so are *you*.'

'I know.' He saw my face. 'MG TF, 1500cc model, one of the rarer ones. Bought it in 1955. Original owner, low mileage.'

'Black?' I said. 'I didn't know they came in black.'

'Nope.' His eyes sparkled over the congee. 'Racing green. Only car I've ever owned that wasn't black.'

'Take me for a ride in it, please,' I begged.

'I will if I have a chance, Emma, I promise. But I can't guarantee anything.' His face softened as he remembered. 'All my friends thought I was crazy to buy it. They said it was much too cheap and old-fashioned.' He looked down at his congee and his voice softened. 'Michelle loved driving it.'

Leo cleared his throat uncomfortably and poured himself some coffee.

After Mr Chen had gone out, Leo sat next to me at the table. 'That's the first time he's mentioned his wife's name since the funeral.'

'Michelle,' I said. 'There're no photos or anything in the apartment.'

'He shouldn't have kept it bottled up for so long, poor dear,' Charlie said. 'It's good to hear him talk about it. He's changed.'

'In what way?' I said.

Charlie stopped and mused. Then, 'I think he just seems happier. Last time he came, he didn't talk much, he didn't laugh, he didn't want to do anything. It's good to see him so happy.'

'I wanna go to the Science Museum!' Simone yelled.

Leo and I groaned.

The next day we all went shopping in Harrods so that Simone could see the toys and Leo could check out the menswear. After the third time through the toy department Simone was becoming restless, so we went back to the menswear section.

Mr Chen called Leo over. 'How much longer will you be?'

Leo glanced back at the racks and the shop assistant he'd been talking to. 'Just a bit more.'

'You've already been more than an hour,' I said, exasperated.

Leo glared at me.

'We'll take Simone to the big toy shop in Regent Street,' Mr Chen said. 'Take your time, and we'll meet you back at the house.'

Leo didn't hesitate. 'Yes, sir.' He returned to the shop assistant without looking back.

Mr Chen and I shared an amused glance.

'I just prefer to be comfortable,' I said.

'Me too.'

'Yeah,' Simone said. 'Both of you are really scruffy. Leo says he's embarrassed to be seen with you, and I should never let either of you buy clothes for me.'

Mr Chen grinned. 'Good.'

On the final day, we all went to the zoo in Regent's Park.

'I'll have to take you to the zoo in Sydney one day, Simone,' I said. 'It's heaps bigger than this one, and it has a great view of Sydney Harbour.'

'*Turtles*!' Simone squealed and ran to see the Galapagos giant tortoises. She leaned over the fence, delighted. 'I love turtles. They're so *ugly*.'

Mr Chen came and stood between us, leaning on the railing. 'You think they're ugly?'

She grinned up at him. 'Yes.'

'What do you think, Emma?' Mr Chen said.

I suddenly realised that he was standing very close to me. Very, very close: his whole body was stretched alongside mine. He put his arm around me to lean on the rail and the shock of the chemistry went right through me.

I took a deep breath and tried to control my reaction.

'I like snakes better,' I said. 'I had a pet carpet snake back in Australia.'

Mr Chen moved closer and leaned into me. His long hair brushed over my shoulder. I found it extremely difficult to concentrate.

Simone didn't seem to notice. 'Was it poisonous?'

'Was what poisonous?' I said.

'The snake, silly.'

'Uh, no, it was a python.'

Mr Chen pulled his arm closer around me. 'What did you feed it, Emma?'

Leo made some throat-clearing noises behind us. Neither of us paid him any attention.

I turned and looked up into Mr Chen's glowing dark eyes. 'Live mice.'

He shifted even closer. His whole body was pressed into mine. 'Where did you get your mice from?'

I caught my breath. 'I bought them from the pet shop. Monty only ate about one a week. Then they found out what I was doing with them, so I had to breed my own.'

'Monty?' Simone said, still watching the tortoises.

'The snake.'

Leo snorted. He was the only one who understood the joke. Then, 'My Lord ...' he said softly, warning.

'I wonder if they have any poisonous snakes here, Simone,' I said without looking away from Mr Chen.

Simone pushed her father out of the way and he snapped out of it. She took my hand. 'Let's go and see.'

Mr Chen took Simone's other hand. 'Okay, let's go.'

'I hate snakes,' Leo said as we moved towards the snake house.

Mr Chen stopped and spoke over his shoulder. 'Some of my best friends are snakes, Leo.'

'No offence, sir,' Leo said sheepishly.

About three hours out of Macau, the jet pilot called for Mr Chen on the intercom. Mr Chen went into the cockpit and talked to him for about ten minutes.

When he returned, he sat and picked up the Chinese book he'd been reading.

'Is there a problem, sir?' Leo said.

'Not at this stage,' Mr Chen said without looking up.

About an hour later, Simone fell asleep on my lap and Leo carried her to the back of the plane and put her in the bunk.

The pilot called Mr Chen over the intercom again. When Leo returned he looked questioningly at me. I pointed towards the cockpit and he nodded.

Mr Chen came back, sat in his chair, picked up his book and bookmarked his page. He closed the book and put it to one side. 'A typhoon is headed straight for Macau. It will be a direct hit in the next two hours.'

A direct hit from a typhoon would close the airport. The winds would be ferocious. A small plane had tried to land during a typhoon in Hong Kong a couple of years before, and had flipped over on the runway. Three people had died. And that hadn't even been a direct hit.

'So we'll divert to Taipei or Manila?' I said.

'I have to be in Hong Kong later today,' Mr Chen said. 'I have an appointment that I must fulfil, regardless of the circumstances. We'll land in Macau.'

Leo threw himself out of his chair and towered over Mr Chen. 'If you're planning what I think you are, you are completely crazy!'

Mr Chen glared up at Leo, irritated. 'I must be in Hong Kong later today. I have no choice.'

'You'll undo all the good work the Lady Kwan did for you!'

'I'll probably need to see Mercy about a month earlier.'

'Wait a minute.' I pointed at Mr Chen. 'You're going to fiddle with the weather?'

Both of them looked at me.

'Don't point at a Chinese, Emma, it's very bad luck,' Leo said.

'Don't be ridiculous, Leo,' Mr Chen said. 'I am far too big for any fung shui to affect me. I *am* water. I *am* shui.'

I dropped my hand and glared at Mr Chen. 'You're going to use all that energy that Ms Kwan gave you to move a stupid typhoon? Leo's right — it had better be damned important if you're going to waste your energy like that.'

'I have a meeting with the Jade Emperor,' Mr Chen said grimly.

Leo sat down, stricken.

'The Jade Emperor,' I said softly. 'The Jade Emperor is so ...' I searched for the word '... so awesome, they don't even have statues of him in the temples.'

'Believe me,' Mr Chen said, 'I would much prefer to divert to Taipei and wait. But the appointment is for this evening at seven and I must be there. The Celestial has come down to the Earthly Plane, to Hong Kong, to see me. It is the first time he's done this in hundreds of years.'

'So what are you going to do?' I said.

'Move the typhoon, make it hit land about two hundred kilometres from Macau, and make it hit in the next thirty minutes.'

'You can do that?'

'I'll need to change my form, but yes.'

Leo hissed with frustration.

'Move the chairs, Leo, give me room,' Mr Chen said. He rose and kicked off his shoes, then pulled his hair from its ponytail and shook it out. 'Emma, sit with Simone in the back. If she wakes, keep her quiet. I'll need to concentrate. Make sure she doesn't come in here. Understood?'

'Don't worry, I'll make sure she doesn't come in.'

He smiled. 'I am more impressed with you every day.'

I felt a rush of professional pride at the compliment. Yep, that's all it was: purely professional.

Mr Chen sat cross-legged on the floor of the cabin. Leo moved the chairs along their rails, then leaned against the side of the plane. Mr Chen closed his eyes, concentrating, and Leo nodded for me to go out.

Simone had slept through all of Leo's yelling; she was completely worn out. I knelt on the carpet next to her bunk.

The plane rocked slightly, then shuddered. A brilliant white glow lit up the main cabin and shone through the galley. It was as if somebody had turned the lights up very bright.

Simone shot upright and scrambled to the end of the bunk. She hopped out before I could stop her and ran to the door of the galley. The light formed a halo around her and her hair floated with static.

I quickly went to her and held her to stop her from going in. She didn't attempt to move; she stood at the door of the galley, frozen, watching her father. Her breath quickened when she saw him.

It had to be him, but he was huge and dark and unrecognisable. He still sat cross-legged on the floor of the plane, but had grown so large that his head nearly brushed the ceiling. His long hair floated around his square, ugly face. The glow came from him; it was all around him. He held one hand in front of his chest and the other in his lap. His eyes were closed, concentrating. Any doubts I had held before completely vanished. What sat in the middle of the cabin was definitely a god.

I gently pulled Simone back into the bunk room and sat her on the bed.

'Is that his True Form?' I whispered.

'No,' she whispered back, her voice trembling. Her little face screwed up with fear. 'That's his Celestial Form, for when he's doing his special things. He's not supposed to do that.'

'Lie down and go back to sleep,' I said. 'He's just stopping the big wind outside so that we can go home.'

She threw her little arms around my neck and clutched me. I pulled her into my lap.

'He's so scary,' she whispered.

'It's just your dad.'

'He's scary.'

I sat with her for about twenty minutes as the plane shuddered and rocked. She buried her face in my chest and wouldn't move.

Then the light blinked out and I heard something hit the floor with a sickening thump. I quickly rose, still holding Simone, and went to the door.

Mr Chen lay on the floor in his normal form, his long hair spread around his head. Leo was bent over him, his face a mask of misery. When Leo saw us he nodded. I gently lowered Simone and led her to her father.

Mr Chen was unconscious. Leo picked him up like a child and gently placed him into a chair.

Simone took her father's hand and ran her other hand over his face. 'Daddy. Daddy!'

'Will he be all right?' I said.

'Yes,' Simone said, with an expression that belonged on a much older face. 'He'll wake up soon.'

Leo rubbed his hands over his face and went into the bathroom.

Mr Chen's eyes flickered open and he looked around. He saw Simone and pulled himself to sit more upright. 'Where's Leo?'

'In the bathroom,' I said.

He nodded and relaxed. Simone crawled into his lap and put her head on his chest.

The intercom clicked on. 'The typhoon made landfall about two hundred kilometres south of Macau, Mr Chen,' the pilot said. 'It will be choppy, but we'll land in Macau on time. I'll tell you when it's time to put on your seatbelts.' The intercom clicked off with an audible pop.

'You're a very silly daddy.'

He kissed the top of her head. 'I know.'

CHAPTER TWELVE

The wind was still blowing fiercely when we landed in Macau, but the pilot handled it easily. We piled out of the plane and took our bags through the nearly deserted airport; every other plane scheduled to land had been diverted.

We raced through customs and immigration. Mr Chen didn't even bother putting our bags on the X-ray machines; he just hypnotised the staff and they waved us through.

Leo glowered.

We hustled onto the boat and took off through Macau's muddy water, under the enormous spanning bridge that joined the three islands. The water was completely flat.

When we hit the open sea the water still didn't have any waves at all, and Leo's expression went even darker.

'Not my doing, Leo,' Mr Chen said. 'The water is always like this after a typhoon, you know that.'

Leo didn't say anything; he just stomped into the cabin at the front of the boat and sulked.

The boat ride back to Hong Kong only took an hour; as fast as one of the Macau Ferry's jetfoils — the jet-propelled hydrofoils that carried the gamblers between Macau and Hong Kong. I glared at Mr Chen when we reached the pier, but he ignored me. It shouldn't have been such a quick trip. The jetfoils travelled much faster than ordinary boats.

Leo jumped off the boat and charged through the afternoon Central crowd into a nearby office building to collect the car from its parking space underneath.

When he pulled the car into the lay-by under City Hall, we threw the bags into the boot. I put Simone in the back with me, Mr Chen sat in the front with Leo, and we raced up the overpass to take us to the Peak.

Mr Chen kept glancing at his watch.

'Will you make it?' I said.

He checked his watch again. 'If I'm quick. I'll need to shower and change first — I can't go like this.'

'Where's the meeting?'

Leo hissed under his breath.

'Sorry,' I said. 'You don't have to tell me if you don't want to.'

'Grand Hyatt,' Mr Chen said. 'Next to the Convention Centre.' The Convention Centre was shaped like a flowing sea creature, jutted into the Harbour and was clearly visible from all over Hong Kong. 'He's taken a suite there for this meeting.'

'What's the meeting about? It must be important.'

'Emma!' Leo snapped.

Mr Chen sat silently, his face grim. Then he shook his head. 'No.'

'Okay,' I said.

Leo visibly relaxed.

When we reached the Peak apartment building, Leo left the car running in the ground-floor car park. We went into the lift lobby, and Leo brought the bags.

Mr Chen lowered his head and disappeared.

'He's not supposed to do that,' Simone said.

'He's in a big hurry,' I said.

'No excuse,' Leo said, glowering.

'At least he waited until we were in here,' I said.

When we reached the apartment, the door was already hanging open. Monica came out of the kitchen to help Leo with the bags, and I took Simone into the living room out of the way.

Mr Chen came charging down the hallway in a pair of black silk pants and a black T-shirt, pulling on a stunningly embossed black silk robe. He stopped at the front door and fiddled with the silk toggles and loops on the robe. The toggles fastened across the front of his chest and then down the side. The robe had a stiff mandarin collar, long sleeves, and fell to the floor.

I rushed to help him with the toggles. He nodded his thanks and tied back his hair as I quickly straightened the collar around his throat, then brushed his shoulders.

I was very close to him, with my hands on his broad shoulders. I looked up into his dark eyes and I saw every detail of his noble face.

He reached up, took my hands and lowered them. He looked into my eyes as he held my hands, and something inside me leapt.

He gently pushed my hands away. 'Thanks.'

'You're welcome.'

He grabbed his sword from its hooks on the wall, then spun to pull his shoes out of the shoe cupboard. He tugged them on and raced out the door, his long hair flying behind him — it had already started to come out of its tie. He pressed the button for the lift, fidgeting with impatience as he waited for it.

'You'll make it,' I said.

He turned and smiled. 'I think I will.'

The lift came and he went in. He smiled into my eyes as the doors closed.

Damn! He looked incredible in that outfit.

Then there was a most satisfying bellow from inside the apartment as Leo discovered the rubber snake in his suitcase on top of his clothes.

We all slept late the next day, even Leo. I checked Simone; still sleeping. If I let her, she'd sleep the day away and be up all night. I would have to wake her soon.

Mr Chen was already locked in his study. I went into the kitchen for a cup of tea.

'What time did he come in, Monica?'

'I don't know, Emma, it was very late.'

When I'd finished my tea, I woke Simone and took her into the kitchen. She didn't want to eat, but she drank the juice I gave her and asked for more. She sat in my lap with her head on my shoulder, drowsy. The poor child was exhausted, dehydrated and jet-lagged. I didn't feel much better myself; I had a massive headache.

Simone suddenly perked up and jumped out of my lap. She went to the kitchen door, poked her head around it, then rushed out. The front door banged and I raced after her.

Mr Chen's personal assistant and his accountant had arrived. I didn't know their names; I'd just watched them go in and out during the months I'd been working there. They'd never spoken to me before, and now I had some idea why.

The accountant was a smartly dressed woman in her twenties. She never seemed to smile, and completely ignored me whenever she saw me. She wore a beautifully tailored pale green silk suit, expensive shoes and carried a slim designer briefcase. Her hair was tied into a severe bun, but she had a round, elegant face and a slender, petite figure. I'd tried to speak to her in the past but she was always ice-cool and refused to reply.

Mr Chen's personal assistant was a slim, charming young man of about the same age, with light brown hair. He wore a tan suit and a jolly expression; he had cute dimples when he smiled. He crouched to say hello to Simone.

Simone kissed the young man on the cheek; she obviously really liked him. He smiled up at me from where he was crouched on the floor and I smiled back.

The girl stiffly told him in Chinese to hurry, and he rose, still smiling warmly.

Leo came out of his room, nodded to both of them, and went into the kitchen. They nodded back and headed down the hall to Mr Chen's study.

I took Simone into the kitchen. Leo sat at the table with a huge mug of coffee and eyes like road maps. My head began to throb. Simone pulled herself to sit in one of the chairs and asked for more juice.

I heard a sound behind me and turned. Mr Chen was leaning with one hand on either side of the doorframe in his scruffy black cotton pants and T-shirt, his long hair coming out over his shoulder and a huge grin on his face. He looked as if he'd just woken from the best sleep in the world.

'I thought you might like to come for lunch with Jade, Gold and me,' he said, 'but looking at you I think I might skip it.'

'Go away, Daddy,' Simone moaned. She crossed her arms on the table in front of her and rested her head onto them.

'Maybe next time, Mr Chen,' I said. The headache was getting worse.

Leo didn't say anything; he just glowered into his coffee.

Mr Chen snorted with amusement. 'I think I'll leave you three at home next time I go to Paris.' He threw himself upright and went back down the hall.

My head shot up as I realised what he'd said. 'Jade and Gold?'

'Yeah,' Leo said. 'That's Jade and Gold. They're his lieutenants or something. On the Mountain.' He nodded towards Monica to indicate that he couldn't say more.

'Gold's nice, but Jade doesn't like me,' Simone said into her arms.

'That's not true and you know it, sweetheart,' Leo said. 'Jade loves you.'

'Geez,' I said, 'I've seen them going in and out for months and I didn't even know they were anything different.'

'Stay away from them,' Leo said. 'Particularly Jade.'

'I have been. I'm not completely stupid.'

Leo looked as if he wanted to snap back something nasty, then dropped it as a waste of effort.

Mr Chen came down the hall. He had changed into a smart dark business suit with a black shirt and tie. He grinned at us through the kitchen door, but didn't say anything. Jade and Gold followed him out of the apartment.

'Black shirt again,' Leo said to his coffee. 'One day I'm going to pull all of them out of his closet and throw them in the trash.'

'Does he have any other ties besides black?' I said.

'Of course,' Leo said. 'But he won't wear them.'

Simone fell asleep on her arms and I had to wake her. She whined, pulled herself into my lap and started to cry into my shoulder. I tried to explain about the time difference but she wouldn't listen. It was going to be a wonderful day.

I checked the bedside clock: 3 a.m. It was 7 p.m. London time and I was starving. I rolled over and tried to go back to sleep.

Eventually I gave up and pulled on an old pair of shorts and a T-shirt. I tied my hair roughly out of the way and went out to find something to eat.

The light in the kitchen was already on. Leo sat at the table wearing shorts and a ratty T-shirt. He had a huge mug of coffee and looked as miserable as I felt. He grimaced as I went in.

'You're mad drinking coffee this time of night,' I said.

'Decaf.'

I nodded and sat across from him. 'I've never had jet lag before.'

'Marvellous feeling, isn't it?'

'I'm starving.'

'Me too,' he said. 'And there's absolutely nothing to eat in this kitchen. Monica only buys one day's worth of food when she goes to the market. You know how Chinese are about fresh food.'

'Yeah. Any ramen? Instant noodles?'

Leo grimaced. 'Nope. Simone ate them all.'

'Any biscuits left in the tin?'

'Biscuits? Oh, cookies. Nope.' He straightened. 'Want to share a pizza? The pizza place is still open, we can get one delivered.'

'I want ham and pineapple.' Simone yawned in the doorway, then climbed into Leo's lap.

Simone fell asleep with her head on Leo's chest. Leo's head dropped onto the top of Simone's, and he began to snore lightly. I sipped my tea.

The intercom buzzed in the hallway and I answered it.

'Pizza man,' the security guard said.

'Send him up,' I said, and returned to my tea.

The doorbell rang and I opened the door. The teenaged pizza guy was on the other side of the gate with the boxes. I opened the gate and he handed me the pizza and the docket. I checked the docket. 'Wait here.'

He grinned and nodded. His pimply face had a sheen of moisture; the pizza uniform had long sleeves and he was obviously suffering from the heat. 'Toilet?' he said in very accented English with a goofy grin.

I gestured down the hallway. 'Sure. Come on in.'

I took the boxes into the kitchen and put them on the table, waking Simone and Leo. Simone crawled out of Leo's lap and sat in another chair.

I flipped through my wallet, looking for a hundred-dollar bill.

Simone shrieked. I spun to see her; the pizza guy had come into the kitchen and grabbed her. He hoisted her into his arms and carried her out of the apartment into the lift lobby. He stopped and looked around, searching for the stairwell.

Leo was slow to react, but once he moved he was like lightning. He charged into the lobby. I followed him.

The pizza guy pulled a knife from the back of his pants and held it at Simone's throat. Simone watched us from under his arm, wide-eyed and silent.

Leo hesitated, his fists clenching.

I turned to run and get Mr Chen, but I was too slow.

Mr Chen charged down the hallway so fast he was a black and tan blur. He was bare-chested, in black pyjama pants. He shouldered me into the living room, grabbed the sword from the wall, ripped it from its scabbard, elbowed Leo out of the way so hard he nearly knocked him over, then spun and took the demon's head off.

The demon dissolved into black streamers and Simone fell onto the floor.

Mr Chen dropped his sword, crouched over her and touched her hair. 'Are you okay, sweetheart? Are you hurt?'

'I'm okay, Daddy,' she said, then picked herself up and threw her little arms around his neck. 'I'm not hurt.' She leaned her forehead on his bare chest and burst into tears.

He flicked back his long braid, then gracefully rose, still holding Simone. He buried his face in her hair and squeezed his eyes shut. He turned and carried her down the hall, then stopped and turned back to where Leo and I stood frozen.

'Don't open the boxes. Don't eat the pizza. Take the boxes downstairs and put them in the trash immediately.' He dropped his voice and spoke with chilling calmness. 'I will deal with you two in the morning.' He went into his room, still carrying Simone.

Leo silently collected the boxes and carried them to the lift lobby. He pushed the button for the lift, the doors opened, and he went in.

I sat on the floor, stunned. My brain just wasn't working at all.

The lift doors opened and I cringed away. But it was only Leo. He picked up the sword from where it lay on the floor of the entry hall and took it into the kitchen to rinse it off. He dried it on a towel. Then he put it into its scabbard and clipped it onto the wall. He closed the apartment door.

Then he sat next to me and put his arm around my shoulders. We stayed there on the floor of the living room in silence for a long time.

CHAPTER THIRTEEN

I tried to be cheerful the next morning as I played with Simone, but I was losing the battle. She didn't seem to notice and played happily with her modelling clay.

She was the one who brought the subject up. 'I was hungry. And we couldn't eat the pizza.'

'I know,' I said. 'I shouldn't have let him in.'

'You didn't know he was a demon, Emma, it wasn't your fault,' she said. 'We'd be okay anyway. Leo's killed lots of demons for me — he's really good.'

'Really? Lots?'

She nodded and returned to the clay. She made a wobbly pony and waved it around, delighted.

Leo poked his nose in and gestured for me to follow him. Monica was behind him. She stayed to mind Simone, while Leo led me to the training room.

The mats were soft under my feet. He gestured for us to kneel on the floor facing the mirrors.

I knelt, then curled up over my knees. 'That monster nearly had Simone and it was all my fault.'

'You didn't know, Emma.'

'I should have,' I whispered, and then we both stiffened. We heard Mr Chen coming down the corridor towards us.

He wore a black silk robe with his hair in a long braid. He stopped in front of us with his back to the mirrors. His face was like thunder; his dark eyes blazed with fury. He stood silently for a while, then he spoke. His voice was soft and icy. 'You let a demon in, right through my front door.'

Neither Leo nor I moved.

He was chillingly calm. 'You let a demon leave a trail right into my house. You let a demon take ...' his voice changed slightly '... *Simone*, and nearly let it have her.'

Leo sagged over his knees.

'You have broken every seal on this house. I built those seals over many years, and they will never be the same again.'

He was silent for a while, watching us.

'Give me one good reason why I should not dismiss both of you immediately.'

'You can't fire me because I quit,' Leo said without looking up. 'I can't do this any more. I keep failing you.'

'You resign your station?'

Leo dropped his head. 'I resign.'

Mr Chen took a step forward and stood over Leo. 'You are aware of your fate if you leave my household.'

Leo hesitated, then nodded once, sharply, without looking up.

Mr Chen turned away. 'I accept your resignation.'

Leo dropped his forehead onto the floor.

Mr Chen turned his blazing eyes to me. 'Miss Donahoe?'

Leo broke in. 'She didn't know, my Lord, don't blame her.'

'No, I should've known better, Leo.' I looked up at Mr Chen. 'But you can't fire Leo — please don't fire him. He loves her. It was my fault. Don't send him away.'

'You are not dismissed, Miss Donahoe. You didn't know. But Leo knew the consequences of inviting a demon into my house.'

'Don't fire him!' I cried.

He turned away. 'I haven't fired him, he has resigned.'

My voice broke and I struggled to control it. 'Don't send him away. You know how much he loves Simone. And she loves him. You can't send him away, it will break her heart.'

'I know.' Mr Chen took a few steps and stood over Leo. 'Tell Simone, pack your belongings and leave.'

Leo's head shot up. 'No.'

'You can't do this,' I whispered. 'He's the best man for the job. Nobody else would be as dedicated as he is.'

Mr Chen didn't appear to hear me. 'Tell Simone. Go.'

Leo shook his head. 'Please don't make me tell her.'

Mr Chen sighed. 'If you want to go, then you must be the one to tell her. I won't.' His voice softened. 'Emma's right. If you were to go, it would break her heart.'

Leo gazed up at Mr Chen. 'Will you fire me if I don't resign?'

Mr Chen smiled grimly. 'Of course not. You are the best man for the job.' He backed away slightly to see both of us. 'Leo, you are the most talented student I have had in nearly fifty years. Better even than Li. He would have had the edge over you in speed because of his small size, but in all other aspects you are his superior.'

Leo watched Mr Chen silently for a while, then dropped his head. 'I withdraw my resignation. This will not happen again.'

'It had better not,' Mr Chen said. 'This is done and finished. It will not be mentioned again. Return to your duties.' He started towards the door.

'Wait!' I said.

Mr Chen stopped.

I pulled myself to my feet. 'I didn't know about letting demons in. I didn't know how to help defend Simone.' I spoke more fiercely. 'You have to tell me what I need to know! Stop keeping me in the dark. Teach me. Teach me about the demons. Teach me martial arts. I want to help!'

Mr Chen watched me silently for a while, then glanced at Leo.

Leo rose as well. 'It's a good idea, my Lord. Teach her.'

I walked up to Mr Chen and glared into his face. 'Teach me!'

His expression softened slightly. Then his face hardened and he turned away. 'No.' He stalked out.

I rounded on Leo. 'Why not? Is it because I'm a woman?'

Leo smiled slightly. 'Of course not.' He went out the door and looked down the hallway after Mr Chen. 'Leave it with me. I'll talk to him. Be patient — it may take a while.'

'Whatever,' I said.

He smiled. 'You know what you said about being crazy?'

'Yeah, I'm a complete nutcase.'

'You're not the only one,' he said, and headed after Mr Chen.

Life settled into its usual routine, but with some slight differences now we were back from Paris and I was in on the Big Secret. More people came and went, and although some of them appeared to be perfectly normal Chinese, others were remarkable.

Mr Chen occasionally pulled all-nighters playing mah jong very loudly with a variety of unsavoury characters that Leo assured me were Chinese demi-gods. Sometimes the games would go for more than two nights straight and Leo would go into Intense Disapproval Mode, sulking and glowering around the house for hours.

Jade's dislike for me seemed to intensify, if that were possible. She went from cold to glacial.

The students who came to learn from Mr Chen were now given permission to talk to me, and their stories were fascinating.

A pair of teenage Chinese boys arrived shortly after we returned from Paris. I quizzed them during Simone's violin lesson. Their names were Zhou and Ling.

'Your English is wonderful,' I said. 'Where did you learn?'

Both of them grinned. 'Nowhere,' Ling said. 'Neither of us can speak English.'

I waved one hand at them. 'But ... but ...'

Their grins didn't shift. 'Living in the Dark Lord's household gives you certain privileges. You can understand any language while you're here.'

'But I can't understand much Cantonese out on the street,' I said.

'Only in the household,' Zhou said.

'Did he bring you in from China then? Are you both from China?'

'Both of us are from China. I'm from Fujian, Ling is from Shanghai,' Zhou said.

'What happens with the light? Sometimes there's a bright light in the training room. Is that him or you?'

They shared a look. 'We can't talk about that, sorry,' Ling said. 'Orders.'

I nodded, understanding. I didn't want to get them into trouble.

Both of them stiffened and their eyes glazed over, then they snapped back and their smiles returned.

'Talk to you later,' Ling said. They dropped their plates into the sink and went out.

I left Simone in the music room for her piano lesson and wandered down the hall. The door to the training room was open.

'Emma,' Mr Chen said from inside.

I went to the door and poked my nose in. He stood in the middle of the room, holding the sword from the entry hall. 'Come in.'

I went inside.

'I'm not going to close the training room door any more,' Mr Chen said. 'I much prefer it open. But don't come in unless invited — you could be injured.'

'Sure,' I said. 'Why is it better open?'

'I can hear what's going on outside.'

'You know what's going on anyway,' I said. 'You know exactly who's coming and going.'

'That uses my energy, and I've been told by a certain Lady in White that if I do it too much I'll be in serious trouble.'

I giggled. 'I don't think she's capable of being cross with anybody.'

He moved through the first few steps of a graceful sword set and I watched with awe. 'It's worse than cross,' he said. 'She becomes sad, like a suffering mother. It's painful to see.'

'I believe it,' I said.

He spun and swung the sword through a perfect horizontal arc. The blade sliced through the air with a clearly audible sound. 'That's all, Emma, thank you.'

I hesitated.

He stopped with the sword above his head. 'What?'

I shrugged. 'I just like to watch you.'

He shook his head and looked away. 'Not from inside. Out.'

I went out, but remained quietly next to the doorway, watching him. He didn't seem to notice.

Leo came up the hall in black track pants and a white T-shirt. 'What are you doing here?'

'Watching,' I said. 'Why don't you wear a black uniform like the students?'

'They don't have one to fit me and I couldn't be bothered getting one made,' Leo said.

He moved to go inside and I stopped him with my hand on his arm.

'Talk to him about teaching me,' I whispered.

He bent to speak in my ear. 'I have been. I'll get there. Leave it with me.'

He patted my arm, then went inside and fell to one knee, saluting Mr Chen.

Mr Chen moved to the weapons rack and handed Leo a long staff. Leo moved through a graceful set while Mr Chen watched, occasionally correcting him. After five minutes Mr Chen handed Leo a different staff; this one had a long blade on the end, like a very broad sword.

They worked slowly through a set of moves together a few times; Leo with the staff, Mr Chen with the sword.

Then they ramped up to full blurring speed. The sound of clashing steel echoed through the apartment.

Monica charged out of Mr Chen's room, rushed down the hall and scurried into the kitchen.

I checked my watch. Time to collect Simone.

Mr Chen and Leo fell silent while I saw the piano teacher out, then the sound of ringing steel echoed again. I took Simone into the kitchen for a snack.

Monica was cowering at the kitchen table with her head in her hands.

Simone patted her shoulder. 'Don't worry, Monica, they never get hurt.'

Monica shook her head without saying anything.

It was quiet when I took Simone back down the hall. We stopped at the training room door. Mr Chen sat cross-legged, alone, in the middle of the mats. His hands were cupped in his lap and his face was rigid with concentration, his eyes closed.

'He's guarding his energy,' Simone whispered. 'We have to leave him alone.'

I could have sworn he smiled slightly without opening his eyes before I guided Simone away.

About a week later I heard shouting as I walked past the training room after dropping Simone at her Putonghua lesson in the music room.

'She can help guard Simone!' Leo yelled.

'She will become a target,' Mr Chen said.

'The more people around who can protect Simone, the better.' Leo saw me in the hallway and gestured for me to go in. 'You want to learn?'

I went inside. 'More than anything.'

I stood in front of Mr Chen and looked up at him. He held his sword in front of him, point down. It was very plain, with no decoration on either the hilt or the blade. 'Mr Chen, I officially request time off on Wednesday afternoons and Saturday mornings.'

'What for?'

'I've found a school of martial arts in Wan Chai that has a teacher that speaks good English. I'll be learning tae kwon do twice a week.'

He stared at me.

Leo snorted with amusement. 'Tae kwon do is really useful if you're ever attacked by a bunch of wooden blocks.'

Mr Chen stiffened and glared at Leo. 'All Arts are of value.'

Leo gestured dismissively. 'If she goes to classes

142

down there, she won't learn anything. Teach her. Teach her the true Arts.'

'No.'

'Why not?' I moved closer to Mr Chen. 'Is it because I'm a woman?'

He smiled slightly. 'No, of course not. Some of my best students have been women.'

'Well then, *why not*?'

His face softened. 'If they know you are trained, Emma, you become a target.'

I stared at him.

'If you are not trained, there is no honour in coming after you,' Mr Chen said. 'As long as you are unable to defend yourself, they won't touch you.'

'And the minute they know I can defend myself, they'll come after me too?'

He nodded, and I understood. He was keeping me safe by not teaching me.

'Simone's safety is more important,' I said. 'I want to be able to help defend her. Teach me, and we'll keep it a secret until I'm up to speed.'

Mr Chen glanced at Leo.

'You think she'll let you get away with *not* teaching her?' Leo said. 'Emma's made up her mind, my Lord, she won't back down.'

Mr Chen laughed softly and shook his head. His eyes sparkled with humour. Then he sighed. 'Very well. If you must learn, I'll teach you. I have to warn you though: if you don't have the talent then it will be a waste of time.'

'Let's see if I have the talent then.'

'All right, we will,' Mr Chen said. 'Come back in about half an hour.'

'I can't. Simone will be finished her Chinese lesson then and I have to mind her.'

'I'll take her to the playground up the hill from here,' Leo said. 'You stay and learn.'

143

'Will you and Simone be okay? What if a demon attacks?'

Leo grinned. 'I can take out just about anything that tries for us. And this time I'll be fully awake.'

'You'd better be.' Mr Chen turned and raised his sword horizontally above his head, the point towards Leo. He held his other hand in front of him, the first two fingers pointed towards the ceiling. 'Ready?'

'Move out of the way now, Emma,' Leo said, and moved into a defensive stance. 'Ready.'

I made a quick dash for the door before my head could be sliced off.

I returned exactly half an hour later, nervous but determined.

Leo gave me a quick, kind pat on the shoulder as he passed me to go out. 'You'll be fine.'

Mr Chen gestured for me to enter. I stood next to him.

'Have you done any martial arts before?' he said.

'No.'

'Good. Hold out your hand.'

He took my hand and concentrated. His eyes seemed to go right through me, sharp and dark. Something ice-cold went from his hand to mine. It shot up my arm, into my head like a freezing black blade, then back down into my hand. He didn't release my hand and I shivered.

'Was that you?' I whispered.

He nodded, still concentrating. Then he released my hand and the cold thing snapped off. 'Interesting.'

'What?'

He shook his head, then gestured towards my jeans. 'Those clothes are unsuitable, they're too tight.'

My face flushed; I could feel the heat.

'We will see if you have the talent, and if you do, Jade can find you a uniform of suitable size.'

'Really? A wudang uniform?' I said with delight.

He looked at me piercingly. 'How do you know it is wudang?'

I shrugged. 'Research.'

He eyed me silently, then turned to face the mirrors. 'Watch what I do. Then we will do it together.'

He raised both arms to shoulder height with his elbows bent and his palms face down. Then he slowly dropped them. He turned to me. 'Try.'

I raised my arms and dropped them. Easy.

He sighed.

I choked back the laugh. 'That bad?'

He didn't say anything, but his eyes shone with amusement as he turned back to the mirror. He raised his hands and crossed them in front of his chest with the palms in, then moved his hands out and down.

I tried to follow his movement more closely. He had bent his elbows and relaxed his hands; I tried to do it as well. He watched me silently, then nodded.

He performed the crossed-hands move again, followed by the floating-arm move, then finished it with a kind of gentle push.

I followed, but screwed it up badly. I shook my head, flustered, and dropped my hands.

'Don't worry if you don't have it right,' he said gently. 'If you want to move slower, or redo a move, just tell me. You are the one in control. You set the pace.'

I nodded, and relaxed. He wasn't pushing me. 'I thought you would just perform the moves and I would follow. That's the way they learn in the park.'

'The best way to learn is the one that works,' he said. 'Every student is different. Try again.'

We performed the moves together again, and this time I had them reasonably right.

'Good,' he said, warm with quiet approval.

I couldn't stop the huge grin that spread over my face. This wasn't just interesting, it was great fun.

He continued the moves, each time adding a slightly more complicated manoeuvre.

When we had done about five different moves in a row, he nodded and stepped back. 'Do you think you can remember?'

'I don't know.'

'Try.'

I turned to face the mirrors and took a deep breath to relax. I still felt nervous about performing the moves alone. I raised my hands and threw myself into it, much too fast, and did the moves completely wrong.

He stepped forward and put his hand on my arm to stop me. 'Wait, slower. Much too fast.'

I froze. The warmth of his body pressed all the way down my back. He stiffened. But he didn't move away.

I looked up into the mirror. He gazed into my eyes.

His hand rotated around my arm and dropped to my hand, but didn't let it go. He shifted slightly to look down at me, still pressed into me.

'Slow down, Emma,' he said softly, his dark eyes glowing. 'We have all the time in the world.' His other hand moved to my back and my heart leapt to my throat. I shifted closer to him.

He dropped his hands and moved away. 'Try again. More slowly. Don't hurry it, take your time.'

I nodded, took a deep breath and turned back to the mirrors.

I tried again, and had it.

'Good,' he said. 'Well done. A yin focus for you, to start off with.'

I turned back so that I could see him. 'Is that like yin-yang?'

He nodded. 'You have been learning. Yin is the more

dark and soft, yang is the more bright and hard. That's two in a row now.'

'Two in a row of what?'

'Leo was also more suited to a yin style at the beginning as well.'

'I can't see Leo as soft.'

'We are not here to discuss Leo,' he said, closing the topic. 'Now we will learn a set of moves, one flowing into another. In Japanese it is called a kata.'

'You know some Japanese martial arts?'

'I know all martial arts,' he said. 'I invented most of them.'

'You are extremely scary sometimes.'

'Good,' he said, perfectly serious. 'I thought you were doing some research on me.'

'I did,' I said, 'but I gave up. It's all contradictory. The only thing that everybody agrees is that you're some sort of turtle-snake thing. Are you?'

I flushed. I hadn't thought about what I'd said. Calling a Chinese man a 'turtle' to his face was incredibly insulting. Would he take it the wrong way?

He held his hands out from his sides. 'I am what you see.'

I saw him. There was so much I wanted to say.

I grinned. '"Ugliest creature in creation".'

He seemed shocked for a moment and opened his mouth to say something, then smiled. 'Jade will find a uniform of a suitable size for you.'

I felt a thrill of excitement. I would be learning from him.

CHAPTER FOURTEEN

'Roundhouse kick,' Mr Chen said, watching me perform the kicks. 'Front kick. Side. Good.' He gestured. 'Here, now.'

We stood side by side in front of the mirrors.

'There are twenty-three standard punches, but we'll do some drills first.' He rolled his fists over the top of each other for the punches. 'Kicking out with the knuckles at the end of the punch.' He stopped and gestured. 'Try.'

I rolled the punches and stopped.

'Is there a problem?'

I shook my head, confused. 'We just started this. But it feels like I've been doing it all my life.' I performed a three-punch set. 'It's like I already knew how to do this.'

'How long have I been teaching you?'

I worked it out. 'We started when we came back from London, end of August. It's late September now. Only about a month.'

'That's about usual for a student of mine,' he said. 'We did the tai chi for three weeks, then we started the harder stuff. So you already know it.'

He demonstrated, performing a slow punch from the

tai chi set. 'It's the same moves, we are just doing them faster.'

'You're right. It's exactly the same moves.'

I performed the punches.

'Slowly to start,' he said. 'Don't attempt to be as fast as me.'

I shook my head. '*Nobody's* as fast as you.'

'You're quite correct. Stop.'

I froze.

He came to me and pushed my elbow down slightly. 'Keep your elbow bent. If it's straight then your opponent could hit the end of your arm and break it. Yin at all times; absorbing.' He left his hand on my arm and smiled into my eyes.

'Thanks,' I said softly.

His other hand came up to my face, but pulled away before he touched me. 'Punches. A hundred, rolling drill, go.'

I watched him.

He moved back, smiled, and gestured with one hand. 'Punches, Emma.'

I sighed, took up a narrow horse stance and started punching.

Maybe it was because he still missed his wife. Maybe it was because he thought an employer-employee relationship wasn't appropriate. Maybe he felt it was too soon.

A lot of maybes.

I sighed and continued to punch. Maybe one day he would get over the maybes and I would see something more definite. I wouldn't push it. I respected his feelings far too much.

I walked out of the MTR station underneath Times Square in Causeway Bay, the upmarket shopping mall. Louise and April were waiting for me at the bottom of the enormous escalators that led up into the mall.

'Where we going?' I said.

April indicated the dirty tenements across the road. 'Shui gow okay?'

Both Louise and I nodded.

We walked through the square at the front of the mall with its huge video screen and crossed the road. The four-storey tenements on the other side were grey with pollution and exhaust fumes. We could catch glimpses through the uncurtained windows of squalid rooms with steel bunk beds.

A noodle shop occupied the ground floor of one of the tenements. We walked past the glassed-in area at the front of the shop where the sweaty chef prepared the shui gow and won ton, dumplings in soup, and searched for a table with three spare chairs. We found one but had to share with a workman by himself, wearing a filthy singlet, and a pair of young office girls in pastel business suits.

The restaurant was tiny, with rubbish on the floor and a ceiling black with grease, but it was packed to the rafters with people eating the dumplings so it had to be good.

April pulled the green plastic chopsticks out of the metal holder in the centre of the table. 'Shui gow or won ton?'

'Shui gow,' I said.

'Won ton mien,' Louise said.

April ordered for us. The waiter plonked three glasses of black tea onto the table, scribbled the order and ran off.

Louise and I pulled out our notebooks.

'Desman,' I said.

'Portcullis,' she said.

'Whoa, high stakes,' I said. 'Vincci.'

'Had that one,' she said. 'Rolls.'

'Whyman,' I said, 'a girl.'

'Porky.'

'Wimpy,' I shot back.

'Window.'

'Lemon,' I said. 'I have no idea why, and neither did she.'

'Cynic,' she said. 'Pronounced "Kainic".'

I closed my notebook. 'You win.'

April watched us with her usual bewilderment. 'What is that all about? You keep doing that.'

'Geez, April, you should have worked it out by now,' Louise said. 'How's everything?'

'I'm going to Australia soon,' April said. 'Another week or so, I'm off.'

The noodles arrived. 'What about Andy?' I said.

She waved the chopsticks dismissively. 'He went to Thailand on holiday with a friend, but he'll be back to see me off.'

Louise stopped dead. 'Wait a minute. Is he still spending most of his time in China?'

The dumplings arrived. April used the chopsticks in one hand and her spoon in the other to fish one out and try it. 'Still good,' she said.

The other people at the table stopped and watched Louise and me carefully as we ate the dumplings. When they saw that we could handle chopsticks competently they returned to their own food.

'Still most of the time in China,' April said. 'Very busy at work. A lot of sales work around Guangdong.'

'Why did he go to Thailand with his friend, and not you?' I said.

She shrugged. 'He just wanted to go with his friend. They went water-skiing or something.'

Louise and I shared a look.

'Is this friend a guy or a girl?' Louise said.

April stiffened, shocked. 'Of course a man! Don't be silly.'

Louise and I shared another look.

'I talked to him about having a baby when we're in Australia, and he thinks it's a good idea.' April beamed with satisfaction. 'Very soon.'

'You need to have your husband around to make a baby, April,' Louise said.

'I know that, we'll get there.' April looked over at me. 'Aunty Kitty wants you to call her.'

'Geez, that bitch really won't drop it, will she?' Louise said.

'You should talk about her with more respect,' April said. 'She's a very important person.'

'I'm happy where I am, April,' I said. 'I enjoy working for Mr Chen.'

April's phone rang with a noisy canto-pop tune. She pulled it out of her bag. It had a pink furry Hello Kitty case and a special aerial with lights that flashed as it rang.

She put the phone to her ear, still holding the spoon with the other hand. '*Wei?*'

She listened for a long time, occasionally nodding and grunting. Then she said, 'Ho ak,' and closed the phone. She looked blankly at us.

'What?' I said.

'Andy's just back from Thailand, he's at the airport,' she said. 'He's flying straight out to Shanghai and he needs me to collect some stuff for him from the airport. I'd better go.' She pulled out her wallet and handed me a hundred-dollar bill. 'Pay for me?'

'Sure,' I said, taking the money.

She nodded to us, rose and went smartly out of the restaurant, her stilettos clicking on the grey tiles.

'What do you think?' Louise said.

'Probably gay, and she's a cover for him. The guy he went to Thailand with is his real partner.'

'Could be; happens all the time. Or he could be straight and that trip to Thailand was a sex trip,' Louise said. 'He could have married her just to get an Australian passport. He's pushing her hard to go there.'

'You think she's aware either way?'

'Look at her.' Louise pointed her chopsticks towards the door of the restaurant. 'No idea. Quite happy to be married to this man who treats her like shit.'

She turned to me and grinned. 'Now, there's something up at the Peak that you want to give me. Hurry up and finish the noodles so you can take me up there.'

'What the hell are you talking about?'

She leaned over the table and spoke quietly. 'There's something up there that I just have to see.'

'What?'

'*Mr Chen.*'

'I have to clear it with Leo before I take you up.'

She stared at me.

'I mean it.'

She waved her chopsticks over the remains of her soup. 'Whatever. Come on, I want to see.'

I pulled out my mobile phone and called home.

'Chen residence.'

'Monica, is Leo around?'

'Wait.'

The phone clicked. 'Yeah?'

'Leo, I want to bring my friend Louise up. The one we had yum cha with. Is that okay?'

'The loud Australian?'

'Yeah. The other one besides me.'

He chuckled. 'Yeah, sure. We know she's not a demon.'

'Oh yes, she is, you have no idea.'

'I believe it.' He was silent for a moment. 'Mr Chen's here — he can mind Simone. Where are you?'

'Times Square.'

'I'll pick you up. I can check at the same time, be doubly sure. Be there in twenty or thirty.' He hung up.

'Leo will be here in twenty or thirty minutes,' I said.

'Let's go across the road to look at the shops while we're waiting.'

'Oh no. No way. Last time I went shopping with you we spent two thousand dollars each and you blamed me for the next six weeks for forcing you to spend your money.'

'No idea what you're talking about,' she said, eyes full of mischief.

'At least you don't wear those business suits all the time like April.'

'These jeans cost eighteen hundred dollars,' Louise huffed.

'Finished?' I asked. I nodded to the waiter and he started to come over, but I drew a circle in the air with my finger and he nodded and turned back to get the check. I pulled my wallet out to pay, opened it and slammed it shut again.

Louise saw. 'What?'

I lowered my wallet so that she couldn't see it.

She snatched it out of my hand and checked inside. A huge grin spread across her freckled face. 'I don't think he's really your type, darling.'

'It's a joke,' I growled. 'I'm going to get him.'

'Let me have it, I have some ideas,' Louise said.

'No way.'

I opened my wallet again and pulled out the money, Leo's ugly face grinning at me from the photo pocket.

We waited at a lay-by area under Times Square for Leo to pick us up. Louise nudged my arm.

'Guys watching us,' she said softly. 'Shame they're not too cute. They keep leering at you.'

I looked around; she was right. A group of young Chinese men were watching us from across the road. They all had dyed hair — blond and red — and were wearing filthy cargo pants and white undershirts. One of them had tattoos all over his bare arms, disappearing under the shirt.

'They look like triads,' Louise whispered. 'Why are they watching you?'

'No idea,' I said. 'Maybe just because I'm cute.'

'I'm cuter than you.'

A huge black Mercedes blocked the view. 'This is our ride,' I said, and opened the back door for Louise to climb in.

Leo put the car into gear, but I stopped him with a hand on his shoulder. 'Leo,' I said softly into his ear, 'are those guys across the road what I think they are?'

'What is it, Emma?' Louise said.

Leo studied them carefully. 'At this distance it's hard to tell. But it would probably be a good idea for us to get out of here.' His voice went softer. 'Don't worry, Emma, as long as they don't know you're learning the Arts they'll leave you alone.' He pulled the car away from the kerb.

I glanced through the back window. The young men watched us go, then casually strolled away.

'Wait a second,' Louise said at the lift lobby on the eleventh floor. 'He has the *whole top floor*? How big is this place anyway?'

'Big enough.' Leo opened the gate and the front door for us. 'Remove shoes, please.'

Louise didn't hesitate; she'd been in Hong Kong long enough to know.

Leo bowed slightly to her, turned and walked away.

Louise grinned at me. 'Why do I get the impression that he doesn't like me?'

'He's a complete bastard who doesn't like anybody,' I said, hoping he could hear me. 'Come on, I'll show you my room.'

'This isn't a room, it's a suite,' Louise said when we reached my room. 'It's nearly as big as our whole flat. Three generations of local people usually live in something this size.' She moved closer and whispered, 'Well, where is he?'

'Probably next door with Simone,' I said. I tapped on the door joining our rooms.

'Come on in, Emma,' Mr Chen said from the other side.

I opened the door and Louise grinned with anticipation.

Mr Chen was sitting on the floor with Simone in his lap, reading a book to her in Putonghua.

'This is Louise, my Australian friend,' I said.

Mr Chen nodded to her and rose. 'I have to make a call. Can you mind Simone for me? I'll be here, so Leo can drive your friend back down the hill later.' He nodded to Louise. 'Nice to meet you.'

Louise grinned. 'Lovely to meet you too, Mr Chen. Emma has my number.'

He stared at her for a moment, then smiled, shook his head and went out.

'I cannot believe you just did that,' I said.

'Don't know what you're talking about. Hi, Simone, remember me?'

'Yes,' Simone said. 'Louise. Emma's silly friend. Can I draw while you talk about your boring stuff?'

'Sure,' I said.

Simone went to her little desk and pulled out her drawing equipment. Louise and I sat on the floor on the pink rug.

'Why haven't you made a move?' Louise whispered. 'The guy's gorgeous, rich and available. I saw the way he looked at you; all you have to do is take the step. What the hell is wrong with you?'

I moved to sit closer to her so that Simone wouldn't hear. 'He won't take it further. I've made it completely clear that I'd like to, but he just won't go there.' I dropped my head with exasperation. 'I really like him. *Really* like him. It's obvious he feels pretty much the same way, but every time we get close he pulls back.'

'Push him,' Louise said.

I glanced up at her. 'No. I respect his feelings, Louise. If he wants to keep it professional, then it's his choice.'

'God, you are a stupid bitch, Emma.'

'He might feel it's too soon after his wife died.' I gestured towards Simone behind me. 'And there's Simone's feelings to think about.' I dropped my head again. 'And there's something else too.'

'What?'

I spoke very softly. 'He's dying.'

She put her hand on my arm. 'He isn't. He looks fine.'

'He is. He has a few years, no more than that.'

'Plenty of time,' Louise said. 'Don't be stupid. Don't throw something good away just because it's not going to last forever, Emma. Nothing lasts forever anyway.'

'I know.' I shrugged. 'He's made his choice and I have to respect it.'

Louise smacked her forehead with her palm. 'I don't know which of you is stupider.'

I smiled with misery. 'You know what? Neither do I.'

CHAPTER FIFTEEN

Monica looked after Simone before dinner while I had a session with Mr Chen. I stopped dead halfway through the set I was working on; I'd forgotten the next move. I frantically searched through my memory, but I couldn't remember what came next.

Mr Chen waited quietly next to the mirrors. He would only help me if I asked.

I took myself two steps back through the set and performed the moves again. Again I stopped.

I dropped my arms and sagged. 'I'm sorry, I don't remember what comes next.'

'Your performance of the set is very untidy, as well,' Mr Chen said. 'You should be practising more.'

'I can only practise when Simone's doing something else. It's hard to find the time.'

'What about the evenings?'

'Hey, that's my time,' I snapped. 'You have no right to ask me to work then.'

He wasn't fazed by my outburst. 'I've seen you come in here in the evening.'

'Yeah, okay, I practise in the evenings sometimes,' I said. 'But most of the time Simone's worn me out by the end of the day.'

Mr Chen watched me silently for a while, then Leo tapped on the door and entered. He saluted Mr Chen. 'I can take Simone sometimes, not a problem.'

'Emma, arrange a roster with Leo for him to care for Simone so that you can practise,' Mr Chen said. 'If you are to gain this useful skill, you will need to work with it. Practise at least an hour every day.'

'You sure that's all right, Leo?' I said.

'Not a problem. The more skilled people, the better.'

'I've been called,' Mr Chen said. 'Emma, stay here and practise the set while Simone is with Monica. Leo, Emma was about halfway through a level six Southern Mantis set — remind her of the next part.'

'My Lord,' Leo said, and both he and I saluted Mr Chen. He nodded to us and went out.

'You should have mentioned it if you didn't have enough time to practise,' Leo said. 'Start from the beginning, see how far you go.'

I moved through the first part of the set. 'I don't like taking so much time off work to do this.'

Leo nodded as he watched me. 'Very nice. It's not time *off* work, it *is* work. If you are skilled enough then you can defend Simone as well as I can.'

'Oh come on, Leo. I'm just a tiny woman. How could I possibly be as good as you?'

'Wing chun was invented by a woman.'

'That's one of the most lethal styles of all,' I said with wonder. 'A woman? Really?'

'That's the story.' Leo moved forward to correct my stance slightly. 'Women are smaller and faster. In battle you have the advantage over someone bigger like me, because I have to come down to you.'

'Do you think those guys this afternoon were demons?'

'Hard to tell. But as long as they don't know you're learning the Arts, they won't come after you.'

'That's reassuring,' I said. 'I'll just have to make sure they never find out that I'm learning.'

'It'll be fine. Don't worry.'

'I'm not worried about them coming after me,' I said. 'I'm thinking of Simone's safety. If they don't know I'm trained, I'll have the advantage of surprise. All the better for me to defend Simone.'

'Excellent,' Leo said.

I stopped. 'This is as far as I can remember.'

Leo moved next to me, so I could see him in the mirrors, and took up the same position. 'Okay, I'll show you the next bit. Tell me when to stop.'

'I really appreciate this, Leo,' I said softly.

He smiled at me in the mirror. 'You're kidding, right? It'll be great to have somebody else in the household to practise with, who won't always be knocking me on my ass.'

'Down, Emma,' Mr Chen said, gently pushing my arm down. 'Don't imagine your opponent higher than you are. You are smaller than most demons, you have the advantage. Make them come down to you.'

I nodded and lowered my blocking arm, then spun and punched, punched with the other hand, and blocked again.

'Good,' he said. 'Again.'

I went through the set again. Step, punch, block, punch, punch.

'After this week we can't train on Saturday or Wednesday mornings,' Mr Chen said, watching me. 'Now that the weather's cooler, I'm having my horse moved back from China, from his summer turnout. I'll be riding with Simone twice a week.'

'I didn't know you had a horse,' I said, blocking too high and correcting myself before he could do it for me.

'I bought him for my wife; she chose him and named him Dark Star. He raced for a few years and was quite successful, but he pulled a tendon. They wanted to put him down but I wouldn't let them; he's all right as a saddle horse. I feel I owe him a decent life, after all the happiness he gave us.'

I stopped with my hands still raised and grinned at him. 'Your horse isn't black too, is he?'

'Of course he is.' He moved beside me. 'Add three palm strikes at the end of the last block.' He demonstrated, moving with the fluid grace that always made me watch with awe. 'Block. Punch, left, right, then three palm strikes.' His hands were so fast they were a blur.

'Again. I didn't see your hands. Will you for God's sake *slow down* for me, please? You're just too damn fast.'

He took my chiding with his usual good humour. He slowed for me, moving carefully through the strikes, then turned and grinned. 'How about that?'

'That's more like it,' I said, and moved through the set, adding the palm strikes.

'Down, Emma,' he said, reminding me.

I performed the set again, adding the palm strikes lower, and he nodded with approval. 'Well done.'

'Can anyone ride there?' I said.

'No. Only club members are allowed.'

'Damn,' I said softly, performing the palm strikes and spinning to perform the set the other way. 'All the places I've tried have waiting lists a mile long. The places that don't have waiting lists are out in the New Territories, at least an hour and a half away.'

'You ride?'

'I had a pony I loved dearly back in Australia. I really miss him.'

'Faster,' he said. 'Would you like to come along? I can arrange a school horse for you. That would be perfect — you can ride with Simone while I work Star.'

I tried to control my huge grin but failed.

'Do you have suitable footwear? Leo can take you to the tack shop in Star House if you don't. Simone would love for you to come.'

'Sure.' I moved through the set again. 'You spend a lot of time with Simone.'

'I spend as much of my time with her as I can. I want to make every second count.'

I deliberately did the block too high, and he put his hand on my arm, gently pushing it down.

'You're a wonderful father,' I said without looking at him.

He froze completely, his hand on my arm. Then he wrapped his other arm around me and pulled me into him, his chest against my back. I closed my eyes as my body responded.

'You're a wonderful nanny.' He released me, moved back and spoke more briskly. 'And very talented. You learnt that set very quickly. How about some weapons?'

I turned and gazed at him. I knew what I wanted to do.

And he knew it as well. He gestured towards the weapons rack. 'Weapons, Emma.'

I shrugged, went to the rack and pulled out my sword. If he didn't stop giving me these damn mixed signals I was going to use my sword on *him*.

I pulled Simone's little jodhpurs over her bottom. 'You're getting too big for these already.'

'Leo says I'll be taller than him when I grow up.'

'I don't think so.'

She threw her arms around my neck. 'I'm glad you're coming, Emma.'

I pulled her close and held her. 'So am I.'

Mr Chen appeared in the doorway, wearing a black T-shirt and a pair of cream breeches. 'Ready to go?'

I stared at him.

'What?'

'Couldn't you find any black riding pants?'

He grinned. 'No. I nearly had some made.'

'You should,' I said. 'You look strange in any other colour.'

'Everything Daddy wears is black. He's *boring*,' Simone said.

'You think I'm boring?' he said with delight.

She threw herself at him. He hoisted her to sit on his hip. She nodded, very serious. 'Yes. Boring.'

He squeezed her. 'What colour's your favourite pony?'

'Black.'

I went to them, put my arm around her, and pressed myself into both of them. 'Then you're just as boring as he is.'

'You're boring too,' Simone said.

'I don't think you are, Emma,' Mr Chen said. He put his free arm around my shoulders and guided me out. 'Come on, ladies, our black ponies are waiting.'

He held me around the shoulders as we waited for the lift. Neither of us said a word.

It was delightful.

Mr Chen drove us to the country club. I hadn't been there before — Jockey Club membership was incredibly hard to come by.

'How long have you been a member?'

'I was one of the first Chinese to be nominated,' he said. 'Something over a hundred years, I'm not sure.'

I choked back the laugh. 'Sorry. How do you deal with the passage of time?'

'I keep "inheriting" the membership — I have legal staff who handle that sort of thing for me.'

He led us down the drive to the stables. The sparkling white building had a red tiled roof and seemed to stretch forever.

A beautiful red-headed woman rode past on a spectacularly shining chestnut thoroughbred. She wore expensive breeches and a bright green cotton shirt. 'Hello, John.' She stopped her horse and bent to speak to us with a very cultured English accent. 'Hi, Simone.'

'Hello, Claudia. I'm going to ride.'

'I'll see you at the arena later then.'

'Bye.'

Claudia shot a sharp glance at me, from my feet to my head, and rode away.

Mr Chen took Simone's hand and we went into the complex, past a cleaner with a broom and dustpan who was carefully collecting every stray piece of hay or straw. We entered the stable building, with its large looseboxes on either side of the corridor. Fans on the ceiling kept the horses cool.

'How many horses here?' I asked.

'About two hundred,' Mr Chen said.

I whistled under my breath. 'And they're all retired racehorses?'

'There are a few riding ponies as well, for the children.' He nodded to a Chinese man leading a grey thoroughbred through the stables. 'It's a shame, not many of the racehorses make it this far. By the time they finish their racing career, most of them are either lame or too unruly to be decent saddle horses. These are the lucky ones. The Jockey Club does its best for them.'

'You're not joking,' I said. We passed a groom leading a wet horse that had just been washed and Mr Chen pulled Simone out of the way. 'This is like the horsy Hilton.'

'No turnout for them though,' Mr Chen said. 'There

isn't enough space. They're in the stables all the time, except when they're ridden or on the exercise machine.'

'So your horse needs to be ridden every day?'

'I have somebody to do it for me when I can't. The son of a friend.'

We reached Star's stable. The horse must have been seventeen hands high; he was enormous. The groom had already saddled him for Mr Chen.

Mr Chen nodded to the groom and shared a few words with him in Cantonese. The groom led the horse out and we followed.

We returned to the forecourt of the stables. An Olympic-sized indoor arena with viewing stands and a dark earth floor stood in the centre of the complex.

'This is like something out of a movie,' I said.

A European man on a very solid grey thoroughbred rode past and casually greeted Mr Chen.

Mr Chen waved back. He looked around, then nodded to some grooms holding ponies. 'These are for you.'

Simone ran to the groom holding a cute black pony. He helped her on and adjusted her girth and stirrups for her.

'The white one for you, Emma,' Mr Chen said.

'Thanks.'

The groom led the horse to the mounting block for me. When I was on I tried to adjust the stirrups but he wouldn't let me; he had to do it. I wasn't allowed to fix the girth either. Eventually I just sat, feeling extremely spoilt, while the groom did everything for me.

Mr Chen swung onto a dancing Star as the groom held the horse for him. He buckled his helmet, then took up the reins and nodded to the groom. 'Come with me,' he said. 'We'll have a walk around the cross-country course and then a run in the outdoor arena.'

The cross-country course was about ten hectares of beautifully manicured lawns and hedges with flowers. A few gardeners worked on the hedges as we rode past.

Star fidgeted all the way, baulking at every sound and trying to trot away. Mr Chen held him effortlessly; he was a fine rider.

'How long have you been riding?' I said.

'On and off,' he said cheerfully, 'about sixteen hundred years.'

'I have to stop asking questions like that,' I said under my breath.

The European woman we'd seen earlier, Claudia, rode towards us. She turned her horse to join us. 'Hello, John. Where have you been all the summer? We missed you.'

'Star has turnout in China during the summer,' Mr Chen said. 'I only ride him in the cooler months.'

'Lucky you, I wish I could do that.' She smiled at me, friendlier now. 'Who's this?'

'This is Emma, she looks after me,' Simone said.

'Oh, does she?' Claudia's smile gained a very slight edge and she spoke with a hint of disdain. 'Nanny, I suppose.'

Simone nodded, serious. 'That's right.'

'You English, dear?'

'No, I'm Australian.'

Her nose tilted up. 'Oh. Australian.' She put both reins in one hand and the other on Mr Chen's arm. 'Dear John, the club is having the first competition of the season next week, why aren't you competing?'

'You know I don't compete,' Mr Chen said.

'But your horse is so *good*. And so are *you*. I've seen the Chinese boy ride Star, he can jump anything you put him at.'

'I don't jump.'

'But why not? You're *such* a fine rider.'

'Because I don't want to,' Mr Chen said with exasperation. 'Weren't you heading back to the clubhouse?'

She looked at her watch. 'Oh, goodness, yes.' She patted him on the arm, then turned her horse. 'Give me a call sometime. We'll have lunch or something together.' She pushed her horse to a canter and rode away.

Star spooked and rabbit-jumped sideways for a while, then settled back to a walk. Fortunately Simone's pony and mine were placid and didn't join in.

'Are they all like that?' I said.

'Sometimes.' Mr Chen sighed. 'They're moving in.'

'Not much you can do about it, is there?'

He shook his head.

We approached the pond. Simone pushed her pony to a trot and rode him straight through the middle of it. The water only came up to her pony's knees.

'It's worth putting up with that, to see this,' he said as Simone raced back through the pond, laughing.

Simone and I were sitting in the living room reading a book together after dinner when the doorbell rang. I didn't move from the couch; Simone was in my lap.

Monica didn't come out of the kitchen to answer the door. Nobody appeared.

The doorbell rang again. I was about to shift Simone from my lap when Leo came charging down the hall, grumbling.

A chorus of thumps nearly knocked the door off its hinges just as Leo reached it and threw it open.

'Let me the fuck in!' a gruff male voice shouted from the other side of the metal gate. 'Fucking new seals,' the voice continued more softly.

Leo opened the gate to let the visitor in. 'Simone's right here and can hear you.'

'Whoops.' The man entered and grinned at us from the entry hall as he kicked off his shoes. He looked in his mid-thirties, but had a shock of snow-white hair with matching enormous sideburns framing his gold-skinned face. He was Chinese, wearing old-fashioned pants and a white jacket trimmed with gold, but his eyes were unusual: tawny and glowing. He was tall, muscular and incredibly graceful, moving with controlled elegant power.

I knew exactly what to do if someone like this turned up. I just ignored them and did my job, and they ignored me. Sometimes I felt like an item of furniture, but it meant that I didn't have to worry about complex Chinese social hierarchies.

Leo shook his head, closed the front door and went back down the hallway.

Simone threw herself out of my lap and ran to the visitor with her arms up. 'Uncle Bai!'

He hoisted her up until she nearly touched the ceiling and she shrieked with delight. He held her in front of him and tickled her face with his sideburns.

'Give me a ride!'

'Not in front of everybody,' he said meaningfully.

'Give me a *ride*!' Simone demanded. 'Don't worry about Emma, she won't be scared.'

'Emma, eh?' 'Uncle Bai' grinned evilly at me from the entry. 'And what does Emma do?'

'Emma looks after me,' Simone said.

'Oh, does she.' His voice went softer and deeper as he looked me right in the eye. 'And who looks after Emma? I wonder if she's being looked after properly? I know *I'd* like to look after her.' He was still gazing into my eyes and his voice became husky. 'I could look after you very well.'

I could feel myself blushing.

Simone pulled at his sideburns. 'Give me a *ride*!'

Mr Chen strode down the hallway and stopped in front of them. 'Leave Uncle Bai alone, Simone.'

The visitor gently lowered Simone, then fell to one knee and saluted Mr Chen. 'Xuan Tian Shang Di.'

Mr Chen nodded back. 'Bai Hu.'

'Tell Uncle Bai to give me a *ride*, Daddy!' Simone demanded.

Mr Chen glared down at her. 'Chen See Mun! Who do you order?'

Simone's eyes went wide. She bowed to Bai Hu, then bowed to her father. 'Please forgive this small person.'

'You are forgiven. Go to Emma.' Mr Chen gestured for Bai Hu to follow him.

'I'll give you a ride later. Promise.' Bai Hu shot me a wicked grin and winked, then followed Mr Chen into the dining room.

Simone climbed back into my lap and we returned to the book.

The doorbell rang again.

'Monica's not here,' Simone said.

Leo came back down the hall, grumbling loudly. He opened the door and the gate.

A striking Chinese woman with long scarlet hair came in. Her traditional flowing red robe was shot with brilliant colours that shimmered as she moved. She stopped and watched us from the entry hall.

Simone climbed out of my lap and bowed politely. 'Madam Zhu Que.'

'Hello, Simone,' Zhu Que said.

Leo opened the dining room door and she went in. He closed the front door and went down the hall, still grumbling.

'You have some unusual visitors today,' I said to Simone.

'Do I? Who?'

The doorbell rang again and Leo shouted something angrily unintelligible from the training room. He stormed down the hall and threw the front door open.

It was another man. He towered over Leo; he must have been seven feet tall, slim and elegant as a dancer. His silk robe was brilliant turquoise with a pattern of reptilian scales shot in silver. His long turquoise hair floated behind him. He came in and watched us from the doorway, his long serene face expressionless. He scared me to death; his turquoise eyes were ice-cold and merciless.

Simone clambered out of my lap and bowed politely. 'Lord Qing Long.'

Qing Long went into the dining room without saying a word.

Leo closed the doors and stomped down the hallway towards the training room.

'That's all of them now,' Simone said, and returned to my lap.

'Won't Leo be in trouble for being rude to them like that?'

Simone giggled. 'They're used to him.'

I laughed with her and we returned to the book.

About an hour later Mr Chen shouted for Monica from the dining room. Monica came into the living room carrying the folding mah jong table and proceeded to set it up near us.

'Does he want us out, Monica?' I said.

'He didn't say, Emma,' Monica said.

'It's nearly your bedtime anyway, Simone,' I said. 'Let's pack up.'

Mr Chen and his visitors came out of the dining room as we were putting the toys back into the box. Black, white, red and blue. Something clicked inside my head and I tried to remember what it was, but it escaped me.

Simone giggled. 'They're the same colour as my Lego,' she whispered.

I laughed with her. 'Only yellow's missing.'

She nodded. 'Yellow's the Jade Emperor.'

I stopped and stared at her.

The four of them chatted amiably as they sat at the table.

'So the Jade Emperor himself came down,' the red lady, Zhu Que, said.

'You are privileged in having a visit from the Celestial,' turquoise Qing Long said. 'He detests the Earthly.'

They pulled the tiles out and shuffled them on the table, rattling them loudly.

'I was nearly late for my appointment,' Mr Chen said, and they chuckled as they turned over the tiles.

'The Elite Guard is a rare gift indeed,' Zhu Que said.

'It's the least Ah Wu deserves. He provided most of those bastards with their basic training anyway,' Bai Hu said.

'Mind your mouth. My daughter is in the room,' Mr Chen said.

'My Lord,' Bai Hu said, smiling slightly.

'Throw for North,' Qing Long said.

'No need,' Bai Hu said with a broad grin. 'Ah Wu's always North!' He banged his hand on the table, threw his head back and roared with laughter at his own joke.

The other three glared at him, unamused.

'That joke stopped being funny a long time ago,' Zhu Que said.

'Lighten up, Fong.' Bai Hu grinned evilly. 'Or it's chicken for dinner.'

Zhu Que shot to her feet, trembling with rage. 'I should expect as much from one who spends so much time with the Barbarians of the West,' she hissed. 'Perhaps you should spend time with Lord Xuan here in the South, where we are civilised.'

She saluted Mr Chen. 'Xuan Tian. My Red Warriors are yours.' Her robes spun and expanded. She disappeared.

Qing Long rose and saluted Mr Chen. 'Xuan Tian. You have us if you need us.' He faded, and was gone too.

Mr Chen glared at Bai Hu. 'Thank you very much.'

'Hey.' Bai Hu spread his hands. 'You got what you wanted. With my Horsemen, the Dragons, the Elite Guard and the Red Warriors on our side, your Dark Disciples won't have a problem.'

'*You threatened to eat the Phoenix*,' Mr Chen said with feeling.

'She needs to lighten up.'

Mr Chen glowered.

'All right, all right, I apologise.' Bai Hu saluted without rising, just shaking his hands in front of his face. 'My Lord.' He threw his arm over the back of his chair and glanced around. 'Now, where will we find two more legs?'

'We can't have a game now,' Mr Chen said.

'How about we invite a couple of the Immortals?'

'That lot?' Mr Chen said with disdain. 'Last time I had them here they nearly destroyed the apartment. Took my housekeeper a week to recover. She almost resigned.'

I choked back the giggle as I put the last of the toys in the box. Simone and I shared an amused look. The Eight Immortals were astonishing. The havoc they created was unparalleled. Monica *had* almost resigned.

'Kwan Yin?' Bai Hu said more softly.

'She's retreated from the world,' Mr Chen said. 'Leo? Leo can play.'

'Your earthly Retainer? Really?' Bai Hu grinned.

'We still need a fourth.'

'What about the white chick?' Bai Hu gestured towards me. 'My favourite colour. Maybe I *will* have chicken for dinner.'

I froze.

'One more inappropriate comment like that and I will throw you out,' Mr Chen said, a menacing rumble.

'Try me.' Bai Hu leaned across the table and glared at Mr Chen. 'I can take you.'

They faced off for a while, then both smiled and leaned back.

'You are absolutely incorrigible. The Red Lady was right.' Mr Chen turned to me. 'Can you play, Emma?'

'Sure. But I'm not very good.'

Mr Chen and Bai Hu shared a look, then Mr Chen gestured towards the tiles. 'Would you like to join us?'

I shrugged. 'Okay. Just let me put Simone to bed and I'll be right back.'

Bai Hu opened his mouth to say something but Mr Chen glared him down. 'Fetch Leo while you're at it,' he said to me.

'I'll come too,' Bai Hu said. 'I promised Simone a ride.' He came over and lifted the box of toys for me. 'I'll take this.'

'Don't let Monica see you, she would die of shock,' Mr Chen said. 'And Bai Hu,' he added pointedly, 'behave yourself.'

Bai Hu raised a hand and followed me down the hall to Simone's room.

I pulled back the bedcovers, turned, and stepped back.

An enormous white tiger, easily half as big again as any natural animal, seemed to fill the room. He grinned up at me and winked. 'Better give her a ride, eh?'

Simone climbed onto his back, holding onto his shaggy tiger mane. He gave her a couple of turns of the room while she crowed with delight.

They were extremely cute. I decided I liked him, despite his crass behaviour.

'Finished now,' he said kindly. 'Go to bed, little Princess.'

She leaned to hug him around the neck from his back, then loudly kissed the top of his head. I felt his fur as I lifted her off; it was plush and thick and silky soft.

He changed back into a man, gave her a hug and a kiss on the cheek, and went out. I popped her into bed. Her eyes were shining.

'Bai Hu is great,' she said contentedly. ''Night, Emma.' She turned over and closed her eyes with a sleepy smile.

I turned off the light, half-closed the door to her room, and nearly walked into Bai Hu where he was lounging against the wall of the hallway.

'Did I freak you out?' he said, grinning.

'I think I'm getting used to it,' I said.

He moved closer to me and I backed up until I hit the wall.

'You know why they use tiger parts in medicine? Our *stamina* is famous. But you won't get skills like mine from cutting up a tiger.' He moved closer to me and pressed his body into mine, pinning me against the wall. 'You like my fur?' He rubbed his hands against my arms and I felt the silky fur. I shivered at the velvety sensation. 'How'd you like to feel it rubbing you all over?' He slipped one arm behind my neck and pressed his cheek into mine, the silken sideburns brushing my face. He turned his head to gaze into my eyes, very close. 'I'd love to show you what I can do.' He thrust himself gently against me, his voice a low husky rumble. 'You wouldn't believe some of the things I can do.'

'*Bai Hu*!' Mr Chen roared from the entrance to the living room, and both of us jumped.

Bai Hu pulled back, grinned, and winked at me. 'Later.' He strode up the hall towards the living room.

I turned and knocked on the training room door.

'Come.'

I opened the door. Leo was working with double daggers. 'Mr Chen and Bai Hu are going to play mah jong,' I said. 'I'm joining them, but we need a fourth. Up for it?'

Leo quickly put the daggers away, smiling grimly with satisfaction. 'You bet. I finally get my chance to put that damn cat in his place.'

Leo and I returned to the living room and sat at the table. The tiles had already been built into the wall.

'How many women in your Western Palace right now, Ah Bai?' Mr Chen said.

'More than a hundred,' Bai Hu said with pride. 'And that's just the humans.' He pointed at his nose. 'I'm the best. None of my women ever wants to leave.'

'Good. You have plenty. So leave my woman alone.'

I opened my mouth to say something loudly, but Leo put his hand on my knee under the table. *Trust him*, he mouthed silently.

I subsided and glared at Mr Chen, but he didn't notice. He was too busy glowering at Bai Hu.

Bai Hu backed down and raised his hands. 'Sorry, Boss, your household, your staff, your rules.'

Mr Chen nodded, his face expressionless. He stole a quick glance at me, but his face remained frozen. 'Let's play. Throw for North.'

* * *

I pulled out my drawer and sighed. 'Cleaned out again.'

'You can owe me,' Leo said. He eyed Bai Hu. 'But from you I want cash.'

'Both of you are cleaning me out. Emma's the only one who's showing me any mercy.' Bai Hu leaned sideways, pulled a white leather wallet from his hip pocket and opened it. 'US or Hong Kong?'

'Hong Kong,' Leo said. 'I'll spend it tomorrow.'

The Tiger grunted, pulled out a thousand-dollar note and handed it to Leo, who took it with grim satisfaction.

Mr Chen checked the clock on the wall. 'It's nearly 3 a.m. and Leo and Emma are human, Bai Hu. We need to let them rest.'

'Give me a chance to win my money back from this black bastard,' the Tiger growled. 'One more round.'

'Which black bastard do you mean?' I said. 'They're both black.' I gasped as I heard what I'd said. I opened my mouth to apologise, but it was too late.

All three of them collapsed over the table laughing.

'Definitely time to let Emma rest,' Mr Chen said.

Leo wiped his eyes. 'I cannot believe you said that.'

Bai Hu reached across the table and took my hand. He smiled into my eyes. 'You have just completely made my night. My week. My decade. Ah Wu has my number, sweetheart. Give me a call, any time.' He shook his head. 'I think I'm in love.' He disappeared.

After we'd packed up, Mr Chen followed me to my room. 'Can we talk?'

I let him in and sat on the couch. He sat with me.

'I am so sorry about that,' I said. 'It just came out ...'

'I haven't laughed like that in a long time,' he said. 'And I wanted to apologise for calling you "my woman". But I had to do something.'

'Why? He was just being facetious.'

He tilted his head slightly. 'No, he wasn't. He usually has about a hundred women in the West. And that, as he said, is just the humans.'

'A hundred?'

'He is irresistible, that is his nature. Even Leo has been in trouble with him. But if you were to fall for him, he would take you to the Palace in the West. You would be content for the rest of your life, serving him. As one of a hundred. Would you want that?'

I opened my mouth and closed it again. I shook my head. Of course, he'd been protecting me. 'Thanks for looking out for me.'

'The Tiger found you particularly interesting because you didn't throw yourself at him. The others always do. You are very remarkable sometimes.'

'Thanks.' I glanced up at him. 'Why are they giving you their armies? Are you expecting a war?'

He hesitated, watching me. 'You are very perceptive.' He took a deep breath. 'The answer is: yes.'

'Even the Jade Emperor gave you his army.'

He smiled slightly. 'I am profoundly honoured. The Elite Guard is a very great privilege.'

'That's why you met with the Jade Emperor. You're all expecting something to happen.'

He just watched me and didn't say anything.

'How long do we have?'

He looked down. 'I don't know.'

'Will they attack us here?'

He shrugged. 'While I am with you, you are safe. But I have not been in the Northern Heavens or on my Mountain for more than two years. It has become obvious exactly how weak I am. They all know. It is only a matter of time before they try me.'

'We need to defend Simone, Mr Chen. You need to stay close to her.'

'I know.' He gazed into my eyes, very serious. 'Emma . . .' His voice trailed off.

'Yes, John?'

Something shifted in his eyes when I called him by his first name.

'I don't want you to stay if you're worried,' he said. 'If you're scared, then resign. Go. If you leave my service they won't come after you.' He looked down. 'You should go.'

'Are you firing me?'

He smiled gently, still looking down. 'No.'

'Do you want me to stay?'

He looked up and gazed intensely into my eyes. 'Yes.'

'You like having me around?'

He didn't say anything, just looked into my eyes. Then, 'I want you to be safe.'

I moved closer to him. 'I'm safe with you.' I took his hand and he didn't pull away. 'I feel very safe with you.'

I raised my other hand to his cheek. His skin was like silk. 'We could have years, John. I don't need more.' I slid my hand behind his neck and pulled him closer.

He closed his eyes and lowered his face to mine.

Then he froze. He remained completely immobile, then gently removed my hand from my neck and held both of my hands in his. 'It can't happen, Emma, I'm sorry.' He dropped my hands and rose. 'Friends. Nothing more. I enjoy your company, and Simone loves you. Stay with us, you make us both happy.'

'We could have years,' I said again, without moving from the couch. 'I don't need more than that. Don't throw something this good away just because it will have to end.'

'I have no choice. Friends. That is all. Nothing more.'

He turned away, but I could see the pain in his face.

He went to the door and opened it. 'Goodnight, Miss Donahoe.'

I tried to hide my disappointment as I rose to see him out. 'Are you sure?'

He nodded without looking at me, went out and closed the door behind him.

I flopped back onto the couch and put my head in my hands. Okay. Friends. I ran my hands through my hair. Nothing more. If that was what he wanted, then I had to respect his wishes.

That ache inside me wasn't my heart breaking. I was glad to have what I did.

CHAPTER SIXTEEN

Several weeks passed without any incident, taking us to mid-October.

I'd put Simone to bed and waited until she finally nodded off. I went into my room, changed into a pair of black track pants and a white T-shirt, and wandered over to the training room.

The door was closed so I tapped on it.

'Come,' Leo said from inside.

I opened the door and poked my head in. Leo was working with the sword that usually resided on the wall next to the front door.

'When are you finishing?' I said.

Leo saw that I was dressed for practice, rather than in the black Mountain uniform I wore for lessons with Mr Chen. 'Come in, we can share.'

'You don't mind?'

'No, of course not,' he said. 'Come on in.'

I entered and closed the door. 'I wanted to do some tai chi. Simone's worn me out.'

'What style?' Leo put the sword back into its scabbard. 'How many styles have you learned?'

'I've learned Chen and Yang, and I've just started Wu.'

Leo put the sword onto the weapons rack. 'I'll do it with you. Nice change of pace.'

'Yang?' I said.

He nodded and moved into position. 'Sure.'

About a quarter of the way through the set Leo roused me out of my concentration by speaking. 'Don't get too attached to him, Emma.'

I didn't stop my performance of the set. 'Friends. Employer-employee. That's all. We enjoy each other's company. We both love Simone.'

'You should be able to touch your hands by now when you do the heel kicks,' he said. 'Friends is good. Be his friend, but don't try to be anything more. It can't happen.'

'I know that, Leo, we talked about it. I accept his decision. I'm happy the way it is.'

'Don't try to make it more, because if you do then you won't have anything.'

I silently continued the set.

'Just enjoy his company for as long as you have him,' Leo said. 'He likes your spirit. He loves teaching you. But it can never be more than that.'

We moved together through the final part of the set.

'Friends,' I said. 'That's all.'

'Good.' Leo turned and went out of the room without another word.

I moved into position to start a Chen set. We were friends, and that was all, and I was happy to have his company as long as he was there to give it to me. I didn't need anything more. I was profoundly privileged to have what I did.

I just wished that damned ache inside me would go away.

The next day, in the afternoon, I dropped Simone into the music room for her Chinese lesson and headed up the hallway.

They were in the training room, and I heard them shouting from two doors away.

'Just ask her!' Leo shouted. 'She wouldn't mind at all!'

'No,' Mr Chen said. 'And that is final.'

'She wouldn't care, my Lord, she'd probably enjoy it.' Leo snorted with exasperation. 'I don't know why I bother, sometimes. Just *ask* her!' He threw the door open and banged it into the wall, nearly knocking it off its hinges.

He saw me. 'Here she is. Ask her.'

'Ask me what?'

Leo pointed. 'Go in there, and don't let him get away with not asking you. It's not like it's a suicide mission.'

'A suicide mission?'

He took my arm and pushed me into the training room. 'Just *ask* him!'

I went further into the training room. Mr Chen stood to one side, scowling, one hand on his hip and the other holding the sword from the entry, point down.

'What's all this about?' I said.

He didn't say anything, just looked irritated.

'Okay,' I said, and turned to leave the room.

'For God's sake, ask her!' Leo roared from down the hallway.

I couldn't help it; I had to laugh.

Mr Chen chuckled as well, and rubbed his hand over his face. 'All right, come with me and I'll show you.'

Leo grumbled loudly down the hallway, then the door to his room banged.

Mr Chen put his sword back into its scabbard and replaced it on the rack. 'Come with me.'

I followed him into his office. It was even worse than usual. The pile of papers on his desk was in serious danger of toppling onto the floor, adding to the stacks of documents already there.

He sat behind his desk and tied his hair back. Then he shuffled through the papers on his desk.

'You should do some filing in here. Or get someone to do it for you,' I said. 'How do you find anything?'

He looked at me sharply, then returned to shuffling through the papers. 'You want to sort this lot out for me?'

'You bet. I could probably have it all fixed up in a day.' I peered over his desk. 'Even that pile of rubbish on the floor over there.'

'"That pile of rubbish",' he huffed, 'is a set of priceless ancient scrolls handwritten by Wu Cheng'en himself.'

I nearly fell off my chair. 'Not *Journey to the West?*'

He glanced sharply at me.

'And it's *on the floor?*'

He ignored me and continued to shuffle through the papers. Some of them fell off the desk and he caught them, then added them to the top of the pile.

'Tomorrow morning,' I said, 'you are going to tell me how you want this disaster area organised, and then you are going to take your daughter out for the day.'

He stopped and glared at me. 'Who are you giving orders to here?'

I leaned over the papers and glared back. 'You.'

'Oh, all right.' He sat back. 'I suppose I shouldn't have them on the floor like that.' He grunted as he found what he was looking for and pulled out a large embossed card. 'Look.'

I turned it over. It was an invitation to a classical concert, a charity fundraiser organised by Kitty Kwok. Mr Chen went to these things all the time; sometimes he appeared in the social pages of the newspaper with gorgeous young socialites draped all over him. '*Mr John Chen Wu donated a large amount of dollars and was thanked by the hostess.*'

I looked up at him. 'So?'

'It's more than two years now since I lost Michelle.' He grimaced. 'The vultures are starting to circle. These ... *women* are chasing me.'

'Lucky you.'

'You're joking, right? You know what these people are like?'

'I know very well what they're like, I used to teach their children. Some of them are lovely, generous souls.'

'Not the ones that are after me,' he said acidly. 'You saw Claudia at the Jockey Club.'

'Claudia is completely beautiful and would look fantastic on your arm,' I said. 'Even though you *are* a Chinese boy.'

He snorted with amusement. 'You don't know what it's like.'

I tried to control my face. 'It can't be that bad.'

'You have no idea. I get rid of one, another one's right after her, chasing me. They won't take no for an answer. They're all over me.'

'Sounds like guy heaven to me,' I said unsympathetically.

He banged his hand fiercely on the desk. 'You are no help at all, you know that?'

That pushed me over the edge. I completely lost it. I crossed my arms on the desk, buried my face in them and laughed until the tears came.

He sighed loudly and looked away.

When I'd regained control I sat up and wiped my eyes. 'But what does this have to do with me? What do you want to ask me? I don't know how to shake women off.'

'Could you come with me and be my shield?'

'What?'

'Come with me to the concert. It's for a good cause

and I'd like to help out. If you come along, they won't chase me nearly as much.'

'See, that didn't hurt, did it?' Leo said from the office door.

'Go and perform twenty-five stage one sword katas immediately,' Mr Chen snapped.

'Whoa, excuse *me*.' Leo spun to return to the training room.

I turned my attention back to Mr Chen. 'You want me to go along with you and pretend to be your girlfriend?'

'No. It was a bad idea. Forget it. Dismissed.'

'Don't you dare. You want me to pretend to be your *girlfriend*?'

He sighed loudly. 'This was a very bad idea.'

I rose and closed the door to his office. I sat again and searched for what to say. 'Do you want me to be your girlfriend?'

He just watched me silently.

'Well? Obviously Leo thinks this is a good idea.'

'Leo's opinions have absolutely no bearing on this situation.'

'Well? Mr Chen? John?'

He winced.

'Do you want me to be your girlfriend? No, wait.' I raised my hands and took a deep breath. 'John ...' I dropped my hands onto the desk and studied them, then looked up into his dark eyes. His face was rigid with control as he watched me. 'There is nothing I would like more than to take our relationship a step further. Nothing I want more. Nothing.'

He didn't say anything. He just watched me.

'Both you and Leo have said that it can't happen. Is it because you want to protect me?'

He studied me carefully. 'Yes. I am protecting you.'

'If the demons know that we care for each other, I'm a target as well.'

He watched me.

'If the demons don't know, then I'm not a target.'

He sighed gently.

'But you still want me to come and pretend to be your girlfriend. You want me to pretend to love you in public, and be nothing in private.' I leaned forward over the desk and rested my hand on his. 'How about we try it the other way around? Be nothing in public and love each other in private?'

He jerked his hand away as if he'd been stung. His face didn't shift.

'Okay,' I said.

He put his elbows on the desk and buried his face in his hands. 'I am sorry, Emma. I should never have asked you this. We can never be anything more than friends. I have my reasons.' He dropped his hands and looked into my eyes. 'Please accept this. Be my friend. I love your company, but it can never be anything more. If you continue to push it, then I think it would be better if you left.'

I took a deep breath. 'Okay. I'll come with you and pretend to be your girlfriend, and I'll be happy. I'd love to have my photo in the social pages.'

He gazed into my eyes. 'Are you sure?'

I snapped myself out of it and tried to sound as cheerful as possible. 'Sure. I'd better go and buy something glittery enough to wear.' I grinned at him. 'And *you're* paying for me to have my hair done on the day.'

'Whatever it takes,' he said, relieved.

'See? That didn't hurt, did it? All you had to do was ask.'

'You want to go and do sword katas too?'

'Don't mind if I do. Simone can come with me; we'll do them with Leo.'

He breathed a sigh of relief. 'Thanks, Emma. I really appreciate this.'

'Oh, don't worry, you're going to pay,' I said, and went out.

After Leo and Simone had finished performing the twenty-five katas, I stayed behind and did them for a while longer. A long while longer.

Nobody said anything.

Later I went to Leo's room and rapped on his door.

'Come.'

He was curled up on his sofa, watching a dreadful American action movie. He turned down the volume and I sat next to him.

'Tripe,' I said.

'Yep.' He pulled himself upright. 'What is it?'

'I need to buy a dress. For the charity thing.'

He glowered.

'Help me buy one, please, Leo.'

He crossed his arms over his chest. 'Slap me with a stereotype, why don't you?'

'Come on, Leo, I need you.'

'Damn straight you do.' He uncrossed his arms and pulled himself sideways on the sofa to speak to me. 'It's a wonder you haven't been listed in "Hong Kong's worst dressed". You're as bad as Mr Chen for wearing clothes that are way past their use-by date.'

'He's always impeccably dressed when he goes out; he's only scruffy at home.'

Leo grinned.

'You don't!'

His grin widened.

I collapsed over my knees, laughing.

'Actually it was Michelle who did the buying to start off with,' he said. 'The job sorta fell onto me afterwards. I don't think he even looks at what's in his closet; he just grabs whatever's hanging up, as long as it's black.'

His smile softened as he remembered. 'I don't even know if he was human to start off with, but it took him a lot of adjusting.' He put his hands behind his head. 'You should have seen some of the expressions on his face. Michelle thought it was charming.'

I laughed. I thought it was charming too. 'I wish I'd seen some of them.'

Leo shrugged.

'So?' I said.

'Okay. Looks like I'll have two wardrobes to manage now.'

'You *did* throw those black shirts away.'

'Nope.' He gestured towards his own room, darkly masculine in its decoration. 'They're in *my* closet, and he'll get them back when he's worn the white ones for a while.'

'The minute you give them back, he'll wear them again, you know that.'

Leo sighed. 'Yep.'

I rose to go out. 'When are you free to take me shopping?'

'I'll clear it with Mr Chen.'

I opened the door. 'Thanks, Leo.'

He raised his hands. 'I have to warn you, we won't be buying anything black.'

We arranged to go shopping the next morning, and Mr Chen took Simone out so we could do it. I went to Leo's room and poked my head around his doorway. 'Ready to go?'

He crossed his arms over his chest and glared at me, then pointed at my jeans and shirt. 'You going like that?'

He ducked into his bedroom and came out with a shopping bag.

I waved my hands. 'No. No way.'

He pushed the bag at me. 'If you want to be taken seriously where we're going, you wear this. Otherwise you'll be ignored so bad you'll think Jade is a perfect sweetheart.'

I snatched the bag out of his hand and checked the contents. I nearly dropped it. 'Shit, Leo, you even bought freaking *underwear* for me!'

'Of course I did. I have a pretty good idea what's under there, and if the shopgirls see it they'll be laughing so hard you won't be able to buy anything.' He hustled me to the door. 'Go and change. Make sure you carry that nice designer handbag you picked up in Paris.'

'You mean the handbag you *forced* me to buy.'

'Yeah, that one.'

We met at the front door after I'd changed.

'Go on, admit it,' he said.

'It looks okay.' Actually, it looked terrific, but I wouldn't give him the satisfaction. The tailored designer slacks and polo shirt fitted like no others I'd ever worn, and their muted shades of cream and tan suited me perfectly. 'But you *ever* buy me underwear again and you are in *serious* trouble.'

'You'll be begging me to one day, sweetheart. I'll bet you love that black lace.'

I shoved him when we reached the shoe cupboard.

He passed me a pair of designer loafers. 'These too.'

'I hate you,' I whispered as I pulled them on. 'Did you go through my wardrobe or something? How come you knew the right size for everything?'

'I would never risk my sanity by entering the disaster area that you so casually refer to as a room,' he said.

'Whoa, big words,' I said. 'So how did you know my size?'

His voice softened and he looked away. 'You're about the same size as Michelle.'

'Do your best to be rude to me when we're down there,' he said in the car. 'Treat me like staff.'

'Not a problem, you ugly bastard.'

He grinned at the road. 'Not *that* rude.'

'Damn.'

'Emma.' He became more serious. 'I bought you the lingerie for a reason. Go out. Meet people. Don't mooch about at home all the time. Get your friend to set you up. Find somebody to show it to.'

I didn't say anything.

'Find somebody, Emma. Don't for a minute think that you have any sort of chance.'

'I don't. Friends. That's all.'

'Good.'

We went to Central, where all of the most famous designers had their shopfronts. We had a ball. Leo crossed his arms and glowered, playing the ugly bodyguard, and the girls in the shops fawned all over me.

Leo gave me surreptitious signals: thumbs up; thumbs down; the very slightest nod or shake of his head. When he finally agreed to a dress that he thought was suitable we had a ferociously whispered argument; the dress cost nearly a month's salary. Eventually Leo called Mr Chen and asked him to pay for it.

Mr Chen agreed, but Leo had to promise to give the black shirts back.

We threw the stuff into the boot of the Mercedes. As Leo opened the door for me, I stretched up to kiss him on the cheek. 'Thanks.'

He could have been blushing, but it was impossible to tell.

On the night of the concert I spent a lot of time in my room preparing after I returned from the hair salon. I wanted to be sure that I looked good enough.

I studied myself in the mirror. I hardly recognised the Emma I saw. I was slim and toned from the martial arts training. The gold lamé dress fell to the floor in a slinky shimmer. I vowed to give Leo a hard time about stereotypes later; I would never have chosen such an extravagant dress for myself, but it was perfect. Surprisingly it didn't look too bad on me, but the shoelace straps were going to drive me completely nuts all evening; they were slightly too long and were sure to fall off my shoulders constantly.

I pulled on the high-heeled gold sandals. I would never have chosen these either — they would be painfully uncomfortable — but they complemented the dress perfectly. Fortunately the training had improved my balance so I wasn't at risk of breaking an ankle by falling off the heels.

I shook out my shoulders and turned. Definitely good enough to be seen on the arm of a god.

I grabbed the matching small gold purse, which was far too tiny to put anything useful in. As I went out the door of my room, I wondered how I would ever remove the thick caking of hairspray from my hair, which was all piled on top of my head.

Mr Chen, Leo and Simone were waiting for me in the living room. Mr Chen wore a black tuxedo, his hands in his trouser pockets, his broad shoulders accentuated by the cut of the suit.

When I entered the room they all fell completely silent.

I raised my arms. 'What?'

Simone came to me, her little eyes shining. 'You look really beautiful, Emma.'

I knelt and put my arm around her waist. 'Thanks, sweetheart.' I moved closer to whisper in her ear, 'I can't kiss you, I'll get lipstick all over you.' She giggled.

I rose and grinned at Leo and Mr Chen, who were both still watching me. 'Snap out of it, guys, we'd better move. This thing starts soon.'

I took Leo's hand and gave it a gentle squeeze. 'Thanks for giving me the help.'

'I think I did too good a job,' he whispered back.

Mr Chen stood like a statue next to the front door. I went to him and waved my hand in front of his face. 'Earth to god.'

Simone giggled behind me.

He smiled down at me and his eyes wrinkled up. 'Let's go.'

Mr Chen drove us to Wan Chai. I sat in the front and grumbled all the way down the hill.

'This dress is far too tight,' I said. 'I can't even do a low kick. How am I supposed to defend myself?'

'You think we'll be attacked?' Mr Chen said without looking away from the road.

'I just don't like feeling so helpless.'

'You're with me. You're safe.'

I sighed. 'You're right.'

He smiled slightly at the road. I pushed my feet further into the strappy high-heeled sandals. My feet would kill me later, I should never have let Leo talk me into anything so completely frivolous.

'I look ridiculous.'

'I think you look just fine.'

That compliment silenced me.

He parked the Mercedes under the Convention Centre, and we walked out to the edge of Hong Kong Harbour. The Convention Centre hovered above us like a creature about to take flight. Music floated from inside. The dark water hissed against the concrete breakwater.

A pair of elderly Chinese men in dirty grey shorts and singlets sat at the edge of the water. They talked loudly in Cantonese and smoked as they held their fishing lines.

'I'd rather be with them,' Mr Chen said.

'Just your age.'

He smiled down at me, his eyes very dark. 'You're quite correct.' He turned back to watch the water.

Hong Kong Harbour was always busy with traffic. Ferries lumbered past, and tugboats towed barges carrying stacked containers from the ships to the shore. The lights of Tsim Sha Tsui on the Kowloon side rippled on the water.

The clouds had come down low enough to brush the tops of the tallest buildings and glowed in the lights. I remembered that I hadn't seen a star for a very long time. The breeze across the harbour was fresh, but it was not so cold that I needed a jacket over my stupid glittery dress.

Mr Chen held his elbow out. I took it. We went inside.

Everybody stood around drinking champagne and eating finger food, chatting and laughing artificially. A few Chinese paparazzi clustered around a pop star wearing a ridiculous designer outfit, shouting questions. A gorgeous young movie starlet floated in and they dropped him to race to her.

I wondered how Mr Chen tolerated it.

A camera appeared in front of us and I was dazzled by the flash.

'Mr John Chen Wu, yes?' the journalist with the photographer said. He appeared to be in his late teens, and was pimply and poorly dressed in a tired T-shirt and a pair of worn-out jeans.

'That's right,' Mr Chen said smoothly.

The journalist moved closer to me. 'And you are?'

'This is my friend, Miss Emma Donahoe,' Mr Chen said.

'How to spell?'

Mr Chen spelt my name for him and he noted it down.

'Nancina Wong just came in,' Mr Chen said, and they disappeared.

Mr Chen squeezed my arm. 'Thanks.'

'What for?'

'That was *Next* magazine.'

'Oh.' The news of his companion would be all over Hong Kong in no time flat. Some of the gossip magazines were so thick that the contents couldn't be fitted into a single binding, and they were presented as two or even three thick magazines with a rubber band around them.

I swore under my breath as Kitty Kwok raced towards us, arms and grin wide. She was like a shark about to strike. Her smile was razor-sharp.

'Dear Emma,' she said, giving me a huge tight hug. She pulled back to beam at me. 'What a *wonderful* dress. You look *fabulous. Such* a change, who would have thought our little mousy Emma would be here? Please come back to the kindergarten, dear, we really need you. We couldn't find anybody qualified to do your job for a long time, and eventually we had to hire a Filipina.'

Mr Chen stiffened. I squeezed his arm. It was only an insult if you believed that Filipinas were good for maids and nothing else.

'That's wonderful,' I said. 'I'm sure there are plenty of competent women from the Philippines who could do a fabulous job.'

'Oh, I wouldn't know about that, dear,' Kitty said. 'The only Filipinas *I* know are *maids*.'

She turned to Mr Chen, making sure that she had her back to me. 'Dear John. Come with me and meet the gentlemen from the Mainland. Some of them are members of the Central Committee. They'd love to meet you. I was lucky to have them here; they're very busy. Came all the way from Beijing.' She held her arm out to him.

Mr Chen glanced at me. I nodded and took my arm from his. It would be a dreadful loss of face all around if he didn't meet the politicians.

He smiled apologetically and took Kitty Kwok's arm.

She grinned triumphantly over her shoulder. 'Try to stay out of trouble, *dear* Emma. There are a lot of wealthy, important men here, and you look *so* gorgeous.' Her smile gained an even more vicious edge. 'Our John must have paid a *lot* for that marvellous dress. I *do* hope he gets his money's worth.'

Mr Chen's face darkened. I gave him another gentle shove on his arm and nodded.

Kitty didn't notice. She dragged him away to a group of Mainland officials loudly discussing politics in the centre of the room. They were delighted to see him, grinning and shaking his hand. He was gracious to all of them; chatting and sharing jokes, making them laugh. They offered him a large balloon glass of expensive cognac but he refused, taking a glass of mineral water from a passing tray instead.

I sighed. Kitty's reaction to seeing me was amusing; she was clearly threatened by me. I shook my head. She was the one who'd given Mr Chen my phone number in the first place. Didn't she regret it now! I smiled with satisfaction.

I felt a presence next to me and turned. It was a well-dressed, good-looking Chinese man of about thirty. He leaned on the wall and watched the people in the room. 'Tedious, isn't it?'

'It's not too bad.'

He turned and held his hand out. 'Simon Wong.'

I shook his hand. 'Emma Donahoe.'

'You're with John Chen?'

'Uh ... yes.'

'Good. We were all wondering who he'd hook up with after Michelle died. Half of Hong Kong's eligible women are sharpening their knives and eyeing your back.' He bent forward. 'And it's a very pretty back too. That dress shows it off well.' He studied my back. 'Lovely and white.'

I took a step back to lean against the wall. 'I'm not really hooked up with him, I'm just a friend.'

'I heard you were *staff*.'

I sighed. So it was out. Kitty Kwok was chatting with the patriarch of one of the Indian dynasties nearby. She saw me watching her, raised her glass and smiled spitefully.

'I'm Simone's nanny.'

'Simone? His daughter?'

'Yes. She's four years old and an absolute treasure.'

'A treasure, I'm sure she is.' He spoke more softly. 'Has he been teaching you?'

'What?' I turned to study him.

He smiled at me. 'If he has been teaching you, then you are very lucky. You look like you've been learning.' He turned back to watch the crowd. 'Do you know who he really is?'

Something started to feel wrong. 'I'm sorry, I don't know what you're talking about.'

'Oh, okay.' He shifted slightly closer to me. 'You are very beautiful, you know. That dress is spectacular.'

I didn't say anything.

'I know a lot about him. I could tell you exactly what you want to know — about the Mountain, about the Celestial, about everything. How about we go for a walk down by the Harbour and you can ask me anything you like? The lights are spectacular.' He turned, put his hand on my arm and smiled into my eyes. 'Come with me. I can show you some things that you wouldn't believe.'

I brushed his hand off and moved slightly away. 'I think I'll just stay here for now, thank you. Don't you have other people you need to talk to?'

'No, I'll just stay here too. So, tell me about yourself, Emma. You're from Australia? Which part? I've never been there.' Then he stiffened.

Mr Chen had seen us. He placed his mineral water on a passing tray and ambled towards us. He stopped in front of Wong with his hands clasped behind his back. 'Is he bothering you, Emma?'

Wong held his hand out. 'Hello, John. My name's Simon Wong.'

Mr Chen eyed the hand as if it were toxic, then smiled grimly and reached to take it.

Wong snatched his hand back. 'We can take you. You are weak.'

I moved slightly closer to Mr Chen. Thought so.

'You didn't even know I was here,' Wong said.

'Try me,' Mr Chen said. 'You will face the armies of the Four Winds and the Elite Guard of the Jade Emperor.'

'Because you are too weak to fight us yourself,' the demon hissed. 'You cannot even protect your own woman and child.'

'Be glad you are in a public place,' Mr Chen said, his voice a menacing rumble. 'Otherwise you would be in two pieces by now.'

'There is a private place by the waterfront,' the demon said. 'The woman can be the prize.'

I opened my mouth to say something loudly, then closed it again and moved closer to Mr Chen, slightly behind him. I'd let the expert handle this.

'You really think you can take me?' Mr Chen said. 'You are extremely stupid.'

'I am the One Hundred and Twenty-Second son of the King.'

'Still alive? How many of your brothers have tried to kill you?'

'Fifty-seven,' Wong said with pride. 'I have destroyed them all.'

Mr Chen smiled slightly. 'I could just sit back and let you destroy each other.'

'That's what you *are* doing,' the demon said. 'You are so weak. I will take your head to my father and be promoted to Number One.'

'I have much better things to do with my time than deal with you,' Mr Chen said. He linked his arm in mine and turned away. 'Say hello to your father for me.'

'I will say hello and present your head as a gift,' the demon hissed behind us.

'Are you okay, Emma?' Mr Chen said as we walked away.

'Is he following us?'

'No. He's gone.'

I breathed a sigh of relief and relaxed. 'I knew something was wrong there. He asked me to go outside with him.'

'Then he has excellent taste.' Mr Chen studied me carefully. 'He didn't do anything to you, did he?'

'He shook my hand. I think I need to wash it.'

'He's in human form; touching him won't hurt you.'

'That's not why I want to wash it. Oh,' I said as I remembered, 'I told him Simone's name.'

'They all know who Simone is; they are just too scared to come after her. That one, though ...' He glanced back. 'An ambitious prince. The worst sort. It is talented, to have killed so many of its nest mates.'

'Should we go home?'

He hesitated, then shook his head. 'No, I don't think Leo would have a problem with that one. Its mouth is much larger than its sword. It's not big enough to break through the seals. It won't be able to get in.'

We stopped next to a railing. Nobody was nearby. 'Why does he want your head?'

'The Demon King made a very foolish promise. Any demon that brings him my head will be promoted to Number One.'

'What's so good about being Number One?'

'Number One is second in precedence only to the King himself. Every demon in Hell would have to obey him. It is an extremely powerful position.'

'Oh my God, every demon in Hell is after your head?'

'Or Simone, to swap for it.'

'Or anyone you care for.'

He gazed into my eyes. 'Yes.'

'He can't hurt you, can he?'

'He could remove my head, but it would not be permanent.' He shrugged. 'There is very little chance he is that good.'

'He cuts your head off, takes it to his father and it's *not permanent*? Sounds pretty damn permanent to me.'

'I would revert to my True Form.' He saddened. 'But then I would be gone for a very long time. You would probably not see me again.'

'Well then, let's make sure he doesn't get your head.'

'I've grown rather attached to it myself.' He looked at me intently. 'Are you sure you're all right?'

'Of course I'm all right.' I linked my arm in his and pushed myself into him, ribbing him. 'I'm with you.'

During the intermission we stood next to the large windows at the back of the Convention Centre and watched the Harbour.

We were silent, our arms still linked.

'Would you like a drink or something?' he said quietly.

'No,' I said, just as softly. 'I'm happy here.'

'Thanks for helping out,' he said. He looked down at me, his eyes very dark and shining.

'I don't mind at all,' I said. I moved closer to him. He didn't move away. He didn't move at all.

The strap of my dress fell off my shoulder again, and before I could move to fix it he swept his arm over my back and slipped it into place. His hand remained on my shoulder, then dropped to wrap around my waist. I leaned into him and he held me. I rested my head on his chest and closed my eyes, relishing the feeling of him holding me. I wanted to stay there forever.

The bell rang for the end of intermission.

'Let's just stay here like this,' I whispered without moving.

'I would love to,' he said, his voice rumbling through his chest. 'There is nothing I would like more. But I'm afraid they will expect me inside.' He gently moved his arm away. 'Come on, Emma. Things to do.'

He pulled his hair out of its tie; it had come loose again.

'Let me.'

Before he could protest I took the tie out of his hand and moved behind him. I smoothed his hair back neatly, resisting the urge to linger as I ran my hands through the long dark strands. It wasn't coarse as I'd expected; it was smooth and silken. It smelled fresh, like the sea. It came at least to his waist. I carefully retied it for him.

'Why do you have it so long?' I said over his shoulder. 'Isn't it a nuisance in battle? It keeps coming out all the time.'

'It is a part of what I am,' he said. 'I have no control over it.'

'If you braided it, it would stay put longer.'

'I tried that for a while. But it comes out so quickly it's a waste of time. I only do that when I want it to stay neat for slightly longer.' He smiled down at me. 'Thank you.'

I silently chided myself. I would be thinking about how that had felt for a very long time.

He held his arm out. We linked arms, turned together and went back into the hall.

CHAPTER SEVENTEEN

We walked back through the car park together after the concert. I was edgy; the place was deserted and our footsteps echoed eerily. Mr Chen didn't seem bothered. The car park was below the level of the water and the sea hissed loudly as it surged against the outer walls.

When we reached the car he stopped and took my arm. He moved me to one side, near the wall. 'Stay there.' He pulled off his dinner jacket and handed it to me. 'This won't take long.' He loosened his tie and turned away.

Simon Wong appeared about five metres away.

Mr Chen moved forward to meet him, but didn't take a defensive stance. 'Don't worry, Emma,' he said, 'this one's mouth is definitely bigger than its sword.'

'Please stay to one side, dear,' Wong said. 'I hear that you're very good at looking after the little one. You'll need to come with me when we're finished and I go to collect her.'

'Get him,' I said softly.

Mr Chen moved a couple of steps further away from me, closer to Wong. Then he stopped, relaxed and waited.

Wong held his hands out and a long curved sword appeared in them. He raised it and it glittered in the harsh neon light of the car park. 'I don't think you can do that right now.'

Mr Chen didn't move. 'I don't need to.'

Wong made a sweeping swing at Mr Chen's head.

I didn't see Mr Chen move; one minute he was in the path of the sword, the next he was hitting Wong. He struck the demon lightly on the face and moved back, so fast he was a blur.

'Fast,' Wong said, then grimaced and swung again.

Mr Chen dodged each blow as Wong swiped the sword at his head. He moved back, leading the demon away from me, easily avoiding each swing of the blade. When they were about three metres further away, he casually threw his hand out and knocked the sword from the demon's hand. It hit the ground with a sound like breaking glass.

Wong stopped and concentrated. He held his hand out and the sword flew back into it. He swung fiercely at Mr Chen again, and Mr Chen dodged out of the way. On the third or fourth sweep Mr Chen again knocked the blade out of the demon's hands.

Wong raised his arm and the sword flew back into his hand. He poised, ready to strike.

'That is a modified wudang style. Where did you learn it?' Mr Chen said.

'They do not have you to vet students on the Mountain any more,' Wong said. 'Gold will now take anyone.'

'You learned this on the Mountain?' Mr Chen said with a slight edge of dismay.

'I have spent the past two years on the Mountain,' the demon said. 'Gold asked me to instruct.' He raised the sword and turned it over in his hand. 'Gold gave me this sword as a parting gift. It is Wudang's finest.'

'Emma,' Mr Chen said without looking away from the demon, 'remind me to have a talk to Jade and Gold later.'

'Sure, Mr Chen,' I said. 'Can we hurry this up? These shoes are killing me.'

'Don't worry, this won't take long.'

'Gold is extremely good in bed,' Wong said viciously. 'But too easy a conquest. Jade ...' He grinned. 'Surprising how much that one warms up, eh? When you have her going, she doesn't stop. I never had the chance to hold them together and force them to perform though. That would have been fun.' He gestured towards me. 'First Michelle, now this bitch. You like them white. You are becoming predictable.'

Mr Chen waited quietly, not rising to the bait.

'So Simone is four now? I've never had a child before. So small, it must be very good —'

Mr Chen flew into motion. He attacked before Wong had a chance to move and hit him on the face over and over, snapping his head back with each blow. As he hit the demon, it was forced backwards towards me. I moved to the other side of the car.

Mr Chen held the demon by the throat against the wall. Wong turned the sword around to stab Mr Chen in the back. Mr Chen's hand snapped out and again knocked the sword from the demon's grasp.

'Are you all right, Emma?' he said.

'Finish this little creep so we can go home.'

'My pleasure.' He shifted his feet in preparation for the kill.

The demon grew into something huge with black scales and three eyes. 'I yield. I am yours.'

Mr Chen's face went blank with shock. 'What?'

'Later.' It disappeared.

Mr Chen shook his head. 'It surrendered then ran. What a coward.'

He hurried back to me. 'That one is strong. I think we should go home.' He took his jacket from me and pulled the parking ticket out of the pocket. 'Damn.'

'What?'

'I've passed the fifteen-minute limit for getting the car out after paying. I need to go back and pay again.'

He put the parking ticket into the pocket of his trousers and threw the jacket into the back seat of the car. He slammed the door shut and hurried back to the Shroff Office with me trailing.

'You can wait at the car,' he said over his shoulder.

'If it's all the same, I'd rather stay with you,' I said.

He nodded, paid the ticket and we returned to the car. I pulled myself into the passenger side and he took off before I'd closed my door properly, the wheels of the Mercedes squealing on the concrete.

'Any way to know if they're all right?' I said as we dodged through the traffic and merged onto the overpass to take us back up to the Peak.

'Not really,' Mr Chen said. 'If he's attacked, Leo won't have time to call me.'

'You think the demon will try for Simone?'

He stared at the road silently for a while. Then, 'I think it will. It is strong. It's killed many of its nest mates. It's studied on my Mountain for two years.' He thumped the steering wheel with his palm. 'That demon has been on *my Mountain*! Every single Master there has a great deal of explaining to do. Some of them are *Immortals*, and they should have recognised it.' He froze, his eyes unfocused.

I could see what had happened from his face. 'Is she okay?'

'Yes. Leo is down. Gold is injured.'

He floored the accelerator and we raced up to the Peak. When we got to the apartment building, he didn't wait for the security guards to open the big gates, he just parked the car in the middle of the drive and ran through the pedestrian entrance.

He stopped in the lift lobby. 'I'm going directly up. Stay here. I'll send someone down to get you when it's safe.' He lowered his head and disappeared.

'Oh no you won't,' I said, and pressed the button for the lift.

The front door was hanging open when I arrived at the top-floor lift lobby. I raced into the apartment and stopped.

Mr Chen was kneeling next to Leo's body in the middle of the living room. Simone stood behind her father, her little face pale and streaked with tears. When she saw me she ran and threw herself at me. I held her.

'It hurt Gold. It hurt my Leo,' she sobbed, shoving her wet face into my neck.

I moved forward to see, and stopped dead. Leo lay on his back on the carpet, covered in blood. I fell onto my knees next to Mr Chen and pulled Simone down to sit in my lap. The front of Leo's shirt was saturated with dark blood and his laboured breathing bubbled. Blood soaked the carpet around him.

'Have you called an ambulance?' I said.

'It's too late for that,' Mr Chen said.

Gold came out of the kitchen. His left arm was gone; the torn sleeve of his shirt hung limply, but there was no blood. He held a kitchen knife and a cup in his right hand, and some bandages under his arm.

'Dear God, Gold, you need a hospital,' I said.

'No, I'm okay,' Gold said, giving the knife and the cup to Mr Chen. Mr Chen took the bandages as well and put them on the carpet next to him.

Gold fell to kneel on the other side of Leo and took Leo's hand. 'Don't worry about me, it doesn't even hurt. I'll be fine.' He glanced up at Mr Chen.

'This may not work in human form, you know that, my Lord.'

'It's the only chance he has,' Mr Chen said. 'Emma, move back.' Then he raised his hand to stop me. 'No, wait, can you help?'

I nodded. 'Whatever you need.'

'Good.' Mr Chen rolled the sleeve of his dress shirt up to above the left elbow. 'My blood in True Form has miraculous healing powers. It may also work in human form, but I've never tried it. When I had the Serpent I never needed it.'

'Your blood?' I moved Simone out of my lap; she didn't protest.

'He has to drink it,' Mr Chen said, passing the cup to me. 'Hold the cup under the joint, we'll need a good cupful for this.' He moved my hand holding the cup under his left elbow. 'Hold it still.'

I held the cup very still. He sliced the inside of his elbow with the kitchen knife. Blood oozed out and he pumped his hand. The blood trickled into the cup in a small stream.

'Where's Monica?' Mr Chen said.

'In her room, hiding,' Gold said. He glanced down at Leo. Leo's face was ashen and his breathing was almost undetectable. 'We're losing him.'

'We need more than that,' Mr Chen said, pumping his hand. He dug the point of the knife into the wound and more blood came out. 'Good.'

'Save him, Daddy,' Simone said, her voice very small.

'I'll do my best, sweetheart.' The cup was about three-quarters full. 'That will have to do.'

He closed the joint of the elbow and reached for the bandages. 'Emma, give him the blood very slowly. Watch him. If he starts to fight you, then stop. The blood of the Turtle is very powerful, and if you take it past the point of healing you could kill him.'

I raised Leo's head slightly and dribbled the blood into his mouth. He swallowed, and some of the blood appeared at the corners of his mouth.

'Slowly,' Mr Chen said. He wrapped the bandage around his arm.

'Come on, my friend,' Gold said, clutching Leo's hand.

Leo jerked as if he'd been shocked. His whole body went rigid and he gasped into the cup.

'Stop,' Mr Chen said. I pulled the cup away.

Leo exhaled, a huge breath, but didn't move otherwise.

'How much have you used?' Mr Chen said, kneeling behind me.

I looked into the cup. 'About half.'

'Give him half of what's left.'

I dribbled the blood into his mouth, then pulled the cup away.

Leo shuddered again, then took a deep breath and his eyes snapped open. He coughed, gagged, then looked around.

'Hold, Leo,' Gold said, his voice full of warm affection.

Leo saw Gold and his eyes widened. 'Simone!' he croaked.

'I'm here, Leo,' Simone said.

Leo sagged back. 'Is everybody okay?'

'We're all fine, Leo,' Mr Chen said. 'Move back, Emma, let me see him.' He took Leo's hand.

'No!' Gold's voice was urgent. 'I can. Let me.'

Mr Chen nodded and released Leo's hand. Gold lowered his head and concentrated. 'He's healed.' He looked up at Mr Chen, full of wonder. 'It worked.'

Mr Chen rocked back on his heels and sighed with relief. Simone burst into tears and threw herself into his lap. He buried his face in her hair, then glanced up at Gold. 'Can you carry him into his room? He'll be weak for at least twelve hours. He needs to rest.'

Gold nodded, lowered his head and disappeared. Leo disappeared as well.

Mr Chen flopped to sit on the floor, holding Simone in his lap. Her sobs petered out to sniffles. I put the cup on the bloodied carpet next to me.

'You were remarkable,' Mr Chen said.

I smiled slightly and shrugged. 'I'm just glad he's okay.'

'How did the demon get in?'

'Gold let it in,' Simone said into his chest. 'Gold knew it.'

Mr Chen nodded into her hair and pulled her closer.

'Is Leo really going to be okay?' Simone said.

'He'll be fine,' Mr Chen said.

'What about Gold?'

'I'll just let him take True Form and he can grow his arm again,' he said. He pulled back to see her. 'Are you okay?'

She nodded, then sniffled. 'Did you have fun at your party?'

He chuckled and held her close. 'Yes, Emma and I had a lot of fun.' He smiled at me. 'Simone has blood on her. She needs a bath.' He glanced down at his bloodied sleeve. 'We all do.'

'Can you take me?' she said into his chest.

He gracefully rose, still holding her. His smile turned sad. 'Goodnight, Emma. If you have trouble sleeping, tell me. I'll fix something for you.'

'I'm fine,' I said. Then I inhaled sharply. Gold's arm lay on the carpet next to the bloodstains. 'How are we going to clean this up?'

'Gold can fix it; it will be gone in the morning.' He studied me closely. 'Are you sure you're okay?'

I shrugged. 'Never a dull moment in the House of Chen.'

'You were completely calm through all of this. You are very cold-blooded sometimes, Emma.'

'I know, all my friends say that.' I rose. 'You can be pretty cold-blooded yourself.'

He shrugged. 'I can't help it; it's what I am.'

He took Simone down the hall to his room, then stopped at the door. 'Let Monica know she can come out now.'

'Okay. 'Night, Mr Chen. Goodnight, Simone.'

''Night, Emma. Don't worry, Leo and Daddy will look after us.'

'I know,' I said, and went into the kitchen to find Monica.

After I'd showered and changed I opened the door to Simone's room to check on her. She wasn't there.

I slipped down the hallway to Leo's room and tapped on the door.

'Come,' Leo said.

He was sitting up in bed in maroon silk pyjamas. Gold sat beside the bed, apparently fully healed. Even his clothes were new. He was holding Leo's hand and gazing into his eyes.

I suddenly understood. 'Oh, sorry. I'll leave you two alone.'

They shared a look, then laughed softly. Gold raised his hand. 'No, no. We're just good friends. Friends. For a long time.' He nodded towards Leo. 'I'm just making sure he's okay.'

'Is he?' I knelt on the floor next to the bed.

Leo smiled slightly. 'Yeah. I feel like I've been hit by a truck, but I'll be fine tomorrow. And boy, is Gold in serious trouble, letting the demon in like that.'

'I *gave* it a Wudang sword,' Gold said. 'The demon came in and asked to use our whetstones to sharpen the sword. When I went into the storeroom to fetch the stone, the demon attacked Leo.'

'Stabbed me in the back, the lousy little coward,' Leo said.

'I came back in time to stop it, and it took my arm off and ran.' Gold shook his head, full of remorse. 'The Dark Lord will probably take my other arm off tomorrow.'

'Your arm's okay?' I said.

He raised his left arm and moved it, demonstrating. 'Good as new.'

'That's incredible,' I said. 'How do you do it?'

Gold shrugged. 'I just grew it back.' He gestured towards me. 'Your lovely dress was ruined.'

He was right. The blood would never come out of the gold lamé. I'd have to throw it away. 'Not important,' I said.

'That dress cost a small fortune. It was a designer original.' Leo sighed with exasperation. 'I don't know why I bother. With either of you. Where's Mr Chen's dinner jacket?'

'Screwed up on the floor in the back of the car,' I said.

Leo sighed again.

'Go out and let him rest, Emma,' Gold said. 'He's fine.'

I rose and turned.

'Emma,' Gold said behind me.

I turned back. Both of them were watching me with admiration.

'You were fantastic,' Leo said. 'You stayed calm, you helped — any other woman would have freaked out.'

'He's right,' Gold said.

'You are a pair of sexist pigs and you will both keep,' I said, and went out.

CHAPTER EIGHTEEN

Simone and I were putting a jigsaw together on the dining table the next morning when Mr Chen came into the dining room. He was wearing his scruffy T-shirt and torn pants and holding a sheaf of papers under his arm. He was barefoot as usual, with his hair falling out over his shoulder.

'Pack up, please, ladies,' he said, 'I need to use this room for a meeting.'

Simone and I scooped the pieces back into the box.

'Did you find everything in your office?' I said.

'Thanks for that. The Sanskrit texts are in the wrong order, but everything else is terrific. I must have you go through my office more often.'

'My pleasure.'

'What happened to *Journey to the West*?'

I gestured towards the dining room's side table where I'd placed the scrolls open on display. I glared at him. 'They should be under glass. Even better, they should be in a museum where they can be cared for properly.'

He saddened. 'About fifty years ago, when China was becoming more politically stable, I donated a large part of my collection to museums in Beijing. Many of the treasures were destroyed during the Cultural

Revolution. Some were sold to overseas buyers. I keep the most valuable things here with me now, where they are safe.'

'You've had to live through a lot, haven't you?' I said.

'I am a part of China. It hurts me when China suffers. Right now things are not perfect, but in such a large and varied land they never can be. The people are fed and housed and have hope for the future. Often in the past they did not even have that.'

The doorbell rang.

'Why are Jade and Gold here, Daddy?' Simone said.

'Just for a meeting.'

'Come on, Simone, let's move out of your dad's way,' I said. 'He has an unpleasant job to do.'

'Thanks, Emma,' he said softly. 'You understand.'

I put the jigsaw on the coffee table in the living room and we sat on the carpet together to finish it. Monica let Jade and Gold into the apartment and they went into the dining room.

I listened carefully for him shouting at them, but I never heard a thing.

About ten minutes later the dining room door flew open. Gold charged out of the room, down the hall and out the front door without stopping to collect his shoes. He closed the front door and the gate behind him.

Jade walked stiffly into the living room and sat on one of the sofas.

Mr Chen came out of the dining room, closed the door softly behind him and went into his study.

I checked Jade; she sat motionless on the sofa. Simone and I shared a look and decided to continue the jigsaw as if Jade wasn't there.

I heard a soft sound behind me and turned to look at Jade again. She sat rigid on the couch with her hands on her knees. Tears ran down her face as she shook with silent sobs. Simone's face filled with concern and she opened her mouth to say something.

I put my hand on her arm to stop her. 'Go and practise your piano.'

Simone nodded, rose and went out.

I sat on the sofa next to Jade. She didn't appear to notice my presence.

My heart went out to her and I put my arms around her. She buried her face in my shoulder and let go. She cried for a long time.

When she quietened I grabbed a box of tissues from the coffee table and passed it to her. She nodded her thanks and wiped her face.

'Do you want a drink of water?' I said.

She shook her head. 'Thanks, Emma. Do you know what happened?' She raised her hand. 'Of course you do. You were there.'

'It worked out all right in the end,' I said.

'We are not capable,' she said. 'We cannot do this. He has left his beloved Mountain in the hands of two incompetents.'

'He trusts you, Jade.'

'And see how we betrayed that trust!' she cried softly, bent over her knees with pain. 'We allowed a *Demon Prince* to study on *Wudang*! We *gave* it a *Wudang* sword!'

I didn't know what to say so I just held her hand.

She wiped her face with the tissues. 'Simone needs you. And I have work I need to do.' She rose and straightened her green silk jacket. 'I'll see you later, Emma.' She cast around. 'My briefcase. My briefcase.' She dissolved into tears again and went out the front door without looking back.

'Emma!'

I raced to the hallway entrance.

Mr Chen stood in the doorway of his office, leaning one shoulder against the frame. 'All of you are to meet me in the training room at five this afternoon. Dress for training.' He stopped. 'Does that fit with Simone's schedule?'

Piano lesson was at four. She would have plenty of time to change into her little Mountain uniform. 'Yes. Shouldn't be a problem.'

'Good. Tell Leo.'

He went into his office and closed the door.

At five o'clock I took Simone to the training room. Leo met us there, looking as bewildered as I felt. Mr Chen usually trained us alone or in pairs, not all three together.

'Come in,' Mr Chen called from inside.

We went in. Jade and Gold were already there, dressed for training. Jade wore a pale green cotton pantsuit and her braided hair fell to her knees. She smiled sadly at me and I smiled back.

Mr Chen gestured towards the long wall. 'Line up.'

We all took places along the wall, facing the mirrors. Small stacks of hand towels sat on the floor next to the wall behind us. There was only just enough room for the five of us to stand side by side.

Mr Chen walked out of the room without saying a word.

'What's going on?' Leo whispered.

'Demon training,' Gold said.

'I can see why.'

'I am so sorry, Leo,' Gold moaned.

'We have failed. We have failed together. We have failed most miserably,' Jade said.

'Yes, you have,' Leo said. 'Both of you are supposed to be much better than that.'

Gold moaned again, a soft sound of misery.

We heard Mr Chen coming down the hall.

'Master present!' Leo bellowed.

As Mr Chen came in we all fell to one knee and saluted, even Simone. He carried a huge jar, about waist-high on me and at least 30 centimetres across. Its top was held down with a complicated metal seal and it appeared to contain large black beads.

It was the jar from the storeroom.

Mr Chen placed the jar carefully in the corner of the room and turned to face us, linking his hands behind his back. 'Emma is the only one who has not had this training before. *Apparently*,' his voice gained a slight edge of irritation, 'Simone is the only one who does not need it. I was hoping to hold off this training until I was sure you were ready, Emma, but as we are doing it now I thought I might as well include you.'

'I'm ready,' I said.

He smiled slightly. 'We'll see. I won't ask you to do anything at this stage, just watch and learn. Now.' He opened the jar with a hiss of escaping air. 'Let's see just how bad things have become.'

He carefully removed three of the black beads and tossed them onto the floor next to the mirrors. Each bead grew and stretched and became a young Chinese man wearing plain jeans and a T-shirt. They stood immobile in front of the mirrors.

'Number them left to right, Western style,' Mr Chen said.

'Which is left, Emma?' Simone whispered quickly.

I pointed for her.

Mr Chen frowned, but his eyes lit with amusement. Then he glared at Gold. 'Gold!'

Gold straightened. 'Number One.'

'Jade!'

'Number Two.'

'Leo!'

Leo hesitated, then, 'Number One.'

'Emma.'

I hesitated, confused. He stopped me with a raised hand. 'I know at this stage that you won't be able to tell the difference. Come forward.'

I stepped up to him.

He gestured towards the three young men. 'One of these is a demon. The other two are shadows. Study them carefully. Touch them if you need to; they're bound and they can't hurt you. Try to tell the difference.'

'How do you tell?'

He smiled without humour. 'How do you explain colour to a blind man? It is something you must learn from experience. Try.'

I studied each of the young men carefully. I did touch each on the hand, and none of them moved. I couldn't see any difference. I stepped away from them and shook my head.

'Can't tell?' he said.

It hurt to admit that I'd failed. 'I'm sorry.'

'No, that's fine. You have all the time in the world to learn this valuable skill. Move back.'

I moved back to the line.

'Don't worry, Emma, it's hard,' Simone whispered.

'Simone!'

Simone stiffened and squeaked. Then she realised she'd been asked. 'Number One.'

Jade sagged slightly.

'Jade and Emma, come forward. Have another look.'

I studied Number One carefully. As far as I could tell, there was no difference.

'Move back, Emma,' Mr Chen said. He gestured towards the demon. 'Jade.'

I moved back. Jade shifted into a defensive stance in front of Number One and nodded.

Numbers Two and Three disappeared.

'Ready?' Mr Chen said.

Jade nodded again without looking away from Number One.

Number One threw himself at her. She was ready for him. She ducked and used his momentum to throw him over her shoulder. He rolled and spun to face her.

I moved back further; the demon was very close. I overbalanced on the towels behind me and Leo caught me before I fell.

The demon lashed out with its right foot in a spinning roundhouse kick. I didn't see what Jade did; she was too fast. Inhumanly fast. She was a green blur. Somehow she tipped the demon over to hit the floor. She was on top of it before it could move, and she quickly rammed her fist through its face. She backflipped and landed on her feet in a long defensive stance, again so fast she didn't seem to move at all.

The demon dissipated.

Jade held her right hand away from her; it was covered in the black gooey demon stuff.

'Towels next to the wall,' Mr Chen said.

Jade nodded, returned to the wall and picked up a towel to wipe her hand.

Mr Chen selected three more beads from the jar.

After about forty-five minutes of demon-spotting, Jade and Gold became very good at it. Jade missed most of them at the start, but after about fifteen minutes she had all of them right. Leo could pick about three-quarters of them. Simone never failed.

True to his word, Mr Chen didn't ask me to identify the demons, but he gave me plenty of chances to study them.

After the demons had been identified, Jade, Gold and Leo took turns destroying them.

Mr Chen put his hands behind his back. 'We will revise this in one week's time. Jade, Gold, dismissed.'

Jade and Gold fell to one knee and saluted Mr Chen. Jade shot me a small smile as she went through the door and I smiled back.

'You are doing very well, Leo,' Mr Chen said.

'Sir,' Leo said, his voice soft and deep.

'Well, Emma?' Mr Chen said. 'Are you beginning to tell the difference?'

'I think I am,' I said. 'It's impossible to describe, but I think I can see it.'

He gestured towards the jar. 'Would you like to try?'

I shrugged. 'Sure.'

He pulled two beads out of the jar and they materialised into women. Half of the demons he'd used were male; half were female. All appeared in human form of different sizes and ages, but all Chinese. These demons were in their mid-thirties.

'Any idea, Emma?' he said.

I studied them carefully.

'Touch them if you wish.'

I moved forward, touched each of them on the hand, then returned to the line. 'Number One,' I said, sounding much more confident than I felt.

'Leo?'

'Number One.'

'Simone?'

Simone smiled up at me. 'Number One.'

I whooped with triumph and clapped my hands. Then I remembered where I was and ducked my head with embarrassment. 'Sorry.'

'Leo,' Mr Chen said.

I broke in. 'Let me do it.'

Everybody stared at me.

'Let me destroy the demon.'

'Do you think you are ready, Emma?'

'Yes.'

'Very well.' Mr Chen went to the rack and selected the short sword he'd been teaching me to use. 'You identified it; it is your privilege to destroy it.'

I took the sword, pulled it from its scabbard, tossed the scabbard to one side and readied myself. I nodded without looking away from the demon.

'Go, Emma,' Simone said softly behind me.

Leo hushed her and she squeaked with indignation.

The shadow of the demon disappeared. Something changed in the demon's eyes and I knew she was free.

She raised her hands, palms up. 'I am unarmed. Are you that much of a coward?'

No, I wasn't. I stepped back and passed the sword behind me to Leo without looking away from the demon.

'Be very sure, Emma,' Mr Chen said.

I moved forward, faced the demon and moved into a left guard stance.

I felt uncertain for a moment, then it hit me like a lightning bolt. I'd been waiting all my life for this moment. It just felt so damn *good*. I couldn't hold back the huge grin that spread across my face. I didn't feel a hint of fear; only the thrill of battle.

The demon didn't move. I gestured a come-on. Leo hissed under his breath and Simone hushed him.

The demon wasn't trained in the Arts. She threw a fist at my face and I blocked it easily, and tried to hit her in the face with the other hand at the same time.

It didn't work. She was faster than me. She somehow thrust through me but I blocked it again. I did a spinning kick to take her feet from under her, and she fell onto her back.

I lunged forward to hit her in the face but her palm lashed out and struck me in the nose. My eyes were full of blood and my face was a mass of pain but my fist went through her and she dissolved.

I straightened to stand upright and the floor moved under me, making me stagger. I tried to wipe the blood out of my eyes, but before I could, strong hands grabbed me and tipped me gently onto my back. A towel swept over my eyes, clearing the blood, and I saw Mr Chen. He was holding me with his hand behind my neck.

He put his other hand on my forehead, took it away and smiled gently. 'It's not broken. You'll be fine.' He looked up. 'Leo. Icepack.'

Leo went out the door.

Simone appeared over her father's left shoulder. 'Is Emma okay? She's bleeding!'

'Emma will be fine,' Mr Chen said. 'Go to Monica. Change out of your uniform. We're finished now.'

Simone pulled herself up and went out.

'You have the makings of a fine warrior, Emma,' Mr Chen said. 'You have a great deal of raw natural talent, combined with the courage of a tiger. It is just a shame that you have come to me so old.'

'Positively geriatric,' I quipped. 'I'll be thirty soon.'

He stroked my hair.

Leo reappeared with the icepack and Mr Chen put it on my face.

'You were terrific,' Leo said.

'Yeah, look what I let it do to me,' I said. 'It nearly broke my nose.'

Leo grinned over Mr Chen's shoulder. 'The first one I faced broke my nose, my jaw and my left arm. I win.'

'I remember,' Mr Chen said without looking away from me. 'You threw your sword away as well. You two are as bad as each other for heedless valour.'

Leo and I shared a smile. We were probably both thinking the same thing though: how stupid we were.

Mr Chen moved the icepack away. 'It's stopped bleeding now. Do you think you can stand up?'

'I can try,' I said.

Leo took one arm and Mr Chen took the other. They raised me easily. They released my arms, then stood ready to grab me if I went down again.

I swayed slightly and steadied myself. I raised my hands as they moved to help me. 'I'm all right.'

'I'll call Monica,' Mr Chen said.

I shook my head. Bad move: stars sprang up around me, but they cleared quickly. 'I'm okay.'

'Have a shower. Have a rest. We will mind Simone,' Mr Chen said.

'I'll be fine.' I moved to the door. Once I started walking I felt okay. 'I am fine.'

They followed me to my room anyway. When I reached the door I turned back. 'I'm all right, really.'

'Tell me if you need help. I'll call Monica,' Mr Chen said.

'You sure, Emma?' Leo said.

'I'm *fine*!' I turned and opened the door, went in and closed it in their faces.

I stormed to the bed, grabbed the fake rat off it, went back to the door and slammed it open. I shoved the fake rat at Leo, who took it sheepishly.

'You left the demon jar open,' I said.

Both of them cursed and ran.

CHAPTER NINETEEN

One morning in mid-November, we all sat down together for breakfast. The men didn't usually eat breakfast with us girls; Mr Chen, particularly, was a very early riser. But that morning he smiled indulgently at Simone as she sat at the table.

Monica came in and ceremonially presented Simone with a boiled egg that had been dyed red. Mr Chen watched, delighted, as Simone ate it. Then he gave her a lai see, a red paper envelope filled with lucky money. She jumped out of her chair and climbed into his lap to give him a hug and a messy kiss. He held her close for a while, his eyes closed and a huge smile on his face. Then he pushed her away slightly so he could stroke her hair.

Monica and Leo both gave her gifts too: Monica gave her a storybook and Leo gave her a toy tea set.

'Happy birthday, Simone. I'll have a present for you later,' I said. 'You're a big five-year-old now. Are you going to have a birthday party?'

'Some of Simone's favourite aunts and uncles will be coming for dinner,' Mr Chen said. 'They all have red packets for Simone.'

Simone clapped her hands with delight. 'Is Aunty Kwan coming?'

'Yes, she is,' he said.

'Mr Chen,' I said, 'can I talk to you privately later?'

'Come into my study when you've finished eating.'

I tapped on the door of his study. 'Come in, Emma,' he said.

I went in and sat down. I'd left the door open; this wouldn't take long. Mr Chen turned away from the computer, leaving the spreadsheet open, and leaned on the pile of papers in front of him.

'Thanks a lot for telling me,' I said.

He looked sheepish.

'Her birthday on her documents is 20 November, not 15 November,' I said. 'You could have at least told me you were planning to celebrate it today.'

'Today is her birthday on the Chinese calendar,' he said. 'I apologise. I forgot to tell you.'

'What else haven't you told me that I need to know?'

He looked guilty.

'Geez,' I said. 'If you think of anything else that I need to know, you'd better tell me. Right now though, that's beside the point. Simone's five years old and she needs to go to school.'

'Yes,' he said. 'She can start school next September. I would like you to find a suitable place for her.'

'Would you prefer a Chinese or English curriculum?' I said, relieved. I had expected a battle about sending Simone to school and was surprised by this easy acquiescence.

'I'd prefer an International school,' he said. 'Any one will do. She will be wealthy when she grows up, I will see to that. She will be a citizen of the world. She may want to study overseas. It is important that she goes to a school that will give her that wider viewpoint.'

Leo was passing as Mr Chen said this and he stopped at the door to listen.

'I'll start looking for a school for her right away,' I said. 'Any particular preference for International schools? The English schools were originally founded for the colonial kids, but they provide a good all-round British education, and you have a lot of links there.'

Mr Chen nodded.

'French? Korean? German/Swiss? The Japanese one is out in the New Territories, but it's good as well —'

'Emma,' he said, cutting through my babble, 'I am leaving this entirely up to you. You choose. I trust you. Leo can assist you; he is an expert on security and that will be a consideration.'

I was silenced. He was placing an enormous amount of faith in me.

'Simone should be home-schooled,' Leo growled from the doorway. 'She'll be in constant danger at school, and we won't be there to protect her.'

'We will arrange something,' Mr Chen said.

'You'll waste your energy keeping an eye on her?' Leo said. 'It's not worth the risk.'

'Leo,' Mr Chen said patiently, 'you knew this time would come. We have had this discussion many times already. Simone will go to school. That is final.'

'This is a very bad idea.'

'Leo,' I said, breaking in, 'how many friends of her own age does Simone have?'

'Being alive is more important.'

'She needs to learn to function socially. Right now she doesn't have a single friend her own age. She hardly knows anybody who's even *human*.'

'We're human. Monica's human.'

'We're staff, Leo. We're *servants*. She needs to learn how to interact with children her age, ordinary kids that she can't boss around. She'll have to learn how to keep her father's strange nature a secret —'

'Oh, thank you very much,' Mr Chen huffed.

'Look me in the eye and tell me you're not strange.'

He glared at me but didn't say anything.

Leo snorted with amusement, then became fierce again. 'Yeah. She'll tell everybody about riding the Tiger and be thrown out of school.'

'She hasn't done it yet, Leo,' Mr Chen said.

Leo sounded desperate. 'She won't be *safe*!'

'Simone *will* go to school. You will accept it. That is an order,' Mr Chen said.

Leo scowled and stomped out.

I turned back to Mr Chen. 'I'll get onto it.'

'Sorry I didn't tell you about her birthday. After I'm gone, just use her Western birthday. Don't bother trying to keep up with the Chinese calendar, it's too complicated.'

'I know. Some years you have a leap *month*.'

'The second August is a very lucky time.'

'How do you do it?' I said. 'You talk about your going, and leaving that wonderful child all alone, as if it was ...' I swallowed it.

He seemed to understand. 'Read the Tao.'

'I have. It's like a set of clues for a cryptic crossword.'

He made a soft sound of amusement. 'You have hit the nail exactly on the head.'

'Why haven't you been teaching me about the Tao? I thought it would be integral to the training.'

'It is.' He leaned back. 'The Tao cannot be taught with words, it is wordless. The minute you try to encompass its nature with words, its nature will escape you. Those of us who are already there can assist you, but you must all find your own way.'

'You're already there?'

'Of course I am,' he said without a hint of impatience. 'That is how I came to be. In human form though ...' He hesitated, thinking. 'I am not pure Shen, and sometimes the human needs and feelings overcome me. It is quite exhilarating. I have not remained in human form this long since attaining the Tao. It is an experience.'

'Shen?'

'Read the Tao. Go and buy Simone a birthday present — I'm sure you were planning to. I'll mind her. Go to Causeway Bay or Tai Koo Shing.'

'I'll take her with me. She can spend the lai see money you gave her.'

He nodded. 'Good idea.'

I looked at him. 'How much money did you give her?'

'Three thousand dollars.'

I gasped a huge sucking laugh.

'Is that too much?'

'Just slightly. Then again, I suppose it's average for a child of a wealthy family. My other clients' children would get similar amounts. More at Chinese New Year.' I rose to go out. 'Who's coming to the birthday dinner?'

He ticked them off mentally, using the Cantonese and Putonghua names indiscriminately. 'About ten of the Generals, about five of the Eight Immortals, Kwan Yin of course, Bai Hu, Sun Wu-Kwong —'

I waved my hands in front of me. 'Oh, no. No way. I'm out of here.'

'The White Tiger will behave, I promise, Emma. It would be nice if you could attend Simone's birthday dinner. As a member of the family.'

'The White Tiger is a perfect gentleman now we've set some ground rules. But if the Monkey King is coming, I'm not going to be there.'

'He intensely dislikes being called the Monkey King, and you know it.'

'Yep.'

Mr Chen sighed. 'They will all be on their best behaviour, even the Monkey King. I have rented a room in Tsim Sha Tsui; there isn't space here for them all. When they're out in public they behave, Emma. It's just here at home that they tend to let their hair down.'

'Speaking of hair, yours is all over the place,' I shot over my shoulder as I went out.

'Damn!'

I went back to my room and did some more research on Shen. Shen wasn't mentioned in the translation of the *Tao Teh Ching* that I had. I wondered why he had asked me to read it to find out about Shen. Shen was the spirit in everybody; the soul. But it had another meaning: it meant a person who existed on the higher plane. Some of them were Raised humans, like the Eight Immortals. They had been born human and found the Tao, the Way.

Others were more like forces of nature; for example, Xuan Wu, Emperor of the Northern Heavens, Dark Lord of the Martial Arts, Right Hand of the Jade Emperor, one of the Four Winds in physical form, and my employer. The literature claimed that he was, paradoxically, both a force of nature and a Raised Immortal. He was a prehistoric totem-like creature, a black turtle, or a combination of a snake and a turtle, two animals together. But he was also a human Emperor who had lived in ancient times and been taught and then Raised to Immortality by his friend, Kwan Yin.

Much of what was said about him was contradictory. I wondered which twenty-five per cent was true.

It was the strangest feeling in the world to read the literature about these people on an intellectual level and then match them up to the visitors who wandered in through the front door. It was weird to see statues of Kwan Yin all over the place and then remember that she was the same delightful woman who had cared for us all so well in Paris.

There were some stories about Bai Hu in which he appeared almost demonic. That fitted.

There were some insinuations that the Jade Girl was half Dragon. The Golden Boy was also called the Clever Boy. They seemed to serve every major deity in the Taoist pantheon. I began to wonder exactly how old Jade and Gold really were; both of them looked in their mid-twenties.

I looked up some of Mr Chen's many names in the dictionary. I knew the characters for them and I had an excellent Chinese–English dictionary, so I flipped through to find them.

'Xuan' meant 'dark'. Not 'black', which was a completely different word. Definitely 'dark', as in lack of light. When they called him the Dark Lord, they really meant it.

'Wu' didn't really seem to have a proper translation, but generally came out as 'martial arts'. It was the same 'Wu' as in Wu shu.

'Xuan Wu' meant 'Dark Martial Arts'.

At some time during his history, his name 'Xuan' had been too close to the dynastic name of the presiding royal family and he'd somehow been changed from 'Xuan Wu' to 'Zhen Wu'. 'Zhen' meant 'truly' or 'absolutely'. No messing around: he was *really* the God of Martial Arts.

In some places in Southern China he was known as 'Chen Wu', the 'Chen' being another form of 'zhen'. He wasn't even using an alias.

But why John? Why such a dead-common English name? Was he trying to avoid too much attention?

No, he wasn't. 'John' sounded like 'Xuan'.

Leo took us down to Causeway Bay in the Mercedes to buy Simone's birthday presents. We parked in one of the older, smaller car parks. Mr Chen owned the parking spot outright; it had probably cost him upwards of a million Hong Kong dollars.

We took Simone around the shops, and let her take her time. She didn't want to spend all of her money. Sometimes she seemed much more mature than her five years. I wondered if it had something to do with her mixed parentage — and not just the Chinese/European mix; possibly something to do with the martial arts training and the discipline involved too. She would grow up with wisdom and strength that would give her an edge over anybody her age. All she needed were the social skills she would gain from going to school.

We stomped up the car park stairs carrying all of Simone's shopping bags and laughing together. Leo leaned against the door to open it for us. Simone went through the door and stopped dead. I nearly crashed into her.

Leo dropped all the shopping bags and pushed us both behind him. 'Stay here.'

A group of six young men with dyed hair, blond and red, lounged against the car waiting for us. They were all covered in elaborate tattoos and looked like gangsters.

'Are they demons?' I whispered.

'Yes,' Simone said. 'Not very big, about level twenty.'

'Can Leo handle them?' I said. 'Should I call your dad on my mobile phone?'

'Leo should be okay.' Simone moved forward and I stopped her. 'I wanna help Leo.'

I pulled her next to me. 'You stay here with me where you're safe.'

Leo walked casually to the demons and stopped about two metres away from them.

'Get off the car,' he said, perfectly calm.

One of the demons grinned and levered himself off the car. As soon as he was upright he threw himself at Leo. The other demons didn't move.

Leo ducked under the demon's outstretched arms, grabbed it around the middle, turned and effortlessly threw it into the wall of the car park.

It exploded into feathery black ribbons that dissipated quickly.

I pulled Simone closer to me. I thought about running, but decided it would be better for us to stay where we were, with Leo protecting us. There were probably demons waiting to grab us at the bottom of the stairs.

'We'll be okay, Emma,' Simone whispered.

I sincerely hoped so. I had faced some demons in the training room, but I wasn't capable of taking out anything bigger than level two or three with my bare hands. These ones were much too big for me.

I vowed to try valiantly anyway, if I had to. I straightened and held Simone behind me. I would protect her at any cost.

The remaining demons slowly pulled themselves upright, still grinning. There were five left.

Leo readied himself, moving into a standard defensive position. Four of the demons threw themselves at him at the same time.

He moved so fast he was a blur.

His left fist crunched into the face of the demon in the centre as his right hand came out and blocked the blow of the one next to it, pushing it so that it blocked the one on the far right. He let the one on the far left strike him as he dealt with the other three, and didn't even seem to notice the blow to his face.

As the first one he had struck dissipated, he grabbed the one to the right and slammed it into the one on the end, destroying both together, at the same time pivoting and lashing out with his foot to take out the one on the far left.

I didn't see any more because the remaining demon had sneaked around Leo and was approaching Simone and me. He grinned viciously as he came closer.

Simone moved next to me and took up a long defensive stance, her little face set with determination.

I grabbed her and pulled her behind me.

'I wanna fight,' Simone said, but I pushed her back and she didn't resist. I moved into a defensive stance and readied myself to defend Simone, with my life if necessary.

Leo's dark forearm appeared around the demon's throat and yanked. The demon's face filled with astonishment, then horror, then it dissipated as well.

Simone ran around me to Leo and he knelt to check her.

I knelt with them. 'Are you okay?'

'I'll have a shocking headache later, but otherwise I'm not injured,' Leo said. 'Are you all right? Simone?'

'I'm fine. Leo, you were great,' Simone said, and moved to hug him.

He pushed her away, keeping her at arm's length. 'Sorry, sweetheart, there's demon stuff on me. I need to go home and wash it off. Don't touch me until then.'

Simone nodded, understanding. 'Okay.'

Leo rose and I did as well. I took Simone's hand.

'Are you okay, Emma?' Leo said.

I shrugged. 'Sure. You were tremendous.'

'All part of the job.' He collected the shopping bags from the ground and checked the contents. 'Nothing broken.' He turned back to the car. 'Let's go.'

I guided Simone to sit in the back. Leo threw the

bags into the boot, pulled out a towel and wiped his arms and face. 'Better get home and wash this stuff off.'

He got into the car and started the engine.

'How many of them could you take bare-handed, Leo?' I said.

'What level were they, Simone?' Leo said. 'Fifteen? Twenty?'

'Twenty,' Simone said.

'I could probably take about ten of them with my bare hands,' Leo said. 'More than that, they'd get through me and do some damage. I could take down twenty or thirty of them before going down myself.' He shrugged. 'Used to happen all the time, but they eased up a couple of years ago.' He lowered his voice. 'They stopped coming after they took Michelle. Obviously they've found out about Simone and they're coming after her now. We need to go home and tell Mr Chen.'

'You should let me help,' Simone said. 'I can kill level ten demons. I wanna fight too.'

'You are a remarkable little girl,' I said, giving her a squeeze. 'But you should let Leo do the demon killing for you right now, because you're too small.'

Simone crossed her arms in front of her chest and made a face.

Leo eased the car gingerly into the car park lift. 'I hope your dad's home to guard you, Simone, 'cause I'm gonna have to clean the interior of the car now. There's black demon stuff all over the front seat here.'

'Does that stuff have a proper name?' I said.

Leo shrugged. 'Not as far as I know. There may be a word for it in Chinese, but I've never heard anybody use one. Everybody just calls it demon stuff, demon essence.'

'I'm *hungry*,' Simone said loudly. 'I wanna go home and have some ramen.'

'You're always hungry,' Leo said.

A group of young men were lounging around the exit of the stairwell. They grinned menacingly at us as we passed them, but made no move to attack.

'Are those demons, Simone?' Leo said.

'Yes.'

I recognised one of them. 'Oh my God.'

'What?' Leo said.

'One of them was Simon Wong.'

'Who?'

'The guy that attacked us at the charity concert. The one that took off Gold's arm and nearly killed you. He was at the bottom of the stairs with the rest of the demons.'

Leo stiffened. 'Let's get home.'

CHAPTER TWENTY

After Leo had showered and changed we all met in the dining room to discuss the attack. Simone noisily slurped her ramen.

'How many?' Mr Chen said.

'Five. Level twenty, according to Simone,' Leo said.

'Appearance?'

'Young male humans. Looked like triads.'

'Do you know what their True Form was, Simone?' Mr Chen said.

Simone shook her head, still slurping the noodles. She swallowed quickly. 'I don't know, Daddy.'

'No demons more senior than that? No indication of who sent them?'

'The Demon Prince that attacked us at the charity concert was at the bottom of the stairs with more demons,' I said.

'Waiting for you to run,' Mr Chen said. 'If you'd run out of the car park he'd have grabbed you. You did the right thing in staying together.'

'Emma's really good,' Simone said.

'I know,' Mr Chen said, smiling into my eyes. 'Nobody was injured?'

'Leo was hit in the head,' I said.

Mr Chen glanced sharply at Leo.

Leo shrugged. 'I'm fine.'

'I'll check you,' Mr Chen said. 'Give me your hand. I'll have a look.'

Leo leaned over the table and banged it softly. 'Don't you dare waste your energy trying to heal me. I'm fine.'

'If your head is injured it may not show up for days, Leo,' Mr Chen said, unfazed.

I leaned over the table as well. 'Don't waste your energy. If Leo's unwell, he can see a doctor. Trying to heal him is total overkill. You need to look after yourself.'

Mr Chen looked from me to Leo, then smiled and shook his head. Both Leo and I relaxed.

Simone giggled. 'There're two of them shouting at you now, Daddy.'

'He needs it,' I said without looking away from Mr Chen. He smiled into my eyes again and I felt a rush of affection for him. I slapped it down. Friends.

Mr Chen rose. 'I have work to do. Believe it or not, there are people who work for me who do as they're told. Stay vigilant, Leo, it appears that the demons are starting to move in. This one in particular appears to have made Simone a target. And mind your head; if you feel unwell tell me immediately.'

After he had gone I studied Leo. 'Are you really okay?'

He shrugged. 'Yeah, I'm fine. I know what to look for, don't worry about me.' He rose, pushing his chair back. 'Mind Simone, I'll go down and clean the car up. I made a hell of a mess in the front, and if Mr Chen wants to use it and finds it like that he'll skin me alive.'

'You're the one that shouts at him, silly Leo,' Simone said, grinning through the noodles.

'Emma's pretty good at shouting too,' Leo said, amused.

'He needs it,' I said.

'Yep,' Leo said as he closed the door.

Leo drove us to Tsim Sha Tsui for Simone's birthday dinner. Simone was excited and jiggled all the way through the Cross-Harbour Tunnel.

We pulled into the lay-by in front of one of the five-star hotels and the doorman came to open the doors for us.

'Whoa, I thought you said you rented a room,' I said over the back of the seat to Mr Chen.

'I did,' Mr Chen said. The doorman opened the car for him and he got out.

Leo grinned triumphantly as he opened the door for me. 'Told you to wear that dress I bought you.'

'Buy me another item of clothing and I will delete every single file on your computer.'

His grin widened. 'You wouldn't dare.'

I shook my head and followed Mr Chen and Simone into the high-ceilinged lobby of the hotel. I had worn plain jeans and a shirt because I thought we'd just be going to a rented room in a restaurant. I hadn't realised it would be a five-star hotel restaurant.

When Mr Chen led us into the ballroom I hung back. Leo grabbed my arm and escorted me. 'Come on, Emma, this is going to be fun.'

Mr Chen had taken the whole ballroom. About twenty-five huge twelve-seater tables were set up around the hall under the glittering chandeliers. The main table had a red tablecloth instead of white.

Leo led me to our table. As staff, we were put out on the edge of the hall. That was the way it worked. Simone and Mr Chen sat at the red table with the senior notables. Kwan Yin was there and greeted Simone with a warm hug.

Most of the guests were in Western business suits, but quite a few wore traditional Chinese floor length robes: mandarin collars, long sleeves, with trousers underneath.

'This won't be as much fun as one of their usual parties,' Leo said as we sat at our table. 'The staff here are human and don't know about them. They'll all have to behave.'

'You talk like you do this all the time,' I said.

'Before ...' He took a deep breath. 'Before Michelle died, we went to a lot of dinners like this. Simone's one-month birthday party was a night I'll never forget. They completely let their hair down. Some of the Shen took True Form and scared Michelle half to death.'

'Is this the first one since then?'

He looked wistful. 'Yeah. Even for Simone's fourth birthday, he only had a couple of them over at our place.' He smiled. 'Looks like he's finally starting to come out of his shell.'

I turned to watch some of the other guests arrive. Qing Long came in; he'd shed the long turquoise hair and settled for standard Chinese short and black, but he was still more than six feet tall. He wore a silver robe embossed with turquoise scales.

'It's good to see Mr Chen getting out more,' Leo said. 'He's been a lot happier since you came.'

I looked at him.

'Don't even think about it though. It can't happen,' he said.

'Don't know what you're talking about.' I turned back to the guests.

A young European man in a tan suit came in. He had sandy hair and tawny eyes. He came straight over to me, dragged me out of my chair, hugged me and kissed me on the cheek. 'Hello, Emma.'

I pulled back to see him properly. He grinned evilly at me, and suddenly I knew who he was. 'Bai Hu. What the hell are you doing looking like that?'

He shrugged. 'Don't you like me better like this? As one of you?'

I moved closer. 'I liked you better with fur.'

'I knew you liked my fur,' he said.

I glanced at the main table. Mr Chen had seen us. His face was rigid.

'You should see the look on his face,' I whispered.

'I know. We should do this more often.' He clasped my hand and pulled away.

'Are you going to spend the whole evening like this?'

He shrugged. 'Sure. Drives the waiters nuts. They can understand me, so they think I'm speaking Cantonese. Like a native. Confuses the hell out of them.'

'What language are you speaking?'

'No idea. I just talk and they understand. For all I know, I could be speaking Tiger.' He stiffened. 'Whoops. He wants me. Probably going to tell me to lay off his staff again.' He turned away. 'Later.'

'Don't go falling for that one either,' Leo said.

I snorted with amusement. 'Not likely.'

'Zhu Que hasn't turned up.'

'The Tiger threatened to eat her last time she was over. She's probably still mad with him.'

A group of stern-looking middle-aged men in standard Western business suits came in, accompanied by aloof women. They went to Mr Chen and paid their respects, saluting him.

'Generals,' Leo said. 'There are thirty-six of them altogether. Only about ten of them here tonight.'

I could see from her face that Simone thought they were really boring.

Jade entered and came straight to me. She wore a beautiful green silk cheongsam with embroidery of gold peonies. It had three-quarter sleeves and swept nearly to the floor, with short splits up the sides. The mandarin collar framed her slender neck beautifully.

'That's a gorgeous dress, Jade,' I said after we'd said hello. 'Where did you have it made?'

'I know a place in Central where you could have a lovely cheongsam made, Emma.'

'You think I could get away with it?'

'Anything would be better than what you're wearing now,' Leo said from behind me. I swiped a kick at his shins without looking back, but missed.

Jade's smile widened. 'Let me take you shopping. I'm sure you would look lovely in one.' Her eyes became unfocused. 'I've been summoned.' She took my hands and squeezed them. 'I'll call you, we'll have lunch and have a dress made for you.'

'That sounds like great fun, thanks, Jade.'

She waved me down and went to Mr Chen.

I sat and pulled my chair in, then saw that Leo's face was rigid with restraint.

'What?'

'Leo. A pleasure,' an elderly male voice said behind me.

I turned to see a tiny ancient Chinese man in a threadbare suit three sizes too big for him.

'Great Sage,' Leo said, saluting.

'Lord Sun,' I said, also saluting.

'Emma.' The Monkey King pulled his staff from his ear and expanded it from the size of a toothpick to a full-sized bo. He spun it in front of himself and leaned on it.

'The staff here are human, my Lord,' Leo said.

The Monkey King shrugged. He didn't care.

'My Lord.' I twisted in my chair to face him and he grinned down at me, still leaning on his staff. 'Lord Xuan has a copy of *Journey to the West* in Wu Cheng'en's hand, the original. I thought it would be more appropriate if he gave it to you. It's your story, after all.'

He threw his head back and roared with laughter, attracting the irritated attention of some of the nearby Shen. When he'd stopped laughing he shook his head. 'I gave it to him.'

I watched him, bewildered.

'I love it that you offer it as if it were your own,' he said, leaning further down to watch me intently. 'You are very presumptuous.'

I struggled to explain. 'I just thought, that it's your story, and that you would probably —'

'She only wishes to assist you, my Lord,' Leo said, breaking in to defend me. 'Emma has the best interests of everybody in mind.'

The Monkey King turned his attention to Leo. 'You, me. Any time. Think you could take me?'

'Your skills far outweigh mine, my Lord,' Leo said, carefully polite. 'I would not presume to challenge you.'

The Monkey King grinned. 'One day, Leo. One day we'll know.'

'My Lord,' Leo said.

The Monkey King disappeared.

'Geez, he's going to blow it and be in *so* much trouble,' Leo said.

'For him, that's behaving himself,' I said.

'I know.'

The celebration was a huge multi-course vegetarian dinner that seemed to go on forever. By the end of it Simone was falling asleep.

I quietly vowed that for her sixth birthday, Simone would have a proper children's party with plenty of kids her own age and absolutely no Shen.

CHAPTER TWENTY-ONE

Simone's face was serious as she sat in the living room with Leo and me after visiting the schools. Their brochures were spread on the coffee table.

'I don't know, Emma,' she said.

'Which one did you like better?' I said.

Simone tilted her head. 'I like them both.'

'The Australian one has the big playground,' Leo said.

Simone didn't say anything.

'You'll be safe in the American one, sweetheart,' I said. 'You saw the big walls.'

Simone glanced quickly up at me. 'Where are *you* from, Emma?'

'Australia.'

'You went to an Australian school?'

I hesitated, then, 'Yes. But Leo went to an American school.'

'I think you should go to the Australian one, sweetheart,' Leo said.

Simone picked up the brochures and looked at them, then up at me again. 'I want to go to the Australian one. I liked the teachers there better.'

Leo tried to hold back a triumphant grin.

'You sure?' I said.

'Yep.' Simone dropped the brochures. 'I like the Australian one. I want to go there.'

I shrugged. 'Okay, your choice. I'll ring the headmistress and arrange it.'

Simone smiled at Leo and he smiled back. He would be unbearable for ages now that he'd won.

Mr Chen drove us to the school with me providing directions. When we arrived he walked across to the opposite side of the road from the school and stopped. I waited patiently while he studied the school silently. Then he nodded and we both went in.

The headmistress was waiting for us in her office. She sat us down and closed the door, then sat herself and pulled out Simone's file.

'Emma hasn't told me much about your line of work, Mr Chen,' she said, opening the folder. 'Exactly what business are you involved in?'

'Mostly government work,' Mr Chen said. 'Administration, management. Occasionally fieldwork, but not since Simone was born.'

She raised her head and stared at him. 'Emma said that you had a private import–export firm in China. Not government work at all.' Her eyes widened. 'Oh.'

Mr Chen opened his mouth to say something and I kicked him under the table. He glanced at me and I shook my head.

'Which government?' she said, smiling. 'China or Hong Kong?'

'Neither,' Mr Chen said. I wondered if it was a speech that he'd worked out over time. 'The truth is, a much higher government than either.'

'Oh my,' she said. She flipped through the pages of Simone's file. 'No wonder security is such an issue for you.' She grinned at me. 'Universal Exports, eh, Emma?'

I grinned back. 'Precisely.'

'Chen Enterprises,' Mr Chen said, missing the point entirely.

'Would you like to see around the school?' the headmistress said, rising.

'What was all that about in the office?' he said as we returned to the car.

'She thinks you're a spy,' I said.

'What?'

'"Government work". She thinks you're a spy. Let her — it means they won't give us as much hassle about the security.'

He closed the car door. 'I hadn't thought of that.'

'Oh, come on, it's obvious,' I said. 'That's what I thought when you gave me that line.'

'Did you?' he said, bemused.

'That's why she said "Universal Exports". That's James Bond's cover company. Used all the time in the films.'

'Who?' he said.

I sighed and closed the car door. 'I'll rent some videos,' I said. 'I can't believe you've never heard of James Bond.'

When we returned to the Peak, Mr Chen, Leo and I sat together and discussed the logistics. I had the school timetable and a rough plan of the area from the handbook. We examined the alternatives.

'It is extremely likely that the demons will try something the minute Simone starts school,' Mr Chen said, very calmly. 'We will need to be ready right away.'

'What sort of attack should we prepare for, sir?' Leo said.

'Probably through the front door to start off with,' Mr Chen said. 'We'll be looking for someone walking in off the street, wandering through and then grabbing her. They'll try the direct approach first.'

I was horrified and made a small choking sound. They both ignored me.

'Any suggestions on how to handle this securely, Leo?' Mr Chen said.

'I think I should be stationed outside the classroom, sir,' Leo said, studying the plans carefully. 'And follow her when she's not in class.'

I exploded. 'No *way*! You will wait outside that school and watch for suspicious people going in. You will *not* go inside while she's there unless she's attacked!'

'If she's attacked it may be too late,' Leo said.

Mr Chen cut through us. 'Both of you, listen. I will teach Simone some skills that will make this point irrelevant. She will be able to tell if a demon is nearby and contact you to come and defend her. You won't need to be inside the school grounds.'

He glanced sharply at me. 'I just had an idea. The school is quite new. Emma, I would like you to ask the headmistress if she wants a free fung shui consultation, as a donation from me. Push it hard, tell her it is very important for Chinese. If she's already had one done, tell her I said it wasn't very good.' He paused, concentrating. 'She has, and it wasn't. You must get her to agree. The fung shui master will be one of mine. He won't just do an assessment; he'll set seals on the school building, to stop demons from materialising there and to keep large numbers from entering at once. Similar to what we have in this apartment.'

I listened carefully and nodded. I knew there were seals on the Peak apartment, but I wasn't sure exactly what was involved. Putting seals on the school was a brilliant idea. 'You can count on me, Mr Chen.'

'Once the seals are set, Leo, you won't need to be inside the school building. You can stay outside and watch for demons entering the grounds. Simone will be able to tell you if they are approaching her.'

'How about on the street outside then?' Leo said, studying the plans.

'That would probably be close enough,' Mr Chen said.

'I'll stake out the school in the car,' Leo said. 'And if you're right about this skill of Simone's, then I'll be nearby if she senses anything and I can be there right away.'

'Is there a place on the street outside where you can do that?' Mr Chen said. 'There were only parking meters nearby, with a two-hour limit.'

'How about we wave the chequebook at the headmistress and ask for a space to be allocated in the car park?' I said.

'Good idea, Emma,' Leo said. 'And if that doesn't work, there are places on the street where I can wait. But the car park would be better.'

'Is everybody happy with this solution?' Mr Chen said.

Both Leo and I nodded.

'Good.' Mr Chen placed his hands firmly on the table. 'I will ensure that Simone is trained in the required skills before September. Emma, talk to the headmistress about getting a parking space for us. I think this will work out rather well.'

As I returned to my room I heard a most satisfying squawk. Leo had discovered that I'd made all the colours on his computer fluorescent greens and pinks, with a photo of myself for wallpaper. He'd have to ask me how to change it back, or wait until Gold turned up. I was the only one in the household apart from Gold who knew how to change the colours. Yes!

* * *

'No, Emma, look,' Mr Chen said patiently. 'Don't be intimidated by my size. That has nothing to do with it. Use my size against me. Again.'

I tried again. I failed. I brushed my hair out of my eyes, then tied it back. He tied his hair back as well. We had been struggling with this for twenty minutes and I still couldn't do it.

'It's just not possible, Mr Chen,' I said, exasperated. 'You're huge. There's no way I could throw you like that.'

'Once you master the skill you will be able to throw Leo,' Mr Chen said. 'You will be able to throw me in Celestial Form.'

I stopped dead. 'Was that what we saw on the plane?'

He looked piercingly at me. 'You saw that?'

'Simone wanted to go to you. She nearly got away from me — I grabbed her just in time. She can be really strong when she wants to be, Mr Chen.' I smiled and shrugged an apology. 'Sorry about that. I did manage to stop her though.'

'I'm sorry if I frightened you, Emma,' he said. 'I know that my Celestial Form scares Simone.'

I grinned up at him. I couldn't believe him sometimes. I shoved him on the arm, ribbing. 'Hey, you were really cute. The big black face is really attractive.'

He smiled gently down at me, amused. 'You weren't frightened?'

'No, of course not,' I said. 'I know it's you. What's to be frightened of?' This was a good opportunity to ask. 'That wasn't your True Form?'

'No,' he said. 'That was more like,' he paused, thinking, 'a working form. When I'm on the job, it's easier to manipulate the weather, fight demons, work with energy, things like that, when I'm in that form. Does that make sense?'

'Perfect sense. So I could throw you when you're that big?' The Celestial Form must have been more than ten feet tall.

'Of course. Once you get over this idea that I'm too big to throw. I'm *not*, Emma. You can do it. Try again.'

'If I do it right,' I said, 'will you let me try to throw the Celestial Form?'

His face went expressionless.

'Oh, too much of a drain on your energy. Sorry.'

'It's a deal.' He bent to whisper to me. 'Just *don't tell Leo*.'

I bent towards him as well. 'Don't worry, I won't.' Our faces were very close. 'I'd be in just as much trouble as you would.'

He nodded and rose. 'Okay.' He reached out and stroked my shoulder affectionately. 'Now you have some real motivation, let's see you do it, Miss Donahoe.'

I grabbed his hand where it lay on my shoulder, pushed, twisted, put my own shoulder into him and threw him onto his back.

He stared up at me from the floor. 'You *vixen*! You knew how to do that all along.'

I bent over him and smiled down. 'No, I didn't, I swear. But the idea of having a go at throwing you when you're that big was too much of a challenge to ignore.'

He chuckled and shook his head with amusement. I put my hand out to help him up, and he took it, still laughing quietly. I pulled him up hard, he was big. But I didn't realise how strong the training had made me and I jerked him straight into me.

We both froze. He was pressed hard against me. He didn't move away. His face went expressionless as he gazed down at me.

He brushed a stray lock of hair from my face, then dropped his hand onto my shoulder.

My heart leapt into my throat.

I put my arms around his waist. I pushed closer into him. He didn't move away.

'I suppose I have to transform now so you can have another go at me.' He moved his hand from my shoulder to my back. His other hand moved to my back as well and pulled me into him.

I looked up into his glowing dark eyes. 'Later,' I whispered. 'Let's just stay like this for a while.'

I put one hand up behind his neck to pull him down. His face went very intense as he dropped it to mine.

Yes!

A swift expression of pain swept across his features. 'I'm sorry, Emma,' he said urgently as he jerked himself away, 'that would be a very bad idea.'

'No,' I said, trying to wrap around him again, 'don't stop now.'

He shook my hands free and backed up. 'It really can't happen, Emma.' His voice became more brisk. 'You'll need to move back and give me some room so that I can transform.'

'Why not? What's the big problem?' I tried to move closer to him, but he backed away even more. I nearly had him pinned against the wall. It was like there was a bubble around me.

He raised his hands defensively. 'Trust me, Emma, it would be a very bad idea. I don't want to hurt you.'

'How could you hurt me?'

'Believe me,' he said, and the pain showed again in his face, 'it can't happen. I have my reasons. We should be nothing more than friends.' He turned away.

'If you're worried about protecting me, you don't need to be,' I said fiercely. 'I'm not frightened of the demons, and besides, it would be worth it. We could still be employer-employee when we're out. Nobody would have to know. If they didn't know, they wouldn't have a reason to come after me.'

He didn't say anything.

'I know you feel the same way! Don't throw it away! Even if it is only a short time, even if it's only at home. I don't need more than that.' I sagged, desperate. 'Don't try to protect me. I don't need protecting. What I need ...'

He didn't look at me. He stood facing away from me, head bowed.

'What I need is *you*.'

He flinched as if I'd hit him.

'It could be wonderful, John. Even for a short time.' My voice broke and I tried to control it. 'I know you want it too.'

'It can't happen, Emma,' he said softly without turning towards me. 'Go to Simone.'

I hesitated. I could see his miserable face in the mirror. His eyes were full of pain.

'I'm not finished with you!' I shouted, then turned and stormed out.

I ran all the way around the Peak trail by myself. I was gone for nearly an hour. It wasn't mentioned when I returned. Mr Chen insisted on behaving as if nothing had happened at all. I had no choice: I had to respect his wishes.

What I really wanted to do, though, was kill something.

CHAPTER TWENTY-TWO

I sighed as I went through my email. Leo had subscribed me to a number of alternative lifestyle lists. It took me nearly twenty minutes to unsubscribe from most of them, but Leo was an active participant on some and they seemed worthwhile.

My phone rang and I picked it up. 'Hello?'

'Emma.'

'April! Where are you? Are you in Hong Kong?'

'Yes, I came back to visit Andy. Lunch tomorrow? I'm meeting Louise. Want to come?'

'Sure. How about the little Japanese place under the hotel in Causeway Bay?'

'I don't know it.'

'Meet me outside the World Trade Centre, I'll take you there. The teppanyaki's good.'

I met Louise and April outside the World Trade Centre and led them past the entrance to the hotel. Early December weather could be very pleasant, and today was particularly good: the fresh breeze blew across the harbour and the sky was clear blue for a change.

The Noonday Gun sounded across the road; all of us ignored it.

We turned right after the hotel and walked down a filthy alley lined with garbage bins.

'Where the hell are you taking us?' Louise said. She picked her way through the puddles of water. 'It'd better not be a dai pai dong, I get sick every time I eat at one of them.'

'You do?' April said. 'I don't. I missed them. No dai pai dong in Australia.'

'Spoilt Westerner,' I said. 'Delicate digestion.' I stopped at the end of the alley. 'Here.'

A tiny Japanese garden nestled under the towering wall of the hotel. I walked along the waist-high bamboo fence to the gate and showed them in. To the right a small fountain splashed into a pool of golden koi carp. A tiny lawn stretched the length of the restaurant, bordered by stands of bamboo.

April was delighted. 'This is so cute! I never knew it was here!'

I opened the door for them and we went in. The restaurant had about twenty booths under the large picture windows overlooking the Japanese garden. At the end of the restaurant the large steel plates of the teppan sat on the marble benchtop.

We sat together at the teppan. The waitress poured us some Japanese green tea and gave us the lunch menu. Typically for Hong Kong restaurants, it had a set-price lunch menu for the office crowd. We all ordered the same thing. Then Louise pulled out her notebook and I felt a jolt of dismay.

'Uh, Louise,' I said as I raised my hand, 'don't bother about that. I haven't had time. I've been flat out busy and haven't even been collecting names. So you win by default. I'm paying.'

'Humph.' Louise put her notebook away. 'I had some really good ones too. There's a guy in a shop in Mong Kok called Circus Wong.'

'So how's life in Australia, April?' I said. 'Andy's not joined you there yet?'

'He's always having emergencies at work, he can't leave yet,' April said. 'Soon.'

'It's nearly three months since you went yourself, April,' Louise said. 'He should be making a move.'

'When he's back in Hong Kong we'll talk about it,' April said. 'He said he'll see me again before I go home to Australia.'

Louise and I stared at her.

The chef came out from the back of the restaurant. He bowed to us and we nodded back. He turned on the teppan and polished the plate completely clean with a wet cloth.

'Did you just say that your husband isn't in Hong Kong?' Louise said.

April watched the chef. 'He had another emergency at work. We had a couple of days together, then he had to rush off to China.' She brightened. 'But he says he'll definitely come to Australia to see me at Chinese New Year. Because I'm his family.'

Louise and I shared a look.

'Are you still working as nanny, Emma?' April said.

'Yep.'

'What about your study?'

'Still doing that.'

'What gym do you go to?' Louise said.

'Gym?'

The chef put some prawns on the plate and expertly moved them around.

'You've been working out,' Louise said. 'You've lost a lot of weight.'

'I run around the Peak,' I said. 'That's all.'

'Not learning martial arts off your Mr Chen?' Louise said.

I didn't reply.

Louise grinned. 'I want some good news soon, Emma.'

'Never going to happen.'

'How about you come along with me on Saturday night then and I introduce you to a couple of new guys at the bank? Both of them are really cute.'

I hesitated, then, 'Not Saturday. I'm busy.'

'Don't moon over him if he isn't going to do anything about it, Emma.'

'I have study to do.'

The chef placed the cooked prawns on our plates. April picked up a piece and delicately dipped it into the garlic sauce. She popped it into her mouth. 'Eat. This is good. Fresh.'

Louise and I tried the prawns as the chef cooked some chicken fillets.

'You have to go and see Aunty Kitty, Emma, she has something for you,' April said.

'Geez, April, I resigned from the kindergarten nearly a year ago,' I said. 'Why doesn't she just give up?'

'She says you have an award or something. Because you were such a good English teacher. She says you have to go to her house and collect it,' April said. 'Apparently it's a prize or something. A holiday.'

'You can have it, whatever it is.'

'You mean it?'

'Yeah.'

'You're too generous, Emma,' April said. 'I'll go and collect it for you.'

'Okay, whatever,' I said. 'I don't have time to take a holiday right now anyway.'

The chef placed thinly sliced beef on the plate, then put long-stemmed enoki mushrooms in the centre and rolled the beef around them. It cooked very quickly.

My mobile phone rang and I answered it. 'Emma.'

'Hello, Emma. It's Jade. Can you talk?'

'I can talk, but nothing special.'

'Okay. I was just wondering — I have an appointment with the tailor tomorrow afternoon and thought you might like to come along and have some cheongsams made at the same time. We could have lunch, then go and choose some silk and have some dresses made for you.'

'Sounds great. When? Where?'

'Can you meet me at the Princes Building? Noon?'

'Sure. But I need to clear it with Mr Chen first.'

'Don't worry, I just asked him, he said it's okay. He said something about buying your own clothes for a change. What does that mean?'

'Don't worry about it. Is he there? Let me talk to him.'

'No, he's not here, I just talked to him. I need to run. See you tomorrow?'

'Sure. Bye, Jade.'

I snapped the phone shut, then checked to see if it had recorded her number. The call wasn't there.

The chef broke a couple of eggs on the teppan, stirred them around, and made fried rice for us. 'Last dish.' He bowed crisply. 'Thank you.'

'I have to go soon,' April said. 'I need to go to the Consulate and do some paperwork for Andy.'

While April was in the ladies' room Louise and I shared speculation.

'Do you think it's possible that he's genuine?' I said. 'And that the emergencies are for real?'

'Not in a million years,' Louise said. 'Something is definitely going on here. He's avoiding her.'

'If he married her for the Australian passport, he'd have been over there months ago. She must be a cover for him.'

'The funny thing is,' Louise said, 'she doesn't really seem to care. She's quite happy to be married to a man who avoids her, provided he visits her at Chinese New Year.'

After lunch I wandered through the shops of Causeway Bay for a while. I went to the computer mall in Windsor House to buy a few pieces of hardware for my computer, a new DVD drive and some more memory. I'd asked Gold to upgrade the machine but he never seemed to have time.

I felt a coldness behind me as I walked back through Causeway Bay to the lay-by where Leo would collect me. I knew what it was. I quickened my pace without looking back, then dived into a tiny below-ground shopping centre selling Japanese collectibles and video games. The shopping centre had glass everywhere and I could see them following me.

They looked like perfectly ordinary Chinese men in their mid-twenties, but they were definitely following me. Two of them. I felt a jolt of panic, then calmed myself. As long as they thought I wasn't trained in the Arts they wouldn't come after me; it wasn't honourable. I checked them: they were only small, about level five or six. I could take them if I had to.

The shops were in a loop and I wandered casually through, pretending to look at the collectible trading cards and gundam figures in the windows. The demons followed me.

They were still further back in the shopping centre when I reached the entrance again. I trotted smartly up the stairs into the busy Causeway Bay street and hauled my mobile phone out of the pocket of my jeans.

'Yes?' It was Leo on his mobile in the car.

I headed quickly down the street towards the lay-by where he would pick me up. 'How far away are you, Leo?'

'About five minutes. Is there a problem?'

'There's a couple of demons tailing me. About level five or six. If you don't turn up soon I may have to face them.'

'*Don't take them on, whatever you do*,' Leo said fiercely. 'Go to the pick-up point and wait. I'm on my way.' He hung up.

I hurried to the lay-by. Fortunately there were a large number of people there, waiting for taxis. There was the usual scramble every time a cab appeared; Hong Kong people would sometimes conveniently forget how to queue.

I nervously stood at the lay-by and waited. The demons positioned themselves across the road at the entrance to one of the shoe shops, leering at me. They didn't make a move towards me.

The car appeared and I quickly climbed in.

'Why did they follow me?' I asked Leo when I was in the car. 'They shouldn't be coming after me; as far as they know, I'm not trained.'

'They may try you out, Emma,' Leo said. 'It's becoming obvious from the way you move that you're trained.'

'*What*?' I cried, horrified. 'They'll attack me?'

'I'm surprised they haven't had a go at you already,' Leo said. 'I think it's only a matter of time before something small gets sent against you, just to see if you really are learning from Mr Chen.'

I thumped the back of his seat, furious. 'Why the hell didn't you tell me?'

He shrugged. 'We didn't want to freak you out.'

I leaned back, crossed my arms over my chest and looked out the car window. 'You will both thoroughly keep.'

'He knew you'd react like this, too, and he was scared.'

I glanced at Leo. 'He was *scared*?'

Leo's expression didn't shift. 'When you get mad, you are extremely scary.'

I glared at him, then I couldn't help it. I collapsed over my knees, laughing. The four-thousand-year-old God of the Arts of War was scared of *me*!

'You are more and more scary every day.'

When I returned to the Peak I stormed straight into Mr Chen's office without knocking. I leaned on the mess on his desk and glowered at him.

'Don't tell me — you were attacked,' he said.

'No,' I said, 'I was followed. Why didn't you *tell* me?'

He just watched me silently.

'You *are* scared of me.'

He smiled slightly.

'You're a *god*, John,' I said, exasperated. 'What the hell can I possibly do that you could be so scared of?'

He didn't say a word.

I spun and opened the door.

'You could leave us,' he said softly as I went out.

The next day at noon I didn't see Jade arrive; it was as if she had been there all the time. She smiled and quickly embraced me. 'Where would you like to go for lunch?'

'How about yum cha?' I said. 'I haven't had any in a long time. Mr Chen doesn't go; nothing vegetarian. Are you vegetarian?'

'Absolutely not,' she said. 'I know a good place nearby, excellent yum cha. Come with me.'

After lunch we dodged through the taxis and cars and went into the Landmark.

'I bought that gold dress here,' I said. 'It cost a fortune. Since we're doing these charity things all the time now, having something more comfortable would be good.'

Jade stopped and looked at me. 'You go out with him all the time?'

I stopped as well. It had never occurred to me that she might be jealous. 'As friends. That's all.'

'Good.'

She walked to the escalators and we rode them past the enormous Christmas tree that had been set up in the atrium.

'What do you do for Christmas?' I said. 'What does Mr Chen do?'

'Christmas?' Jade looked at me blankly. 'Christmas is about the same time as Winter Solstice, so we get together with family. But for Christmas?' She shook her head as we stepped off the escalator at the top. 'No. Nothing.'

'It's a big thing in Australia. It's different, because it's in the middle of summer, but we have a lot of traditions.'

'It is a big festival?'

That stopped me dead. I'd never thought of Christmas as a festival. 'I guess you're right. It would be fun to share it with you.'

'You are very generous, Emma — willing to share your family time with me.'

'We're all family. You, Gold, Mr Chen, Monica, Simone, Leo, everybody. We're all family.'

She took my hand and squeezed it. 'You're right.'

She stopped in front of a tiny tailor's shop with a couple of faded mannequins wearing tuxedos in the window. 'This is it.'

She led me inside. The shop had bolts of cloth along the walls and a desk against the back corner. A door next to the desk opened and a tiny wizened old Chinese man came out. He grinned broadly and approached us. 'Princess Jade. Welcome.'

'Princess?' I said, glancing at Jade.

She smiled and waved him down. 'I am very low in precedence, Mr Li. Just Jade.'

'How is your father?'

'My father is well, thank you.' Jade touched my arm. 'This is my friend, Emma. Cheongsam, please.'

'May I have your hand, please, miss?'

I held my hand out and Mr Li took it. He turned it over so that it was palm up and stroked it with the other hand. He didn't stop grinning at me the entire time. It began to feel creepy, him holding my hand like that.

'No need, Mr Li, Emma is human,' Jade said. 'The Dark Lord's human nanny.'

'I see,' Mr Li said, the grin not shifting. 'But she is trained. She has been trained by the Dark Lord himself.' He gave me my hand back and gestured towards the back of the shop.

'That's right, she asked to learn,' Jade said, smiling sideways at me.

'Excellent,' Mr Li said, grinning over his shoulder. 'This way.'

He led us through the door at the back of the shop and I stopped dead.

We were in an enormous factory room. The far wall was so far away it was almost invisible. Rows and rows of young women worked on old-fashioned industrial sewing machines. Sunlight streamed in from windows set high on the walls. Outside, it had been a grey and miserable day.

'Jade, this room is bigger than the whole shopping centre. Where the hell are we?'

'This is the back room,' Jade said. 'Come. The silk is at the end.'

Some of the girls smiled up at us as we passed them. When we reached the far wall Mr Li sat us at a large high work table covered with books of fabric. He gestured towards the bolts of silk covering the entire wall behind us. 'I will let you take your time and choose. Tea?'

'Bo lei,' Jade said. 'We just had yum cha.'

Mr Li barked orders to the staff in Cantonese.

Jade sat next to me and pulled the fabric books closer. There must have been at least twenty of them.

'God, there are so many,' I said, overwhelmed.

'No, it's easy,' Jade said. She flipped one of the books open. 'This is embossed, not embroidered. Longevity.' She studied me. 'Do you know what that is?'

I shook my head, flipping through the pages of different-coloured silk, all embossed with stylised circular patterns.

'Each pattern is a character for longevity.' She pulled another book out and flipped it open. 'Flower brocade.' Another. 'Dragons.' She held the book up at the green dragon brocade. 'I like this. I may have one made as well.'

'Feel free to take a sample if you wish to make your own, Princess,' Mr Li said as he passed behind us. 'You know you do not require my services.'

'Are you sure?'

Mr Li stopped and gestured towards the rows of busy young women. 'I have quite enough work as it is.'

'Is the Dark Lord's suit finished?'

Mr Li's face lit up. 'Of course. I forgot. Let me fetch it for you.' He chuckled. 'Who would have thought of such a thing. The Dark Lord Xuan Wu himself requiring the services of a tailor. I must have a plaque made.'

'You should see what he wears at home,' I said, studying the silk in front of me.

'He is the scruffiest Immortal on *any* plane,' Jade said, and we giggled together.

Mr Li tutted and raced away to fetch the suit.

Jade turned to look at me. 'We should choose a colour that suits your complexion first, and then you can select the design. You have beautiful white skin, Emma, what do you use to whiten it?'

'Whiten it?'

'You know, make it a lighter colour.' She smiled and touched my arm. 'Of course. I forgot. You're European.'

'You forgot for a moment that I'm not Chinese?'

She nodded, still smiling.

I threw my arm around her shoulder and gave her a quick friendly squeeze, making her smile widen. 'I am absolutely delighted. I'll take it as a compliment. Now ...' I flipped through the book. 'How about this white silk? It's beautiful.'

Jade's face went strange.

'Oh, of course, white is for funerals.'

'Tai chi chuan uniform,' Mr Li said as he charged past. 'Suit coming.'

'He is quite correct.' Jade raised her voice. 'And the suit had better hurry, we are nearly ready to choose.' She lifted a book of silk and flipped it in front of me. 'Dark blue suits you. Pink is lovely.' She raised another book and opened it. 'This.'

I looked down. She held a sample of black silk with large golden chrysanthemums against me. 'The gold flowers bring out the highlights in your hair.'

'And the black brings up her pale complexion.' Mr Li dropped a linen bag onto the table next to us. 'Lord Xuan's suit.' He nodded at the book of silk. 'Lord Xuan's colour. His livery. Most fitting.'

I hesitated.

'Oh, black is for mourning in the West,' Jade said, pulling the book away.

'No, we wear it all the time anyway,' I said.

She put it against me again. 'It really is perfect.'

Mr Li turned and barked some orders in Cantonese, and a whole bolt of the black silk floated off the shelves towards me. I backed away; the bolt was easily big enough to crush me

'Stay still, it won't hurt you, I have it,' Mr Li said. He guided the silk to wrap itself around me, then waved one hand. A mirror appeared, floating next to the work table. It had no frame; it was as if the air itself was suddenly reflective.

'Look, Emma,' Jade said, and I turned to see.

They were right. The black silk suited me perfectly. The golden chrysanthemums shimmered against me, making my hair glow.

But it was Xuan Wu's ... John's colour. I realised then, there was nothing I wanted more in the world than to stand side by side with him, wearing the black silk. Both of us in black. And have him smile down at me.

I wanted it so much it hurt.

'I'll have blue embroidered with small flowers, and pink embossed longevity,' I said, pulling the black silk away. The silk unwrapped and floated from me.

'You should take the black, it's perfect,' Mr Li said.

'No. No black.'

'Are you sure, Emma?' Jade said, disappointed.

I sat at the work table and opened the books I'd chosen. 'This. And this. No black.'

'The black is lovely on you,' Jade said.

'Maybe next time.'

'Would you like a lift home, Emma?' Jade said as we walked back through Central.

'Leo is collecting me from Theatre Lane,' I said. 'I didn't know you had a car.'

'I don't, I can't even drive.' Jade stopped at one of the designer shopfronts. 'That jacket is beautiful.'

'Oh my God, that's real fur!'

'The shoes are beautiful too.'

'Animals had to die for that coat, Jade.'

Her eyes widened. 'I never thought of it like that. Of course. And the shoes are snakeskin.' She shook her head. 'I didn't even think of it.'

'Some of my other Chinese friends are like that too,' I said. 'They didn't connect the leopard-skin coat that pop star wore at those awards with —'

'I saw that,' Jade said. 'Stunning.'

'— with the fact that the pop star was wearing a dead protected animal. That was so wrong.'

'You Westerners eat your pre-packaged cuts of meat, all clean and tidy, without thinking of the dead animal behind them.'

'I suppose you're right.'

'It's a cultural thing.'

'I guess. Still like the coat?'

'I adore it, but I wouldn't buy it now.' Her eyes turned inwards. 'Leo is at Theatre Lane to collect you.'

My mobile phone rang.

'How do you do that?'

'Do what?'

I shook my head and flipped my phone open. It was Leo.

CHAPTER TWENTY-THREE

I pulled away from the computer and stretched. I rose and went into my bedroom to look out the window.

The low grey clouds roiled across the sky; it was probably only about eight degrees outside. It never dropped below freezing in Hong Kong, but in mid-January the wind could become bitter. Although Hong Kong was nearly in the tropics, sometimes it was colder than my home in southern Queensland.

There was a tap on the door. 'Emma?'

I opened it and let Mr Chen in. His black cotton pants seemed to be more shredded every time he wore them.

He took a seat on the couch. I leaned on the desk next to my computer.

'You spend a lot of your free time in front of your computer,' he said.

I shrugged.

'The weather's going to be fine, clear and quite warm tomorrow. I'll take Simone for a hack around the hills at the club. We'll be longer than we usually are. Do you still want to come?'

I glanced at the grey cloudy day outside my window. He smiled slightly.

I sat on the couch next to him. 'Sure.'

He moved a short distance away from me on the couch. 'Good.'

'Why do you do that?'

'What?'

I gestured towards him. 'You never want to be too close to me.' I shifted closer and he quickly stood and went to the door.

'Is it that unpleasant being close to me?'

He hesitated with his hand on the doorknob. Then he shook his head. 'The problem is exactly the opposite.' He opened the door. 'Early tomorrow, Emma.' He went out and closed the door.

I sighed loudly and returned to the computer. His freaking choice. I changed my mind, threw myself out of my chair and stomped into the training room to hit something for a while.

Of course he was right. The breeze had shifted and it was warm and mild as the sunshine streamed through the bauhinia trees on either side of the trail.

After half an hour of riding I broke the silence. 'It's nearly six months since we went to Paris, Mr Chen. We need to go back.'

He pushed Star to walk slightly ahead of me.

'I wanna go to the Science Museum!' Simone called at his back.

'You need to see Ms Kwan,' I said.

He ignored us. Simone and I shared an exasperated glance and trotted our horses to catch up.

Mr Chen stopped his horse. His eyes turned inwards and his face went rigid. Star danced sideways, but he paid no attention.

'What, Daddy?' Simone said.

He raised his hand to hush her.

He listened for a while, then snapped back to the *here*. He held Star with his knees and the horse stopped, his ears flicking backwards and forwards. Mr Chen ripped his mobile phone out of his pocket and quickly dialled.

'I need you here now,' he said. 'I don't care if you have to steal a car or hijack a taxi. Nobody can carry you, you'll have to make your own way here, but I need you here within twenty minutes. I'll meet you outside the stables.' He closed the phone and grimaced.

'Are you okay?' I said, but he raised his hand again. He listened for a long time, his face becoming more and more intense.

He snapped back and grabbed Simone's reins. 'We need to go back to the stables right away.'

He turned Star and trotted along the path, then slowed to a walk because Simone's pony couldn't keep up with Star's long strides.

'What happened?' I said.

'My Mountain is under attack.'

'How bad?'

'Very bad. An army of demons. My Dark Disciples are holding them off, but it is an extremely large force and they need me there.'

'Can you go? Without losing your human form?'

He hesitated, still leading Simone's pony. He didn't look at me. 'I hope so, Emma.'

'Go now,' I said. 'I'll mind Simone.'

He turned but didn't really see me. 'No. This may be a diversion so they can grab Simone. I need to see her safely with Leo before I go.'

I nodded, understanding. If anything really big came after us I didn't have the skill to hold it off. We needed Leo.

When we returned to the stables the grooms for Simone and me were already waiting. Mr Chen threw himself off Star and cast around; his groom was nowhere to be seen. He hissed with frustration and gently led the horse into its stall. Then he took us out to wait at the entrance to the stables.

His eyes unfocused again. He listened for a long time. 'They've broken through the wall. My Palace is on fire,' he whispered, stricken. 'They are desecrating my halls and pavilions. They need me there *now* to make some rain to put out the fires.' He refocused. '*Where the hell is Leo?*'

'There he is, Daddy!' Simone shouted, and ran to Leo who was charging down the drive towards us.

Mr Chen turned to go, but I stopped him with a hand on his arm. 'John.'

He hesitated.

'John. This could be goodbye.' I swallowed. 'I just want to say ...' I struggled to find the words. 'I just wanted to say ...'

He took my hands, raised them to his face and kissed them. He gazed into my eyes, full of pain. 'You don't need to say anything. I know.' He released my hands and ran into the stables.

Leo approached me with Simone on his hip, carrying her easily.

'— and Daddy said there's a lot of demons up there and he's going there now and we have to stay here and we'll be just fine with you, Leo,' Simone finished without taking a breath.

'Let's get her home and safe, Emma,' Leo said grimly. 'How bad is it?'

We turned and walked back up the drive towards the car. 'Very bad.'

'Damn.' We reached the car and he unlocked it with the remote. He gently dropped Simone into the back seat. 'This may be it, Emma.'

'I know,' I said softly. I buckled Simone in and Leo pulled himself into the driver's seat.

'It? What, Leo?' Simone said.

'Lunchtime.'

'Oh, yeah. Daddy will be hungry after killing all the demons. We should make him some tea. I wonder if he'd like some bean curd? Or some noodles?'

'I'm sure he would,' Leo said. He choked and tried to turn it into a cough.

When we arrived home Leo pulled down Dark Heavens, the sword in the hallway. He turned to me and spoke softly. 'Emma, take off now. They don't want you, they want her. Get yourself out of this now; as long as you're not here you'll be completely safe.'

'Don't be ridiculous.'

'Go, Emma.'

I moved closer and glared up into his face. 'No! I'm staying here with Simone!'

He bent and studied me carefully. 'Are you sure?'

'Of course I'm sure!' I took Simone's hand. 'Where's the safest place?'

Leo shook his head. 'You are amazingly stupid sometimes.'

'I know. Where?'

'Training room. Monica!'

Monica came out of the kitchen wiping her hands on a towel. She saw the sword in Leo's hand and her eyes widened.

'Monica,' Leo said, 'Mr Chen won't be needing you for the rest of the day. Take the afternoon off.' He hesitated, then spoke with force. '*Out.*'

Monica nodded and returned to the kitchen, undoing her apron.

'I'll see her out and lock up.' Leo followed Monica into the kitchen.

I led Simone into the training room. 'You know what's happening, Simone?'

'Daddy's Mountain,' Simone said.

'We'll be safe with Leo.'

'I know.'

Leo charged into the training room and stopped. He took Simone's hand and led her to the mirrors. 'Sit here.'

Simone sat cross-legged in front of the mirrors, unafraid.

Leo gestured towards the weapons rack. 'Anything in particular he's been working on with you?'

'Yeah.' I selected the short sword from the rack. 'But what I'd really like is a machine gun and I don't see one here.'

'Guns don't hurt them,' he said. 'Knives, poles, bladed weapons. You need to cut them or break them.'

'What else didn't he tell me?'

'Probably a lot,' Leo said with grim humour. He turned to me, raised Dark Heavens and lowered his voice. 'If I go down, take this. It's his. It will do a great deal of damage.' He gestured. 'In front of Simone.'

I moved into position. Leo stood in front of me. They would have to make it through both of us to get to her.

'Sharpened your sword recently?'

'Yep. Mr Chen showed me how. But I'd prefer not to have to use it.'

'I'd prefer you didn't have to use it either.' Leo faced the door. 'Ready?'

I prepared myself in front of Simone. 'Bring it on.'

'Have I told you how stupid you are?'

'Yep.'

We waited silently.

I began to feel ridiculous, standing over the child with a sword, when it was possible that nothing would happen.

Leo lowered Dark Heavens. 'Maybe we'll be lucky and they won't —'

The door crashed open. Simone squeaked, then, 'Demons coming, Leo.'

'Good girl, you remembered.' Leo unsheathed Dark Heavens and threw the scabbard to one side. 'How many?'

'I don't know,' Simone said.

'They can only come in one at a time,' Leo said. 'The seals stop them.'

I pulled my sword out and readied myself.

The demon appeared in the doorway. It was only about four feet tall, skinny and as black as Leo. It had huge ears and a grotesque, almost comical face. It grinned at us and disappeared.

'Small one,' Leo said. 'Saw its own reflection. How many more are there, Simone?'

Mr Chen walked in the door, holding his sword and smiling. I dropped my arm with relief. 'Thank God.'

'That's. Not. My. Daddy,' Simone said loudly and clearly.

The demon smiled, raised its sword in a salute to Leo, and moved into a defensive position.

Leo didn't move at all in front of me.

The demon rushed forward and Leo sprang to meet it. Their swords met over their heads then moved together to lock at the hilts with a painful grating sound. Leo and the demon were face to face. The demon's smile widened. Its other hand shot out to hit Leo's head, but Leo dodged the blow, spun and jumped back, twisting the demon's sword away at the same time.

The demon's smile disappeared as it leapt forward to strike. Leo blocked the blow, the swords ringing together, but the demon continued to come at him with lightning-fast attacks. Leo moved back as he parried the blows, but when Simone cried out behind him he stood his ground and blocked the demon's thrusts without shifting his feet.

The demon became concerned as it saw that Leo had no difficulty dealing with its attacks. Leo didn't miss the shift in control and pressed forward, still parrying the blows.

The demon jumped back out of Leo's reach.

Leo didn't give it time to recover. He tore straight into it with a series of fierce attacks. The demon grimaced and fell back. Leo hit it harder each time and the demon blocked with difficulty.

Leo feinted into the demon's face with his left fist, and at the same time ran it through with his sword. He twisted the blade inside the demon, then slashed upwards through the demon's body and out its shoulder.

The demon smiled. 'Now you will meet my mother.' It dissolved.

Something came down the hallway. A sickening wet slither.

'Mother, Leo,' Simone whispered.

'Oh my God,' Leo said under his breath.

I readied myself and hefted my sword. 'I'm right behind you.'

'Stay there. Don't get in the way. If I go down . . .' He hesitated. 'Don't let it have you, Emma. It won't hurt her, she'll be okay. But whatever you do, don't let it take you.'

'I understand.'

The demon appeared in the doorway.

Its back end was a slimy snake that oozed toxin over its black scales. The front end looked like the top half of a man with the skin taken off. It had to lower itself on its coils to fit through the door; it was enormous.

It came halfway into the room and raised its body on the coils. Its skinless head nearly touched the ceiling. 'You are the Black Lion? Disciple of the Dark Lord?'

'I am just an ordinary man.'

The demon smiled and its red eyes flashed. 'I like your skin. I think I will take it.'

Leo readied himself. 'Come and get it.'

It moved incredibly fast for something without legs. Leo stepped forward and spun to strike it with the sword, but it was too fast. Its right hand snaked out and wrapped around Leo's sword hand at the wrist.

Leo dragged his hand back and tried to free it but the demon had him. It raised itself on its coils and lifted him easily.

Leo struggled. He tried to prise the demon's fingers loose with his left hand. His muscles bulged as he attempted to free himself. His feet hung just above the floor.

The demon's one-handed grip slid on Leo's wrist so it used both hands. Its forked tongue flicked out and snapped over Leo's face, tracing his features. He screwed his eyes up and grimaced.

I lunged forward to attack it, but Leo was ahead of me. His free left hand flashed out, grabbed the demon's tongue and, with a twist and a snap, pulled it out.

The demon dropped him and screamed. It held its hands to its face, still screaming.

Leo landed on his feet, spun and sliced the demon in half. The human part hit the floor and exploded into black demon stuff. The snake part writhed for a long time before dissipating.

Leo took a deep shuddering breath and backed to stand in front of us again. 'Any more?'

Simone took a gasping breath and screamed. She collapsed over her knees into sobs. I wanted to comfort her but stayed where I was.

'I'll take that as a yes,' Leo said. 'Don't move.'

'I'm still here,' I said.

'You're still stupid too. Looks like the Mother blew the seals. This is a really big one, isn't it, Simone?'

Simone whimpered something unintelligible.

The demon appeared in the doorway. It was of average human height. It appeared to be a perfectly ordinary Chinese human male.

Leo hissed under his breath. It was Simon Wong.

Wong leaned one shoulder on the doorframe and crossed his arms over his chest. 'Hello, everybody. Been having fun with my little pets?'

Leo shifted his grip on the sword.

'Three little girls.' Wong didn't move from the doorframe. 'Kissed any nice boys lately, girls? Got a new boyfriend, Leo? Still haven't made out with the boss yet, Emma? And dear little Simone —'

Leo swung at Wong's head. He disappeared. The sword took a chip out of the doorframe.

Leo backed to stand in front of me.

Wong reappeared, leaning on the doorframe. He held the Wudang sword. 'I have a special place in my harem for all three of you, but you will require minor surgery, Leo, before you may take your place. I will not have Entires guarding, regardless of their preference.'

Leo swung at the demon again, and again it disappeared.

'That is some piece of work,' he said.

'Freaking coward,' I said, hoping that Wong could hear me. 'It keeps running.'

Wong appeared in the middle of the room. He gestured a come-on. 'Black Lion. You first.'

'Get him,' I said softly.

'Oh, don't worry, Emma, you're next,' Wong said. He moved so fast he was a blur. The sword was almost invisible as it swept straight for Leo's head.

Leo blocked easily, swept Wong's sword down in a parry, then twisted away to take a spinning swing at Wong's neck. Wong ducked under it and jumped back.

'You're as good as they say you are,' Wong said. He held back and grinned at Leo. 'They tell stories about you, you know? You should hear what they have to say.'

Leo swung at Wong's head. Wong blocked it, swept Leo's sword down, and attempted to twist it out of his hands. Leo managed to keep his grip on the sword and pulled back. He took a deep breath and readied himself again.

Wong shifted his feet and lifted his own sword. A hint of his true nature appeared on his face. 'You've improved, Leo. You're much better than last time.' His grin widened. 'I mean the time before. Remember? When I got through you and grabbed little Simone's darling mother? I had a lot of fun with her, you know. But she *broke*.'

Simone sobbed once, loudly.

Wong swung at Leo's head again. Leo blocked the blow and the swords locked. Leo planted his feet and struggled to free the blade but Wong didn't shift. 'I'm better too, aren't I? I've been working out.'

It became a test of strength. They were evenly matched. Leo trembled with the effort of holding Wong's sword away from his throat.

Wong stiffened and his eyes turned inwards. He snapped back and grinned. 'Close enough to kiss you, Leo. What a shame. It would have been fun to have you beneath me, but that pleasure will have to wait until next time.'

Leo grunted with the effort of holding Wong back. His feet slipped slightly on the mats. His arms shook as he struggled to keep the sword from his throat.

Wong turned to grin at me without shifting his grip on the sword. 'Emma, dear. Why don't you go to him?

You could have years together, you know. Sneak in with him. Wake him up. He'll give you everything you want, and a whole lot more. You don't know what you're missing.'

He disappeared.

Leo lurched forward, then straightened. 'Is it gone, Simone?'

'Yes. No more right now,' Simone said, her voice trembling. 'That was a really scary one.'

I dropped my sword and rushed to hold her. 'We're all right now, darling.'

She buried her face into me.

'Stay here,' Leo said. He charged out of the training room. A few furious bangs sounded as he tried to close the front door. He returned, shaking his head. 'Front door's useless. We need a new one.' He moved his mouth next to my ear and spoke very softly. 'Emma, if they win on the Mountain, they'll be straight here. Go. Go now.'

I stopped with my arms still around Simone. 'Here?'

He nodded. 'Get out now. If you're here when they come, they'll get you too.' His face softened. 'Believe me, you don't want that. You have no idea what they're capable of.'

I held Simone tighter. 'No way. I'm staying with you.' I raised one hand to stop him. 'You don't need to tell me. I know. I'm stupid.'

Simone stiffened and gasped.

A loud thump resounded in the hallway.

Leo snatched up Dark Heavens and stood in front of me. I dropped my arms from Simone, grabbed my own sword and stood behind him.

'This could be what scared the prince away,' Leo said. 'Is it a bigger demon, Simone?'

Simone didn't say anything. We both checked her; she sat wide-eyed and silent.

We heard it coming down the hallway with dragging footsteps. The strong smell of burning filled the room.

He appeared in the doorway. He was blackened and bleeding. His smouldering armour hung off him. He staggered halfway into the training room and fell to his knees.

Simone shrieked, '*Daddy*!' and threw herself at him.

'Simone.' He collapsed.

CHAPTER TWENTY-FOUR

Leo pushed Simone gently to one side and tipped Mr Chen onto his back.

He was soaked with water and covered in mud and blood. His long hair was plastered to his face. Leo pulled the hair away and tilted his head back. He felt his neck, concentrating, then put his ear next to Mr Chen's mouth. 'At least he's breathing and he has a pulse.' He checked Mr Chen's head, turning it from side to side, then opened his eyes one at a time. 'Looks okay, probably just exhaustion. He has a lump on his head — maybe a concussion.'

Simone hovered. 'Will he be all right, Leo?'

'Give me time to look at him, sweetheart, but I think he'll be okay.'

Leo pulled the shredded black lacquer armour away and pushed it to one side. Mr Chen still had his riding clothes underneath. They were soaked with water and blood. Leo ripped the shirt open, revealing his chest, and Simone squeaked. His skin ran with water, blood and thick transparent goo. He had one large angry gash about halfway down his abdomen, and was covered in smaller bleeding cuts and blistered burns.

Leo ripped off his T-shirt and pushed it into the large wound. He ran his hand over Mr Chen's abdomen, sweeping the blood away to see the injuries. 'Ugh. Venom.' He wiped his hands on his pants. 'But he hasn't been poisoned. Stroke of luck; I don't think the hospital could handle a demon poisoning.'

He checked Mr Chen's arms, stopping at the left. He gently probed it. 'This is broken in two places.' He ran his hands down Mr Chen's sides and twisted his slim hips. 'Good. No fractures here.' He checked Mr Chen's legs and pulled off his boots. The left foot was severely swollen and Leo gently pressed his fingers into it. Mr Chen flinched without regaining consciousness. 'Broken ankle.' Leo smiled grimly. 'Don't know how he made it down the hallway on that.'

Leo pulled his T-shirt out of the large abdominal wound to check it. 'He's lucky this wasn't deeper.' He packed the T-shirt over the wound again, then rocked onto his heels. 'We need to get him into a hospital. He must have defeated them and then come back here to check on Simone. If we can get him to a hospital I think he'll make it.'

He smiled sadly up at me. 'All over.'

I sighed with relief and flopped to sit on the floor.

Simone fell into my lap. 'Everything's okay?'

'I think he'll make it, sweetheart,' Leo said. He pulled his mobile phone out and dialled. He listened silently, then said, 'Ambulance.'

Simone moved to her father's head while Leo gave the emergency line the details of where to send the ambulance. She knelt, lifted his head into her lap and shook with sobs. 'The demons aren't supposed to be able to hurt him. They can't. They can't.'

Leo closed his phone. 'The ambulance is coming. Don't worry, Simone, I think he'll be okay.'

'But he's so weak,' Simone whispered, still cradling her father's unconscious head. 'There's hardly anything in there at all.'

'I know, sweetheart,' Leo said, full of pain. He glanced up at me. 'We'll need a story. Robbery? Burglars broke in and he stopped them?'

'That won't explain the burns,' I said.

'Damn, you're right. What do we tell them?'

Inspiration hit. 'Kidnapped. Beaten. Tortured.' I checked my watch. 'We paid the ransom, we got him back. He's only been gone a couple of hours and ordered us not to contact the police.'

Leo's eyes widened with admiration. 'That's perfect, Emma. There was a similar case in the papers not long ago. It happens all the time.' He checked Mr Chen again. 'But the others weren't beaten.'

'Take one look at him, Leo, and tell me he wouldn't have fought back. Hard.'

Leo nodded. 'Hope the ambulance comes soon.'

'They won't find out about him? They won't be able to tell?'

'What we have here is a perfectly normal human being. They won't be able to tell anything, provided we keep our mouths shut.'

Simone rested her cheek on Mr Chen's bloodied forehead. 'Don't worry, Leo, I know what to say.'

'I know you do, sweetheart.'

'I'll go with him,' I said. 'You stay here and guard Simone.'

Simone's head shot up. 'I'm going with my daddy!'

'We'll all go,' Leo said. 'I'll ask one of the security guards from downstairs to mind the flat. They're good about that. They can arrange for the door to be fixed while we're gone.'

The doorbell rang. 'It's the ambulance men, Leo,' Simone said.

'That was quick,' I said suspiciously.

'No, there's a hospital only five minutes away on the Peak,' Leo said. 'Everybody know what to say?'

Simone and I nodded.

Leo went to show them in.

We sat on a couch outside the ward. Simone lay across Leo and me, her feet on me and her head in Leo's lap. I pulled off her little riding boots and dropped them to the floor. The hack on the horses seemed like days ago.

A slim young doctor came out carrying a clipboard. He looked around.

'We're with John Chen,' I said.

He came to us and flipped the paper on the clipboard. 'Family only, please.'

We all rose. Leo picked up Simone and put her on his hip.

'We're all family,' I said.

Leo glared down at the doctor, daring him to disagree.

'Right, now you can come,' the doctor said, unfazed. 'The police want to talk to you as well. You'll need to give us his ID card number and details later.'

'Will he be okay?' Leo said.

The doctor studied the chart. 'He's lost a lot of blood, and he's very weak, but there doesn't appear to be any critical damage. We want to keep him overnight for observation. He took a severe blow to the head and we need to keep an eye on it.'

Leo and I shared a look. Leo nodded, very slightly.

'Can we see him?' I said.

The doctor gestured towards the ward. 'Don't stay too long.'

A couple of policemen waited for us inside the ward. Leo and I shared another look.

'Go and see him first,' one of them said. 'Then we'll take statements.'

I took a deep breath and followed Leo into the room.

Mr Chen's hair was a mess, tied back roughly out of the way. He appeared to be asleep. His left arm was in a cast to above the elbow, and a drip fed into his right forearm. Pieces of tape covered the cuts on his face. He was very pale.

Simone clambered onto the chair next to the bed and whispered, 'Daddy.'

He didn't move. She took his hand. 'Daddy.'

His eyes slowly opened. He saw her and smiled. 'Simone. Thank the Heavens.' He saw Leo, then me. He breathed a sigh of relief. 'Are you all right? Everybody's okay?'

'We're fine,' Leo said, moving to stand behind Simone.

'Leo was great, Daddy,' Simone said. 'He killed the demons for me.'

Mr Chen glanced up at Leo.

'House. Shape Shifter. Snake Mother,' Leo said softly.

'A Mother,' Mr Chen said. 'A challenge for you. Well done.'

Leo hadn't mentioned Wong. I didn't mention him either.

Mr Chen raised his good hand. Simone scrambled onto the bed and held it.

'Careful,' I said. 'His foot is broken.'

'I have stitches in here too,' he said, pointing at his abdomen.

Simone carefully eased down to lie on the bed with her head on the pillow next to his, and held his hand. 'I'm glad you're okay, Daddy.' She touched his hair. 'You need to wash your hair. There's mud in it.'

He smiled sadly. 'I know. When I come home tomorrow.'

He turned his head to see Leo. 'Take her home. Guard her well. It's finished. Major damage — not just to me — but the attack was fended off.' He gestured with his head towards the police and lowered his voice. 'What are we going to tell them?'

'You were kidnapped,' I said softly. 'We paid the ransom. They gave you back. You fought them and they did this to you.'

'Well done, Emma, that's perfect,' he whispered. He raised his voice loud enough for the police outside to hear. 'I don't remember anything. They must have broken in and knocked me out. I don't even remember what they looked like.'

Simone snuggled next to him. He stroked her hair with his good hand.

The doctor came in. 'The police want to talk to you, Mr Chen. Then your family should go home and let you rest.'

'Can one of us stay with him?' I said.

The doctor nodded.

We all shared a look.

'You take Simone home,' I said to Leo. 'I'll stay here and watch him.'

'I wanna stay here with my daddy!'

'Your daddy needs to sleep without any wriggling lumps jumping on him,' I said. 'Go and help Leo get the house ready for him to come home tomorrow. I'll stay here and look after him.'

'Go, Simone,' Mr Chen breathed.

'Okay, Daddy,' Simone said. 'We'll make sure everything's ready for you.' She clambered off the bed and took Leo's hand. 'Daddy will be all right with Emma.'

'I know, sweetheart,' Leo said. He moved closer to me and spoke softly. 'Call me if anything happens. But I don't think anything will; it's all finished.'

I turned to see the police. 'Let's talk to them and get this over with.'

Mr Chen tried to pull himself upright and failed, falling back onto his pillow.

Leo grabbed the controls for the bed and raised Mr Chen's head. I went to let the police in.

'Don't talk to them for too long,' the doctor said. He clipped the chart to the end of the bed and went out.

The police glared at us but had to accept our statements. They seemed accustomed to wealthy people fabricating stories for them. They made us promise to go back and tell them more if we remembered. They also made us promise to take Mr Chen to the police station as soon as he was well enough. They wanted to catch the perpetrators of this particularly brutal crime.

The irony wasn't lost on either me or Leo. The last thing these guys wanted to catch was a Mother.

The dim hospital night-lights and the warm hum of the equipment lulled me and I dozed in a chair next to him, holding his hand.

He snapped awake and cast around, waking me. He gripped my hand so tightly it was painful. 'Simone!'

'Simone's safe,' I said. 'She's at home with Leo.'

His eyes were wide and unseeing. 'Michelle?'

My heart twisted. 'No, John, it's me. Emma.'

He relaxed, his voice full of warm relief. 'Emma.'

'I'm here.'

He shifted, trying to be more comfortable, and grimaced.

'Are you in pain? Do you want me to call the doctor?'

'No.' His voice was very soft. 'No more drugs. More drugs could push me over the edge. I don't want to lose it.'

I grasped his hand. 'Hold on.'

'I am. For Simone. And for you.' He smiled up into

my eyes. 'My Emma.' He raised my hand to his face and kissed it. 'Dear Emma.'

'I'm here, John.'

He released my hand and pushed it away. 'I can't hold it. Don't. Touch. Me.'

'Why not? Why can't I touch you?'

'I will tell you when we're home,' he said, his voice thick with sleep. 'I should have told you a long time ago. But I didn't want to lose you. I will tell you. I should tell Emma, but I don't want to lose her.' His voice was very soft. 'Dear Emma. Don't leave me.'

'I won't leave you, John.'

He drifted away.

Leo and Simone returned the next morning to pick him up. The doctor tried to make him stay longer, but he insisted that he was fine and wanted to go home. Leo backed him up and together they bullied the doctor into releasing him.

He couldn't use crutches with a broken arm. The hospital lent us a wheelchair. Leo wheeled him down to the car, but he climbed clumsily into the passenger seat himself. He wouldn't let Leo carry him. Leo shook his head, folded the wheelchair up and put it in the boot.

Mr Chen was mortified when he was wheeled past the smiling security guards back at the Peak. 'This is not fitting.'

'Deal with it,' Leo said unsympathetically. 'You won't need it after you call the Lady.'

Mr Chen's face went rigid and he didn't say anything.

Leo wheeled him into his room. I hung back in the hallway, but Simone dragged me in with her.

Leo bent to assist Mr Chen into bed, but Mr Chen raised his hand. 'Leo, I need your help. This is not an order, this is a request.'

Leo stopped.

'The hospital staff tried to clean me up, but there is still mud and blood on me. There is also demon venom and it needs to come off. Will you help me?'

Leo silently watched him.

Mr Chen's face was full of regret. 'I would understand if you declined.'

They looked at each other for a long time.

Leo turned to me. 'Emma, have a look in the kitchen and see if you can find some plastic bags and rubber bands. We'll need to keep the plaster dry.'

Leo came into the kitchen later. Simone was noisily slurping the ramen that I'd made for her.

''Bout time you ate something,' Leo said.

Simone slammed her chopsticks onto the table. 'I want to see Daddy.'

'Daddy's sleeping.' Leo pulled a coffee mug out of the cupboard. 'Leave him alone.'

Simone returned to the noodles and ate them more slowly.

'Where's Monica?' I said.

'Gone to the market,' Leo said.

When Simone had finished the noodles I took her for a nap. She fell asleep almost immediately; she'd been awake most of the night with Leo. I went into my room, showered and changed, and returned to the kitchen. Leo was still there, glowering at his coffee.

I sat across from him. 'He's not out of the woods yet, is he?'

Leo shook his head without looking up.

'He needs Kwan Yin.'

He nodded.

I inhaled sharply as I understood. 'He's too damn proud to call her.'

'He drives me completely crazy sometimes.'

'Do you have the number for the house in Montmartre?'

He smiled at me. 'That house doesn't exist.'

'What?'

'Ms Kwan made it for him. It's not real. It's about as far from the demons' power centre as you can get, that's why they do it there. But the house isn't real at all.'

'What about London? Charlie? James?'

'Oh, they're real all right; he's had that house for years. But they'd have even less chance of contacting her than we would.'

I ran my hands through my hair. 'Jade? Gold?'

'Yeah.' He grimaced at his coffee. 'I asked him why he didn't want Gold to help clean him up instead of me.' He shrugged. 'The demons killed them. They're dead.'

'No!' I rubbed my hands over my face. 'No, Leo, they're Shen, I know they are. You can't kill Shen. They just go away for a while and then come back.'

'He says about three or four months.'

'That long?'

He nodded.

'What are we going to do?'

He studied his coffee, full of misery. 'Hope that he has the sense to call her before he fades away.'

I crossed my arms on the table and flopped my head on them. 'No.'

He sighed with feeling, finished his coffee and rose. 'I'll be in the training room.'

When Simone woke she was listless and uninterested in everything I tried to do with her. Eventually I planted her in front of the television and she watched it, eyes wide and unseeing.

I pulled a book out and attempted to read. I kept reading the same page over and over without comprehension.

I jumped; I'd heard a noise. I rushed to the door and looked outside. Nope; not Ms Kwan at the door.

I went to Mr Chen's room, opened the door slightly and checked on him. He appeared to be asleep, his face peaceful. He looked very, very old. He didn't move.

I returned to the television room and tried to read the book.

A couple of hours later Monica prepared lunch for us and we sat around the table looking at it.

Simone picked up some vegetables in her chopsticks, then put them down again.

I sipped my tea.

Leo threw himself up and went back to the training room without saying a word.

Simone and I returned to the television room.

Half an hour later I heard another sound and rushed out. Ms Kwan wasn't there. I sat on the couch in the television room and put my head in my hands. Leo was still in the training room doing a level one sword kata over and over.

I'd had enough.

I grabbed Simone and took her into his room. I dragged a chair from beside the wall, jammed it next to the bed and sat in it. I pulled Simone into my lap.

He turned his head to look at me without saying anything.

'You see this?' I hissed. 'This is the reason all of us are here.'

His eyes flicked to Simone and something changed in them.

'Think of what would happen to her if you were to go now.'

He didn't say anything. I wanted to slap him.

I half rose so that I could get closer to him, still holding Simone in my lap. 'Call her. Get her here *now*.'

His eyebrows creased and he turned his face away.

Simone obviously didn't understand, but didn't say anything. I stood and gently lowered her to the floor. 'And you think *we're* stupid!'

The doorbell rang and Simone shrieked with delight. 'Aunty Kwan's here! Aunty Kwan's here!' She raced out the door.

I poked my finger into the air at him. 'I am not finished with you.'

He ran his good hand over his forehead and smiled with some of the old sparkle. 'I sincerely hope not.'

Ms Kwan appeared in the doorway. 'Out, Emma.'

I went to her and took her hands. 'Thanks for coming.'

She pushed my hands away. 'Go. Quickly.'

I went out and closed the door behind me.

Leo came out of the training room, the sword still in his hand. 'Was that her?'

'Yep.'

He fell to lean against the wall and wiped his hand over his face.

'Get some rest,' I said.

'After I have something to eat,' he said. 'Suddenly I'm starving.'

'Me too!' Simone said.

'Yeah,' I said. 'I wonder if Monica's thrown our lunch away yet.'

'She doesn't throw food away, Emma, you know that.'

'Let's go and see.'

CHAPTER TWENTY-FIVE

I heard them coming and sat upright on the sofa, groggy. Leo was sprawled across the living room's other sofa. I checked my watch: 5 a.m. They'd been in there together for more than twelve hours straight.

Ms Kwan led him into the kitchen, her face like thunder. The plaster was gone and he could walk by himself.

Leo woke, and we opened the kitchen door to check on them. Mr Chen sat staring at the table, expressionless. She pulled a saucepan out of the cupboard and found some ho fan in the refrigerator. She poured some vegetable stock into the saucepan and put it on the stove. She didn't look at us. 'Out.'

Leo and I shared a look and closed the door.

Leo rubbed his eyes. 'Thank God.'

I grabbed him and held him tight. He buried his face in my hair. We held each other for a while, then separated and returned to our rooms without saying a word.

About an hour later, Leo and I came out for breakfast. The kitchen was deserted so we sat at the table together and waited. Monica appeared, bustled through the kitchen and made breakfast for us as if nothing had happened.

Ms Kwan came in and sat at the table with us. Monica made a pot of tea for her and she nodded her thanks. The three of us sat together for a long time without looking at each other.

Eventually she stirred. 'Leo and Emma — here is something I should have given you a long time ago.' She held her hand out, palm up, and a soft glow appeared. It coalesced into a pearl so large it filled her palm. She placed the pearl on the table with a soft metallic click.

'If he should ever be this bad again,' she said, 'hold this and call me. I will come.'

'Thanks,' I said. 'You don't know how much we appreciate it.'

Leo nodded, speechless.

'I will need to stay at least a week, day and night,' she said. 'Do you have room for me?'

'You can have my room, I'll take one of the student rooms,' I said.

'I don't want to put you out,' she said, concerned.

'I would be honoured.' I hesitated, but I had to know. 'How bad is the Mountain?'

'We all knew this was coming. It was inevitable. The Demon King led an enormous army of demons to attack the Mountain. The other three Winds and the Elite Guard of the Jade Emperor fought side by side with the Dark Disciples. All of the Dragons in the Heavens rallied to his aid. The Tiger's Western Horsemen cut through the demons. But they were overpowered. Every demon in Hell joined the attack.'

'All of them?' Leo whispered.

'Every single one. Even though he was nearly incapacitated in his own weakness, the Dark Lord donned his black armour and led his disciples under their black banners. He must have destroyed hundreds of demons by himself. Eventually they overcame him and threw him from his own wall.'

Leo looked away.

'He fought his way back up and defeated them. It was a mighty battle, and I was unaware. I was in retreat. I did not know.' She smiled sadly. 'I am sorry. They cut through the Mountain Palace of Yuzhengong. They desecrated the temples and killed the clergy. Much of the Palace has been burned to the ground.'

'No,' I whispered.

'When the battle was over, he came directly here. But he knows that his Mountain, his Palace, is ruined. He has been building the Mountain for centuries, adding to its elegant halls and pavilions. Even its Earthly shadow was magnificent. And now it is all gone. It is breaking his heart.'

I took her hand and she smiled sadly at me. 'I will spend the rest of the day with him. Do not disturb us. He was very close, and we should not be interrupted.'

'We understand,' I said.

She released my hand, rose and went out.

I woke and cast around, confused, then remembered. I was in a student room. I rose and went into the hallway. It was very late.

I went to the small picture window at the end of the hall. The carpet was soft under my feet.

The window overlooked the eastern part of Hong Kong Island. The ridge that was the top of the island stretched in front of me, leading down to Causeway Bay and North Point. The lights were still on; Hong Kong buzzed with activity, even though it was so late. The streets of Central were a flurry of traffic.

A lone car drove past, going down the tree-covered

hillside of the Peak. The Peak Tower had closed up for the night. The shopping centre next to it was dark.

The hills and highrises of Kowloon shimmered over the harbour in the distance. The clouds were low overhead, and glowed in the reflected light of the city.

I touched the glass. The surface was cold; the temperature would be less than ten degrees outside. It was warm inside.

I turned and looked along the hallway. Closed doors in the darkness. Shadows. Quiet. I was right next to his door.

I went to his door.

I touched the handle.

Wong had asked me: why don't you go to him?

And I asked myself: why not?

I knew he felt it too. Something was holding him back. If I went in and slid into bed beside him, what would he do?

I wanted so much to climb in with him, pull the covers over both of us and run my hands over his golden skin. To feel the muscles of his arms, his back. To run my mouth over his silken shoulders and bury my face in his neck. To feel his hair slide between my fingers, fresh with the smell of the sea.

To have him turn to me and hold me, his strong arms around me. To feel him next to me, to press myself against his warmth . . .

I grasped the door handle.

No. It wouldn't be right. He'd made his choice and I had to respect it.

I just wanted to find a cup to have a drink of water, that was all. I took my hand away and headed towards the kitchen.

After I woke the next morning I quietly checked on Simone. She was still asleep, so I left her. She needed the rest.

I passed the training room on the way back to the kitchen. The door was ajar; I moved to close it.

They sat cross-legged on the mats, facing each other, their hands out and their palms together. Their eyes were closed and a glowing nimbus of silvery energy surrounded them.

I quietly closed the door and went into the kitchen to find some breakfast. Leo was already there. I poured myself some coffee from his pot.

When I sat he showed me an article on page five of the newspaper.

A fire has severely damaged the palace of Yuzhengong at Wudangshan in Hubei province. Because of the remote nature of the palace, many parts of it were burned to the ground before fire crews could arrive. No one was hurt, but many Ming Dynasty (14th- to 17th-century) structures were destroyed.

The palace is one of the pinnacles of Chinese art and architecture, representing the finest examples from a period of over 1000 years. The palaces, halls and temples are some of the greatest achievements of the Yuan, Ming and Qing dynasties. The palace is situated on the slopes of the Wudang Mountains in Hubei province and contains Taoist buildings from as early as the 7th century. The palace was a World Heritage Listed site.

'What, the journalists didn't see the demons? Are they invisible or something?'

'The demons attacked the Mountain on a higher plane,' Leo said. 'The one at Wudangshan reflected the damage. At least that's my understanding of it. You ever been there? Wudangshan?'

I shook my head.

'It's a really amazing place. The whole Palace clings to the side of the mountain. There's a little temple right on top of the mountain, made of gilded copper with a gold roof, with a statue of *him*,' he nodded towards the door, 'inside. Love to see that. The one on the Celestial Plane, I mean.'

'Maybe one day he'll be able to take you.'

'He won't be taking anyone,' Leo said with bitter finality. 'He'll hang around until Simone's ready, and then he'll go.'

I sighed. 'Most of the Mountain on the higher plane is gone anyway.'

'It'll be killing him,' Leo said. 'It was bad enough when he couldn't go there. Now that it's been destroyed I hate to think how he's being affected. The Mountain is a part of him.'

'And that part of him has been destroyed with it.'

Leo dropped his head.

Ms Kwan came in, and Monica made her a pot of tea. Ms Kwan seemed tired.

'Are you okay?' I said after Monica had moved away. 'You've been holding human form for a long time.'

'I spend most of my time human,' she said. 'I wander the world. I care for you all.'

I nodded understanding. It was one thing to give your life for another, but she gave her whole Immortal *existence* to serve humanity.

'Ms Kwan,' Leo said, 'there's something we haven't told him. About the attack.'

'What, Leo?'

Leo fiddled with his coffee mug. 'I didn't tell him about one of the demons that attacked us. It was a Demon Prince.' He tilted his head, still studying his cup. 'It was the one that killed Michelle.'

'Do not tell him,' she said sharply. 'I will be the one to tell him. He is not ready yet. I think I know the one you mean. It does not have the skill to defeat you, Leo, but it is learning.'

'It broke in and stabbed me in the back in October.'

'I am not surprised,' Ms Kwan said. 'It is quite a piece of work.'

'You have no idea,' I said. 'It said some things you wouldn't believe.'

'I would believe it,' she said. 'I wish the King had not sworn that foolish oath. To be Number One is a very grand prize for them. They know Ah Wu would swap his head for anything he loves. We must not let it have its hands on Emma or Simone, Leo. You must protect them.'

'So far they've only sent small ones to try me out, and I've managed to avoid facing them,' I said. 'I don't need Leo's protection, I can handle it.'

Ms Kwan hesitated, looking at me, then turned and glared at Leo. 'She doesn't know?'

Leo smiled wryly.

I looked from one to the other. 'What don't I know?'

Ms Kwan sighed. She picked up the teapot and two cups. 'Come with me, Emma, we need to talk.'

'Sorry,' Leo said as we went out.

'You will very shortly receive the sharp edge of my tongue,' Ms Kwan said without looking back.

Leo's voice followed us down the hallway. 'You don't have one, Ms Kwan, and you know it.'

Ms Kwan led me to my room. There was very little evidence of her residence there. She gestured for me to sit on the couch and sat next to me. She poured the tea.

'Now.' She turned to face me. 'It is obvious that these *stupid* men have not told you.'

'Told me what?' Then I understood. 'Why he won't have me. Why won't he, Ms Kwan? We could have years together! I don't need anything permanent. I don't need promises or grand sentiments. If I could just have him for the short time we have left ...' My voice broke and I tried to control it. 'I don't need more than that.'

She passed me the box of tissues from my desk.

I pulled one out and wiped my eyes. 'I know he feels the same way! Even the demon said I should go in and wake him up!'

'Emma. Dear Emma.'

I dropped my head with misery. 'That's what he called me in the hospital.'

'I cannot believe these two useless men have not told you, but I should not be surprised. They really will receive the sharp end of my tongue.'

I shook my head. 'Leo's right. You know you don't have one.'

'In this case I do. Emma, listen carefully. This is most important. Your life is at stake here. You must understand.'

I glanced up at her.

She smiled sadly. 'His feelings for you are as strong as yours are for him. Stronger, if that is possible.' She sipped her tea. 'It is strange. After such a very long time without finding someone worthy, he has encountered two, one after the other. It is far too unlikely to be a coincidence. But we must deal with what Fate hands us.'

'I'm worthy? Wait, *he feels the same way too?*'

'Of course. But he cannot act on his feelings. It would kill you.'

This stopped me dead. It would *kill* me?

'If you had gone to him as the demon suggested, you would be dead.' She poured more tea for us. 'Emma, if you were to go to him, he would not be able to control himself. He would take you in a second. He would not

297

think twice. He would completely lose control. It is his nature, because of what he is.'

'A Shen?'

'No, a Turtle.'

I gasped.

'You know it is an insult?'

I nodded.

'You are learning quickly.' She sipped her tea, then placed her teacup on the table, took my hand and looked into my eyes. 'Emma, the sharing of love is a sharing of energy. You are young, he is old. You are strong, he is drained. If he were to take you, he would take your energy. He would suck the life out of you and kill you. He would not be able to stop the drain. He would not be able to think at all. Sometimes even the sharing of your feelings through a touch can start the drain. He must be very careful.'

I stared at her.

'Do you understand, Emma? If you two were to act on your feelings for each other, it would kill you.' She sighed. 'He is a fool. He should have dismissed you the moment he knew how he felt for you. But he has kept you here, because he cares so deeply for you, and because Simone loves you. But you must know, Emma. The more he loves you, the less he will be able to touch you. If he loved you completely he would be unable to touch you at all.'

'He loves me,' I cried softly. 'He loves me. I love him. And it can't happen.'

'It can never be. Do you understand what the demon was trying to achieve when he suggested you go to him?'

'He was trying to get me killed.' I thumped the table. 'Damn it! They should have told me! He should at least have asked Leo to tell me! Why didn't they *tell* me? You know I nearly went to him? It was a close thing, Ms Kwan, I had my hand on his door.'

She watched me with compassion.

'If I'd gone in there, I would have been dead by now.'

I picked up my tea and put it down again. 'Those two are such *idiots* sometimes! I am going to *strangle* them!'

'No,' Ms Kwan said. 'I will strangle them first.'

We shared a smile.

'I should have known,' she said. 'I had to tell Michelle as well. They were too embarrassed to tell her.'

'Wait,' I said. 'He had a child with Michelle. He could touch her. Why could he touch her and not me?'

'He returned to the Mountain regularly while he was married to Michelle,' she said. 'He was able to rebuild his energy on the Mountain. Even so, he still had to be very careful.'

'They are so *useless*!'

She smiled slightly. 'Then Simone was born, and he carried both of them to the Mountain. A child may travel to the Celestial Plane under the protection of its mother. Movement to the plane is very stressful for mortals, but the mother protects the child, lends her energy, ensures the child's safety. Now that Michelle is gone, he cannot return to his Mountain. He cannot leave Simone here without his protection.'

'If that demon had never killed Michelle, none of this would have happened. Simone would still have her mother, and her father would be able to stay with her forever.'

'That is true.'

'I am going to get that demon one day.'

'You are quite remarkable sometimes, Emma.'

'He touches me when we're training together, Ms Kwan.' I sighed. 'I should tell him to stop, shouldn't I?'

'He knows how far he can take it. While he is teaching you he must concentrate on his beloved Arts and will not hurt you. He has very good control. You can trust him. He knew you would respect his wishes and would not push it.' She poured more tea. 'He has spoken of nothing but you since you arrived, Emma. Your courage, your talent, your total devotion to Simone . . .'

I could feel my face reddening.

'He is a man in love. And men in love do foolish things.'

'He loves me.' My heart leapt at the words. 'He does love me.' My throat thickened. I lowered my head and shook it. 'He does.'

'I think we would all understand if you were to decide to leave now, Emma. There is no future in this. I think it would be best if you were to leave and find another.'

'No. Simone needs me. And I want to be with him for the short time we have left.'

'It can never be, Emma. You can never share your feelings. You must be especially careful when you are alone together. Do not show your affection for him too much, dear, you could push him over the edge.'

'I think I must be the happiest woman in the whole world.'

Her eyes turned inward. 'Simone has woken. You must care for her, and I must care for him.'

'Let's go,' I said, and rose. I couldn't stop my smile.

'I think,' she said, smiling sadly, 'you are as great a fool as he is.'

'Oh, I sincerely hope so.'

She bundled me into her arms and held me for a while. Then we went out together.

I returned to the kitchen with the teapot and cups. Leo sat at the table, still watching his coffee. I placed the pot and cups into the sink for Monica.

I stopped as I passed him on the way out of the kitchen and smartly slapped the back of his bald head.

'Keep anything important a secret from me *ever* again and I will tear your arms off.'

He didn't move or look up. 'You are extremely scary sometimes, you know that?'

'You have no idea,' I growled, and went out.

CHAPTER TWENTY-SIX

A week later we all sat quietly at the dinner table. Mr Chen brooded. Simone fiddled with her vegetables. Leo was monosyllabic.

'You need to swim in the sea, Ah Wu,' Ms Kwan said.

Mr Chen didn't look up. 'The water is unclean. It would undo everything you have done for me.'

'We are going to Australia the day after tomorrow,' Ms Kwan said. 'All of us. Ah Wu, arrange it.'

He glared at her. 'I can't go anywhere.'

'You will swim in the sea. It is summer there. You will take Simone to the playgrounds.'

'The Northern Heavens must be administered, Mercy. I can't leave.'

'Your Generals are quite capable, Ah Wu. You are going.'

He glowered.

'That's a great idea, Ms Kwan,' I said. 'I'll arrange the plane.'

'You'll arrange the plane?' Leo said, incredulous.

'I've been through his office. I know what to do.'

'Good,' Ms Kwan said. 'I have a place for us to stay, but you will need to bring Monica. I do not have staff there.'

Mr Chen glared at his vegetables.

'I will brook no argument, Ah Wu. You need to swim in the sea.'

He opened his mouth to say something.

'You're going,' I said. 'You need it.'

He closed his mouth.

And that was that.

As we walked out of Coolangatta airport to the van the fresh warm breeze hit me and ruffled my hair. I breathed deeply; it was good to be out of the pollution of Hong Kong.

Leo took the keys, opened the van and put the bags in. 'Road rules?' he asked me.

'Pretty much the same as Hong Kong, but you can be more polite about waiting at intersections,' I said. 'It's not as busy as back home, so you won't need to push in. But apart from that, almost identical. You want me to drive?'

'Don't be ridiculous,' he said, and opened the door for me and Ms Kwan. 'Get in.'

As I buckled Simone up I had a sudden realisation: I'd called Hong Kong home.

Ms Kwan provided directions. The apartment building we were staying in was massive; it must have been more than twenty storeys. It was south of the main tourist area in a part of the Gold Coast that had fewer highrises, and it overlooked the beach. The penthouse took up the entire top floor of the apartment building, and had a small roof garden with a spa.

As soon as we entered the apartment Mr Chen went straight out onto the balcony and leaned on the railing, watching the surf below. The fresh breeze lifted his hair.

The sky was a deep blue, without a single cloud, and the air was clear enough to see the container ships on the horizon. The sea was a deeper blue, and the surf pounded below us. The wide beach stretched to the horizon in both directions.

I stood in the open-plan kitchen in the centre of the apartment and watched him.

After Leo had put the bags into the rooms, he came to check out the view. 'Amazing place. Don't you miss it?'

'I've never lived in anything as exalted as this. We used to come down and stay in pokey hotels. But I miss the fresh air and sunshine.'

'His element is water,' Leo said. 'He can't go into the water at all in Hong Kong. The sea is too polluted. Swimming pools are chlorinated, and poisonous to him. Ms Kwan is a genius to get him here. He probably can't wait to go in.'

'Well, let's take him down and put him in the water,' I said, turning to smile at him.

'We'd better take him shopping first.' Leo grinned. 'Unless you want to see him arrested.'

'I need to do some shopping too,' I said. 'None of my swimsuits fit me.'

'Yeah, you have lost weight. I didn't really notice.'

'Too busy looking at the guys. Don't worry, there'll be plenty to look at here.'

Monica came in and checked the refrigerator. 'I hope I can find the right Chinese ingredients here.' She bustled through the cupboards. 'All Western.'

'I know my way around,' I said. 'Leo can take us to the shops. I know where you can buy everything you need.'

'I need to buy some swimmers!' Simone yelled. She ran out of her bedroom and threw herself at Leo. 'Pick me up, Leo, I want to see outside!'

Leo hoisted her on to his hip. She clapped her hands in delight. Mr Chen turned to look at us from the balcony and smiled. It was the first time he'd smiled since the attack on the Mountain. It was wonderful to see.

'We're going shopping,' Leo said to him. 'You have to come along.'

Mr Chen came into the living room and closed the sliding door behind him. 'Let's go.'

'You coming, Ms Kwan?' I shouted.

'Yes! Wait for me!' She hurried out with a white straw hat in her hand, still wearing the silk pantsuit. 'The sun is very strong here. I want to find a hat.'

'Oh, come on, Kwan Yin,' I said. 'You need a hat?'

'The sun is very strong.' She linked her arm in Mr Chen's. 'Come, Ah Wu, this hat is very old and I need to buy a new one.'

I directed Leo to the enormous shopping centre across the road. Leo and I took Simone to buy swimwear; Mr Chen and Kwan Yin wandered off together; and Monica disappeared into the supermarket.

Leo stood inside the door of the shop, on guard duty, while Simone and I tried on swimsuits.

I showed Simone the solar swimwear and she giggled. 'This is strange.'

'The sun is strong here, and if you don't cover up you'll burn,' I said.

One of the staff came over and crouched to speak to Simone. 'Hello, darling, my name's Jo. You want to try them on?'

Simone nodded with enthusiasm. 'Can you help me while Emma tries on some swimsuits too?'

'Sure.' Jo smiled up at me. 'We'll be just fine. Go and try on some suits, Emma.'

'You sure, Simone?' I said.

Simone pushed me. 'We'll be fine. Leo can see us.'

I glanced at Leo. He nodded.

I shrugged and went to the racks.

As I tried on the suits I heard the staff asking Simone questions about Hong Kong, and her answering in her sweet, piping voice. I went out to find a smaller size and discovered that she had three assistants helping her. This happened wherever we went, whatever country we were in. She charmed everybody just by being her usual sweet self.

I grabbed a few more suits off the rack and held them up, one at a time, to show Leo. He shook his head at all of them. I took them into the change room anyway and he snorted with disdain.

One of the staff checked on me. 'You okay there? I saw you going in and out a few times.' She looked me up and down. 'You an aerobics instructor or something?'

I looked at myself in the mirror. I was quite muscular from the martial arts work. Nothing tremendously obvious, but it was apparent that I was in good shape. 'No, I'm just the little girl's nanny.'

'Nanny and bodyguard,' she quipped.

'Nah,' I said playfully, 'that's her bodyguard next to the door. The big black guy. See him? Six foot six and massive?'

She laughed and turned to look, then stopped dead. 'Bodyguard? Is her father a movie star or something?'

'Nope, just a rich guy from Hong Kong.'

'So he pays you well then?'

I didn't say anything.

She patted me on the arm. 'Good on you. Good to see people making their way.' She gestured towards the swimsuit. 'How about I show you some of our nicer stuff?'

'That would be great, thanks.'

'You're lucky — the little girl is a delight.'

'Her father's a sweetheart too.'

She laughed. 'Oh. Very lucky.'

I turned back to the mirror. 'I think I must be the luckiest woman in the whole wide world.'

'Wait there, I'll be right back. Oh. Here she is.'

Simone came in wearing bright orange solar swimmers with a lurid green and purple frill around her little behind. She wriggled for me. 'These are so cool!'

'I need sunglasses to look at you,' I said. 'Go and ask Leo to pay for them.'

'Okay. Hurry up, Emma, I want to go to the beach.'

I finally settled on a pale blue and white striped bikini with a matching wrap that even Leo approved of.

Jo and a couple of the other women hugged and kissed Simone. 'Enjoy Australia, Simone,' Jo said. 'Have fun.'

'Thanks, Jo,' Simone said.

'Are all Australians like that?' Leo asked as we walked back to the car park.

'Yep. Pretty much. It took me a long time to become accustomed to Hong Kong; we're much more friendly and relaxed here.'

Leo grinned. 'I think I'm gonna like this place.'

Monica was waiting for us with a mountain of groceries. Leo loaded them into the van for her and just as he'd finished, Mr Chen and Ms Kwan arrived. Both were smiling broadly.

'Find something in black?' I teased.

Leo scowled as he climbed into the driver's seat.

'Yes,' Mr Chen said. 'The people here are quite remarkable. Very friendly.'

'Now you know where I get it from.'

We all rushed to change when we returned to the apartment. Monica chose to stay behind. 'I don't like the beach,' she said. 'I don't like sand, and I can't swim. Let me sort out my kitchen.'

Simone and I waited in the living room for the others. Leo came out first. He wore shorts with the second-loudest Hawaiian print I had ever seen. His fluorescent pink shirt was absolutely the loudest. A pair of expensive sunglasses perched on his American team baseball cap.

'You Hawaiian, Leo?'

'Nope, Chicago.'

I was about to give Leo a hard time about the shirt when Ms Kwan came in. She wore a white one-piece swimsuit with a large white shirt over it, a huge white straw hat and sunglasses. She looked like a movie star. She twirled for us. 'What do you think?'

Mr Chen came out behind her. 'I think you look gorgeous.' He wore his new black swim shorts with a towel thrown over his shoulder.

He was magnificent. Smooth golden skin over toned muscle, graceful and sleek. Tall and chiselled and not an ounce of fat on him. He had an angry red mark on his abdomen where he'd been injured, but apart from that he was glowing with good health.

He stopped in the living room and stared at Leo and me. Then he grinned, shook his head and walked past us.

Ms Kwan stopped in front of us. 'Put your tongues back in, you two,' she whispered.

It was near the end of the day and people were packing up to go. A woman power-walked along the wet sand past us. Further along the beach a man flew a large acrobatic kite, its fabric fluttering loudly. A helicopter roared overhead, following the line of the surf. The breeze was still warm and the sun was crisp against my back as we faced the waves.

'We have to swim between the flags,' I announced. Everybody looked at me as if I was completely crazy.

'The current here can be really strong,' I explained. 'The lifeguards are professionals, and they mark the parts of the beach that are safe, and patrolled by them, with flags. You swim between the flags, you're safe. You go outside the flags, you're quite likely to get swept out and drown.'

'That can't happen to me,' Mr Chen said quietly. He looked up and down the beach. 'I don't see any flags, Emma.'

'They must have finished for the day,' I said. 'You just go out and swim, if you're sure you'll be okay.'

Mr Chen nodded. 'Simone can stay out of the water today, and swim tomorrow. Stay with Emma and Leo, Simone.'

'Okay, Daddy,' Simone said. 'Look at all the sand! I want to play.'

'Keep an eye on her,' Mr Chen said. 'Don't let her into the water if it's dangerous.'

'It's not that dangerous,' I said. 'You just need to be careful.'

He studied the waves. 'Let me go out and see what it's like.'

'Well then, go!' Ms Kwan said, waving him away with one hand. She pulled a beach mat out of her bag and spread it on the sand. 'Come and sit with me, Emma, Leo.'

Mr Chen dropped his towel onto the mat and went towards the water. 'Be careful, Daddy,' Simone called. He didn't hear her. He went straight out into the surf, dived into one of the far breakers and disappeared.

'He's not coming back up,' I said urgently.

'He doesn't need to, dear,' Ms Kwan said.

The sun set behind us. The highrises along the beach made elongated shadows on the sand. The sky turned a delicate shade of lilac and the breeze became cooler. The beach was almost deserted. I pulled on my wrap.

Simone chatted in front of us as she played in the sand.

'He's been in the water for nearly an hour, Ms Kwan,' I said. 'Are you sure he's all right?'

'He is in his element, Emma.'

Mr Chen emerged from the waves and fell into the shallows. He lay in the water, his sides heaving, then flopped onto his back. The waves covered his face.

Both Leo and I rose to help him.

'Hold,' Ms Kwan said. 'No need.'

He pulled himself up to sit in the shallows. He untied his hair, shook it out and tied it back again. Then he sat with his hands around his knees.

Simone ran to him. She slammed into him from behind and wrapped her little arms around his neck. He smiled over his shoulder, pulled her into his lap and rocked her.

'He is a lucky man to have so many who love him,' Ms Kwan said.

Neither Leo nor I said anything.

'But you know it can never be as you wish, for either of you.'

'I am content to serve as Retainer,' Leo said. 'If he were able to return my feelings, he would not be the same man. He would not be *him*.'

I glanced up at Leo. I'd probably known from the start. He saw me watching him and smiled slightly.

'You know there is nothing I can do for you once he is gone,' Ms Kwan said.

'I know. Once he's gone, it's not important anyway.'

'What, Leo?' I said.

He rubbed the back of his head. 'Do you have to know absolutely everything?'

'Only if someone's safety is at stake.'

'Well, then, in this case you don't need to know.'

I shrugged and turned back to watch Mr Chen and Simone. 'I respect that, Leo. If it's your private business then you don't need to tell me anything.'

He watched them as well. 'I thought you were being curious, wanting to know everything that's happening. But you're just looking out for them, aren't you?'

'Of course.'

'And you, Emma,' Ms Kwan said. 'Living to serve. Content, as Leo is, to love without expectation.'

'I wish it could be different for you, Emma,' Leo said. 'For both of you. I should have told you sooner — given you the chance to leave. Both of us should. And now you're stuck here, just like I am. You should go.'

'How would he feel if I left, Leo?'

Leo was silent.

My throat was so thick I had difficulty with the words. 'I feel the same way you do. I am content.'

Ms Kwan's hand appeared under my nose, holding a packet of tissues. I took one and nodded my thanks, then wiped my eyes.

'Normally I try to give people hope,' she said. 'In your case, there is none. It can never be.'

'I know,' I whispered. 'But I'm happy with what I have.'

She wrapped her arms around me and her power moved through me. I was filled with a warm, glowing feeling of comfort.

After a while she pulled back and smiled into my face. I nodded; I was okay. She turned her gaze to Mr Chen. 'He will be fine now. Stay here for as long as you need. The apartment is yours.'

'Is it real, Ms Kwan?' Leo said.

'Quite real. I own the apartment outright, and as long as you need it, it is yours. Take care of him. Take care of them both.'

I looked up to thank her but she was gone.

Leo moved closer and wrapped his arm around my shoulders. 'I think we must be the two stupidest people in the whole world.'

'I think we're the luckiest.' I leaned into him. 'It must have killed you when he married Michelle.'

'I was very happy for them. They loved each other very much. It was wonderful to see. And then Simone came along. I think that was the happiest time of his life.' He smiled at me. 'And now he has you.'

I took a deep breath and let it out slowly.

'I really wish it could be different for you, Emma. For you and him. You should hear him sometimes when he talks about you. I've been telling him for ages that he's mad to keep you around. He'll only end up hurting you.'

'Right now I'm happy, Leo. I'm with him. That's all that's important.'

He stroked my arm. 'I understand.'

'Does he know?'

He chuckled and his arm shook on my back. 'Of course he does. He just puts up with me.'

'No, I don't think he puts up with you, Leo. I think he loves you like a son.'

He stared at me, then his face lit up with genuine delight. 'Maybe you're right.' He turned back to watch the water. 'You're really wise sometimes, Emma.'

'Wise? I think we've just established exactly how stupid I am.'

'Both of us.'

'Yeah.'

Simone dragged her grinning father up the beach towards us. 'I'm *hungry*!' she yelled.

CHAPTER TWENTY-SEVEN

After I'd put Simone to bed I went out to the living room. Leo was sprawled on the sofa, sleeping. Monica was wiping the kitchen benchtops. I wandered into the kitchen and saw Mr Chen sitting at the large table on the balcony, watching the waves.

'You should be having a holiday as well, Monica,' I said. 'There are some excellent Chinese restaurants around here. If you like, we can take him out and give you a couple of nights off.'

Monica stared at me with horror. 'Not cook?'

'You should have a break.'

She continued to wipe the cabinets. 'This *is* a break. This apartment is very small. But if I didn't have to cook, I wouldn't have anything to do. Please don't take him out, Emma.'

'You would have preferred to stay in Hong Kong, wouldn't you?'

She wiped over the cupboards without looking up. 'This is a strange place. Everything is so far away from everything else. How do you find your way around? And it's so *quiet*.'

'I know,' I said. 'Some of my Chinese friends don't like Australia; they say it's so quiet they can't sleep.'

She busily rinsed the cloth in the sink. 'We look after him. I look after him.' She smiled at me. 'We care for Simone. That makes me happy.'

I patted her shoulder. 'Me too.'

She removed her apron. 'Goodnight, Emma.'

''Night, Monica.'

She went to her room, smiling contentedly.

I knelt by the couch, next to Leo's head. 'Leo.'

He grunted and grimaced.

I patted his shoulder. 'Wake up, Leo.'

His huge fist lashed out towards my head and I dodged it. 'Hey, Leo, it's me!'

He pulled himself upright and wiped his hands over his face. 'Sorry, Emma. Don't do that again. If you wake me suddenly I can attack you.'

'I moved out of the way in time.'

'Don't take the risk. Ask Mr Chen to wake me, or just leave me where I am. Gold once woke me in the middle of the night and I broke his neck.'

'You should have warned me.'

He looked sheepish. 'Yeah, I know. But I didn't think we'd ever be in that sort of situation.'

'Me either, I suppose.' Then I heard what he'd said. 'You and Gold were attacked in the middle of the night?'

He smiled gently and I understood. 'But Gold said you were just good friends.'

'We are now. That was a long time ago.'

'I'm sure breaking his neck put a slight damper on the relationship.'

'Nope. He thought it was hilarious. He kept waking me to try and get me to do it again.'

I nodded towards Mr Chen where he sat on the balcony. 'What did *he* think?'

'He hoped it would become something more permanent. He wanted me to be happy. Same as he wants you to be happy, Emma.'

'I am happy, Leo.'

I stood, took his hand and raised him to stand in front of me. He pulled me into his arms and held me tight. I stretched up to kiss him on the cheek. 'Go to bed, Leo. You're buggered.'

He stared at me, speechless, then shook his head, released me and went out.

'It just means "tired" in Australia,' I said to his back.

He raised one hand and went into his room, still shaking his head.

I took a teacup from the cupboard in the kitchen and joined Mr Chen. The cloudy sky merged with the dark sea. The waves were a dull roar below. The warm humid breeze blew strongly over the balcony and lifted the loose strands of his long hair.

He poured some tea for me and I tapped the table next to the cup in thanks.

'Do you know the origin of that gesture?' he said.

'No, do you?'

'Of course I do. I was there.' He rested his chin on his hand. 'Once an Emperor went out incognito, just with a couple of guards. He wanted to see what life was like outside his palace, without the layers of formality that separated him from the ordinary people.'

'The Jade Emperor did that?'

He glanced at me. 'You are very perceptive sometimes.'

'Go on. Tell me. It's fascinating.'

'We went to a teahouse. The Celestial poured the tea. We were horrified — to have the mighty Emperor pour tea for us, two lowly guards.'

'Not that lowly.'

'I'm never going to finish this, Emma,' he said, with amusement.

'Sorry. Go on.'

'One of the guards thought quickly. He bent his fingers and placed them on the table.' He demonstrated, bending his first two fingers and putting them next to the teacup. 'To signify himself kneeling to the Emperor. The Emperor was impressed by the guard's quick wit and promoted him to senior advisor.'

'That was very clever of you,' I said. 'And over time it's just become a tap on the table. How long ago was that?'

'About five hundred years.' He smiled wryly and put his chin back on his hand. 'And it wasn't me. It was Er Lang. I was the guard who *didn't* think to do it.'

'Does he really have three eyes?'

'Er Lang? Yes. Most of the time you can't see the third one; when it's closed it's not really noticeable.'

He turned to watch the waves and sipped his tea. 'You can see the lights from here.'

'What lights?'

'There is a building.' He gestured inland. 'It has flashing lights on the roof.' He sounded bewildered. 'It's keeping me awake.'

'You're not accustomed to being kept awake?'

He shook his head, his eyes shining. 'One day I will tell Simone exactly what I have suffered for her. Just when I have overcome one difficulty with being human, another strikes me.'

'You'll be able to tell Simone that yourself?'

'One day. Perhaps. I may be able to return in her lifetime.' He looked down at his tea. 'I sincerely hope I will be able to.'

'Do you know how long you'll be gone?'

He didn't look up. 'Nobody has ever done this before. I have no idea how long it will take, but it will be a very long time. The answer to your question is: no.'

'I hope you'll be able to see her again.' I turned to look at the flashing lights reflected from one of the other highrises. 'That's the casino. They'll turn the lights off soon. Otherwise they'll have complaints.' I grinned at him. 'Hey, why haven't you been over there yet? You're Chinese, aren't you?'

He looked as if he was going to tell me off, then smiled. 'Gambling for money is not interesting when money has no value. The Tiger and I occasionally game for much higher stakes than money.'

'Thought so. Look at the Hong Kong Jockey Club — richest institution in Hong Kong.'

He poured more tea. 'We need to talk, Emma.' He put the teapot down. 'This is very hard.'

'You should have told me!' I yelled, and he jumped. 'Or at least had Leo tell me. I don't know which of you is more hopeless. Ms Kwan is right.'

He gazed into my eyes. 'She told you?'

'Damn straight she did.'

He studied his cup carefully. 'You are dismissed, Emma. When we return to Hong Kong you will pack your bags and leave.'

'Absolutely not.'

'You should leave, Emma. I could hurt you.' He sighed. 'I am hurting you anyway.'

'No! I love both of you too much to leave. I'm not going.'

His head snapped up so that he could see me. 'You love both of us?'

'You think I don't?' I sighed with exasperation. 'You think this will make any difference to me, John? You should have told me.'

'I didn't want to lose you.'

I reached out to take his hand, then pulled back and held my teacup instead. 'You won't lose me. I'll stay with you until you go. I won't leave you.'

His eyes glittered. 'I am making you suffer. You should leave. I could hurt you. Even unintentionally, Emma, I could hurt you. Even now it would not take much.'

'We'll just have to be careful, John.' I straightened. 'Mr Chen. We'll just be careful when we're alone.' I took a sip of tea. 'We'll be friends, we'll care for Simone.' I looked into his eyes. 'I don't need more than that.'

'Eventually I will not be able to touch you at all.'

I gazed into his eyes. Love me completely, and be unable to touch me at all. 'Even if you couldn't touch me at all, John, I still think I would be the happiest woman in the world.'

'We are a pair of fools.'

'I know. But I'm happy to be a fool with you.'

He poured more tea. I tapped the table next to my teacup.

Mr Chen, Simone and I ate breakfast on the balcony the next morning. Simone had already pulled on her new swimmers and was chatting merrily about the beach.

Leo stormed into the kitchen and towered over Monica. He was wearing just a pair of shorts, his dark muscular torso bare. Usually he didn't come out until he was fully dressed in one of his sharp outfits.

He hissed angrily at Monica. Monica protested just as softly. We couldn't hear a word they said.

'What's going on?' Simone said.

Monica shook her head and turned away from Leo. He glowered down at her, then he straightened, looked out towards the balcony and saw my face.

He walked to us with a great deal of aloof dignity. He came right up to me and towered over me, his face a mask of fury, but clearly couldn't think of anything to say. He stormed back into the apartment without saying a word.

I collapsed over the table, shaking with silent laughter.

'What did you do?' Mr Chen said.

'I snuck into the laundry room while Monica was busy,' I whispered, so softly Simone couldn't hear. 'All his underwear is pink.'

'You are very evil sometimes. I look forward to seeing his revenge.'

'I don't.'

The beach had already filled with people, most of them setting up their towels between the yellow and red flags.

'There's the flags, Daddy,' Simone said, pointing. 'We have to go there.'

'Having the flags is a good idea,' Mr Chen said.

'Looks okay to me,' Leo said, sceptical.

'If you came here by yourself, and there were no flags, where would you swim?' Mr Chen said.

Leo looked up and down the beach. Then he pointed. 'Over there. Looks calmer there. Don't know why the flags aren't set up there, there's fewer waves.'

'Most people who are new here think that,' I said.

'Leo, if you were to swim there, you would be quickly swept away and probably drown,' Mr Chen said.

Leo opened his mouth to protest.

'Even with your strength, I don't think you could fight the current there. It's very strong. That's where the water is going out, not coming in. That's why it looks calmer.'

'We call it a rip,' I said. We all walked towards the flags together. 'Last year a young backpacker from New Zealand hopped off the bus, dropped his bag in the hostel, changed into his shorts, walked into a rip and drowned. He'd been here less than an hour.'

Leo studied the waves with new respect.

'They are very useful,' Mr Chen said.

We dropped our stuff near the lifeguards' tent between the flags and flopped to sit on our towels. I put sunscreen on Simone, then had Leo put some on my back. His huge hands covered me in no time at all.

Mr Chen stood watching the waves.

'Go!' I said.

He glanced down at me. 'I may be gone for quite some time.'

'How long, sir?' Leo said.

Mr Chen looked out at the waves. 'A couple of hours?'

'We'll be fine here,' I said. 'Plenty of people around.'

'And we have Leo,' Simone said.

Mr Chen didn't say anything; he just walked towards the water.

'Mr Chen!'

He stopped and turned. I gestured with my head towards the lifeguards' tent. 'The lifesavers here are professionals. Disappear quietly, otherwise they might try to rescue you.'

He nodded, turned and walked down to the water. He waded into the breakers, then dived into one of the metre-high waves. He didn't reappear.

Nobody noticed.

'How come he can swim like that?' I said.

'No idea,' Leo said. 'Something to do with his nature.'

I raised the sunscreen. 'Want me to put some on your back?'

'Don't be ridiculous,' he said with scorn.

'The sun's much stronger here than in Hong Kong, Leo.'

Leo rose and held his hand out for Simone. 'Want to swim?'

Simone jumped with excitement as she grabbed his hand. 'Yeah!'

At the edge of the water Simone shrieked with delight and ran away from the waves. I showed her how to jump over the small breakers and Leo watched with a huge grin.

Simone threw herself at Leo with her arms up. 'Carry me, Leo, I want to go deeper!'

He hoisted her onto his hip, then waded into the deeper water. The waves broke around him but he didn't seem to notice. Simone laughed and he laughed with her. He didn't laugh often and it was wonderful to hear them together.

Simone pointed to some children body-boarding. 'Can I try that?'

'You want a boogie board?' I said.

'That looks like fun. Can I try?'

I touched Leo's arm. 'I'll buy her one across the road at the shops.'

Leo nodded agreement.

I returned to our gear and opened the bag to pull some cash out. I nearly shrieked when I saw the cockroach sitting on the money. I loathed cockroaches and in Queensland they could grow enormous. Then I saw it properly and pulled it out. I looked up; Leo was grinning at me from the surf. This plastic one was going down the back of his technicolour shirt very soon.

I walked through the park and across the road to the shopping centre. A store near the entrance sold small boogie boards and I bought one for Simone.

As I walked back to the beach I realised I was being followed. I watched them out of the corner of my eye: two middle-aged male Chinese tourists, wearing slacks and polo shirts and carrying large leather bags. They were almost like twins, with identical plastic-rimmed glasses and unruly hair. The fact that they were by themselves was unusual enough to be noticeable;

normally Chinese tourists travelled in groups and were bussed around. They didn't feel like demons, and they were close enough that I should have been able to tell, but I could be wrong.

I hurried back across the park towards the beach. They followed me, talking to each other loudly in Putonghua, making no attempt to hide their presence. They had the distinctive Beijing accent, rolling their r's.

I reached the wooden boardwalk at the top of the sand and walked out onto the beach. They stopped on the boardwalk; they wore shoes and socks and would have to pull them off to follow me.

I glanced back. They were sitting on a bench on the boardwalk watching the waves. Waiting for us. Damn!

I took the boogie board down to Leo and Simone. Simone jumped up and down, clapping her hands, then fell over in the water. She pulled herself up again, laughing.

Leo saw my face. 'What?'

'How far away can she sense them?'

'About three, five metres. You think we've got some?'

I gestured with my head towards the top of the beach. 'They followed me.'

Leo looked up at the boardwalk. 'Which ones?'

I looked up as well. They were gone.

I quickly checked the beach; they had taken off their shoes and socks and stood at the edge of the water nearby, grinning.

I backed to stand next to Leo, facing them. 'Those ones. Look like Mainland tourists.'

Leo dropped to one knee and spoke to Simone. 'Look at those men over there, Simone. Are they bad people?'

Simone studied them, eyes wide, then grinned up at

Leo. 'Nope. Just people.' She jiggled. 'Let me try the board!'

'You sure there's none around here?'

Her eyes unfocused then she snapped back. 'Let me try!'

Leo shrugged and rose.

I smacked my forehead with my palm. 'I am so paranoid.'

'It's only being paranoid if nobody's after you. In this case, I'd just call it being careful, and be glad that she has an extra pair of eyes watching out for her.'

I sighed. 'I suppose you're right.'

The tourists approached us, grinning broadly. They had rolled their slacks up and were holding their shoes in one hand. Both Leo and I readied ourselves without moving into a defensive stance.

One held a camera out to us, bobbed his head politely and said something in Putonghua.

'He says I'm beautiful, and you're beautiful, and Australia's beautiful, and he wants to take a picture with us,' Simone said.

Leo and I shared a look.

The tourist bobbed his head again, still grinning. 'Qing, piaoliang xiaojie.'

'Please, pretty lady,' Simone said. 'Sort of.'

'Are you sure, Simone?' Leo said.

'Just people,' Simone said.

I nodded and smiled. The tourist passed the camera to the other man, and stood behind Simone and me. Leo moved out of the frame but the tourist beckoned for him to move back into the picture. He shrugged and turned to face the camera as well.

The other tourist took the photo and the one behind us moved in front of us again. 'Xie xie, xie xie.'

'Bu keqi,' I said, and he smiled even wider.

The two of them waved and walked away.

'That was extremely weird,' Leo said, watching them.

'Show me how to do it!' Simone shouted, grabbing the boogie board.

After an hour of body-boarding Leo and I had to stop; Simone was wearing us out. We built a sandcastle. Leo sat next to us and watched.

Mr Chen waded out of the surf and flopped onto his stomach on the sand beside us. Simone squealed, ran to him and threw herself on top of him. He grunted and grimaced, and she quickly moved off. 'Sorry, Daddy, I hurt you.'

He sat up and put his arms around his knees. 'I'm fine.'

'Let me see,' I said.

He moved his legs down so that we could see his abdomen. 'I'm okay.'

Simone sat in his lap and he wrapped his arms around her. He kissed the top of her head. 'Did you build that?'

'Leo and Emma helped me. The funny men should have taken a picture of it. It's really good.'

Mr Chen glanced sharply at me. 'What funny men?'

'Some Mainland tourists.' I shrugged. 'Wanted to take our photo. All of us, even Leo.'

Mr Chen shook his head.

'Uh-oh,' I said.

'What?' Leo said, concerned. He sat next to me. 'Simone was sure they were just people.'

'Did we do something wrong, Daddy? They were people, not . . .' Simone dropped her voice. 'Demons.'

Mr Chen spoke softly and we all moved closer to hear. 'Sometimes they have humans working for them. It doesn't happen often, but it's been known.' He pulled Simone tighter. 'Don't *ever* let *anybody* take your photo, Simone. If they do, they can show other people what you look like.'

Simone's mouth flopped open and her eyes went wide. Then she turned to Leo and me. 'That's why they wanted your photo too, Leo.'

Leo thumped the sand with his fist. 'Damn!'

Simone turned back to her father, very serious. 'Don't worry, Daddy. Leo will look after me.'

'They could have been tourists, it's possible it was all innocent,' Mr Chen said. He shrugged. 'Don't worry about it. The reason they use humans here is because they are far from their Centre and very weak. An attack here is highly unlikely.'

'Are you okay so far from your Centre?' I said. 'It applies to you as well, doesn't it?'

'Is that right, Daddy?' Simone said. 'You can't leave China for very long?'

He held her in his lap. 'That's right, sweetheart. Because I'm very big, I can travel and stay away from China, but I could never live permanently anywhere else.'

He smiled. 'Let me show you something. Do you want to come with me?'

She brightened. 'Sure!'

He rose, picked her up and put her on his hip. He turned to Leo and me. 'Don't worry about us, we'll be fine. We'll be in the water.' He strode away towards the waves, with Simone talking excitedly into his face.

'He'd better not waste any of his energy,' Leo grumbled.

'Yeah,' I said. 'He'll be in serious trouble.'

Leo and I laughed softly together.

Mr Chen carried Simone into the breakers until he was chest deep, then dropped straight into the water and they disappeared.

'Whoa,' Leo whispered.

'Just when I thought he couldn't astonish me any more,' I said.

'Me too.'

They returned about half an hour later. Mr Chen carried Simone out of the water as if they'd been wading together. He sat on his towel, and Simone fell into the sand and dug a hole.

'Where did you go, Simone?' I said.

Simone pointed. 'Out there.'

'What did you see?'

She shared a smile with her father, then grinned at me. 'Big fish.'

'How big?'

Her eyes widened and she became serious. 'Really, really big. Big enough to eat Leo.'

Leo laughed. 'Don't be silly, Simone.'

'Oh no, Simone's quite right,' Mr Chen said. 'Some of them were big enough to eat you, Leo.'

'You shouldn't take her out if it's dangerous,' Leo growled.

'She was in absolutely no danger. We were in the *water*.'

Leo looked embarrassed. 'Sorry.'

The next morning Leo was so sunburned he could barely see through his swollen face.

We went to the shops and left him at home to harass Monica. Mr Chen didn't even offer to heal him.

CHAPTER TWENTY-EIGHT

Simone shrieked when we entered the theme park. 'I wanna go on *that* one!'

'I'll take you,' Leo said.

'The roller coaster?' I said.

Both Simone and Leo nodded enthusiastically.

'That's as good as some in the States,' Leo said.

'Oh, thank you very much. Nice to know my homeland passes the Leo Alexander Roller Coaster Test of Civilisation.'

'Yep.' Leo grinned down at Simone. 'You sure, sweetheart? It's awfully fast.'

'I'll be okay if you go with me,' Simone said.

'Mr Chen, sir?'

'You go,' Mr Chen said. 'I'll stay on the ground and guard.'

Leo grimaced. 'That's my job. You should take Simone.'

'And spoil your fun? Besides, I think Simone would prefer to go with you.'

'Yeah, Leo, let's go!'

'Emma?'

'I'll stay down here and keep Mr Chen company.'

Leo hesitated. 'Are you sure?'

'*Go!*' Mr Chen and I both shouted together.

They shared a huge grin and ran. We followed them at a more sedate pace.

They returned to us, disappointed.

'Simone's too small,' Leo said. 'And I'm too big. They won't let either of us on.'

'Use your magic to make me bigger, Daddy,' Simone said.

'I don't have magic, you know that,' Mr Chen said.

'Let's go on that one instead,' Leo said, pointing at the pirate ship.

'Okay!' Simone yelled and grabbed his hand.

When we reached the priate ship Mr Chen and I sat on a bench where we could see them waiting in the queue. Simone waved to us, jumping up and down. Then she fell over. Leo helped her up, then put his hands on his hips and told her off, exasperated. She slapped him. He tickled her. She wriggled with delight.

'Tell me about the Mountain,' I said.

He sighed. 'What do you want to know? The damage is extensive.'

'What was it like before the demons attacked?'

He put his elbows on his knees and studied his hands. 'The Celestial Mountain?'

I nodded.

'Wonderful.'

'Tell me.'

He looked up at Simone, wistful. 'The base of the Celestial Mountain is always in clouds. There is no physical way down; you must be carried by a Shen. The top of the Mountain is covered in trees; not much lawn, it doesn't grow well there.'

'How many buildings?'

'I have no idea.' He smiled. 'It would be like counting the buildings in the Summer Palace in Beijing. One leads to another. Walkways through mountain passes, between the peaks. Seven peaks. Arching bridges over the deep gorges.'

'It does sound wonderful.'

'Michelle hated it.'

'Why?'

'She needed an audience. She lived to sing. She demanded that I stay here with her, so I did.' He watched Leo and Simone without really seeing them. 'She was fabulous. Every time I needed to go to the Mountain, to rebuild myself, she kept telling me she would be all right here, with Leo to guard her.'

'But she wasn't.'

'Her family came to Hong Kong to visit her. Her mother, her father, her brother — all of her family. They didn't know about me, what I am, they came to see Simone. Family is important, so I left her and went to the Mountain. The demon came. It took Leo down. Her father and brother tried to defend her and her mother. The demon killed them and took Michelle and her mother. Fortunately, it was unaware of Simone's existence. No attempt was made on her.'

He hesitated.

'Why did it kill them? Why not swap them for your head?'

He didn't look up. 'I don't think the demon knew that humans are more fragile.'

I gasped. The demon had pushed his fun too far and killed Michelle and her mother by mistake. Now I understood why Leo felt the way he did. 'Do you know who did it?'

He nodded without speaking.

'Leo failed you.'

'Despite what he thinks,' he said, 'he didn't fail. He wasn't ready. I knew he wasn't ready, but family is important.' He watched Leo and Simone board a ride. They both waved and he waved back and smiled.

'It was my mistake. One of the biggest mistakes of my life.'

'Leo was your wife's bodyguard before she met you, wasn't he?'

'I am glad we encountered each other. He is by far the greatest warrior of his generation. I have been able to bring his skills to a level he would not have otherwise achieved. Because of his proximity to me, he has been free of the virus and I have helped him to live longer.' He smiled wryly. 'He does not see that as an advantage, though.'

'Virus?' I said; then, 'Oh my God.'

He glanced sharply at me. 'You never need to be told anything twice. Sometimes you don't even need to be told once.' He looked down at his hands. 'I'm surprised he didn't tell you.'

'He shouldn't bring guys home like he does. He should be more careful.'

'Don't worry, he's careful. He's been tested; he's clear. As long as he stays with me, he will be free of the virus.'

'And when you go?'

He didn't look up from his hands. 'He'll probably have about a year.'

'That's awful.' I suddenly realised: 'I have never had a day sick since I joined your household. You did that?'

'If you'd taken a sick day I think I would have dismissed you,' he said. 'One of the perks of the job.'

I turned to him and touched his sleeve, then pulled my hand away. 'How long do we have, John? Until you go?'

He took a deep breath. 'Simone will probably be able to handle anything thrown at her by the time she is eight years old. Then I will be able to release myself from this form and go.'

Less than three years. I would make the most of it.

'Are you sure you can't stay until she's grown up? She needs you.'

'I know,' he said softly. 'I don't know how I will maintain this form for another three years. It will be even harder now that the Mountain is gone.'

'Will I ever see you again?'

He gazed into my eyes. 'It's highly unlikely, Emma. It will take me a very long time to return. That is my nature. I'm not sure how long, but it will be a long time. I don't think you will ever see me again.'

I turned away. Ms Kwan was right. There was no hope.

'Emma.'

I turned back to him.

'I was hoping that you would look after her for me. When I'm gone.'

I stared at him.

'You will do this for me?' He studied me carefully. 'You won't have to do it by yourself — Jade and Gold can help you. But I can't think of anyone more suitable to care for her after Leo and I are both gone.'

I shook my head, speechless. I struggled to find the words.

'Please do this for me, Emma. All of Michelle's family are gone. You will be all that she has left. I will ensure that you have everything you need.'

I choked on the words. 'Of course I will, John. I am so honoured.'

'Thank you.' He looked relieved. 'As soon as Jade and Gold return we will make the arrangements.'

'What happened to them?'

'The demons killed them.'

'So where are they now?'

'Here come Simone and Leo.'

'You're up, Emma,' Leo called as they approached us. 'Missy here requires the services of a female.'

'You have to take me to the toilet, Emma,' Simone said loudly. 'Hurry up, I want to go on some more rides.'

When we returned to the apartment Mr Chen stood on the balcony and watched the waves. I went out and stood next to him. 'Do you want to swim again?'

He turned to me and smiled gently. 'Yes, I do. But I think we've done enough today.'

'Okay,' I said, and went inside.

I found Leo and Simone and rounded them up. 'Come on, guys, we're taking him down to swim.'

'Simone's too tired, I'll stay here with her,' Leo said.

'No, Leo, I should stay near Daddy,' Simone said, serious.

'She's right, Leo. We'll just have a walk along the beach while he swims.'

Leo sighed loudly.

'You're the one that's tired,' I said. 'Just a walk, then we'll sit on the sand. Let him swim.'

'You don't even need to change,' Simone said. 'Let's take Daddy to his water.'

'You're right, it's good for him.'

We all went down to the beach, Mr Chen in his black swim shorts. He hesitated as we neared the water and checked behind us; the sun was setting between the highrises. 'I'll only go for a short time.'

'Go,' I said. 'We'll just sit here and wait for you.'

He passed his towel to me and walked down to the water. The evening breakers were stronger, but he seemed to have no difficulty wading through them. He dropped vertically into the water and disappeared.

The three of us strolled along the edge of the ocean while the sun set. Venus came out over the surf, then more stars.

We stopped and sat together on the sand, watching the waves. Simone sat in Leo's lap and he wrapped his huge arms around her. The sky above the ocean darkened from purple to indigo. The breeze freshened, full of the sound of the waves and the smell of the sea. More stars came out.

A small group of dolphins appeared in the water. They surfed from the large breakers into shore, so close that we could see them clearly. We watched, entranced.

'Does that happen often?' Leo said.

'I've never heard of anything like it happening before,' I said.

Simone pulled herself free and stood to watch them, rapt. Then she sat in Leo's lap again.

'They say hello. Daddy sent them. They say he'll be back soon,' Simone said.

The dolphins turned and leapt above the water as one, high enough for their shining bodies to arc over the waves. Then they were gone.

Later Mr Chen waded out of the surf, his dark eyes shining with contentment. We rose to meet him and I handed him his towel.

He took it and threw it around his shoulders. We walked back up to the apartment together without saying a word.

CHAPTER TWENTY-NINE

I lay awake, listening to the surf. The moon shone through the curtains, making the bed covers glitter as if covered in frost. Simone was an unmoving dark shape in the room's other bed. The curtains billowed in the breeze. I'd left the window open; I liked to hear the sound of the waves.

I rose and went into the dark living room, still wearing my old tank top and tatty shorts.

Mr Chen was leaning on the balcony railing, dressed in black pyjama pants. The breeze lifted his long braid and brushed it over his bare back. A few strands of hair floated around him. He shifted slightly and the muscles moved beneath his skin, glowing in the moonlight.

I could have sworn he was waiting for me.

He turned to me and smiled, his dark eyes shining. I slid the door open and the warm air brushed over me. I joined him on the balcony. The tiles were still warm, with a light dusting of sand on them. Simone's little boogie board leaned against the railing to one side.

I stood next to him and we watched the moon rise over the water in silence. It seemed to fill the sky, the water shimmering below.

Eventually he spoke, his voice warm and low. 'You should be exhausted after the day you've had today.'

'I think I'm through exhaustion and out the other side, Mr Chen.'

He smiled sideways at me. 'I'd really prefer it if you called me John.'

'Not in front of Leo or Simone I won't,' I said, '... John.'

More than anything in the world, I wanted to put my arm around his waist and lean into him. I wanted to touch him so much it was killing me. I moved slightly away.

'The moon is very beautiful tonight, isn't it?' he said. He gestured towards the ocean. 'There is a large amount of sea life out there. Whales are migrating down the coast. The water is full of cetaceans and juvenile billfish, tuna and marlin. I swam side by side with another turtle for a long time. It is wonderful.'

'You saw all that? Hold on — *another turtle?*'

He didn't turn away from the ocean. 'Don't worry, I can hold human form out there, hard as it is for me.'

I bent and rested my forehead on the railing. 'I'm employed by a sea monster.'

He spoke with mock impatience. 'I thought you'd done some research on me. You should have known that by now.'

'What — that you're a sea monster?'

He nodded. 'Hn.'

I straightened and leaned on the rail next to him. 'North, black turtle. South, red phoenix. East, blue dragon. West, white tiger.'

'Four winds,' he finished for me. He turned and leaned one arm on the rail. 'The dragon is blue-green. His name "Qing" means "clear" as in "clear sky". In China he is often depicted as blue. In Japan he is often depicted as green. I suppose you saw what colour he really is.'

'A gorgeous shade of turquoise,' I said. 'His hair is amazing.'

'You should see his True Form. He is exquisite.'

'He scared me to death,' I whispered.

'He wouldn't be a dragon if he didn't.'

'And you're North ...' I didn't finish it; I didn't want to insult him.

'I am a turtle,' he said. 'I am the egg of a turtle.'

I gasped. The 'egg' thing was even more of an insult. He'd just calmly called himself a motherless bastard. I was speechless.

He turned back to the sea. 'And a dog demon is a bitch. It is what we are, our nature. I am a Turtle.'

'What about the snake thing, though? You're often depicted as a combination of a snake and a turtle twining together.'

He watched the waves. 'My Serpent essence is out there somewhere, roaming. I do not know where it is. Nobody else has seen it. It is absolutely silent when I call.' His voice changed slightly. 'Don't ask me what happened, because I have no idea. Half of me is missing and I don't know where it is. Right now I can exist separately. I will rejoin when I regain True Form.'

'Does it hurt?' I whispered.

He didn't answer me. He just watched the waves.

'Does it have something to do with the current situation? Because you're so drained?'

He didn't turn away from the water. 'No. It happened long before all of this. I have no idea why.'

'That is one of the weirdest things I have ever heard,' I said. 'And I have had far more than my fair share of weirdness in the past twelve months.'

'And you have handled it remarkably well,' he said. He turned back to me and smiled slightly. 'Particularly the way you have been dealing with the demons.'

'Are you kidding? Killing demons is great fun.' I

shook my head as I understood. 'Good God! I saw the Four Winds sit down to play mah jong,' I said.

'Until the Tiger once again opened his big stupid mouth.'

'He threatened to eat the Phoenix. She was so . . .'

'The word is "pissed", Emma. I really like English sometimes. There's no word that conveys it quite as well in Chinese.'

I grinned. 'And the Dragon didn't do anything. The Tiger insulted his consort and he just sat there.'

'I think they had a small falling out afterwards. The Phoenix is pissed with both the Tiger and the Dragon. The only one she's not annoyed with right now is me.'

We laughed softly together.

'Are you speaking English right now?' I said.

'Yes. I've learned a few languages.'

'Why? I would have thought you wouldn't need to.'

'I can speak and be understood. But if I write, I must write the language.'

'Oh. That makes sense.' I smiled up at him. 'Your English is excellent.'

'When I want to be clearly understood, I don't bother speaking the language. But I like to keep my skills up, so I speak English to you, Leo and Simone as much as I can. Can you tell the difference? I'd be curious to know.'

I thought about it. 'Yeah, I can tell. When you're speaking English, like you are now, you sound more formal. More old-fashioned. When you're not, you sound like me.'

'That's because then you are hearing the meaning, not the words.'

'You always have a slight English accent, though. It's very charming on top of your old-fashioned way of speaking.'

He raised his eyebrows and opened his mouth to say something, then shook his head. He turned back to the water and I did as well.

We watched the moon rise in silence.

After a while he spoke. 'Would you like to see some energy work? I think you would enjoy it.'

'Yeah, sure,' I said. 'What's involved?'

He gazed into my eyes and held his hands between us, palms up. 'Take my hands.'

I froze, watching him. 'Don't be silly.'

His smile widened slightly. 'While I am doing energy work, I have complete control of the energy. You are safe. I cannot harm you. Trust me.'

I sighed with resignation. I did trust him. I put my hands in his, feeling the hard calluses on his palm and thumb from the sword. I had similar calluses on my hand. We were a matched set.

I held his hands, looked up into his glowing dark eyes, and everything around us disappeared.

His eyes turned inward as he concentrated. He didn't seem to see me. 'Close your eyes.'

I closed my eyes, trusting him completely.

'Don't let go of my hands. This is most important. Wait.'

A slight tingle moved through me, from my hands to my feet and then back again.

'Keep your eyes closed while I tell you what I've done. Don't let go of my hands.'

I nodded with my eyes closed. The tingling stopped.

'I have lifted you above the building,' he said. I gasped. I couldn't feel it; the sandy tiles were still beneath my feet. 'You are now about half a li — about two hundred metres — above the top of the building. Whatever you do, Emma, *do not let go of my hands*.'

'I understand,' I said. 'Can I open my eyes now?'

'Sure.'

I opened my eyes. He stood in front of me, his face rigid with concentration, his eyes unseeing.

I looked down and felt a moment of dizziness when I saw how far above the beach we were. I gripped his hands and closed my eyes.

'Are you all right?' he whispered.

I nodded and reopened my eyes. I just wouldn't look down.

Now that we were higher, the sea seemed to stretch forever. The moon had risen further over the water and a glittering silver road spread over the waves. The beach glowed below us, and the mountains of the hinterland shimmered in the distance.

'This is energy work?' I whispered.

He didn't focus on me, he was concentrating. 'Hn.'

'You can teach me this?'

He seemed to see me for the first time. 'If we had a thousand years, I could teach you this. But I will teach you some simpler things; I think you will find them useful.'

I looked into his glowing dark eyes. 'I wish we did have a thousand years.'

His voice was full of pain. 'So do I, dear Emma.' He inhaled sharply and his eyes unfocused again. He smiled slightly, still concentrating. 'I am a fool.'

'We both are,' I whispered.

Leo's deep voice carried clearly on the night air. 'If you two do not come down from there right now, I will call the police.' He stood on the roof garden, next to the spa, with his hands on his hips. 'Even worse, I may be forced to call Ms Kwan.'

'He's just upset because if he were to try energy work it would probably kill him,' Mr Chen said loudly, still unfocused.

'You are incredibly mean to him sometimes,' I said.

'Don't worry, Emma, he'll get his,' Leo said. 'You two *get down here now*!'

I didn't feel the movement. The tiles were still warm beneath my feet. Mr Chen's face went rigid with concentration and we floated gently back down to the balcony.

Leo ducked inside from the roof garden and thundered through the apartment and out onto the balcony. He stood with his arms crossed over his chest and glowered.

Mr Chen nodded reassurance and released my hands, then both of us turned to face Leo, looking sheepish.

'Do that again and I really will resign,' Leo said. 'I don't know why I bother looking after you when you throw your energy away like that.'

Mr Chen sagged slightly. I felt like a child caught with her hand in the candy jar.

'If Ms Kwan saw you doing that, she'd nail your shell to the wall,' Leo said.

I giggled at the mental image and Leo glared at me. 'Think of Simone,' he said.

That sobered me. 'She's right, Mr Chen. You should rest.' I nodded to Leo. 'I'm glad one of us has some common sense.'

'I wouldn't call it common sense. Look what I put up with!' Leo returned to his room, shaking his head.

Mr Chen and I shared a smile.

'He's right, John. Go and rest.'

We went through the sliding doors and Mr Chen closed them behind us.

'Thanks for showing me that,' I whispered as we parted. 'But don't ever do it again.'

'You are more than welcome,' he whispered back. 'And I'll try not to.'

CHAPTER THIRTY

Mr Chen pulled an old black T-shirt over his swim shorts and stretched out on his towel. 'We've been here a week now, Emma. We'll go back in another three days, after the weekend. There are so many things that need my attention. I can't stay away for too long.'

'I understand.' I didn't need to ask him whether he felt better. He glowed with good health, the scar on his abdomen had nearly disappeared, and he even appeared younger, in his early thirties.

'I wanna stay here,' Simone said without turning to look at us.

'I have to go back to Hong Kong, you know that,' Mr Chen said.

Simone banged her little spade on the sand in disgust.

Leo hadn't said anything and I looked over at him. He was distracted; gazing up the beach. I turned to see what he was looking at.

A pair of good-looking men in swim shorts practised martial arts together. They looked in their mid-thirties, tanned and muscular. They performed high roundhouse kicks on each other; probably karate or tae kwon do.

Two gorgeous young women sat on towels nearby and watched them.

The men stopped and walked down to the water together. One of the women followed them in. She spoke to them and they answered her. They were friendly; I could see them smiling as they spoke. Eventually they walked out of the water and back up the beach together, ignoring her. She gave up and returned to the other young woman, said something. The first woman shook her head.

Leo and I both laughed.

'Go and talk to them,' I said softly. 'They probably know their way around.'

Leo turned back to watch Simone.

'Go, Leo,' Mr Chen said. 'Tomorrow's Saturday. Take the whole weekend. The time is yours.'

Leo didn't move.

I shoved him so hard he nearly fell over. 'Go!'

'That's an order, Leo. Go and talk to them,' Mr Chen said.

Leo growled something unintelligible under his breath, rose and walked over to the two men. He showed them some shaolin moves, demonstrating ways to block the high kicks and take an opponent down with a minimum of effort. The men were delighted and asked him to show them more.

Mr Chen watched Leo with a small smile. Then he turned his attention to me. 'And you, Emma, will visit your family. I have booked a flight for you to return to Hong Kong in two weeks.'

I opened my mouth and closed it again.

'I spoke to your mother and she will be delighted to have you there.'

'What?'

'She's expecting you tomorrow morning. Your sister will be there as well — she says your nephews are dying to see you.'

I raised my hand to shove him and changed my mind. He grinned at me. I dropped my head to my knees.

'You don't want to see your family?' he said.

'I am so embarrassed,' I said. 'I'd intended to spend a day with them, and I haven't even done that. I didn't even *think* of them really.' I looked up at him. 'Thanks.'

He shrugged. 'Family is important.'

I shared breakfast with Mr Chen and Simone before I left.

'Where's Leo?'

Mr Chen stirred his congee. 'He didn't return after meeting up with his friends last night. I don't think he'll be back until late tomorrow night or early Monday morning.'

'Good,' I said. 'Will you two be okay without me?'

Both Simone and Mr Chen snorted with disdain.

'You are a silly, Emma,' Simone said. 'You go and see your mummy and daddy.'

'I'll be gone for two whole weeks, sweetheart.'

'Is that longer than one day?'

'Yep.'

Simone shrugged. 'Me and Daddy are going swimming. And talking to the fish.'

'What do the fish say?'

Her eyes were cheeky over her cereal. 'They're really boring. Nearly as boring as Daddy.'

Mr Chen made a soft sound of amusement but didn't say anything.

I finished my tea. 'I'd better go. I'm supposed to pick the car up at nine.'

Mr Chen rose and came to me. He stood slightly away and looked down. Then he looked into my eyes. 'I will miss you.'

'I will too!' Simone yelled, and ran and tackled me. I picked her up and she threw her little arms around my neck. She kissed me loudly on the cheek. 'Me and Daddy will miss you, Emma!'

'I'll miss you too, sweetheart.' I pulled her close and smiled at Mr Chen over her shoulder. 'I'll miss both of you.'

He turned away. 'Go, Emma. I'll see you back home in two weeks. Enjoy this time with your family.'

I lowered Simone. She pushed me gently. 'Bye, Emma.'

I swallowed, turned and picked up my bag. I embraced Monica, and left.

I took a taxi to the shopping centre to collect the rental car. I was tempted to rent a luxury convertible, but decided against it and got a small hatchback instead. I threw my bag into the back and headed northwest to Montford.

The Gold Coast's huge sparkling mansions faded and the houses became smaller and more unkempt the further west I travelled. Montford was an ordinary suburban town just out of Brisbane; nothing like the expensive glamour of the Gold Coast.

After nearly two hours' driving I arrived at my parents' house. They'd left a space on the drive for me, and two cars were parked in the street in front of the house. Looked like everybody was there. I steeled myself and pressed the doorbell.

I opened my suitcase on the living room floor and pulled out gifts for everybody. Game Boy for four-year-old Mark; less complicated toys for two-year-old David. Silk tops for my sister Amanda; she was older, shorter and rounder than me, with darker hair that fell over her shoulders. Her husband, Alan, was tall and gangly and I gave him some designer T-shirts I'd found in a factory outlet in Kowloon City.

I'd brought handicrafts for my mother: carved balsawood scenes and cloisonné. Her long kind face lit up.

My father received some small electrical things I'd picked up across the border in Lo Wu Shopping Centre. He was thrilled. He hadn't changed at all since I'd last seen him; his generous, leathery face smiled under his greying hair; a working man.

I gave everybody a traditional Chinese silk jacket. Plain navy blue ones with embossed longevity for Dad and Alan; beautifully embroidered ones for Mum and Amanda. I even gave little jackets to Mark and David.

Everybody was thrilled and I was finally allowed to sit on the couch. Amanda passed me a mug of tea and they sat around me, expectant.

'I sent you a Christmas card and your friend Louise said you'd moved out,' my mother said. 'Then this Mr Chen man calls and says you're coming to stay.' She hesitated. 'Is there something you want to tell us, dear?'

'I'm working full-time as a nanny for Mr Chen,' I said. 'Not what you're thinking at all.'

My father was incredulous. 'Full-time nanny, Emma? Surely you can do better than that.' His eyes widened. 'Wait a second, you *moved in* with this man?'

'Let me! I wanna see!' David shouted. Mark had opened the zip pocket in the lid of my suitcase and found my sword. He waved it triumphantly, and David jumped with frustration as he tried to get hold of it. 'Let me see!'

I quickly rose and grabbed the sword from David. Before I had a chance to rezip the compartment, David had pulled my nunchucks out and was squealing over them.

Alan took the chucks from his son and held them, shocked. My father peered inside the case, then reached in and pulled out the pair of butterfly swords: short-bladed weapons with hooks on the guards specifically designed for close combat against long blades. He held the weapons up, his face rigid. 'Emma ...'

I sat on the couch and rested the sword across my knees. I put my head in my hands.

'I wanna play!' David shouted.

'I don't think these are toys,' Alan said softly.

I ran my hands through my hair and glanced up at them. They stood around me, watching me as if I was some sort of monster.

'Please don't look at me like that,' I said.

'I'll take the boys out in the yard so you can talk,' Amanda said. She glanced back over her shoulder as she led them through the door.

After a few moments of uncomfortable silence my father spoke. 'What the hell are you doing with these?'

I opened my mouth and closed it again.

'Are these yours, Emma? Tell us the truth,' my mother said gently.

My father moved to pull one of the butterfly swords from its leather scabbard. I raised my hand. 'Don't take that out.'

'Why not?'

I took a deep breath. 'Because,' I said, and hesitated. 'Because ...'

'Why, sweetheart?'

'Because it's as sharp as a razor and I don't want to see you hurt.'

Alan put the chucks onto the floor in front of him. 'These are all real, aren't they?' He pointed at the chucks. 'These are hardwood. You could break somebody's head with them.'

I nodded.

'Tell us, Emma,' my mother said.

I thought quickly. I needed to put a believable story together, and cursed myself for not being prepared. Of *course* they'd find my weapons. I'd brought them to train with, and Mr Chen didn't mess around with blunt padded training stuff; once we were at a certain level we used the real thing. Blunt weapons were useless against demons. The butterfly swords were my newest weapon and I needed the most practice with them. Ever since Simon Wong had turned up with his Wudang sword we'd done a lot of work on defence against a long sword with the butterfly blades.

I couldn't lie to my father, he'd see right through me. He always had. I looked from one of them to the other, desperately trying to think of a story they would accept.

'You've moved in with this Chinese man. You're working as a nanny — something that you're far too good for, Emma. And now this. Tell us what's going on,' my father said.

'Okay.' I took a deep breath. 'I was working part-time for Mr Chen, looking after his daughter, Simone. But she needed full-time care, so I moved in to look after her.'

'Is there more to this than an employer-nanny relationship?' my father said sternly.

I hesitated, then looked him in the eyes. 'Mr Chen and I do not have any sort of physical relationship. He hasn't touched me, and he never will.'

My father glared at me. He saw straight through my careful phrasing.

'So why nanny?' my mother said. 'Surely you can do better than that?'

'He pays me very well, Mum, and his daughter needs me.'

'How well?'

I hesitated again.

'How much does he pay you, Emma?' my father persisted.

I dropped my head and mumbled, 'Five thousand dollars a month.'

'That's pathetic,' my mother said. 'That's less than a thousand Australian dollars a month. You can't let him pay you so little, Emma. What's going on?'

I dropped my head even further. 'Five thousand US.'

'What's that in Australian dollars, Alan?' my father said. Alan was an insurance assessor and knew the exchange rates off the top of his head.

'Five thousand US ...' Alan worked it out, then stared at me with wonder. 'That's nearly a hundred thousand Australian dollars a year.'

'That's ridiculous!' my father snapped. He glared at me. 'What the hell is going on, Emma?'

'Okay, let me explain.' I looked at them; they all appeared outraged. My father in particular was livid. 'Mr Chen is dying, Dad. He's terminally ill. He only has a couple of years left.'

My mother's eyes went wide.

'His wife's family are all gone. When Mr Chen dies, his daughter will have nobody left. So I'll look after her. The money isn't important, I just love her dearly.'

'And her father?' my father said.

'What about him?'

'Do you love him?'

Something inside me began to hurt. I dropped my head and didn't answer.

'Okay,' my father said. 'That part I understand. He has the sense not to take it further.'

I nodded without looking up.

He raised the butterfly sword. 'But why this?' He gestured with it towards my short sword. 'Why do you have these things? That sword you have there could kill somebody.'

I glanced up. 'I've never used it on a single human being and I hope I never will.'

'Well, then,' he said, 'why?'

I lifted the sword and brushed the gold tassel on the end of the hilt. I'd never really looked at it closely before; to me it was just my weapon. The hilt was made of silver alloy, engraved with entwined serpent-like creatures. Quite fitting for Xuan Wu. Shame there were no turtles on it.

'Mr Chen is a martial arts instructor, and he's been teaching me.'

'Is he involved in the underworld there?' my father said quickly.

I looked him straight in the eyes. 'No.'

My mother sagged with relief.

'So why do you have so many lethal weapons on you?' Alan said.

'Purely to practise with.' I took another deep breath. 'Mr Chen is very wealthy and that makes Simone a target. She already has a bodyguard —'

'The little girl has a *bodyguard*?' my mother said with disbelief.

'Quite normal for the child of a wealthy family in Hong Kong,' I said. 'I've been learning as well, just in case —'

'You are coming home right now,' my mother said. 'I won't have you in danger.'

'The weapons stay at home. I'm mainly learning them because I like it.'

'You *like* it?' my mother said.

I nodded. I smiled slightly and shrugged. 'It's great fun.'

'What does this Chen man do for a living, Emma?' my father said. 'He's teaching you martial arts, he's wealthy. What's his profession?'

I took a deep breath. I could almost hear the wheels rattle as I rolled the story out. 'He does government work.'

'*Government* work?'

'Some administration, some management. He used to do fieldwork too, but nothing like that since Simone was born.'

'Good God, the man's a *spy*?' Alan said. 'For China?'

'Something like that. But not China. A much higher government than China.'

'A *spy*?' my mother said weakly.

'Not really a spy,' I said. 'Just government work. He spends most of his time in front of the computer, and teaching martial arts.'

'And?' Alan said.

'And that's all.'

'Are you in danger, Emma?' my father said softly.

I hesitated. Was I in danger? The demons didn't know I was trained, so I wasn't a target yet.

'Right now,' I said, 'no.'

'"Right now"?' my father asked.

'Right now I'm not in danger. As long as I don't do anything stupid, I won't be.'

'Well, it's obvious there's a lot here that you're not telling us, but I suppose we'll just have to take your word for it.' My father's stern face relaxed a little. 'I'm just glad this guy has the sense not to lead you on when he only has such a short time left.'

'He really is a wonderful man.'

'I am coming to Hong Kong to see this "wonderful man" for myself, as soon as I can get myself organised.' My father passed the butterfly sword to me. 'Make sure the kids don't get their hands on these.'

'I'll put them at the top of the wardrobe in my room,' I said.

'Now let's have lunch,' my father said. 'You keep complaining you can't get a decent barbecue back there, so I have it all fired up and ready for you.'

'About time somebody said something worthwhile!' I cried with delight.

'Can you give us a martial arts demonstration, Emma?' Alan said, his eyes sparkling.

'Do I have to?' I whined like a four-year-old, and everybody laughed.

CHAPTER THIRTY-ONE

We sat in the backyard while Dad and Alan handled the cooking. Mark and David ran around the yard screaming something about Ninja Turtles.

Eventually Mark charged up to me and grabbed my leg. 'Teach me nunchucks!'

'No,' I said.

'Aw, come on.'

'Maybe Aunty Emma can get you some toy ones,' Amanda said.

'Uh, no,' I said. 'I don't really like the idea of kids playing with toy ...' My voice trailed off as I heard what I was saying '... weapons.'

'Good,' my mother said firmly. 'We have you for two weeks, Emma. What are we going to do with you?'

'Take her shopping to buy some clothes,' Amanda said.

'These clothes are perfectly fine,' I huffed. I opened my beer and poured myself a glass. 'I really missed this.'

My father put a plate of greasy lamb and steak on the table in front of me. 'You missed this too, didn't you?'

I hesitated, then took a steak from the plate. 'Absolutely,' I said with false enthusiasm.

I piled a huge amount of salad on my plate as well and took a couple of slices of bread. After a year of near total vegetarianism in the Chen household, I knew that the red meat wouldn't sit well with me.

'So tell us all about it,' Amanda said.

I explained about Mr Chen, and described my life in Hong Kong. They were curious about Leo's role, and I tried to play down the kidnapping angle; I explained that Mr Chen was just being careful. They seemed satisfied with my explanations and didn't push it.

'Where'd you buy your nice handbag?' Amanda said.

'Boulevard Haussmann,' I said.

'Sounds German.'

Uh-oh. 'French. It's in Paris.'

Amanda turned and caught my mother's attention. 'Hey, Mum, she's been to Paris!'

My mother came and sat with us. 'Did you go to England?'

Uh-oh even more. 'Yes.'

'And you visited Jennifer? She didn't mention seeing you.'

I didn't say anything.

My mother sighed with exasperation. 'I don't know what I'm going to do with you two. Is there a reason you don't like each other? Did you have a fight or something a long time ago?'

I shrugged. 'Nope. Nothing much we can do about it, I suppose.'

'You should have gone to see her when you were in England.'

I smiled ruefully. 'I know.'

'Which airline did you fly on?' Amanda said, changing the subject.

Thank you, Amanda. 'It was a private jet.'

Both of them stared at me, wide-eyed.

'Let me get this straight,' Amanda said. 'You have been on a *private jet* to *Paris* with this rich man that you work for.'

'And I just about walked my feet off taking Simone sightseeing. I was *working*, Amanda.'

She looked away. 'All that and you're paid a fortune as well.'

'And I miss you terribly.' I embraced her and that made it all better.

My father came and sat with us. 'Show us the kung fu then.'

'What would you like to see?'

'Nunchucks!' Mark shouted.

I showed them some different styles of kung fu, bare-handed and with weapons. I demonstrated the chucks for the boys, and they were thrilled. I showed my mother some tai chi; some Yang and some Chen style. I pointed out the differences between Northern and Southern styles of kung fu but nobody seemed to be able to tell. Finally Alan passed me my short sword and I performed a low-level kata for them.

'If you were attacked, Emma, could you really defend yourself?' Alan asked as he put the weapons back into the bag for me.

I nearly said 'Humans or demons?' but managed to stop myself in time. 'Uh, yeah, I could defend myself.'

'How many guys could you take down? Without a weapon?'

I hesitated. 'I have no idea.'

'Rough guess,' Amanda said.

'Trained in martial arts or not?'

'Not trained,' Alan said. 'Just ordinary muggers or something. If a couple of guys tried to mug you, could you stop them?'

I thought about it. Untrained humans were about equivalent to level ten or twelve demons. 'Yeah.'

'How many before you'd be worried?'

Last session before we left Hong Kong, I'd taken out nine level five demons barehanded. 'If they weren't armed, there'd probably have to be around six of them before I'd be worried.'

'So you could take down *six* unarmed guys?'

I shrugged. 'Probably.'

'What if they were trained? What if they were black belts in, say, karate?'

'About the same, to tell the truth. The karate they teach in the West is mostly non-contact. Most practitioners aren't that good when it comes to serious combat.'

'What belt are you? Black belt, what dan?'

That stopped me dead. 'Uh, we don't have that. You're either good or you aren't.' I studied him carefully; his face was innocent. 'Why are you asking me all of this, Alan?'

'Our next-door neighbour, Shane, is a black belt in karate,' Amanda said. 'Alan's probably wondering if you'd be able to take him down. He keeps skiting about how good he is.'

I glared at them. 'I am *not* entertainment.'

They shared a look.

'I mean it,' I said. 'What I'm learning isn't for fun. The Arts are serious, they're for self-defence, and I won't use them merely to put your neighbour in his place.'

'You've changed, Emma,' my mother said softly.

I glanced at her. 'You say that like it's a bad thing.'

'I'm not sure that it isn't.'

'Elbow him in the ribs,' I said, demonstrating. 'Then switch hands, step back, over his back and lift his arm behind him.' Shane fell to one knee in front of me. 'If he doesn't go down, you help him along with your toe behind his knee. If you twist his wrist just *so*,' Shane grunted with pain, 'sorry. If you twist his wrist a little, he can't move his arm. His other arm can't reach you, he's effectively helpless.'

Amanda performed the same move and quickly had Alan on his knees in front of her.

'Ease up, sweetheart,' he said.

'Yeah, don't lift his arm too high, you'll break it,' I said.

She glanced up at me. 'I could break his arm?'

'Easily,' I said. 'Dislocate it at the least.'

She released him and stepped back.

Alan shook his head and rose. 'I was completely unable to move.'

'No, you could have moved,' I said. 'You could have fallen on your face on the grass. Apart from that, she had you.'

'Yeah,' Alan said. He grinned at Amanda. 'You're pretty good.'

Amanda watched him silently for a moment, then smiled up at me. 'Teach me another one.'

I laughed. 'Sure.'

Everybody came to see me off at the airport. Amanda noticed that I checked in at the first-class counter, but didn't say anything.

'We're coming to visit you as soon as we're organised,' my father said as he hugged me. 'I want to meet your Mr Chen, this mystery rich man who's changed you so much.'

I pulled back, held his arms and looked up at him. 'I haven't changed that much, have I?'

'You're stronger and fitter, you're doing these martial arts, and you obviously care deeply about them,' my father said. 'But I want to hear the whole story when we get there.'

'Me too,' my mother said. 'Just let me sort myself out, and then we'll come over. I want to buy some more of those pretty things you gave me.'

I smiled at them. 'I'll be happy to show you around.' Inside I desperately willed them not to come. I didn't want to see them in danger.

'Keep in touch, sweetheart!' my mother shouted as I went down the escalator to immigration.

'Miss Donahoe, yes?' the flight attendant said, checking the passenger list. 'Welcome aboard.' She raised the bottle she was holding. 'Champagne?'

'No, thanks.'

'As soon as we take off, I'll provide you with the menu. Just order anything you want, any time you like.'

'Thanks,' I said, and settled into the large comfortable seat. I looked out the window at the clear blue Brisbane sky and felt a wrench. I'd miss the fresh air and the sunshine.

But I was going home. To Simone, to Leo ... and to John.

Something really began to hurt. I'd lost two precious weeks of time with him that I'd never be able to make up.

I leaned back and closed my eyes. He felt the same way too. And there was absolutely nothing we could do about it.

Except enjoy what we had for the little time we had left.

CHAPTER THIRTY-TWO

Leo and Simone were waiting for me when I emerged at the arrivals gate. Simone raced to me and tackled me with a huge grin. I lifted her, hugged her, then put her down again and led her to Leo.

He was subdued. 'Hey.'

I looked around, concerned. 'Where's Mr Chen? Is he okay?'

'He's fine. He's at home in a meeting.' Leo took the trolley from me and pushed it towards the car park. 'Nothing but meetings since we came back. How's your family?'

'They found my weapons. Completely freaked them out.'

'Trust you to goof it up,' Leo said caustically. 'Wouldn't be surprised if you killed one of them by accident.'

I stopped and stared at him. 'That's not like you, Leo. What's the matter?'

He didn't stop pushing the trolley. 'My turn next.'

I rushed to keep up with him. 'Your turn to what?'

'Now that you're back, and it's Chinese New Year, I have to go and visit *my* family.'

'Is that a problem?'

He paid the parking ticket at the Shroff Office and led us to the car. 'You have no idea.'

He opened the car door for me and I buckled Simone into the back. 'Oh. Your lifestyle?'

'That's a delicate way of putting it,' he said sarcastically.

I nodded to Simone.

'Oh,' he said, understanding. He got in behind the steering wheel. 'They may try to *cure* me.'

'Cure you? There's no cure for . . .' I stopped.

'He told you.' He closed the car door.

'I'm sorry if you didn't want me to know. He just came out with it. He said you'd have about a year once he's gone.'

Leo started the car and eased it out of its space. 'He has the right to tell you anything he wants to about me.' He shook his head. 'I did some really stupid things when I was young.'

'But surely your family know there's no cure, Leo?'

'That's not what they're trying to cure. They don't even know about that. No, every eligible girl in the neighbourhood will probably be waiting for me.'

'Oh,' I said softly. 'That's awful.'

He stopped the car to put the ticket into the machine, then turned to me and grinned. 'How about I take a photo of us together and tell them you're my wife?'

'How about I rip your head off and feed it to the biggest demon in the jar?' I glared at him. 'You are a demon that's kidnapped the real Leo. Where did you put him?'

'Don't be silly, Emma,' Simone said patiently. 'That's not a demon, that's my Leo.'

Leo turned to me as the boom gate opened. 'It's good to have you back, Emma.'

'It's good to be back.'

* * *

The minute we entered the front door Mr Chen raced into the hall from the dining room. He came to me and stopped, then gazed intensely into my eyes.

'Careful,' Leo said.

'No need,' Mr Chen said. 'Take Simone.'

'Sir.' Leo led Simone down to her room.

His eyes didn't leave my face. 'Welcome back, Emma. It's good to see you.'

More than anything else in the world I wanted to throw myself into his arms and squeeze the life out of him. Instead I took a deep breath and smiled. 'It's wonderful to be back.'

'When you've unpacked and rested, we need to talk. Let me know when you're ready.'

We went into the training room together and he closed the door. His face was rigid with restraint. He went to the long wall and put his hands behind his back without looking up.

I stood in the middle of the room.

'I have hesitated about taking this step,' he said.

I waited.

'I don't want to do this, but if we are to take the training to the next level, then it must be done.'

'What?'

He looked into my eyes. 'Here in the training room, we are master and student. But I cannot take you to the next level until the relationship is formalised.'

'Formalised?'

'You must swear allegiance to me, Emma. If you are to learn energy work, you must do it as a Retainer. I wish you could learn it as something more, but it can never be. So you must swear allegiance and formally become a Retainer.'

'Is this something terribly complicated?'

'You must go down on your knees, accept me as your Lord, and swear to obey me.'

I relaxed, relieved. 'That's easy.'

He fixed his eyes on mine. 'No, Emma, I don't think you understand. You must promise to obey me if I give you an order. Regardless of what I order you to do. Any order.'

I hesitated. '*Any* order?'

'Any order. If I order you to lie for me, or steal for me. If I order you to commit murder for me: to kill another human being, not a demon. If I order you to fall on your own sword, to kill your friends, to kill your family. You must obey me without hesitation. Even if I were to order you to bring Simone in here and remove her head.'

I sagged slightly. This *was* big.

His gaze was very intense. 'Do you understand the full implications of what I am requiring of you, Emma Donahoe?'

I nodded.

His voice was gentle and full of pain. 'Answer the question, Emma.'

'I understand, sir.'

He looked away.

'Leo's already done this, hasn't he?'

He smiled slightly, then looked back at me. 'Of course.'

'It doesn't stop him from telling you off.'

'He may give advice. He may object. But if I tell him it is an order, then he will obey. Always. Immediately and without hesitation. I wish I did not have to require this of you.'

Our eyes didn't shift from each other.

'I'm glad to be learning from you, John ... Mr Chen. Sir.'

He winced.

'I'm happy to be with you and Simone. I don't need more.'

He took a deep breath and let it out. 'Very well.' He turned away and walked to the weapons rack. 'I will give you time to consider whether you are willing to take the step. Until then, we'll work with the sword.'

But I didn't need to consider anything. I trusted him completely. If he'd ordered me to let go of his hands when we were floating above the building on the Gold Coast, I'd have happily complied and fallen to my death content.

Swearing allegiance was just a formality. I would obey him anyway. I fell to my knees.

He collected my short sword from the rack, then turned and saw me. He froze.

'I swear allegiance,' I said. 'I accept you as Lord. I promise to obey you.'

And I hoped that was all there was to it.

He stood watching me for a long time before he spoke. 'Very well, Emma Donahoe, you may rise. I hope you understand the gravity of what you have just done.'

'I do, my Lord.' And suddenly I knew why Leo called him that.

'Dismissed. Return tomorrow.'

'My Lord.' I rose without looking at him. I hesitated, then went out.

He closed the door quietly behind me.

Two hours later Simone's eyes unfocused while she sat with me. 'Why is Daddy upset, Emma?'

'Is he upset? I haven't seen him.'

'He's in the training room doing sword katas over and over, and he's been doing them for a long time. Do you know why?'

I didn't look at her. 'No, darling, I have no idea.'

CHAPTER THIRTY-THREE

I held Simone's hand as we walked through the airport behind Leo and Mr Chen. Chinese New Year was always a busy time and the airport was packed with people going in both directions.

Leo checked in, and we accompanied him to the immigration gates. He knelt to hug Simone.

She kissed him on the cheek. 'Say hello to your mummy for me.'

'I will, sweetheart.' He rose, hesitated, then pulled me into his arms and embraced me, surrounding me with the musky smell of his cologne. 'Look after them for me,' he whispered into my hair. 'Don't let him do anything stupid.'

I pulled back to smile up at him. 'Don't worry, I won't. I'll look after them.' He embraced me again, then released me.

He turned to Mr Chen and stood rigid without looking at him for a long moment. Then he fell to one knee and saluted. He gazed up into Mr Chen's eyes and for a fleeting second his true feelings showed.

Mr Chen nodded.

Leo ignored the amused looks from passing people. He rose, grabbed his bag and went into the immigration area without looking back.

'I do not require looking after,' Mr Chen growled softly as we walked back to the car.

'Yes, you do, Daddy,' Simone said. 'You're hopeless by yourself.'

Mr Chen smiled and shook his head.

I sat in the back of the car with Simone as Mr Chen drove us home. Chinese New Year had come in early February, and the weather was still quite cold.

'Can you drive, Emma?' Mr Chen said as he navigated the North Lantau expressway.

'I have an Australian driver's licence, but I've never been game to drive in Hong Kong,' I said over the back of the seat. 'Everybody drives so close, it's scary.'

'It's not so bad once you're used to it.' He slid through the auto toll lane and moved into the right lane to pass over the Tsing Ma Bridge. 'There is method to the madness, I assure you.'

I didn't say anything; I wasn't sure where he was headed.

'If you want to borrow the car over the Chinese New Year break, you can,' he said. 'I won't be using it.'

'You won't be visiting anybody?'

'Since I can't travel, they'll all come to me.'

I inhaled sharply as I understood. 'How many freaking gods are coming over?'

'Pretty much all of them, I think.'

I dropped my head into my hands. 'I should have gone to visit my family. Leo's the lucky one.'

'That's what you're supposed to do at New Year — visit your family. For some couples in China, New Year is the only time they see each other.'

'I have a friend like that. She's in Australia, her husband's here, and he'll visit her at New Year and she's quite happy with the situation.'

'They're called "astronauts".'

'Yeah. Is Monica going home to the Philippines?'

'I suggested it, but she wouldn't go. She's arranged to spend time with her sister at her sister's employer's apartment on Stubbs Road. The employer won't be there, so they'll have the place to themselves. Some other members of the family are coming to see them. Even the sister and brother from Singapore, but I think the sister in the Middle East can't make it.'

'How many brothers and sisters does she have?' I said, incredulous.

'I think she's in the middle of about nine.'

'So it'll just be the three of us for the entire New Year break.'

Simone piped up. 'We'll be like a family!'

'We *are* a family,' he said.

'Yes, we are,' I said.

'We're a family,' Simone said softly.

A couple of days later Mr Chen tapped on my door. 'Can I talk to you?'

'Come on in.'

'I was wondering if you'd help us,' he said. 'Monica's done most of it, but my study and the Kitchen God still need to be done, and I'd like to take the mats up in the training room and vacuum underneath them.'

'Oh, the New Year clean-out,' I said. 'Sure. I'll take your paperwork, you do the rest of the study, and then we can do the mats together.'

'Thanks. You know why we do this?'

'Something about the Kitchen God taking the annual report to the Jade Emperor, and coming back with the new good luck for the whole year.' I stopped when I heard what I'd said. 'You saw the Jade Emperor yourself not long ago. Is this really necessary?'

His eyes sparkled. 'Oh, absolutely.'

'So there's another god around here that I haven't noticed — the Kitchen God?'

'You want to see?'

'Sure.'

He led me into the kitchen. One of the cupboards had an open altar underneath. The interior was painted red and contained an inscribed tablet over the top of an incense pot. The pot and tablet were nearly black with the dust from the incense.

'I've seen you put incense in that. That's him?'

'Yep.'

'What does he look like?'

He gestured towards the pot. 'That.'

'You are really annoying sometimes, you know that?'

'Good,' he said with a perfectly straight face.

That evening the three of us went out for a vegetarian meal in a restaurant in Wellington Street. Afterwards, we walked together to the pier and boarded Mr Chen's boat. A cheerful deckhand helped me aboard, and Mr Chen carried Simone. Every boat in Hong Kong seemed to be floating on the Harbour to watch the show, and the promenade on both sides was thick with thousands of people.

We sat on the cushioned top of the boat and leaned on the soft backrest. One of the deckhands provided us with a blanket and a thermos of tea. The wind whistling across the Harbour was bitter and seemed to cut straight through my jacket.

Simone sat between us as the boat moved into position. Three barges had been moored in the Harbour to launch the fireworks.

'I'm cold, Daddy,' she said.

We moved closer together with Simone between us. Mr Chen put his arm around her shoulders and I pulled the blanket up to her chin. All three of us wriggled down under the blanket.

He gazed at me and my heart leapt. It was a look that said everything. He smiled slightly and I knew he felt it too. Both of us sighed and glanced down at Simone.

'Cold,' Simone said.

I bundled her into my lap. Mr Chen moved closer and put his arm around my shoulders, pulling both of us into him. I didn't care about anything else apart from the feeling of having both of them so close to me. I nestled against him and put my head on his shoulder. He squeezed me gently and pulled me closer.

The fireworks began and Simone yelled, '*Wah*!'

Her shout was echoed by everybody around the Harbour. The explosions vibrated through the boat.

Mr Chen brushed my shoulder, then gently leaned over me and pushed his face into my hair.

I didn't move. Simone was busy watching the fireworks and didn't notice.

I turned my head to see him.

He smiled down at me. His eyes were very dark and shining.

'Don't you have to be careful?' I whispered.

He moved his mouth next to my ear. 'I could never hurt my child, even unintentionally. She is your shield.'

'You can't hurt me while we have her between us like this?'

He moved his face further down to the side of my throat. 'No,' he breathed, and I felt the word more than heard it.

I gazed into his glowing dark eyes. Our faces were very close. 'It's wrong to use her like this.'

'I know. But sometimes you have to take the chance when it's given you.'

Another firework went off above our heads. Neither of us noticed. He lowered his face to mine and closed his eyes. Our lips touched. He opened to me.

It was what I had wanted from the moment I'd seen him.

He pushed harder into me, deepening the kiss. The explosions went off over our heads and neither of us cared. I put my free arm behind his neck and buried my fingers into his wonderful silken hair. My whole body was like an electric wire, strumming to his touch.

But both of us were intensely aware of Simone in my lap. It had to end, and he pulled back first. He gazed into my eyes, then moved in and touched his mouth to mine again, a light brush. He smiled. 'We are a pair of fools. Now I must be even more careful about touching you.'

'Tell me it's not worth it.'

He smiled again. I ran my hand through his hair. He drifted his fingertips over my face.

'Why aren't you watching the fireworks, Daddy?' Simone said loudly.

We dropped our hands and looked down at her.

'Why are you looking at Emma and not at the fireworks? Are you okay, Emma?' Simone's little face lit up. 'Oh.' She smiled slightly and looked back to the fireworks, wriggling her little bottom in my lap as she turned. 'Don't mind me.'

We laughed softly together.

I put my head on his shoulder.

He squeezed me around the shoulders and brushed his hand over my arm. 'We will probably never have another chance like this.'

'This is more than I ever hoped for.'

CHAPTER THIRTY-FOUR

On New Year's Day I went into Simone's room to dress her but Mr Chen was ahead of me. He'd dressed Simone in a little red cheongsam and was kneeling to tie her hair into two buns on top of her head. She was adorable.

He wore his black silk robe with his hair braided. He smiled over the top of her head. 'Gung hei fat choy, Miss Donahoe.'

Simone saluted me, serious. 'Gung hei fat choy. Lai see dao loy.'

'Already asking for lai see. You are so cheeky,' I said.

Mr Chen carefully tied a red ribbon around one of Simone's little buns. 'Do you have new clothes you could wear today, Emma? It's traditional for New Year's Day to be a new beginning. Wearing new clothes is a part of that.'

'I don't have anything.' Then I had a sudden inspiration. 'How about one of my new cheongsams?'

'The pink one!' Simone jiggled with delight. Mr Chen lost his grip on the ribbon and tutted at her. 'Sorry, Daddy.'

He didn't look up from her hair. 'If you could wear your new cheongsam, I'd appreciate it.'

'He's just saying that because you look so pretty in it,' Simone said.

'Okay,' I said.

He smiled.

I went back into my room, put on my pink cheongsam, twisted my hair into a neat bun, and applied some make-up just to seal the deal.

They stood together in the living room waiting for me. Mr Chen's face lit up when he saw me. I twirled for him.

'You look prettier than me!' Simone yelled. 'Doesn't she, Daddy?'

'I don't know which of you is more delightful to look at,' he said with a gentle smile. 'So I think I'll settle on seeing both of you together.'

The doorbell rang and he went to open the door.

'Hey, what happened to the seals?' Bai Hu said as he came in. 'Yours were always the best. What happened?'

'A demon blew them completely during the Mountain attack.' Mr Chen closed the front door. 'I'll never have them back to what they were. You can come straight in now.'

'Must have been a hell of a demon.' Bai Hu stopped dead and stared at Simone and me. 'Look at the two beautiful girls. Wanna come home with me, girls?'

'Yeah, sure!' Simone shouted, jumping up and down.

Mr Chen took Bai Hu's arm, pulled him close and growled something softly into his ear.

Bai Hu raised his hand and nodded. 'Don't worry, I get it, I get it, all yours.' He raised the other hand as well. 'Paws off. I promise.'

'Good,' Mr Chen said. 'Come and help me set up the tables. We'll have two mah jong tables in the training room, and one out here.'

'What about Monica? Where's she?'

'Visiting family. Gone for the whole break.'

370

'You're doing all this yourself?' Bai Hu said, incredulous.

'Of course. Come and help with the tables.'

'No. No way.' Bai raised his hands again. 'This is so not fitting it's not funny.'

'Get over it.'

'No.' Bai Hu gestured towards Simone and me. 'They have to do housework?'

'He vacuumed under the mats,' I said. 'I did the study.'

'*You* did housework, Ah Wu? This is ridiculous,' Bai Hu said. 'Let me lend you one of mine.'

'You want to give us a housekeeper?' I said.

'Of course,' Bai Hu said. 'What about the dinner tonight? You have, what, about ten coming over? Who the f—' He stopped. 'Who's going to cook that? You're going to make poor *Emma* cook?'

'If I let Emma cook we'd all be dead of food poisoning by morning,' Mr Chen said. 'I can do it myself. I'm quite capable.'

'I do not believe this.' Bai Hu waved one hand. 'There.'

'That was totally unnecessary.'

'The hell it was.'

A smiling Filipina came out of the kitchen and bowed to each of us in turn. 'How many for dinner, sir?'

'Twelve,' Mr Chen said. 'Vegetarian.'

She nodded. 'Very good, sir,' and went back into the kitchen.

'You shouldn't make her work over the break,' I said.

'Not a problem, Emma, she's a tame demon,' Bai Hu said. 'You know, if word got out about him doing this, he'd never hear the end of it.'

'There is no higher honour than preparing a meal for the ones you care for, and you know it,' Mr Chen said.

Bai Hu growled and shook his head. 'Nobody would eat it, Ah Wu, they'd be too embarrassed. Now, let's set up these tables.'

Later that afternoon the doorbell rang. I ran to answer it.

'Madam Zhu Que,' I said, saluting.

'Hello, Emma,' Zhu Que said. 'What happened to Ah Wu's seals?'

I closed the door behind her. 'A demon attacked us when he was on the Mountain. It blew the seals.'

She held out a bag of oranges. 'Could you take these?'

Mr Chen came out of the training room. Zhu Que fell to one knee and saluted him. 'Xuan Tian.'

He nodded back. 'Zhu Que. Gung hei.'

She rose and held her hands out. A box wrapped in red and gold paper appeared in them. 'Cookies. For the Princess.'

'Daujie,' he said, speaking Cantonese. 'We still have an hour before dinner, and the other game in the training room needs a fourth.'

'Is the Tiger on that table?'

'No.'

She nodded. 'Then I will play.' She held a lai see out to me.

I shook my head and raised my hands. 'Not necessary, my Lady.'

'Take it,' she said, pushing it towards me with a small smile.

'Take it, Emma,' Mr Chen said.

I sighed with exasperation and took the lai see. That was the fourth one I'd received that day.

'Lady,' Mr Chen said, indicating the training room.

She nodded and headed down the hall to the mah jong games.

'They're just having fun,' Mr Chen whispered to me. 'Let them. You're a younger unmarried member of the household.'

'They're just tormenting me,' I whispered back.

'That too.'

'You have any idea how much is in these?'

'If there's less than five thousand dollars in any of them except the Tiger's, tell me.'

'How did you know the Tiger didn't give me that much? He only gave me twenty dollars, a token.'

'You work it out, Emma.' He left me and went into the training room.

'Oh.'

Qing Long and Zhu Que were mortified when I sat at the table with everybody for the New Year feast.

'You always allow Retainers to share meals with your Generals, Ah Wu?' Qing Long said.

'She is a member of the family,' Mr Chen said, and that was that.

Two weeks later we went to collect Leo from the airport. He insisted on driving us home and Mr Chen didn't argue.

'Did you have fun?' I said. 'Did you see everybody? They didn't try anything, did they?'

Leo pointedly ignored me.

'Did you just go to Chicago, or did you go anywhere else?'

Leo drove without saying anything.

'Did you see your brothers and sisters? Do you *have* any brothers and sisters?'

'Leave me alone,' Leo snapped.

'You *will* show us photos though, Leo,' Mr Chen said.

'Yes, sir, I will,' Leo said with resignation.

When we were home, and Leo had put his bag in his room, Simone and I sat on either side of him on the couch. Mr Chen leaned on the back of the couch, looking over our shoulders.

'This is my mother and two of my older sisters.' He pulled out another photo. 'The other sister, and my brother.'

'How many nieces and nephews do you have, Leo?' I asked, seeing all the smiling children.

He quickly worked it out. 'About fifteen.'

'You're one of five?'

'Yep.'

'Oldest? Youngest?'

'Youngest.'

I looked at his mother, a kind, smiling woman. 'Why aren't there any photos of your father?'

'He died when I was fifteen,' Leo said. 'Enough.' He took the photos into his room and didn't come out for a long time.

A couple of weeks later I met April in the lobby of the hotel in Causeway Bay.

'Where's Louise?' I said.

'She's not coming. I wanted to talk to you by yourself.'

We went up the escalators into the upmarket Chinese restaurant and were seated at a table large enough for eight, some distance from the nearest diners. The waiter provided us with a list of the yum cha snacks; there weren't trolleys, we had to fill out the order.

As soon as the waiter left us, April grabbed my hand. She held it so tight it was painful. Her face was rigid with control.

'What is it, April?'

'I'm pregnant.'

'That's wonderful!' I cried. 'Just what you wanted. What does Andy think?'

She looked down at the table. 'He wants an abortion. He wants me to lose this baby.'

'Oh my God,' I said softly. 'He doesn't want you to abort it because it's a girl, does he?'

'He has another wife, Emma. He already has a son with her. He said he doesn't want any more boys. He *wants* a girl.'

I inhaled sharply. 'Another wife?'

'He has a lot of girls on the Mainland, as well as the other wife. He didn't come to Australia at Chinese New Year, so I came here to see him. He picked me up at the hotel *and brought the other wife along*. Just to shame me.'

I was speechless.

'And he says that since he has a son with her, he doesn't want another boy. This child is a boy — I found out from the ultrasound in January. He says lose it, have another. If I have a girl, he'll drop the other wife and come to Australia.'

'I thought boys were better.'

'Not for him. He's in a bad business. If he has a son, then the son may become involved. He doesn't want that.'

'Bad business?'

She dropped her voice. 'Triad business.'

'Oh my God, he's a *gangster*?' I hissed softly.

She waved it away; unimportant. 'I'm his wife. I have nothing to do with his business. That's *his* business.' The despair showed for a fleeting second. 'What am I going to do, Emma? Should I do what he asks? If I have a girl for him, he'll keep me. We'll be a family. Or I could divorce him and forget about it. I had plenty of men ask me out when I was in Australia.'

I shook my head. I didn't know what to say.

'Or I could keep the baby. Once he sees the baby, he'll be happy, I know he will. He loves me. We'll be a family.'

'What do your family say?'

'They say I should stay with him, that I'm the real wife. The other woman is just a mistress. His family, the houses of Kwok and Ho, are very wealthy. Very prestigious. My family gain a lot of face from the marriage.'

'I can't believe it.'

'If I have the child then he can apply for Australian citizenship through the child. I don't want him to be able to do that. Then he won't need me.'

The dim sum arrived and she tucked into them as if nothing was amiss. 'The morning sickness isn't too bad now. It was bad a few weeks ago.' She poured the tea. 'And what about you, Emma? You have a man? Louise said you had something with this Chen man, but I don't think you're that stupid, involved with the employer. You have another man?'

'No. Nobody.'

'You in love with your employer.' It wasn't a question.

I looked down at the table. I didn't know what to say.

'Any chance?'

I hesitated. I shook my head.

'You are a stupid, Emma,' April said.

I didn't move. She was right.

'Eat,' she said, waving her chopsticks at the steamers. 'I saw a fortune teller last week, he said my face is very happy. Both of us will be happy.'

CHAPTER THIRTY-FIVE

Once Chinese New Year had finished and things in the Chen household returned to their usual chaotic normality, Mr Chen started me on energy work.

'Sit,' he said, gesturing towards the centre of the mats in the training room. He sat cross-legged across from me. He was silent for a while, looking down, and I waited.

'If you are able to do energy work, you are exceptional. Only about one in ten thousand humans gains the ability, usually only if they are taught from an early age. But you're extremely talented, Emma, and I think you'll be able to do it.'

'Exactly how talented am I?'

He looked into my eyes. 'You are one of the most talented students I have ever taught, Emma Donahoe. If you can gain the energy work skills, I think you will surpass Leo.'

I inhaled sharply. 'I'd be better than *Leo*?'

'Not in physical ability, though if you continue to learn at this pace it will be a close thing. But if you can learn energy work, you will leave him far behind.'

I was speechless. I couldn't believe it.

'To gain energy work you must prepare. You will prepare for the next two weeks, and then we will begin.'

I was still astounded at the thought of being better than Leo. 'Sir.'

He held his hand up and counted off on his fingers. 'One. We must work on your meditation skills, to bring you into line with Simone. She is far ahead of you.'

That wasn't surprising. I waited.

'Two. Strictly vegetarian from now on. Same as me.'

I opened my mouth and then closed it.

'Do you have a problem with that, Emma?'

'No. If I can learn to do the sort of thing that you did in Australia, then it will be worth it.'

He smiled slightly. 'You will never achieve anything like that in less than a lifetime. But you may be able to gain some interesting skills.'

'Is that all?'

'Absolutely no alcohol or any other drug. Plenty of rest. Sleep at least eight, nine hours a night. When we begin the work you will sleep much more than that; it is exhausting. And ...' His voice trailed off and he looked down.

'Yes?'

He didn't meet my eyes. 'No intimate partners. Do not bring anyone home. You must conserve your energy.'

I'd thought it was completely obvious that there'd never be anybody else.

He glanced up to see my reaction.

'That will absolutely not be a problem,' I said softly.

'Good. Now, we will work on a balance between yang of martial arts activity, very strong, very forceful, and yin of meditation and Quiet Standing.'

I grimaced. 'I *hate* Quiet Standing. At least when I'm meditating I can be reasonably comfortable. Quiet Standing *hurts*.'

'And this is why we must work at it. For the next three weeks, you will spend a great deal of time Standing.'

I shook my head.

'Are you still prepared to try for this?'

I looked him straight in the eye. 'Absolutely.'

'Very well then, Emma, on your feet and let's have you Standing for the next thirty minutes. Try to phase out as much as you can.'

I pulled myself to my feet, moved into a narrow horse stance and put my hands onto my dan tian, my energy centre. I closed my eyes and tried to drift off.

He left me to it.

A week later we were still at it. He'd set me to Standing and leave the room. At least I was skilled enough not to feel that it was torture any more; I could relax down onto my heels and drift away.

He came back in and stood in front of me.

Then he went out again.

He did this three or four times. He was waiting for me not to notice.

After forty-five minutes I felt that I was wasting his time. I wasn't relaxed enough, and that made me more tense.

'You are doing very well,' he said. 'Dismissed.'

I dropped my head and skulked out.

After another week of maddening failure I began to wonder why he bothered. It was becoming obvious that I'd never get there. Nevertheless, he continued to work with seemingly infinite patience.

After a brisk session with the sword he indicated the middle of the mats. 'Standing.'

I sighed with resignation, positioned myself, closed my eyes and drifted off. I was past the point of caring about whether I was getting there. I was just glad for the break.

'Emma.' I snapped open my eyes. He stood in front of me, expressionless. 'Dismissed. Rest.'

I slumped with disappointment. He'd finally given up.

I checked my watch as I went out but it had stopped. I quickly poked my head into the living room to check the clock there, and stopped dead.

I'd been Standing for nearly *three hours*.

He chuckled behind me and I turned. He leaned on the training room doorframe. 'Didn't you know?'

'Not at all. It felt like only a few seconds.'

'I checked on you four or five times. Simone was beginning to worry about you.'

'Is she okay?'

'Yes. Leo took her out.' He smiled into my eyes. 'Leo couldn't believe it. I think you are ready.'

I sagged. Suddenly I was exhausted. My legs were made of lead.

'Go and rest, Emma.' He turned away, then turned back. 'Oh. Do not attempt Quiet Standing unsupervised, you could stay under for a long time. We need you.'

'Yes, sir.'

I dragged myself to my room and collapsed on the bed. I desperately needed a shower but I couldn't move.

We sat cross-legged together on the floor of the training room.

'Visualise your chi, in your dan tian,' he said, very softly. 'Close your eyes, Simone.'

My eyes were already closed as I concentrated on my chi.

'Move it to your hands.'

My hands tingled as the chi flowed through them. They felt very warm.

'Less than that, Simone. Good.'

I took a deep breath and let it out again.

'Release it if you need to, Emma. Do you have it?'

'I don't need to release it. I have control.'

'Good. Now move your chi above your hands.'

I saw the light through my eyelids and snapped open my eyes. Simone had done it. She sat, wide-eyed, watching the little golden ball of chi floating above her outstretched hands. I could feel the warmth from it; it was shot with white fire, about the size of a tennis ball.

'Do you have it?' he said.

She nodded. Her hair floated around her head with the static.

'Can you hold it there?'

'It's hard.'

'Concentrate. Keep it there.'

'I think I have it,' she said, straining.

'Let it go. Gently, Simone, float it back into your hands.'

Her eyes widened slightly and the chi dropped back into her outstretched palms and disappeared. She fell sideways and I caught her.

Mr Chen scooped her out of my arms and clutched her in a huge hug, his face glowing with pride.

He pulled back and smiled gently at her. She was pale and panting, but her eyes sparkled. He brushed her hair. 'Are you okay?'

She nodded. 'I'm okay, Daddy.'

'Good. Now listen carefully. Go into your room, recentre your chi, and then rest. Don't try to do it again, you could hurt yourself. Do you understand, Simone? It's very important. Go, recentre, rest.'

She nodded, serious. 'Don't worry, Daddy, I'll go and rest.' She threw her little arms around his neck and giggled into his throat. 'I'm so tired I need to be carried anyway!'

He lifted her and pulled himself to his feet. 'Stay here,' he said to me, and carried her out.

I remained cross-legged on the floor, furiously beating myself up. I'd failed miserably. I'd let Simone's chi distract me. That shouldn't have happened. I was tempted to try it again, but without his supervision I could easily kill myself. Not that I didn't feel almost suicidal after wasting so many weeks of hard work.

But at least Simone had done it. I felt a warm glow of pride for her.

Mr Chen came back in and sat cross-legged in front of me. He pulled his long hair out of its tie, shook it, and put it back. He sighed and put his hands on his knees. 'Now for you, Miss Donahoe.'

I dropped my head. I didn't know what to say.

'Is the chi still there? In your hands?'

I held my hands in front of me. 'Yes.'

'Good. Relax. Go deeper. Let's try again.'

I glanced up at him. 'It won't drain me too much?'

'No. Close your eyes. Try.'

I took a deep breath, closed my eyes and went down.

'Deeper.'

I dropped further. My hands weren't attached to me any more. My legs were gone. I was a glowing point of light hovering between my eyes.

'Are you still here, Emma?' he whispered.

I nodded.

'Hold out your hands.'

I didn't try to move them. My unattached hands floated in front of me by themselves. They seemed a long way away.

'Move the chi to your fingertips.'

My fingertips glowed with the chi. The concentration of energy in such a small area made them almost painfully hot.

'Now curl your fingers over your palms. Good. Float the chi from your fingertips into your palms. There.'

I opened my eyes. My hands still didn't feel attached to me. I'd generated slightly more than Simone; it was a little more than a tennis ball. I watched it float above my hands with awe.

It was desperately difficult to keep it there. It felt as if a rubber band was trying to pull it back into me. I struggled to keep the chi outside my body.

'How long do you think you could keep it there?' he said, full of warm satisfaction.

'I don't know. Right now I have it, but I could lose it any time.'

'Well done. Let's see how long you can hold it; if you can hold it for a full minute I'll be very pleased. If it feels that it is getting away from you, let it fall. Hold it; I will supervise.'

He put his fingertips on my temple. The touch made me look up. I saw straight into his glowing dark eyes. His face was full of proud adoration and I saw how much he loved me.

And of course I completely lost it.

The chi shot like a rocket straight past his left ear. Everything went sideways and faded. I heard him laugh softly as he caught me, then he was gone.

'You must rest, my Lord,' Leo said. 'She'll be fine.'

'Leave us,' Mr Chen said.

'She'll be furious with you when she wakes up, you know that.'

'Go.'

Leo snorted. The door opened and closed.

I tried to open my eyes but couldn't. I attempted to lift my arms but I was paralysed. I panicked for a second: I couldn't move at all or open my eyes or say anything.

'Don't try to move,' he said.

I relaxed.

'You probably can't move. Don't be concerned. Everything is fine.'

I tried to ask him what had happened but I couldn't. I struggled to say something.

'Don't try to speak, difficult as such a thing is for you,' he said with amusement.

I laughed softly with him. There, I could laugh; why couldn't I speak? I tried again. I gave up.

'Good,' he said. 'You probably don't remember what happened. You tried to take my head off with a bolt of your chi. Well done. The hole in the wall of the training room is one of the best I've ever seen. Most unusual for the chi to shoot away like that on first generation.'

I put a hole in the wall? Go, me. Well, not so great about trying to take his head off, but putting holes in walls with my energy sounded really satisfying. Then I remembered what had happened. He'd touched me and I'd lost it. I'd let my feelings get in the way of the training.

'Don't worry about it, Emma,' he said.

I struggled to speak.

'Leave it,' he said more firmly. 'It was my fault. I should never have touched you while you were holding the energy like that.'

I desperately wanted to tell him it was my own stupid fault.

'Emma Donahoe, this is a direct order. You will relax, you will not worry about it, you will rest. I am here. Simone is cared for. Leo is his usual difficult self. Rest.'

Great. A direct order. I had no choice. I let myself drift away.

I pulled myself upright to sit against the bedhead and looked around. He sat in a chair next to the bed, sleeping, his noble face peaceful.

He woke and smiled at me. 'Are you okay?'

'What happened?'

'Remember the energy work?'

I remembered everything and sagged back onto my pillow.

He saw my face. 'You did very well, Emma. I should not have touched you. I underestimated ...' His voice trailed off. I knew what he'd underestimated: my love for him.

'It's my own stupid fault,' I said. 'I shouldn't have let it get away from me like that.'

'I know you can't control it. I understand perfectly.'

I sighed. We both knew it. And there was not a damn thing we could do about it. I couldn't even hold his hand. Waste of time brooding on it; accept it and get over it.

I remembered what Leo had said. 'How long have you been sitting with me?'

'About three days.'

I raised the blanket and looked down at myself. I was in my pyjamas. I had absolutely no memory of how I'd made it there.

'Monica's been helping you,' he said. 'Every few hours you'd come around for a while, be almost coherent for about ten minutes, let her help you into the bathroom, then return to bed and sleep again.'

I shook my head. 'I don't remember any of it.'

'Perfectly normal.'

'And you've been sitting here with me for three days?'

He didn't say anything, just watched me.

'How much sleep have *you* been getting?'

He smiled slightly.

I tried to pull myself more upright to shout at him, but I couldn't. I pointed my finger at him instead. 'You take yourself out of here *right now*, go into your room and rest.'

He didn't move.

'My Lord.' I softened my voice. 'Simone needs you. Please. Go and rest. Conserve your energy. I'll be fine.'

He wasn't happy, but he rose and went to the door anyway.

Hey, this Retainer thing could work both ways.

'You needed me,' he said from the doorway.

'Not as much as Simone does.'

'But you needed me.'

'I'll always need you,' I whispered. 'And you won't always be there for me. But you know what? I'll survive.'

He opened the door and went out.

CHAPTER THIRTY-SIX

A couple of weeks later I was doing a tai chi set in the training room when Mr Chen came in with Bai Hu. Both of them ignored me completely and I returned the favour, continuing the set.

'There,' Mr Chen said, indicating the hole in the wall. It was close to the ceiling, about the size of a basketball; a huge dent in the concrete. If it had been an ordinary Western plaster wall it would have gone right through and possibly injured somebody. He hadn't had it painted over, and the paint was blistered and blackened around the edges, like a fireball had hit it.

'Whoa,' Bai Hu said. 'Impressive.'

'First time she did it,' Mr Chen said.

'What made her lose it?'

'Broken concentration.'

'Really? That's surprising,' Bai Hu said.

I ignored them.

'Tea?' Mr Chen said.

'Got any beer in this dump?' Bai Hu growled.

'Get your own.' Mr Chen went out.

Bai Hu stopped at the doorway. 'That is the most impressive damn thing I've seen in a hundred years. More than that. Shit, girl, you're talented. Any time you want to give this loser the flick, let me know. There's a nice suite in the Palace waiting for you.'

I still ignored him.

'Move your tail,' Mr Chen said from the hallway.

Bai Hu chuckled, a throaty growl, and went out.

Two Sundays later I was almost back to normal. I sneaked home early from my day off: the finals of the cricket were on and I hoped Simone and Mr Chen were out so I could watch it on the big screen in the TV room.

I stopped in the hallway and listened carefully. Nobody home. I made myself a pot of tea in the kitchen, grabbed some nuts, and settled myself in front of the television to watch the game. I desperately longed for a beer but I stuck with the tea.

About halfway through Australia's innings Mr Chen opened the door and poked his head around, nearly giving me a heart attack.

He glanced at the screen. 'Cricket?'

I shot to my feet. 'I'll be out of your way in a second.'

His hand snaked around the door and pointed at me. 'Don't you go anywhere. You stay right there. That's an order.' He pulled out and closed the door.

I cursed my stupidity as I cleared the table. This was the only day of the week that they didn't have the rest of us hanging around at home with them and I'd spoiled it for them.

The door opened and Simone toddled in, carrying her drawing equipment. She settled on the floor between the coffee table and the television and tipped out her pencils.

Mr Chen came in wearing his torn cotton pants and a faded black T-shirt and carrying a teacup. He threw himself to sit on the couch next to me and filled his cup from my pot.

'What's the score?' he said, pulling his legs up to sit cross-legged.

'India won the toss. They sent Australia in to bat. It's two for a hundred and thirty-two.'

'Bad move, India, letting the Aussies bat first. They'll be thrashed again. The Australian team are so good right now it's disgusting. We don't have a hope.'

'*You* don't have a hope?'

'England.' He leaned to grab some nuts. 'I've half a mind to go bowl for them. Too far from the Centre though. They might even take a Chinese on the national team now. I was selected, but the old ...' He took a breath and changed the word he was about to say. '... *gentlemen* on the board wouldn't have me on the team back then.'

I stared at him.

'Shame the next Ashes series isn't for a couple of years. I hope I can see it before I go,' he said without a hint of remorse. 'Damn. I could really do with a pint.'

That was it. I fell over sideways on the couch laughing. He watched me with bewilderment. 'What?'

I pulled myself upright. 'You've had beer?'

'Right now this old Shen is on a strict diet for health reasons,' he said amiably.

'So you're not vegetarian by choice?'

'Mostly vegetarian, but I do like the occasional bit of high-quality "cat food". Tuna's absolutely no good cooked, but pilchard is particularly tasty. Missed that. I wonder if the tins in the bottom of the cupboard are still good.'

My mouth flopped open.

'Oh, *human form*,' he said, smiling broadly. 'Strictly vegetarian. Right now I have to be careful. Mind my energy, don't you know.'

* * *

Later, we made some noodles for a snack in the kitchen together.

'Which saucepan, Daddy?' Simone said from behind the cupboard door.

'The medium-sized one,' Mr Chen said. 'Emma, there are some boxes of vegetable stock in the cupboard — could you get a couple out?'

'Sure,' I said, and went to the cupboard. The vegetable stock was on the middle shelf.

I quickly checked down the bottom. There were about ten tins of expensive 'cat food' there — mostly pilchards, but some prawn and cuttlefish too. There was also a perfectly ordinary cat's food bowl.

I grabbed the stock and handed it to him. His eyes sparkled as he took it. 'Now there should be ho fan in the fridge. Emma?'

I went to fetch the noodles while he poured the stock into the saucepan and turned on the heat.

'I want to stir, Daddy,' Simone said.

'Are you sure you won't "do a Simone"?' he said.

She paused, looking at him.

I handed him the noodle packet and he turned to open it.

'You'd better stir, Daddy,' Simone said.

We ate the noodles messily on the coffee table. They were even better than Monica's.

There was a tap on the door. It opened and Leo poked his nose in.

'We're watching the cricket,' Mr Chen said through a mouthful of noodles.

Leo snorted with disdain and closed the door.

'Too complicated for an American to understand,' Mr Chen said scathingly.

'I heard that,' Leo growled from the corridor.

I didn't know why we clapped and cheered when the game finished. It was a complete walkover; it was over before the required number of balls had even been bowled.

'You two are silly,' Simone said from the floor.

'Who do you think is more silly?' Mr Chen said.

'Oh, you are, Daddy, definitely.'

'Well, there you have it, Emma: the expert says that I am much sillier than you.'

'It's a close contest though.'

His grin didn't shift. 'Yep.'

The phone next to my computer rang. 'Emma,' I said.

'Call for you,' Monica said, and clicked it through.

I sighed. I hoped it wasn't Kitty Kwok again.

'Hi, Emma, long time no see. What you been doing with yourself?'

'Busy, Louise. How about you?'

'Lunch, Sha Tin, day after tomorrow? We can talk all about it. I want to hear exactly what's keeping you so busy.'

'Sure.'

I put the phone down and went down the hall. When I reached Mr Chen's office I raised my hand to tap on the door. Before I even touched it, he called from inside. 'Come on in, Emma.'

I went in and sat across from him. I sighed when I saw the pile of papers on his desk. 'I only tidied this three weeks ago. You hate me.'

He smiled slightly.

'And you knew I was coming as well. Stop wasting your energy.'

His gentle smile didn't shift.

'I'm going to lunch with Louise the day after tomorrow. It'll be in Sha Tin, so I'll probably be back late.'

'Are you asking my permission?'

'I don't know, am I?'

'You know you don't need to.'

'Yeah, I know.'

'Don't worry, I'll be here to mind Simone.'

'Good.' I rose to go out. 'When will Jade be back? I miss her. And Gold. It's quiet without them coming and going.'

He watched me silently.

'Where are they, John?'

He shook his head.

'How long? They've already been gone for two months.'

'A few more weeks. Give it time.'

'Are they okay? Nobody's hurting them?'

He smiled slightly again. 'Don't worry about them. They're fine.'

I turned to open the door.

'Emma.'

I turned back.

'Don't bother asking them where they were when they return. Don't ask, because if they tell you anything they are in serious trouble.'

I went back to my room and shuffled through my notes on Shen. When Shen died, they were supposed to go to Hell for a while and then return to Earth.

Hell. I had quite a lot of information about Hell. A complicated place; very bureaucratic. Ten levels. Judges at each level, meting out punishment. A lot of Hells.

I wished I'd visited the Tiger Balm Gardens in Causeway Bay before they'd been torn down. There had been detailed depictions of all of the Hells there.

Louise met me at the round atrium connecting Sha Tin station with the shopping mall. She looked just the same: blonde, bony and full of freckles and mischief.

She stopped dead when she saw me and her eyes widened. 'Is that you, Emma?'

'Of course it's me.' I linked my arm in hers.

'You look completely different,' she said. 'You've lost a lot of weight. And you have a great tan. Stop.' She pulled her arm from mine, grabbed my forearm and prodded it like a side of meat.

'What the hell are you doing?' I said, bewildered.

'Muscles. And you walk differently, like you own the world.'

'Well, I don't.'

'Your skin is glowing, your hair is shining, you have muscles — who's your personal trainer? Or are you pregnant?'

'I am definitely not pregnant,' I said grimly. 'Absolutely no chance of that.'

'What a shame,' Louise said cheerfully. 'I lose.'

'What do you lose?'

'I had a bet with April. She bet that you wouldn't be doing it with him by March. Looks like she was right.'

'Have you heard from her?'

'When we're in the restaurant.'

We walked through the central atrium of Sha Tin Town Centre. It was five storeys high, and open to the ceiling. A large oval musical fountain stood in the middle, but we walked past, ignoring it.

I looked around. 'Where are we going? It's all changed.'

'Downstairs,' Louise said. 'New food court. Some nice places.'

'But it has to be vegetarian for me.'

She stopped and stared at me. 'What?'

I shrugged and took her arm to start her walking again. 'Strictly vegetarian. I hope we can find something.'

She shook her head. 'What the hell for? Is it something to do with this Chen man who you're so most definitely *not* sleeping with?'

'Something like that,' I said. 'I'll tell you about it when we get there. Is there anywhere we don't have to wait too long?'

'Don't be ridiculous,' she said, grinning. 'This is Hong Kong, remember.'

'Yeah,' I said. 'You have to queue up for everything. Sometimes I wonder if the kids have to take a number and queue for a room at the love hotels.'

She cackled with delight. 'I love it.'

We found an Italian restaurant serving food adjusted for Chinese taste and took a number to wait. It would only be twenty minutes; not too bad for a weekday lunch.

'So why vegetarian?' Louise said.

I rolled out a story that I'd heard other vegetarians use successfully in the past. 'I eat so much vegetarian in the Chen household that if I eat meat now I don't feel well.' I shrugged. 'It's easier just to stay off it.'

'I couldn't do that,' Louise said.

A gruff male voice with a Cantonese accent interrupted us. 'Hi, Emma, who's your gorgeous friend? Look at the two of you. Good enough to eat.'

I turned to look at him. He appeared to be a perfectly ordinary good-looking Chinese in his mid-thirties, wearing tennis gear and holding a sports bag with a few tennis racquets in the pocket on the side.

Then I recognised him. He looked completely different with black hair. 'Bai Hu.'

Bai Hu bent over Louise. 'Who's your delicious friend, Emma?'

'Louise. Louise Wilson.' She grinned like a predator, then moved closer and held out her hand for him to shake.

He held it for much longer than necessary and didn't let go. I could almost see the sparks flying. 'Hi, Louise.'

'No *way* is she going to be number one hundred and one,' I hissed.

'Don't worry about Emma, she's an old fuddy-duddy,' Louise whispered to Bai Hu.

'Are you two waiting for lunch?' Bai Hu said without shifting his eyes from Louise's. He dropped his voice. 'How about I take you somewhere where you don't have to wait?'

'Disappear, *Tiger*,' I said fiercely. 'I am having lunch with my friend and you will not interfere.'

'No, please, Emma,' Louise said meaningfully. 'Let's go with him.' She used his hand to pull herself in closer and turned to stand next to him. She even nudged him with her hips.

Bai Hu shrugged. 'If the lady wants me along then I must concede. How about some Japanese? I know a good place upstairs, you won't have to wait.' He smiled down at Louise, still holding her hand. 'I'll buy.'

'If you're buying then you can have whatever you want,' Louise purred.

Bai Hu threw his bag over his shoulder and linked arms with Louise. 'Let me show you the way,' he said, completely ignoring me. 'It's really very good. Do you eat raw fish?'

'I'm willing to give it a try,' Louise said. 'I'm willing to give anything you like a try.'

'Get your paws off my friend!' I snarled, but he ignored me. 'Xuan Wu will hear about this!'

'What, Emma?' Louise said, without looking away from the Tiger.

'I'm a friend of Miss Donahoe's employer, Mr Chen,' Bai Hu said. 'Tiger Bak. Pleased to meet you.'

'Oh, very cute,' I said under my breath. 'Tiger White. Excellent.'

Louise glared at me. 'What's the problem, Emma?'

'Yeah, Emma, what's your problem?' Bai Hu said. 'Come and have lunch with your friend, just like you said you would.'

'I'm strictly vegetarian right now,' I said.

'Yes, of course you are. Don't worry, we'll find something for you up there.' He pulled Louise closer as they walked to the lifts. 'How much can you generate?'

'About a tennis ball, slightly more.' I dropped my voice. '*Get your paws off my friend!*'

'What are you talking about?' Louise said, bewildered.

'Oh, didn't you know? Young Emma here is learning martial arts from the Master himself,' Bai Hu said with relish.

'Your tail is in serious trouble,' I growled under my breath.

'No wonder you look so different,' Louise said without shifting her eyes from Bai Hu. 'Where are you taking me?'

We walked out of the lift and through the open-roof area of the shopping mall to the hotel. An upmarket Japanese restaurant was situated directly next to the hotel entrance.

'Here,' Bai Hu said. A large number of people stood around the entrance to the restaurant, obviously waiting for tables. The reception desk was deserted.

Bai Hu strode up to the desk, banged loudly on it with one hand, and shouted something extremely coarse in Cantonese that would require a great many four-letter words to translate into English.

The people standing around the entrance stared at him.

The receptionist stormed out from the back of the restaurant as quickly as she could in the constricting kimono, her face a mask of fury. Then she saw Bai Hu and her expression changed completely to one of warm welcome. She stopped and bowed very low to him, and gestured for him to enter without saying a word. He waved us in front of him.

He walked very close behind Louise as we went inside and she flushed through her freckles. I tried to kick him on the shins but he moved out of the way before I could hit him. He grinned at me, then pushed past me to guide Louise by the arm to a private room.

The waitress was servile, bobbing and smiling at Bai Hu. She opened the shoji screen to the private room and indicated for us to go in. We left our shoes outside the room and walked to the table set in the centre of the tatami mats.

Bai Hu threw his sports bag into a corner of the room, then moved to sit as close as he could to Louise. She nestled into him and gazed up into his eyes. He smiled down at her and took her hand.

'I'll be back in a minute,' I said, but they ignored me. He lowered his face to hers and she closed her eyes.

I raced out of the room, through the restaurant and into the telephone alcove next to the rest rooms. I pulled out my mobile phone and called home.

'Chen residence.'

'Quick, Leo, I need to talk to Mr Chen right now! Put me through!'

'Are you in trouble, Emma?'

'No, I just need to talk to Mr Chen *right now*!'

'Yes, Emma?'

'John.' I sighed with relief. 'You have to help me. I'm here at Sha Tin with Louise, and the White Tiger followed me. He's in the room with her, putting major moves on her. Help!'

'Wait.' He was silent for a moment. 'He said he was just there to play tennis with the general manager of the hotel. It was a coincidence.'

'But he's putting the moves on Louise!' I wailed softly. 'I don't want to lose her!'

'Hold.' Silence again. 'Emma, I'm sorry. If she decides to go with him it's her decision. He says she's actually ...' He hesitated. 'Well, let's just say he didn't need to put any moves on her at all.'

'But she won't know about all the others.'

'Yes, she will,' he said. 'He tells every single one of them exactly what they're getting into before he takes them. They all agree to go, fully aware of the situation.'

I stopped dead at that. 'I do not believe this. They agree to go and be one of a hundred?'

'I don't know how he does it.' He sounded amused. 'He doesn't hypnotise them, he doesn't cloud their minds. All he does is look at them. He's remarkable.'

'How can I get her out of this?'

'I have no idea.' He sounded unconcerned. 'Is it any of your business anyway?'

'She wouldn't have met him if I didn't know him already.'

'Yes, she would,' he said. 'He goes to Sha Tin all the time. He owns the hotel. They would have run into each other eventually.'

'Damn!'

'If she's going out with someone already then he will keep his paws off her. That is the only hope she has. Otherwise, he will regard her as fair game.'

'You are absolutely no help whatsoever, you know that?'

'Sorry,' he said, without a hint of remorse. 'Is that all? No demons or anything otherwise?'

'Good*bye*,' I snapped, and flicked the phone shut.

I stormed back to the private room.

Bai Hu and Louise were gazing into each other's eyes, their faces barely apart. There was a dish of sashimi on the table that both of them completely ignored.

'All right, you two,' I said. 'Bai Hu, get your ugly paws off my friend. I will *not* lose her to your harem. Louise ...' She ignored me so I went to her and shoved her shoulder. 'Don't get yourself mixed up with this bastard. I know him and he's *bad news*.'

Louise snapped out of it and smiled up at me. 'Did you know that Tiger owns this hotel?'

'Don't get involved with him, Louise. I don't want to lose you.'

'Stay out of it, Emma,' the Tiger said, without looking away from Louise. 'It's her decision to make. And I could give her more than she could ever want.'

She gazed up at the Tiger with adoration. 'You're just jealous. You have your Mr Chen, leave me alone.'

The Tiger's head snapped around to me. 'What's this? You and him?'

I turned away and sat in a chair on the other side of the table. 'Nothing.'

'Look at her,' Louise said, still holding Bai Hu's hand. 'Head over heels for her Mr Chen.'

The Tiger dropped Louise's hand. She didn't seem to notice. 'I thought he was joking.'

I ran my hands through my hair. 'He was. Nothing there.'

Bai Hu rose and came around to my side of the table. He sat next to me and studied my face.

I looked at Louise. She sat frozen, smiling at us.

'You've done something to her.'

'Of course. We need to talk.' He saw my face. 'Don't be a fool, Emma. You know it can't happen.'

I dropped my head with misery. 'Too late, Bai Hu.'

'And him?' His eyes unfocused. He snapped back to me and smiled sadly. 'Damn, but you are a pair of fools.'

I shook my head. 'We know.'

He glanced at Louise. 'I'm sorry. I won't contact your friend again. I think you need her.' He turned back to me. 'What are you going to do?'

I sighed with defeat. 'I'll take each day as it comes. I'll enjoy the time I have left with him. I'll be strong when he goes, and I'll survive. And when he's gone, I'll look after that wonderful little girl for the rest of my life.'

'And him?' His eyes unfocused again for a moment. 'He says pretty much the same thing you do, Emma. He says he'll enjoy what he has with you until he goes.' His voice broke. 'He wishes he could tell you how he feels to your face without hurting you.' He shook his head. 'What a pair of fools.'

'Are you communicating with him now?' I whispered.

He nodded without looking up.

'Could you tell him . . .' I hesitated, searching for the words. 'Could you tell him that I know? That he doesn't need to say anything? Because words aren't really necessary between us.'

'Is what's between you really that true?' the Tiger whispered.

'Yes.'

He smiled. 'He said yes too.' He waved one hand.

Louise jerked upright. 'What's going on?'

The Tiger pulled himself to his feet. 'I just remembered, I have somebody I have to meet, but don't worry, lunch is on me.' He smiled down at Louise, who appeared bewildered. 'You're absolutely stunning, Louise, but there's somebody else right now and it wouldn't be right.'

'No, please, Tiger, stay,' she said, desperate.

He grabbed his sports bag, went to the door and pulled his tennis shoes on. 'Order anything you like.

And tell him that next time I see him, I'm going to punch him in the nose.'

'Who?' Louise said.

'Bye, Louise, it's been a great deal of pleasure,' he said, and went out. As soon as he was outside the door, he looked around and disappeared.

Louise rushed to the door. 'Wait!'

'He's gone, Louise.'

She sighed. 'God, he was wonderful.'

'He already has a lot of wives,' I said. '*Lots* of wives.'

'So?' She turned back to me. 'You know his number?'

'No. I have no way of contacting him, and even if I did I wouldn't give it to you. Come on, let's order something.'

'Suddenly I'm starving.' Louise's eyes sparkled. 'Owns the hotel, huh?' She sat down and looked at the sashimi. 'Raw fish? Did we order raw fish?'

'No, *you* ordered raw fish.'

'Oh.' She picked up a menu as if nothing had happened. 'Did you hear about April?'

'I heard she's in some trouble,' I said, wondering how much Louise knew, and how much I could give away.

'Her husband has another wife. That's why he didn't go to Australia. Did she tell you?'

'Yes, I know all about it.'

'Baby too?'

I nodded. 'She didn't have an abortion, did she? I'd hate to think she aborted the baby just because her husband didn't want it.'

'She negotiated with him and they came to an arrangement. He's paying for her to live in a flat in Discovery Bay, a long way away. She's going to have the baby, and he'll pay for the flat and a domestic helper for her. Apart from that, they have hardly any contact at all.' She sighed. 'God, Emma, her life's a wreck. But you know what?'

'What?'

'She's *happy*,' Louise hissed. 'She says that Australia was too boring. She's looking forward to having the baby and going back to work.'

'Well,' I said, picking up the menu to find something vegetarian, 'women do incredibly stupid things for the love of a man.'

'I wonder if Tiger comes past here often,' she pondered quietly. 'Owns the hotel, huh?'

CHAPTER THIRTY-SEVEN

The train taking me home rattled along the outdoor line, through the Lion Rock Tunnel and into Kowloon. Kowloon Tong station was next, and the interchange with the MTR.

I stepped off the train and joined the crowd heading into the MTR station. I felt the coldness behind me and knew immediately what it was. I didn't bother looking back; there were thousands of people all around me, the post-lunchtime crowd.

They followed me all the way to the MTR train; four of them. They stood in the middle of the train and ignored me. They looked like salesmen, in their mid-twenties and wearing cheap suits. I stood at the end of the carriage, next to the driver's cab. I called Leo as the train rushed through the darkness of the Cross-Harbour Tunnel.

'How far away from the pick-up point are you, Leo?'

'I'm already waiting for you. Hurry up, I could get booked again.' Then he inhaled sharply. 'You got some?'

'Four,' I whispered into the phone. 'About level fifteen or twenty. Too big to take by myself.'

'There should be a lot of people around.'

'There are. I'm okay. I'm glad you're there, though.'

'So am I. Stay on the phone — keep me informed. I'm coming down to the platform to wait for you.'

'What about the car?'

'To hell with the car.'

The train stopped, the doors opened and just about everybody piled out to take the Island line. I stayed on the train to go to Central. I stole a glance through the nearly deserted carriage; there were only three or four other people left now.

The demons saw me looking at them and wandered up to me, smiling, acting like they knew me.

'They're coming for me, Leo,' I hissed.

The train stopped at Central station and the doors opened. The remaining people left the carriage. The demons stood between me and the doors. I realised I should never have stood so far from the exit; I hoped I'd have a chance to learn from my mistake.

The doors closed again. Trapped until the next station.

Leo charged through the demons and they scattered. He grabbed my arm and dragged me down the carriage aisle. There were no partitions between carriages on MTR trains, to make it more difficult for muggers. We walked as quickly as possible to the middle of the train, where an elderly couple sat together, asleep on one of the side benches.

The demons followed us.

As we approached the elderly couple they rose. I realised with an ice-cold shock that they were demons too.

I looked back. The other demons were right on top of us. The ones in front of us stood and waited.

The train stopped and the doors opened. We hustled off the train and along the platform to the exit. The demons followed us.

'Damn,' Leo whispered.

Sheung Wan was one of the quietest MTR stations. We had five storeys of escalators and stairs to go up to reach ground level, with endless corridors in between. And nobody around.

We took the escalator, running up the steps to reach the top faster. A long corridor with a curved tiled ceiling lay ahead. Three demons, appearing as young office girls in pastel business suits, waited for us.

Leo and I stopped. The demons behind us came up the escalators and stopped as well.

Leo and I moved back to back. I faced the office girls: they were smaller, only about level ten. Leo faced the others, the four salesmen and the elderly couple. They were about level twenty.

'Looks like they're going to get their answer,' I said.

'Not much we can do, is there?' Leo said.

'Nope.'

The three girls threw themselves at me and I didn't have time to think. I grabbed the closest one by the outstretched arm as she came for me and flung her into the one directly behind her. I kicked the third one in the abdomen at the same time, and I was through her. She dissolved.

The remaining two crashed into each other and staggered back, then recovered and dived at me again. I ducked the roundhouse fist that came at me, hit one of them in the abdomen with my own fist, then dropped and spun, taking the feet out from under the other one.

The first demon exploded. The second hit the floor and stayed there, obviously dazed. I fell on top of her and ran my fist through her face.

I ducked instinctively without even realising. The elderly woman had tried for my head. I grabbed her hand, flipped her over and ran my fist through her face as well.

I quickly checked around me: quiet. Leo pulled himself to his feet. I rose as well.

'Are you okay?' he said.

I wiped my hands on my jeans. 'Yep. Fine. You?'

He shrugged. 'They didn't lay a finger on me. Not even a scratch.' He raised his hands. 'Just filthy.'

I raised my hands as well. 'Me too.'

Suddenly we fell into each other's arms and held each other, laughing fit to burst. Then we pulled back and wiped our eyes with our shirts; the demon stuff was stuck to our hands and would sting like anything if we rubbed it into our eyes.

'You were great,' he said, gasping.

'So were you.' I took a deep breath. 'You think the car's still there?'

'Not a chance.'

'We'll have trouble getting a taxi looking like this.'

'I know.' He wiped his hands on his slacks. 'Damn. Another pair ruined.'

He pulled out his mobile phone and gingerly pressed the buttons, trying not to get too much black stuff on it. 'Mr Chen, please, Monica.'

He paused, then, 'We were attacked by demons in Sheung Wan station, my Lord. It's highly likely that the car's been towed ... Theatre Lane, I went down into the station to meet her. She was being followed ... Nope, we're both fine.' He spoke with more force. 'Sir, we're *fine*. They didn't lay a finger on us, we're okay. Really.' He sighed in exasperation and handed the phone to me. 'Talk to him, Emma.'

Mr Chen sounded desperate. 'Are you sure you're okay? Is Emma all right? She hasn't been hurt?'

'John,' I said, and he went silent. 'I'm just fine. Both Leo and I are okay.'

'Thank the Heavens,' he said.

'But we need to find a way home — the car's probably been towed. We're both covered in demon stuff and we'll have trouble finding a taxi.'

'Hold.' He was silent for a while. Then, 'There will be a white Mercedes waiting for you at exit B of Sheung Wan station. The driver will bring you home.' His voice softened. 'Are you sure you're okay, Emma? You're not hurt?'

'John, I am absolutely fine, and the sooner you stop talking to me, the sooner I can get home and get this disgusting stuff off me.'

'Hurry home, Emma,' he said, and hung up.

'Does this car belong to Bai Hu?' I asked the driver of the white Mercedes.

'Yes, ma'am,' the driver said. 'I just brought it round from the hotel in Western.'

'Sorry about the demon stuff,' Leo said.

'Not a problem, sir. Happens all the time.'

'All the time?' I said.

'I often take the Lord Bai Hu's sons out demon-hunting, and they usually return in a far worse state than you are now.' He glanced in the mirror and smiled at Leo. 'It's an honour to be driving the Black Lion.'

Leo hesitated, then, 'Thanks.'

'Why do they call you that?' I whispered.

'Because they all hate me.'

After we'd showered at home we met in the dining room and told Mr Chen all about the attack.

He sighed and rubbed his hands over his face. 'Well, we knew this day would come.'

'You'll have to cut back on the social activities, Emma, until you can handle about six or eight level twenties yourself,' Leo said. 'Until then, I think you're probably a major target.'

'He's right,' Mr Chen said. 'Don't go out by yourself any more, at least not until you have the energy work mastered. It's too dangerous.'

'Damn,' I said softly. 'Will I be able to go out with Jade when she comes back?'

'Absolutely. But I'm afraid you should only see your human friends if you invite them up here.'

'Well, then,' I said briskly, 'let's get stuck into the training, so I can defend myself if they come after me. I don't want my social life on hold for any longer than absolutely necessary.'

They both stared at me.

'What?'

'You are an extremely remarkable woman,' Mr Chen said.

'To hell with that. You are the most cold-blooded chick I've ever laid eyes on,' Leo said.

'You say that like being cold-blooded is a bad thing,' Mr Chen said.

'Sorry, sir.' Leo looked sheepish.

'What on earth for?' I said.

'Yes, Leo, why are you apologising?'

Leo was obviously desperately embarrassed. Mr Chen and I shared a sly look.

'Dismissed, Leo. Emma, stay.'

Leo rose. He saluted Mr Chen, 'Sir,' and went out.

As soon as he was gone Mr Chen and I collapsed over the table, laughing.

'His face was priceless,' he wheezed.

'We are *so bad*.'

'I've never managed to make him call me a Turtle to my face,' he said.

'Oh, a challenge,' I said. 'Let me work on it.'

He stopped laughing and smiled. He opened his mouth, then closed it again.

'No need to say anything, John.' I rose and opened the door. 'And it's mutual.' I went out.

* * *

'What's this — demon training?' I asked Leo when we met outside the training room the next day.

'No idea,' Leo said, and tapped on the door.

'Enter,' Mr Chen called, and we went in together. Leo closed the door softly behind us.

'Good,' he said when he saw both of us there.

Leo and I saluted, then waited patiently.

Mr Chen went to the staff rack and pulled out two staves, one slightly heavier than the other. He tossed the heavier one to Leo and the lighter one to me. He gestured. 'Leo this end. You both warmed up already?' We nodded. 'Good.'

He linked his hands behind his back as Leo and I moved into position. 'This is not a test of ability. It is a test of skill. Attack the staff, not the opponent. Leo, don't hold back. Emma, I think you're ready.'

I stiffened. This was my first time sparring with Leo. I wasn't worried, though; in fact, my immediate reaction was: *yes!*

Mr Chen looked from me to Leo, his eyes burning. 'If either of you feels it is going out of control, *call immediately*. If either of you is injured, it is your own fault. Now,' He moved to the corner, leaned on the wall and crossed his arms over his chest. 'Even though I know it's a total waste of time, I'm giving both of you the opportunity to back out now. Call now if you don't want to go through with this.'

Leo and I looked at each other. Then we both grinned.

'Bring it on,' I said.

Leo spun his staff and flicked it under his arm, putting his left hand out into a guard. I held mine in front, defence. We nodded to each other, ready.

'Go,' Mr Chen said quietly. Neither of us moved.

Leo came for me first. He attacked with his staff straight out in front, swinging it to hit mine right in the middle. Confident. Thought he could take it in one.

I used my staff to block his, twisted my body, and sent him lurching to the other side of the room with a quick flick, using the staff as a lever. I didn't give him time to recover; I went in after him and tried to sweep the staff out of his hands with an upward attack. He only managed to hold onto the staff because he was stronger.

'Good,' Mr Chen said from the corner.

I let my staff slide up Leo's, spun and jumped back, guarding, ready for him. He put his staff out in front of him and came straight at me. Once again I used my staff as a lever, sweeping along his and trying to swipe it out of his hands. Again he managed to hold it.

I suddenly knew that although he had the edge in strength, I had the edge in speed.

Holy shit. I was faster than Leo, and he was one of the fastest I'd ever seen, short of Mr Chen.

I jumped back, spun my staff with delight, snapped it under my arm and put my right hand out into a guard. Come and get me, Lion. I can take you.

He didn't think. He came for me. He did exactly what I wanted. I watched him carefully as he swung his staff at my lower legs, trying to sweep my feet out from under me. I easily stepped over the staff. I used my own and helped it along, giving it a good push in the direction it was already going, then spun mine in my hands and used it to twist his foot from under him. He fell with a thud.

He flipped himself upright and moved into position again.

'Hold!' Mr Chen shouted from the corner. We immediately halted, turned and snapped to attention, the tips of our staves on the floor next to us.

'Having fun?' Mr Chen growled.

Neither of us said anything. Then we both stiffened with horror.

Oh my God, he said *attack the staff*. Both of us went for *each other*. We were in *big trouble*. I could see from Leo's body language that he was thinking exactly the same thing.

'Emma, you will sharpen every single sword in this room until it will cut a silk scarf dropped on it from the height of a metre. I will provide the silk. Leo ...' Mr Chen scowled. 'You went for Emma first. You will sharpen every other bladed weapon in the room to a similar edge. I will come back in two hours and you will each demonstrate your work.'

He stalked away from the wall, then stopped between us. 'Emma, you are absolutely the fastest damn human I have ever seen in my entire life. I knew the minute I had you sparring with Leo I'd see it. Faster than Li. Faster than anybody. I must start you on larger demons immediately. With that speed you could probably take a level fifteen without difficulty.' He grinned broadly. 'You're amazing,' he whispered. Then his face closed up again. 'Go and get the stones and sharpen those blades. And next time, both of you, *try* to do what I tell you.' He sighed with resignation. 'I really don't know what to do with the pair of you.'

We each saluted, staff in hand. 'Yes, sir.' But I couldn't control the huge grin on my face. Leo was grinning as well.

'He's right. I've never seen a human that damn fast before either,' Leo said as we went through the kitchen to the storeroom to find the whetstones. 'I never knew Li when he was training with Mr Chen — he was gone long before I was here — but everybody knows how fast he was, he was almost inhuman. And you could take him.'

'Are you okay, Leo?'

'Are you kidding? Staves, day off, I know a place — how about it? Full on, no quarter, you and me, what do you think?'

411

'You are damn well on,' I said. 'I can take you any day of the week.'

'We'll see about that. Now I know how fast you are I can deal with it easily. But if either of us gets injured we will be in deep trouble.'

'You won't have a chance to get injured. It will be all over before you even know it's started,' I said, and quickly ducked.

I raised my hand and rested the tip of my staff on the floor. 'Stop, Leo, I'm done. You can best me. I concede.' I stretched my left arm. 'And my arms are ready to drop off.'

Leo lowered his staff, then strode to me and quickly embraced me. 'Mine too.'

We both stiffened when we heard a loud round of applause. We turned to face the glass frontage of the tae kwon do dojo. A crowd of delighted residents of South Horizons, Ap Lei Chau Island's major residential development, had been watching us. They cheered loudly when they saw us notice them. Both of us quickly saluted them, staves in hand, and the cheers became even wilder.

'Did you know we had an audience?' I said.

'No idea.'

'Wonder how many of them are demon spies.'

'Probably at least two or three. They have your number now, Emma.'

I shrugged. 'Completely worth it.'

The owner of the dojo came up to us, his face full of delight. He put one hand on Leo's arm and pumped his hand with the other. 'Thank you, my friend, that was magnificent.' He nodded to me. 'Both of you are magnificent. Can you come back next Sunday? I have had thirty or so people asking to learn tae kwon do because of what they've seen. Will you come and teach? Please?'

Leo and I shared a look.

'I may be able to come in on an occasional Sunday and help out,' Leo said. 'But Emma's not ready.'

'She looks thoroughly ready to me.'

'I'm just a junior compared to Leo,' I said. 'I'm really not qualified to teach anybody.'

'You are as skilled as anybody I've seen,' he said with awe. 'How long have you been learning?'

'Years,' I said.

Leo nodded. If I told Mr Kim the truth, that I had been learning for less than a year, he wouldn't believe me. He'd think that I was playing him for a fool or showing off.

'You sure you won't come in and teach?'

'I'm sorry, I can't.'

He shrugged. 'Very well.' He grinned at Leo. 'Thank you, my friend. Come and let me give you something cool to drink. Both of you are exhausted.'

'Thanks.'

When we arrived home after dinner Mr Chen charged out of his study and pointed at us. 'Both of you, in the dining room, right now.'

We sat across from him.

'Emma, the demons now know *exactly* how good you are. Why have you done this stupid thing?'

I shrugged.

'Leo, was this your idea?'

'Yes, my Lord.'

He glared at us. 'Leo, swords. Emma, bladed weapons.'

'Yes, sir,' we said in unison, saluting.

'Is this going to happen again?'

'No, sir.'

'Shall I pin a target to your back, Emma?'

'I think there's one there already, my Lord.'

He winced, then rounded on Leo. 'How about a sign, Leo? "The God of Martial Arts teaches me; challenge me and see how good I am"?'

'What she said, my Lord. There's one already there.'

He sighed with exasperation. 'Go and sharpen those blades.'

We both rose, fell to one knee saluting him, and went out.

There were twenty-nine swords and sixty-three other weapons with blades. After we'd finished sharpening them, neither of us could move.

But it had been completely worth it.

CHAPTER THIRTY-EIGHT

We stood opposite the mirrors as Simone floated the chi around the room.

'Back to your hands,' Mr Chen said.

The chi returned to Simone's hands and hovered above her outstretched palms.

'Back inside.'

She took a deep breath, her eyes widened, and the chi dropped into her hands.

'Good. How do you feel?'

She glanced up at him. 'I feel okay.'

'Do you need to sit?'

'No, I'm okay, Daddy.'

'Good. Emma.'

I generated the chi and held it above my hands. I had slightly more than Simone had managed.

'To the mirrors.'

I floated it off my hands and moved it towards the mirrors.

'Now. Try something. Walk to the centre of the mats, leaving the chi there. Sometimes you will need to move yourself while you have the chi. Do you think you can do it?'

I concentrated on keeping the chi motionless and nodded.

'Try.'

I took a careful step forward, still holding the chi next to the mirrors. I wanted to say how difficult it was, but I couldn't speak and perform the tasks at the same time.

'Way to go, Emma,' Leo whispered from the doorway, breaking my concentration. The chi snapped back and hit me in the abdomen, knocking me flat.

I came around with their concerned faces hovering above me. I raised my hand. 'Help me up, Leo.'

Leo took my hand and helped me to my feet. I staggered and he put his arm around my shoulders to hold me.

'I'm okay,' I said, pushing him away. 'It goes away very quickly.'

'Sorry, Emma,' he said.

I shoved him. 'I'm ready. Let's try it again.'

'No,' Mr Chen said. 'I think you've done enough for the day. Both you and Simone are ready, Emma. We'll all go to the house on the hill in Guangzhou for a couple of weeks, there's more space for you to move the chi around there. Leo, help Emma back to her room.' I opened my mouth to protest. 'Let him, Emma, that's an order. You are very drained and I think you need the assistance.'

'How do you do that?' Leo asked as he helped me down the hallway. 'Do you just concentrate and it comes out?'

'Something like that,' I said. 'All of the tai chi and chi gung work that we did before leads up to being able to move the energy outside the body.'

'I do them too. Do you think I could do the chi if I tried?'

I stopped and looked up at him. 'You know what would happen if you did, Leo.'

He opened my bedroom door. 'Yeah. But sometimes I think it would be worth it.'

After he'd helped me inside I embraced him and buried my face in his huge chest. 'Leo, if you try to do energy work and activate the virus, you won't die from it because I'll kill you first. Simone and I need you. We all need you.'

He stroked my hair. 'Yeah. I know.'

'Promise me you won't try.'

'I promise,' he whispered, then released me and went out.

A week later we threw our duffel bags into the boot of the Mercedes and headed out to the border. After an hour of driving we reached the riding club where Mr Chen kept his horse. Leo parked the car. Mr Chen grabbed a small rucksack from the floor of the car and went into the club.

'Why are we stopping here?' I asked Leo over the back of the seat.

'Wait and see,' Leo said.

Simone giggled.

My mobile rang and I managed to get to it in my bag before it stopped ringing. 'Emma.'

'Hello, Emma, it's Kitty.'

I sighed. 'Hi, Miss Kwok.'

'Kitty, please, Emma.' Her voice was kind. 'I haven't seen you in ages, where have you been? You haven't been to the last two charity functions I arranged. Have you been sick?'

'No, no, I was there.' Just avoiding her.

'You must come and visit me, Emma. Come up to my house for lunch sometime. I'd love to see you. How about tomorrow?'

'I'm sorry, Kitty, but I'm in China with Mr Chen, and it looks like we'll be here for a while.'

Mr Chen returned to the car, but he looked completely different. He appeared to be in his mid-sixties, overweight and balding, and he'd changed out of his usual black clothes into a poorly fitting navy business suit. He opened the rear door. 'Move over, Simone, I'll sit in the back.'

Simone giggled and shifted over for him.

'I have something I need to do, Kitty. Talk to you when I'm back in Hong Kong,' I said, and hung up. Enough!

Mr Chen climbed clumsily into the car, pulled a ridiculous pair of plastic-rimmed glasses out of his jacket pocket and put them on.

'You look absolutely adorable,' I said.

'He looks *stupid*,' Simone said.

'Why did you change your appearance?'

'My travel document says I'm sixty-four years old. Gold was in the process of arranging a new one, but he never made it in time. Who was that on the phone?'

I glared at my mobile. 'Kitty Kwok. She keeps calling me to talk me into visiting her at her house.'

'She must really like you.'

I shoved the phone back into my bag. 'Well, I don't like her.'

Leo drove out of the club to the border crossing. The car had both Hong Kong and Mainland licence plates; very common for people who often travelled across the border. When we reached the crossing we didn't even need to get out of the car. The officials checked our exit documents at the first gate, then we drove a couple of hundred metres and the guards at the second gate checked our entry documents.

It was strange to be on the right side of the road after so long driving on the left in Hong Kong.

'I'm letting my hair go, Leo,' Mr Chen said. 'I can't hold it. Tell me if we approach a checkpoint.'

'My Lord,' Leo said.

Mr Chen grew his hair back out to its usual length with a sigh of relief, but nothing else about his appearance changed. His hair covered Simone's face and she huffed and blew it out of the way.

'Sorry, sweetheart,' he said and brushed his hair to one side. 'How about that?'

'That's better,' she said, and grinned.

The road was four lanes wide and planted with flowers on both sides; something not often seen in Hong Kong. After about forty minutes on the highway, Leo pulled off onto a narrower winding road that led into some hills. He slowed the car and carefully negotiated the turns.

We passed through a village of ugly brick and concrete houses. There were no sidewalks, only dirt and mud paths. Piles of rubbish and open drains lined the sides of the road. A few bored-looking young women in brightly coloured pants and jackets stood behind ramshackle stalls selling alcohol and cigarettes. We passed a butcher, huge cleaver in hand, with pieces of pig — lungs and intestines — hanging in the open air from the rails of his stall. A few grubby children emerged from one of the houses and ran beside the car for a while, then gave up.

Further up the hillside, past the village, the potholed bitumen changed to gravel that crunched under the wheels of the car. Leo slowed even more.

Close to the top of the hill we turned off the gravel onto a narrow dirt track that twisted through bamboo groves. Leo slowed the car to a crawl and we inched through the cool greenery.

As we approached the top of the hill the bamboo opened up. We passed through a Chinese-style gate topped with green tiles, adorned with complex calligraphy and flanked by a pair of stone lions. Leo drove slowly through and we came to a high red stone wall with similar green tiles on top. A groove of putty ran along the top of the wall, with shards of broken glass set in it.

Mr Chen raised his hand and the black steel gates in front of us swung smoothly open.

'You can get young again now, Daddy,' Simone said.

'Can't,' he said. 'I'd break these clothes and I need them to go back in.'

She giggled.

'You know other kids' dads can't do that, Simone,' I said. 'When you go to school you can't talk about it.'

'I know that, silly Emma.' Simone gazed up at her father with adoration. 'My daddy's *really special*.'

'So are you,' he said.

We drove for about three hundred metres along the driveway then crested the hill. A huge white concrete mansion with a green tiled roof nestled into the hillside on the other side. The view from the top of the hill was spectacular, overlooking the fish ponds and rice paddies below. The haze of pollution from Shenzhen economic zone, where many goods for the West were manufactured, made the horizon a blur.

'We're lucky we're so high here — we're out of the pollution,' I said. 'I should be able to generate twice as much chi.'

'That's why I brought you,' Mr Chen said.

Leo stopped the car in front of the house. Two gardeners who had been trimming a hedge dropped their tools and rushed inside.

A tiny round-faced middle-aged Chinese lady wearing the traditional black pants and white jacket of a servant came out the front door.

Mr Chen leapt out of the car and charged into the house without stopping, his long hair flying. The servant smiled indulgently as he passed her. Simone jumped out of the car and ran to the servant. The woman hugged Simone, then walked to the car holding her hand.

Leo opened the boot. The gardeners and another female servant came out of the house to help him with the bags.

The servant holding Simone's hand came to me and said in perfect English, 'Hello, madam. I am Ah Yat.'

'I'm Emma, and I'm not madam, I'm just the nanny.'

'Yes, Miss Emma.' Ah Yat smiled down at Simone. 'Long time no see, my darling.'

'I'm *hungry*,' Simone said.

'Come with me.' Ah Yat patted my arm. 'I have tea.'

The minute she touched me, I knew. Ah Yat was a demon. I took Simone's arm and pulled her away.

'Emma, stop!' Simone shouted. 'Don't do anything! It's okay!'

Leo grabbed me from behind and held me before I could attack Ah Yat.

'What the hell are you doing, Leo? It's a *demon*!' I shouted.

Ah Yat stood silently and watched us with amusement.

'Emma, calm down, it won't hurt anybody,' Leo said into my ear. 'It's a tame one.'

I stopped struggling. Leo released me.

Simone put her little hands on her hips and scowled. 'Don't you dare hurt Ah Yat! She's a *good* demon.'

I rounded on Leo and stuck my finger into his chest. 'Why the hell didn't you tell me? I could have destroyed her!' I dropped my voice to speak with more menace and continued to poke him in the chest, making him take a step back. 'The next time there is something I should know that is *important enough to save my life*, you had better tell me, Mr Alexander.'

Leo opened his mouth to protest and then realised I was talking about more than just Ah Yat. He rubbed the back of his neck, sheepish.

'Watch my chi,' I said softly. 'It will be out to get you next time.'

I turned back to Ah Yat. 'So sorry, Ah Yat, but these *stupid* people didn't think it would be necessary to tell me about you.'

'Not a problem, Miss Emma. You have done very well to spot me. Master Leo didn't pick me at all when he first met me. Would you like some tea?'

'Absolutely,' I said, and followed her into the house.

Ah Yat sat us in the kitchen and presented us with a pot of Chinese tea.

'How long have you worked for Lord Xuan Wu?' I said.

'About ...' She stopped and her face went strange. Then she snapped back. 'Sorry, Miss Emma. I am the head demon here. I tell the others what to do. I have been in the Dark Lord's service for nearly six hundred years.' She put a saucepan on the stove to make some instant ramen for Simone. 'I am close to attaining perfection and gaining humanity.'

'I don't want you to go, Ah Yat,' Simone said.

'Don't you want me to be human and live a real life?'

Simone screwed up her little face with deliberation. 'Yes, but I want you to stay here and look after us too.'

'The Dark Lord will not release me until he is sure that I am no longer needed.'

'Good,' Simone said, relieved, and slurped her apple juice.

'What do you have to do to attain perfection?' I said.

Ah Yat stirred the noodles. 'There are a number of paths a demon may choose to follow. Serving a mighty lord such as Lord Xuan Wu is one of them. If I serve him well, he will put in a recommendation for me when I am ready. I am nearly there.'

She poured the noodles into a bowl and presented them to Simone. 'Take care, my darling, they are very hot. Wait a moment, I will cool them.' She put one hand over the noodles and concentrated. 'There.'

'Thanks, Ah Yat,' Simone said. She pulled the noodles closer and attacked them with gusto.

'Where do you buy your groceries?' I said. 'You're miles from anywhere here.'

'The Dark Lord has a house in the city. I travel to that house, walk out the door and do the shopping. Then I return to the house and travel here. To others it appears that I live in the city.'

'I can see why he has this particular type of staff up here. Normal people would be limited by its remoteness.'

'We are *demons*, Miss Emma. Do not hesitate to say the word. We are aware of our nature and are working to overcome it, with help from the Dark Lord.' She sighed through her smile. 'It is true bliss to serve in such a manner.'

One of the male demons, Ah Sum, showed me to my room. It was decorated like a colonial-style hotel, with white wicker furniture and a large window overlooking the spectacular view. A fluffy double bed sat under the window, and a pair of rattan chairs flanked a side table. Another chair sat under a desk on the other side of the room, beneath a large mirror with a white wicker frame. It was spotlessly clean, and the demons had already unpacked for me and put my clothes into the dresser.

'Is your name Number Three?' I asked Ah Sum.

'That is correct. Ah Yat is Number One, Ah Yee is Number Two, I am Number Three, and Ah Say is Number Four.'

'You should have real names. Just being numbers isn't really enough.'

'We are delighted to be called anything, ma'am,' he said, and went out.

A while later there was a tap on the door. 'Come in,' I said.

Mr Chen came in, stood uncomfortably for a moment, then flopped down in one of the rattan chairs next to the wall. He raised his hands. 'I don't know what to say.'

I leaned on the desk, facing him. 'Sorry would be a good place to start.'

He rose and bowed slightly. 'My apologies, Miss Donahoe.'

'What else haven't you told me? Things that I need to know?'

'Probably a lot, Emma.'

'Great. One day you'll forget to tell me something important and you'll get me *killed*.' I sighed with exasperation. 'The demon Wong — while you were on the Mountain. Do you know what he said?'

Mr Chen watched me, expressionless.

'He suggested that I pay you a midnight visit. He said we could have years. He was right, wasn't he? We *do* have years. He made sense. So I did.'

He opened his mouth and I stopped him with a raised hand.

'I had my hand on your door. I don't know what stopped me. I was so close to going in to you and getting myself killed.' I banged the desk with frustration. 'It was such a close thing, you know? Ms Kwan told me, she warned me. If she hadn't told me the next day I would probably have gone to you that night. Gone right in there and let you kill me.'

He opened his mouth to say something but I cut him off. 'And you did *absolutely nothing* to warn me! You

424

didn't tell me, you didn't ask Leo to tell me — what the hell is wrong with you?'

The anguish on his face made my heart ache.

'You didn't tell me that the demons might try me out. I was wandering around town blithely unaware of the fact that they could crawl out of the woodwork any minute and have a go at me.'

He looked away.

'*And* you never told me that Ah Yat was a tame demon. She's only a level six, John, I could destroy her with one arm behind my back! Six hundred years of hard work, gone! Enough, all right? You have to *tell me* the things I need to know!'

I dropped into the wicker chair next to him and ran my hands through my hair. The thought came unbidden: I loved this stupid man so much. And I couldn't even touch him.

He rose and moved in front of me. He held out his hand and I eyed it suspiciously. He nodded reassurance, so I took his hand, trusting him completely. I fully expected his touch to kill me, but nothing happened. He raised me so that I stood facing him, both his cool hands holding mine.

He looked into my eyes. His face was still expressionless, a mask of restraint, but his dark eyes were glittering and I could see it all. He was close to losing control. If he did, I was dead.

He quickly dropped my hands and backed to the other side of the room.

'It would be worth it,' I said softly.

'No, it wouldn't. I love you too much to lose you.'

I froze at his words. We stood silently and gazed at each other across the width of the room.

He moved half a step towards me, then moved back again. 'I can't hold it, Emma. There are no more secrets now. But I must go, before I lose control and hurt you.'

I nodded and turned away. He went out, closing the door softly behind him.

I fell back into the chair. I sat for a while, then asked Ah Yat where the training room was. I went in, closed the door and performed sword katas until I dropped from exhaustion.

Leo told me later that he knew something was up, because while I was locked in the training room doing sword katas for many hours straight, Mr Chen was in the garden doing precisely the same thing, heedless of anyone who tried to speak to him.

CHAPTER THIRTY-NINE

The next day, by silent agreement, we returned to training as if nothing had happened.

We went to the top of the hill behind the house.

'First, generate chi,' Mr Chen said. 'Both of you together, we have plenty of room. Move about three metres apart first.'

Simone and I separated and generated the chi. I had about a basketball's worth; more than twice as much as I could generate back home.

'The lack of pollution makes a huge difference,' I said.

'Exactly. Now, both of you, move it as high as you can without losing it.'

I floated the chi above my head.

'Slowly, ladies. Very gently. Particularly when it starts to pull back.'

I lifted the chi three metres, and then four metres. I slowly drifted it until I had it five metres above my head.

'Stop, Emma. Hold it there. Do you feel it? Simone, you too, right there.'

I inhaled sharply. 'It's like I'm up there with it!'

'It's like flying!' Simone squealed, and then screamed. Her chi rocketed back down to her and hit her on the top of the head. She crumpled.

I managed to hold my chi but watched Simone, concerned. Mr Chen strode over and raised her in his arms and brushed her hair.

I couldn't move with the chi so far from me. I floated it back to myself as quickly as I could, reabsorbed it and raced to them. Simone was limp, her face ashen.

I took her little hand as he carried her. It was ice-cold. 'Tell me she's going to be okay,' I said.

'She'll be fine, she's just drained,' he said. I hurried to keep up with his long strides back to the house.

Ah Yat was waiting for us at the front door. When she saw Simone her eyes widened.

'She's all right, she just needs to rest,' Mr Chen said.

He carried her to her room and placed her gently on her bed. We knelt side by side and watched her. He stroked her hair; her little face was pale and serene. He took her hand and concentrated, checking her.

'How long will she be out?' I whispered. 'It won't be three days like me, will it?'

Simone stirred. 'Emma?'

'Not long at all,' Mr Chen said with amusement. 'She has a hundred times the talent that you do, Emma.'

'Exactly how good is she?'

He put his arm around my shoulders and squeezed me. 'When she is grown, she will match any demon and most Shen. I strongly suspect that she will mature to be one of the most powerful creatures in creation.'

I tried to slip his arm off my shoulder.

'No need.' He raised his hand, which was holding Simone's. 'She's your shield.'

I turned to look at him properly. He smiled down at me, his dark eyes full of amusement, then he dropped his face to mine and quickly kissed me. I put my hand behind his neck and pulled him in for more. He closed his eyes and our lips met. We pulled back and gazed into each other's eyes.

'Daddy?' Simone said.

We snapped apart and turned to her. He quickly dropped his arm from my shoulders.

She opened her eyes and smiled up at him. 'Can we go back outside? I'm okay.'

He raised her hand and concentrated. 'Yes, you are.' He shook his head. 'That was the fastest backlash recovery I have ever seen. Let's go outside and try it again.'

After three days of work we took the afternoon off. Simone and Mr Chen hit some tennis balls on the tennis court. Leo and I played with a frisbee on the lawn. We could throw it with a speed and accuracy that surprised both of us; the training gave us skills in other areas that only appeared when we tried them.

A little brown dog wandered up to us with its tongue hanging out. It stopped about five metres away, unsure.

Leo threw the frisbee to the dog and it jumped to catch it, then ran to him with the disk in its mouth. He took the disk from it and it backed up slightly, wagging its tail.

He threw the disk again and the dog charged to catch it, leaping high in the air.

'Good boy!' Leo shouted. The dog ran back to him and dropped the disk at his feet. It gazed up at him and grinned broadly.

Leo dropped to one knee and rubbed the top of its head. It settled and rolled onto its back. He scratched its belly and it wriggled with delight.

I stood back and let him have his moment.

'I wonder if he'd like to stay,' Leo said. 'It would be great to have a dog around.'

'You know we don't have space back at the Peak,' I said. The dog grinned at me and wagged its tail. 'But he really is very cute.'

Leo rose and picked up the frisbee.

The dog's grin widened. Its mouth became wider and wider and its face cracked open into something grotesque and horrible.

'Demon, Leo!' I shouted. 'Get down!'

Leo cast around, looking for the demon.

The dog shot a ball of flame out of its mouth. I generated a huge ball of chi and threw it at the demon, hitting the fireball and ramming both balls of energy straight into its head.

The blast knocked Leo off his feet and enveloped him in a cloud of black demon stuff. He lay unmoving on the grass, covered in the black goo.

I spun to call Mr Chen and crashed straight into him. He shoved me to one side and ran to Leo, falling to his knees next to him.

Leo started to pull himself upright.

'Down, Leo,' Mr Chen said. 'Don't move until you're cleaned up. You're covered in it.'

Leo fell back onto the grass.

'Are you injured?' Mr Chen rose again and looked around. '*Ah Sum! Ah Say!*'

Leo shook his head.

'Where are they?' Mr Chen concentrated. 'Damn! I'll do it myself.'

Leo furiously shook his head.

'Remain still, that's an order,' Mr Chen said. 'You know dog essence is three times worse, it needs to come off quickly. Back, Emma, Simone, give me room.'

I took Simone's hand and pulled her away. 'Enough?'

He nodded. He rose, took a deep breath and lowered his head.

'No, Daddy,' Simone whispered.

He put one hand in front of his chest and the other in front of his abdomen. He closed his eyes and his long hair came out of its tie and floated around his head.

A tiny dark cloud appeared at head height above Leo. Mr Chen took a deep gasping breath and a tornado grew from Leo to the cloud, then a wall of water crashed out of the cloud.

The water seemed to go on forever. It completely soaked both Leo and Mr Chen, and the wind whipped it around and doused me and Simone with the spray too. I tasted the water as it blew into my face: salty.

Then the whole thing stopped as if it had never happened. Mr Chen sagged to his knees on the grass. Simone shook my hand free, ran to him and knelt next to him. 'Are you okay, Daddy?'

'It's gone, Leo,' he said.

Leo sat up. He raised his arms and checked them. He touched his face.

Mr Chen gasped for breath. 'Did you get any in your mouth?'

'No, sir,' Leo said. 'I'm fine.'

Mr Chen nodded. 'Good. Are you injured?'

'No, sir. Emma destroyed the demon before it could hurt anybody. She was terrific.'

'How did it get in?' I said.

Mr Chen didn't get up from the grass. 'It should not have been able to. I have been building the seals on this place for centuries; they are some of the most effective in existence. The dog demon must have had very powerful assistance to break through.'

We all shared a look. Simon Wong.

'Are the seals blown now?' I said.

'No. This one was not big enough. It was just a test. But we will have to be very vigilant; the next one will probably be larger.'

'Where did my chi go?' I said. 'It hit the demon and disappeared, but I'm not drained at all. In fact I feel three times stronger.'

'The chi combined with the demon's energy and fed you. That's what happens when you destroy a demon with chi; you absorb its energy.'

'So that's what the chi's good for,' I said. 'I feel great.'

'We all need to go back to the house and dry off,' Mr Chen said. 'Leo, I need your help. I'm very drained.'

Leo put Mr Chen's arm around his shoulder.

'Will you be okay?' I said.

'I'll be fine. I just need to go back and sleep for a week.'

I had a sudden wonderful idea. 'Stop, Leo.'

'What?'

I generated a ball of chi and held it in front of me. 'Take it.'

Mr Chen glared at me. 'Don't be ridiculous. Take that back immediately.'

I moved the chi closer to him and his eyes widened. 'No, Emma! Take it back! Quickly! *No!*'

Leo dragged Mr Chen a few steps away from me. I understood, and reabsorbed the energy.

Mr Chen sighed. 'That was an extremely foolish thing to do near me in this state. Never, ever try anything like that again, Emma.'

'Sorry,' I whispered.

'You're a damn fool sometimes, Emma,' Leo said. He helped Mr Chen towards the house.

I followed them, head bowed, Simone alongside me.

'What was all that about, Emma?' she said.

'That was just me being a complete idiot, Simone.'

Ah Yat met us in the doorway with a pile of towels and scolded us all for getting the carpet wet.

'You lot all go outside and do something quietly this afternoon,' Mr Chen moaned. 'I need to sleep.'

* * *

Leo and I took Simone outside to play. She chatted to her stuffed toys and we sat on the grass and watched her little tea party.

'So dog demon stuff is more poisonous, Leo?' I said.

'Yep.'

'And you'd be poisoned if you had it in your mouth?'

'I should have told you,' he said, sheepish.

'Nope,' I said. 'I knew that the black stuff has to come off, but he didn't tell me that dog demons were worse. How long can you have it on your skin before it kills you? I know it starts to burn after only a few minutes.'

'Three, four hours completely covered in it like I was and you're dead,' Leo said. 'That was great what you did with the energy.'

'No, it wasn't, it was stupid.'

'I mean destroying the demon. That was great. It was a good idea to try to give him your energy too, but you know he can't take it.'

'It was probably only a tiny amount for him anyway. He must have thousands of times the energy store that I do.'

'Sixty thousand,' Simone said without looking around. 'That's what Daddy says anyway.'

'Sixty thousand? Most of the time he seems to have a similar amount to me when I look at him.'

'He is running on empty all the time,' Leo said. 'He's completely crazy.'

'Sixty thousand times mine,' I said. 'I wonder what he could do with his chi.'

'He uses shen and ching energy sometimes too,' Simone said. 'But he hasn't done any of that in a long time, he's really drained.' She turned to us and glared. 'He won't tell me about ching. He says I have to wait until I'm bigger.'

Leo glanced at me. I tried to describe ching without giving too much away in front of Simone. I pointed at my head. 'Shen. Spirit.'

He nodded.

I pointed at my abdomen. 'Chi. Breath of life.'

He nodded again.

I indicated lower. 'Ching. Essence of life. Grown-up stuff.'

His eyes widened.

'That's what Daddy says,' Simone said, irritated. 'He says I have to wait until I'm grown up.'

'Well, you do.' I grabbed her and tickled her until she begged me to stop. She leapt to her feet and ran away, then came back and ran in circles around us, yelling her little lungs out. Neither of us stopped her. She didn't have space to run around like that back in Hong Kong.

'An expert energy practitioner can convert one type of energy to another,' I said. 'In ordinary people, the ching is a limited amount, and as you run out you grow old and die. If you can generate chi and convert it to ching, you will continually replenish your ching, never grow old and never die.' I realised the implication for Leo and opened my mouth to apologise.

'And I'll never be able to do that,' Leo said. 'Good.'

I stared at him. 'Good?'

'Yep.'

CHAPTER FORTY

Mr Chen, Simone and I sat around the large dining table having breakfast. Leo had already finished and gone out. Both Simone and Mr Chen went rigid, their eyes unfocused.

'Is everything okay?' I said.

Mr Chen raised his hand, then he snapped back.

Simone squealed, hopped out of her chair and raced out of the room. I heard excited voices in the hall and glanced at Mr Chen.

'Go and see,' he said.

I went out to the large tiled entry at the base of the stairs and stopped. It was Jade and Gold.

I embraced Jade, then released her to quickly hug Gold and kiss him on the cheek.

'I missed you guys so much!' I said. 'Welcome home! A lot's happened while you've been gone.'

Simone jumped up and down, clutching Gold's hand. 'You're back you're back you're back!'

'Let me go, Simone,' Gold said. 'We need to pay our respects first.'

'Go, quickly,' Simone said, releasing his hand and pushing him on the behind. They went into the dining room and we followed.

Mr Chen stood next to the wall, waiting for them.

They fell to their knees and touched their foreheads to the floor. 'Wan sui, wan sui, wan wan sui.'

'Hei sun.'

Jade and Gold rose, then bowed and saluted again. 'Xuan Tian Shang Di.'

Mr Chen nodded back, then all three of them relaxed.

'Come into my office, there is something we need to discuss.' Mr Chen shot me a quick smile as he led them out.

They were gone for about fifteen minutes, then Mr Chen returned by himself.

'Where are they?' I said.

'They've both gone to the Mountain to check the damage,' Mr Chen said. 'They're the first Celestials to return, they can report for me. They'll be back tomorrow with some paperwork for us, and Gold will stay to help with your energy work.'

'Hey, I wanted to talk to Jade,' I said. 'When will we have a chance to catch up?'

'I know how you two talk when you're together,' Mr Chen said, returning to his congee. 'You'll get your chance.'

Simone giggled. 'Yeah, you and Jade talk non-stop.'

'We're not that bad,' I huffed.

Mr Chen and Simone shared a look, then both grinned.

The next morning Jade and Gold spent another half hour in Mr Chen's office. Then Jade disappeared, and Gold and Mr Chen took us out to the large open field next to the house for advanced energy training. Leo tagged along to watch.

'Let me demonstrate first,' Gold said. He generated a ball of chi about the size of a tennis ball and threw it into the ground. A series of explosions went off along the ground for about three hundred metres. The chi sailed out of the ground with a huge blast that scattered dirt everywhere and raced back to Gold. He caught it easily.

'Any demon on the ground anywhere near the line of the blast will be destroyed,' he said. 'You need to angle the chi so that it will travel just under the ground; if the angle is too steep it will be swallowed by the earth and you'll lose it.'

Simone and I listened carefully.

'Start with a small amount of chi, ladies,' Gold said. 'You could easily lose it. Use about this much.' He generated a ball of chi about the size of a golf ball. 'Princess Simone, you first.'

Simone made a little ball of chi, gathered herself and threw it into the ground.

Nothing happened.

'Lost it,' Gold said. 'Are you all right, my Lady?'

'I'm okay,' Simone said. 'Let me try again.'

'If you become too drained then we will stop,' Gold said.

Simone nodded. She generated another ball of chi, then hesitated, concentrating. She took her time and lined it up carefully. Then she released the chi into the ground.

A few small bursts erupted for about five metres, then the chi popped out of the ground, swooped towards her and hit her hard. She staggered but didn't fall.

'Careful. When it returns it will be coming fast. Try to slow it as much as you can. Lady Simone should rest for a while. Lady Emma, your turn.'

'Good one, Gold,' Leo said.

'I'm not joking,' Gold said. He gestured towards me. 'Lady Emma.'

437

'What?' Leo said.

'I'm not Lady anything, Gold,' I said, confused.

Gold looked to Mr Chen for guidance.

Both Leo and I turned to Mr Chen as well.

'We will discuss this later,' Mr Chen said. He looked sheepish. 'Sorry.'

I suddenly understood what was going on. 'You'll keep.' I nodded to Gold to indicate that I was ready. I generated a small ball of chi and hesitated. I carefully angled it towards the ground, lined it up, and released it.

A few small bangs erupted from the ground. The chi popped out with a satisfying roar about ten metres away, then sped back to me. I had to concentrate hard to slow it before it hit me, and caught it with a tremendous feeling of triumph. I had it.

They all burst into applause, even Mr Chen.

'Stop it, you guys,' I wailed. 'You're embarrassing me.'

'Well done, Emma,' Mr Chen said.

I put my hands out in preparation. 'I want to try a bigger one. I want to see some serious damage.'

'No,' Mr Chen said quickly. 'At this stage it would not be a good idea. You will still lose about one in five. Start small, and when you have the skill mastered, try larger amounts.'

'Yes, sir.'

'Not any more,' he said.

'What the hell is going on?' Leo said. 'What do you mean, "not any more"?'

'Finish here, then return to my office and we'll discuss it. I have paperwork I need to attend to first. Emma and Simone, practise the skill for another thirty minutes or so, until you're tired. Leo, Gold, guard them. When you're finished, drop Simone with Ah Yat and come to my office. Understood?'

'Yes, sir.'

'Good.' He went back to the house.

'I want another go,' Simone said. She generated a small ball of chi and lined it up. 'Out of the way, Emma.'

'Yes, ma'am.'

Gold tapped on Mr Chen's office door when we returned. Mr Chen opened it himself.

'Just Emma first,' he said. 'The rest of you, wait outside, and when Jade comes ask her to wait too.'

I went in with Mr Chen and sat across the desk from him. Mr Chen's desk was immaculate.

'Who tidied up for you?'

'Ah Yat,' he said with a wry grin. 'She's the only one apart from you who knows how to put things in order.'

'That's ironic.'

'Yes, I'll lose her soon. She's nearly there,' he said. 'Now that Jade and Gold are back, I want to arrange the guardianship for you. I want to do it immediately, so that all the staff know you'll be the one to take over when I'm gone.'

'So that's what it was all about,' I said. 'But why "Lady Emma"?'

'As Simone's guardian, you will have precedence over all my staff. They will become yours.'

'Wait a second — they'll all be working for me? You said they'd be working *with* me, not *for* me.' I inhaled sharply. 'What about *Leo*?'

'Leo is a sworn Retainer. Him too.'

I ran my hands through my hair. 'No. No way. It can't work like that.'

'As Simone's guardian, you will have precedence. There is nothing you can do about it.'

'What will Leo do when we tell him?' I whispered.

'That may be hard. I may have to order him to accept you.'

'No. Don't order him to do anything, please, John. He's my friend. As far as I'm concerned, we'll be working together.'

He shrugged it off. 'There is one other thing.' He leaned forward and studied me over his hands. 'It's about you.'

'What about me?'

He relaxed back and rubbed his hands over his face. He took his hair out and retied it, even though it didn't need it. He threw himself forward again, and clasped his hands on the desk. He looked at his hands.

'Just ask me, John.'

'All right. Here goes.' He studied my face. 'You have picked up the martial arts training very quickly, Emma. Particularly the energy work. You are exceptionally talented.' He hesitated, watching me. 'It's as if you knew it all before.'

'I feel the same way sometimes. It's strange, it feels as if I'm remembering rather than learning. Do you know why?'

'Sometimes, when I am near you, you seem to be more than you appear.' He looked into my eyes. 'It's very small, and very fleeting, and may not even be there at all. Is there something you're not telling me about yourself, Emma Donahoe?'

I gasped with astonishment. 'You think I'm a Shen?'

'There are Shen in Australia. Very old, very powerful. I've never met a single one.' He gazed at me. 'Well?'

'You know what?' I looked down at my hands. 'I wish I was. I wish I was an Immortal and I had all the time in the world to wait for you.' I looked back up at him. 'But I'm not. As far as I know, I'm just an ordinary human.'

'Will you let me look inside you and see if there's something about you that you don't even know yourself? It is possible; sometimes we lose our memories and our identities and become lost. Look at me.' He spread his hands over the desk. 'Half of me is missing, and nobody knows where it has gone. Will you let me look inside you?'

'Sure. It would be great if you found something. If I was an Immortal, then I could wait for you to come back. There would be hope for us.'

He smiled slightly. 'Yes, there would.' He straightened. 'The only problem is that we require a shield. Wait.' He concentrated.

Ms Kwan appeared behind Mr Chen. She smiled sadly. 'Be aware, Emma, that I will know everything there is to know about you. If there is anything you wish to keep a secret, do not do this.'

'I don't have any secrets,' I said pointedly, looking at Mr Chen. He made a soft sound of amusement. I turned back to Ms Kwan. 'John's right. I'm so talented, it's scary. I picked up the energy work in no time flat. If I'm something special, then there's hope for us. I want to know.'

'Very well. Let us see exactly how much trouble you and this young human are in, Ah Wu.'

'A great deal.' Mr Chen rose and came around the desk to me. 'Pull back from the desk, Emma, and sit so that Mercy can hold your hands.'

I moved a little way back from the desk. Ms Kwan stood between me and the desk and leaned against it. I raised my hands and she took them.

'Relax into a light trance,' Mr Chen said. He rested his hands on my shoulders. It was a wonderful, relaxing feeling to sit in this way.

He moved into my mind and I blocked him. He stopped at the entrance to my consciousness.

'Let me, Emma,' he whispered. 'Trust me.'

I tried to stop blocking. I imagined myself *welcoming* him in.

'Thank you,' he said with amusement. 'Don't mind if I do.'

It was like having someone come into my house and look around. He shuffled through me and poked his nose into all my corners.

He stopped dead. 'Well, will you look at this,' he said. 'I seem to recall a young woman shouting at me just a couple of days ago that I keep too many secrets from her. And the first time I look inside her head, I find this.'

I'd completely forgotten that I'd kept this a secret from him. I imagined myself pulling a large hat way down over my head with shame.

'You look very cute like that,' he said. 'Two secrets.' He examined them. 'Your undergrad degree was only just a pass, but you still made it. Why wasn't it on your CV?'

The reason popped into my head.

'It would not have bothered me; in fact I would have been delighted to have a nanny with a degree. But I can understand that many older residents of Hong Kong don't have a degree and would find yours intimidating.'

Yeah. Kitty Kwok doesn't have one.

'She says she does, you know.'

I've been in her office and done her filing. She lies.

'Quite common.' He somehow indicated the other secret. 'And then we have this.'

'A part-time postgraduate degree, Emma?' Ms Kwan said, incredulous. 'How in the Heavens did you find time to do this while you were learning the Arts and caring for Simone? And without telling Ah Wu at all? You *are* remarkable.'

'I honestly wondered what you were up to,' Mr Chen said. 'I knew it wasn't a young man, because your ching level never changed. But you're always locking yourself in your room and asking for leave at unusual times. And this is why.'

He flipped through my MBA studies.

'Only six months of coursework to go. Very impressive. You received a High Distinction for Accounting, I see. Remind me to give you the budgeting spreadsheets for the Mountain when we're back home.'

I flinched with horror and he felt it.

'I don't know which of us hates budgeting more,' he said, amused. 'Why didn't you tell me you were doing a Masters part-time?'

The answer popped into my head.

'I see. You're right, you know. I would have supported you, but I would have expected you to resign the minute it was finished, to look for something better than just being a nanny.'

The real reason surfaced.

'No. Just for the challenge? The woman cannot resist a challenge. Well, I'm sorry, Emma, but those skills will be extremely useful to you after I'm gone. I will help you finish this degree and attend your graduation with a huge proud smile on my face.'

No way.

'All right, if that's how you want it: I won't help you, I'll let you do it all yourself.' He paused, musing. 'Your grades are excellent for part-time study. Exactly how intelligent are you anyway?'

I drew back, but it was too late. He grabbed me, held me down, stretched me out and measured me. He released me and I snapped back.

'That was unnecessary, Ah Wu,' Ms Kwan said.

He bowed an apology to me. I waved it away. As far as I was concerned he could know everything there was to know about me; I trusted him completely.

'You hide your intellect very well. That is probably what I have been sensing in you. I measure your IQ at a hundred and forty-five.'

A hundred and forty-seven last test. But IQ doesn't mean much anyway.

'Very impressive. I've definitely made the right choice.'

He came to my feelings for him.

'Stronger than I expected.' He sighed. 'I should have sent you away a long time ago. Before either of us could reach this stage.' He quietly studied my emotions. 'Very strong. Very true. I am making you suffer.'

It's worth it.

'You should find another, Emma. I will never be anything for you. I will go, and leave you and Simone alone. You should find another love.'

My fierce reaction surprised all three of us.

There will never be anybody else in a million years.

'How long will it take you to return?' Ms Kwan asked Mr Chen.

'I have no idea. I am unique: two separate creatures. This is a unique situation: a powerful Shen almost completely drained. Nobody else has ever done anything like this before.'

'Let me look at you.' Ms Kwan did something but I couldn't see what it was. 'Anything from ten to a hundred years, perhaps more.'

'Ten years?' I cried, full of hope.

'Ten years?' Mr Chen said, full of the same fierce hope.

'There is a small chance of you returning after ten,' she said. 'The chance becomes slightly better after twenty years.'

'At what stage does the chance become fifty–fifty?' I said.

'About twenty-five years. That is far too long to make any human wait, Ah Wu. Do not do this to her.'

'I can wait,' I said.

He squeezed my shoulders and leaned into me. 'You would wait for me?'

'Forever,' I whispered. *Forever. But I would be an old woman.*

'I am already an old man,' he said with amusement. 'I am not even completely human. It makes no difference to me.'

'Do not do this to yourselves,' Ms Kwan whispered.

I tried to hold back my elation. I didn't care how long it was, I would wait for him forever. And now I had a small hope that I could cling to: that he would return, and I would be able to see him again, and we could be everything we wanted for each other.

I began to feel embarrassed by the strength of my feelings.

'Don't be,' he said gently.

He pressed forward into me. I leaned back into him, and felt him against the back of my head. We shared the warmth of our feelings for each other, physically as well as mentally enjoying the touch.

I wondered if he really felt the same.

'Enough to kill you, dear one,' he said. He showed me.

Ms Kwan gasped.

It was like fast-forwarding through a video, except the video was me.

The day I'd agreed to go full-time, when I shook his hand. I saw myself; all he'd seen were my blazing, intelligent blue eyes. He'd been entranced.

Six months later, when Leo and Simone had rushed us home from Central and I'd told him that I'd find the truth. He'd been attracted by my spark and spirit and my complete lack of fear, more than he was willing to admit to himself.

The trip to the zoo, where both Simone and I had been delighted by the reptiles. He'd suddenly found himself right next to me and felt my hair near his face, felt my warmth, smelt my floral shampoo. He hadn't been able to resist the urge to touch me, to savour me. All he'd wanted to do was reach around me and hold me close, pull me into him and bury his face in my hair.

Me kneeling on the floor after the pizza delivery demon had tried to take Simone. Me fighting for Leo's job, unconcerned for myself.

Our first lesson, when I'd managed those first simple moves and a huge, delighted grin had spread across my face. He'd wanted to sweep me up and take me down the hall and throw me onto his bed. Then I'd become flustered and he had grabbed the chance to correct me, to be closer to me, to press himself into me. It had taken everything he had to control it.

'Oh dear,' Ms Kwan said. 'You should have dismissed her a long time ago, Ah Wu. I did not realise it was so strong so soon.'

The first time he'd seen me in my Mountain training uniform. He wanted to pull me close, push his hands inside my black jacket and run them over my skin. He'd had to concentrate on the Arts so that he wouldn't hurt me.

I came out of my room ready for the first charity concert. He hadn't seen the dress; he hadn't seen the hair or the make-up. All of that was a blur in his memory. He had only seen my smile and my glow, and it had pierced him through. My smile was the most beautiful thing he'd ever seen. And then I'd knelt and held Simone, and he had changed his mind; me with Simone was the most beautiful thing he'd ever seen.

He had a fleeting memory of Michelle and Simone, full of pain. I touched him and we shared the grief. I understood. I had helped him to heal. He had stopped living in the past and was living in the present, with Simone and me.

Simone and me. The two women he adored more than anything in the world. One of the happiest moments of his long life was the time spent with us at

Chinese New Year, being able to hold both of us together on the boat. Being able to kiss me, something he had wanted to do from the day he saw me. And after that moment, he knew that his heart was lost forever and both of us would gain nothing but suffering.

He felt a stab of pain. He was immensely guilty that he hadn't told me earlier that there was no future for us, that he would never be able to touch me in the way that he wanted. He felt that he'd betrayed me. He was sure that if he'd told me sooner, I would have been able to leave him and find someone else. Words could not begin to express the remorse he felt at what he'd done to me. He'd selfishly kept me around, keeping me ignorant of the truth. He should have told me; he should have sent me away.

'That is quite correct,' Ms Kwan said.

'I'm sorry,' he whispered. 'I should have told you.'

'Yes, you should,' I said. 'But it would have made absolutely no difference whatsoever, because I would still love you, and I would still have stayed with you. I don't need more than we have.'

Ms Kwan moaned softly. 'You are both such fools.'

I felt humbled that a mighty being like him should harbour such feelings for me. I didn't know what to say, but then I knew: between us, words would never be necessary. I could feel him agreeing and smiling with wonder. The way he felt surprised even him.

He straightened. 'I think we have seen all we need to.'

'Good,' Ms Kwan said. 'I have seen entirely more than I *ever* needed to.'

You know everything there is to know about me now. One day I must do the same to you.

'I couldn't let you, Emma. Inside you is bright and welcoming. Inside me is dark and sometimes cold. I am sure you would not like some of the lower levels. And if you were to go inside me, you would never come out again. You would be lost completely.'

I'd love to be absorbed by you, to become one with you. I'd love to take the time to go through all of you.

'I doubt if you'd live that long,' he said with amusement.

Found anything supernatural?

'Ah Wu?'

'No,' he said. 'You are as you appear. You are a perfectly ordinary human, just very naturally talented. You are not a dragon or a spirit or a Shen. And despite some of your recent behaviour, you are not even a demon.'

Both of us laughed softly.

'She is remarkably cold-blooded for a human, though, Ah Wu,' Ms Kwan said. 'Look at her. After suffering all of this, she is still able to laugh.'

'Emma has some extremely attractive reptilian qualities that I have always found irresistible. I agree with you. She is absolutely fearless. Her courage and spirit are exceptional. She is one of the most cold-blooded human females I have ever met.'

'You say that like it's a *good* thing,' I said.

'That's because it is.'

'Release her,' Ms Kwan said. 'I have seen enough.'

'One thing first,' he said. He dropped his head and kissed the top of my hair. 'I do love you,' he whispered.

'And I love you.'

He dropped to kneel beside me and put his arms around me. 'Don't let go of Mercy's hands.' He buried his face in my neck. I turned my head to him. He put his hands on either side of my face and kissed me. We lost ourselves in each other. I shook one of my hands free from Ms Kwan and put it on the back of his head.

We pulled back and gazed into each other's eyes. He ran his fingertips over my face. 'I think that was one of the last times for us to touch, Emma. I will not be able to touch you again unless it is very brief.'

'I don't need more than I have,' I said. 'I'm profoundly privileged to have you and Simone in my life.'

'You really are a complete pair of fools,' Ms Kwan said. 'I should have told you both right from the start that there was no hope. Now you both will wait for each other, suffering like this.'

'Look,' I said fiercely, glaring up at Ms Kwan. 'Can I explain something here? *I'm not suffering.* I'm *happy.* Okay? I don't want to be anywhere else, with anyone else. I want to be here, with Simone and with John. I don't care if I can't touch him, that's not important. What's important is that I have his company, and his wonderful daughter. Got it?'

'You were correct, Ah Wu,' Ms Kwan said. 'This one is certainly worthy. If she does not find the Tao I will be most surprised. Release her.'

He moved away from me and she disappeared.

'Let's get Leo, Jade and Gold,' Mr Chen said, 'and we'll make the arrangements.'

CHAPTER FORTY-ONE

Leo looked bewildered as he came into Mr Chen's office with Gold. I touched him gently on the arm. 'You'll find out all about it in a minute, Leo. It's not that big a deal anyway.'

He nodded. 'Thanks, Emma.'

We sat around Mr Chen's desk. It was a nice change to have room to move in the large office. Back in Hong Kong all the meetings were held over the dining table.

Mr Chen shuffled the papers on the desk. 'Let's put Leo out of his misery, people.'

Leo grunted.

'It's a simple thing, Leo, and I'm sure you've probably thought about it,' Mr Chen said. 'I only have a limited time here. So do you. Somebody will need to have guardianship of Simone when I go. I've decided to arrange for Emma to look after her.'

Leo leaned back. He didn't say anything. His face was completely expressionless.

'Are you okay, Leo?' I said. 'I hope you're not too upset by this.'

Leo still didn't move or speak. His face was a mask of control.

'I would prefer not to have to order you to accept this decision, Leo,' Mr Chen said.

Leo leapt out of his chair and stood rigid.

Both Mr Chen and I flinched.

Leo studied me searchingly for a long time. I expected him to storm out in disgust any moment.

'She won't be safe after I'm gone,' Leo said without looking away from me. 'Once they know she's Simone's guardian they'll come straight after her, and she won't be able to defend herself.'

I didn't move or shift my eyes from Leo's.

'We have two years, and she is exceptionally talented,' Mr Chen said. 'She will be able to defend herself against smaller attackers, and I will arrange a guard for her.'

'She's not qualified to manage the estate as guardian,' Leo said, still looking straight at me. 'She's just a nanny.'

'She has an undergraduate degree in business, and has nearly finished a part-time MBA,' Mr Chen said. 'But most of all, she loves Simone as her own. She is the most suitable person for the job.'

Leo remained staring into my eyes for a long time. I waited to see what he would do. If he walked out it would break my heart. He was the most loyal and trustworthy friend I'd ever had, short of Mr Chen himself. But the choice was his to make, and I would understand.

Leo dropped to one knee before me and took my hands. 'I take you as my Lady,' he said, his voice thick with emotion. 'I vow to obey you for as long as I live. I will serve you as I have served the Dark Lord. I am yours to command. I only hope that I will prove worthy of you.' He looked up into my eyes and smiled. 'Lady Emma.'

I freed one of my hands to put it on his face, and kissed him on the cheek. I touched my forehead to his and we smiled together. We remained like that for a while, sharing.

'You are my best friend, Leo,' I said quietly. 'And I love you dearly. I really don't know what I'll do without you.'

When I released him he sat down again and wiped his hands over his face. 'That's a big relief,' he said to Mr Chen. 'I was worried you might give somebody else guardianship.'

'Good. Now, let's go through the details of the bequest and then we can arrange the formalities. All of the Earthly fortune will be left to Simone, with Emma acting as guardian until Simone reaches majority. When I lose it I will do my best to leave the human form behind so there will be no legal entanglements about whether John Chen Wu is really dead.'

I winced.

'Emma, Jade is a qualified accountant and Gold is a solicitor registered both in Hong Kong and the Mainland. Jade.'

Jade pulled out a piece of paper and read from it. 'The estate as it currently stands includes the building on the Peak —'

'Wait a minute, the *whole building*?'

'Let her finish, Emma, then ask,' Mr Chen said.

I sat back. But the whole building?

'The building on the Peak, the office building in Central, the office building in Wan Chai, and the apartment buildings in North Point and Happy Valley. The house in London, the house on the Earthly Plane at Wudangshan, the hutong in Beijing —'

Gold cut in. 'That courtyard house was reclaimed for development and demolished. I told you that, Jade.'

'Yes, that's right, I forgot.' Jade drew a line on the paper, then glared at Gold. 'You should have fought harder.'

Mr Chen waved one hand impatiently. 'It was inevitable. It was right next to the Palace. I'm surprised we lasted that long. Continue.'

Jade raised the paper again. 'Other sundry items such as the cars, securities holdings totalling about a hundred and fifty million Hong Kong dollars, cash of ...' She pulled out another piece of paper. 'About fifty million, but the major assets are the properties.'

I quietly vowed that the fortune would be even larger when I handed it to Simone.

'Jade and Gold will help you to manage the assets and run the Mountain when I'm gone,' Mr Chen said.

'Wait a minute, back up there,' I said. 'Run the Mountain?'

'Somebody has to do it while I'm gone.'

'No *way*!' I shouted. 'I've never been there, and as far as I know I can't even go! I don't know anything about running the blasted Mountain! Get the Generals to do it!'

'The Generals will have their hands full running the Northern Heavens,' Mr Chen said. 'They should be okay for a while. I'm sure a quarter of the sky won't fall down without me.'

'The Northern Heavens may not fall, but they could be a bit lower when you return, my Lord,' Gold said, his boyish face alight with grim humour. 'I suggest the Generals defer to Lady Emma as well.'

'Good idea,' Mr Chen said. 'Jade and Gold will come to you for advice, Emma. I'm sure the three of you will be quite capable of administering everything in my absence.' He looked around the table, then back to me. 'Emma, after I am gone, you will have Regency. You will rule in Simone's name until either she has majority or I return. I know I only mentioned you caring for her, but this is part of the responsibility.'

Everybody stared at him, speechless.

He didn't seem to notice our reaction. 'If fortune is on our side, you should have at least two more years before I go. We have plenty of time to bring you up to speed with the management of the family assets and the Mountain. And when I am gone, you will be Regent.'

'My Lord, this is highly unusual.' Jade shuffled the papers. 'You can only offer Regency to one who is family by either blood or marriage.'

Mr Chen gazed silently at me for a long time. Then he looked down at his hands. 'If I could, I would marry Emma in a second.' He looked into my eyes again; his own were full of pain. 'I know she feels the same way. But I cannot marry a woman I cannot even touch. It would not be legitimate; the Celestial would not permit it.'

'You're killing me, John,' I said. 'You know how I feel. I would marry you in a second too.'

'Can you Raise her, my Lord?' Leo said. 'If you can, then you should.'

'Much as I would like to, I cannot. Right now I do not have the ability, and frankly neither does she. But Lady Emma certainly has the potential. In fact she has more potential than anyone I have seen in centuries, apart from Simone. I like to think that the two women I love most in the world will find the Tao together.'

Everybody at the table was silent. Finally Leo spoke softly. 'I wish I could be around to see it.'

Mr Chen rose. He stood motionless and gazed intensely at me. Everything went still. It was as if the entire Universe held its breath.

Mr Chen put one hand on the table in front of him. His voice became loud and firm. 'I swear that one day I *will* marry you, Emma Donahoe. I will return, and I will find you, and I will Raise you, and I will take you to live on my Mountain, and you will be mine. This I swear as Xuan Wu, Xuan Tian Shang Di.'

Jade and Gold shot to their feet. Gold knocked his chair over. They stood shocked and silent, staring at Mr Chen. Jade turned to me, her eyes wide and her mouth open.

Mr Chen smiled slightly and sat.

'What was all that about?' I said. Mr Chen didn't reply. 'Jade? Gold?'

Gold shook his head in wonder. 'If one such as he swears such an oath, Lady Emma, then the Heavens and Earth will be moved if necessary to ensure that it comes about.'

Mr Chen smiled. 'It *will* happen, Emma.'

Gold retrieved his chair, and he and Jade sat, still shaking their heads.

'I never thought I would see such a thing,' Jade said. 'A solemn oath by the Sovereign of the Four Winds, the Dark Emperor himself. It is something to tell my grandchildren.'

Mr Chen and I looked at each other across the table.

'I will be waiting for you,' I said.

'You may have to wait for some time.'

Leo turned away.

'That's all of them,' Gold said, tapping the stack of papers on the table. 'I'll see to it that a copy is sent to the Celestial and one is sent to the Hall of Records. We'll keep a set on the Mountain as well, for reference.'

'Good, my arm is ready to drop off,' I said. 'Can we get back to training now?'

'We have to do the Oaths of Allegiance,' Gold said. 'Everybody who is a sworn servant of the Dark Lord must swear allegiance to you.'

'Okay, let's do it,' I said. 'I don't like the idea of you two going down on your knees to me, but if we do it, we do it. I just want to get it over with and return to the training.'

'It's more than just us, my Lady,' Jade said with a small smile.

'Gold, the Tiger's here at the front gate,' John said. 'Let him in.'

Gold lowered his head and disappeared. He returned a few seconds later with Bai Hu.

Bai Hu saluted John. 'My Lord.' He saluted me. 'My Lady.'

My mouth flopped open. 'Oh my God.'

'Is there a problem, Emma?' John said.

I pointed at Bai Hu, then remembered and dropped my hand. 'No. No way. The other three Winds as well?'

Bai Hu threw himself to sit at the table and grinned at me. 'I think about two hundred people will be swearing allegiance to you, my Lady.' He winked at John. 'I felt that oath all the way from the Palace. Way to go, Ah Wu. I couldn't have thought of a better solution. How long will she have to wait?'

'Between ten and a hundred years,' I said. '*Two hundred people?*'

'I'll take Simone outside to play; this has nothing to do with me,' Leo said. He saluted John. 'My Lord.' He saluted me. 'My Lady.'

'Don't leave me to handle this by myself!' I shouted. He ignored me and went out. I ran my hands through my hair with exasperation. 'No *way.*'

'Use my hotel in Guangzhou,' Bai Hu said. 'The ballroom's free, plenty of space. When do you want to do it? You'll need to give everybody a couple of days to get organised. How about the day after tomorrow?'

'I do not believe this is happening,' I moaned quietly.

'Sounds fine,' John said. 'Jade, could you take Emma upstairs and help her find something suitable to wear? If you can't find anything, we'll need to contact Mr Li in a hurry.'

'You all hate me.'

'Only if you want to, Emma, sorry,' John said.

I threw myself to my feet. 'Come on, Jade. Mission Impossible.'

'You are quite correct, my Lady.'

We went into my room and shuffled through my disaster area of a wardrobe together.

'It doesn't matter what you wear, my Lady, Western or Chinese,' Jade said.

'Please, Jade, just Emma.'

'I'm sorry, my Lady, you'll need to get used to it.'

I sighed and pulled out my cheongsams. Both of them were falling to pieces from being worn so much. They were all I had apart from a couple of plain dresses and my jeans and shirts.

'Do you have anything in black?' Jade said. 'If you and the Dark Lord were to wear his colours together, you would make a most striking couple.'

A *couple*. 'I wish, Jade.'

'It will happen. Even if Heaven and Earth must be moved.'

I sighed. 'I wish I'd had a dress made out of that black fabric at Mr Li's. It would have been perfect.'

Jade held her hands out and a box appeared in them. She put the box on the bed, lifted the lid and pulled out a gorgeous black cheongsam. 'You mean this?'

'Where did you get that?'

'I had it made anyway. He had your measurements, so I just ordered it for you.' Her voice softened. 'Now I know why you didn't want it at the time.' She smiled gently. 'And I understand.'

'I'm glad you're happy for us, Jade,' I said. 'I know how you feel about him.'

'How I feel?' she said, confused.

'I know you disliked me since I started teaching Simone, and you were jealous of me and him.'

She smiled broadly. 'I could never be jealous of you, I could never feel that way about him, he is far too terrifying.'

'He's not terrifying, he's gentle and kind.'

'You haven't seen his True Form.'

'So why did you dislike me so much?'

'Mrs Chen was a truly wonderful woman and I thought that nobody would ever be able to care for either of them as well as she did. When you arrived I thought you were trying to take her place, and hated that. Now I know that I was wrong, you are worthy of both their love.'

'I'm worthy?'

'Yes. Now try the dress on.'

She held it out to me and I took it. 'It's so perfect I can't believe it.'

It was cut conservatively, with low splits up the sides and a high, stiff mandarin collar. The silk toggles and loops were gold, and the ends of the three-quarter sleeves were trimmed with gold. It swept to the floor, and the golden chrysanthemums shimmered as I moved.

Jade guided me to sit in front of the mirror. She pulled my hair up into a high bun. 'I will do your hair on the night. I have some elegant antique hair ornaments that my grandmother gave me; they are well over a thousand years old and the colour is perfect. Do you have any gold jewellery? It would not be fitting for you to attend without any pure gold on you.'

'Twenty-four carat gold? One hundred per cent pure? We don't have that in Australia, Jade. Most of our gold is either nine or eighteen carat. The first time I saw really pure gold I didn't even know what it was.'

'No pure gold?'

'Not a single bit,' I said. 'Not part of the culture.'

'That is entirely not good enough,' she said. 'We must at least find you a nice bracelet.' Her eyes unfocused.

'Don't you dare!' I shouted, but it was too late.

There was a tap on the door and she flitted to open it. John came in, obviously uncomfortable about invading Girl Space. But when he saw me he stopped dead. I rose to show him the dress.

'Exquisite. I love the colour.'

'Do you have anything suitable?' Jade said.

'Not here. I have some on the Peak, but the main collection is on the Mountain. Go and fetch it for me; you can move much faster than Gold in True Form. Carry it, don't try to bring it directly. Some of the pieces are extremely fragile and could be damaged by the transition.'

'My Lord,' she said, and bowed. She went out.

He gestured for me to follow him to the window. 'Come and watch. She doesn't often travel like this, and it will be a thing to see.'

I moved to stand beside him.

'That dress is superb,' he said quietly without looking at me. He was very careful not to touch me.

We looked over the lawn at the front of the house. Jade rushed out the front door, then stopped and lowered her head.

She changed into a dragon.

She was about two metres long, glittering with green scales. She had gold claws, and gold fins on her tail and behind her legs. She raised her head, her green eyes flashed, and she launched herself into the air. She didn't have wings; she flew like a swimming snake, whipping through the air. She accelerated higher until she disappeared.

'That was one of the most beautiful things I have ever seen,' I said.

'I agree,' John said, but he was watching me. 'She will be about half an hour, Emma. Come down to the garden and have some tea with me while we wait for her. Then you can choose something suitable.'

Half an hour later Jade plummeted from the sky in dragon form, a small rosewood casket held in her front claws. She landed lightly on the grass and bowed to us. Then she changed back into a woman. She placed the casket on the table between John and me, then sat next to me and poured herself some tea.

I leaned to speak softly to her. 'Where do the clothes go, Jade?'

'I conjure them as I change,' she whispered. 'I make them as I need them.'

'Your dragon form is beautiful.'

'Thank you. But I am a very small dragon. Wait until you see Qing Long.' She gestured towards the casket. 'Now, let's see what sort of collection the Dark Lord has. This should be interesting.'

'Not very much, I'm afraid,' he said. 'I've never been one for collecting gold. I bought some for Michelle —'

I cut him off. 'Please don't ask me to wear anything that belonged to her, John.'

Jade smiled.

'Very well, then, let's see what we have,' he said, and opened the box.

He pulled out a few very nice pieces. All of them had an interesting history or story behind them. Most had been gifts from friends or rewards for service from the Jade Emperor. John obviously didn't place much value on them in monetary terms.

'This is a piece of gold jade in the shape of Mercy,' he said.

I held it. It was Ms Kwan in her Celestial form, sitting cross-legged and holding the urn that contained the bottomless font of Mercy. It was about ten centimetres long and the jade was a striking shade of amber.

'I thought jade was green.'

'I am,' Jade quipped, 'but the stone can be any colour. Some of the finest jade isn't green at all.'

460

'Here's a chain for it,' John said. He threaded the pendant onto the elaborately carved chain. 'Is this too heavy?'

'No, I can handle it,' I said. I popped it over my head. It sat on the black silk and glowed against the chrysanthemums. 'Perfect.'

He pulled out six gold bracelets and held them out to me. 'Pick a few.'

I took one with triangular links, without touching him. 'I like this.'

'Dragon scales design,' Jade said. She opened the soft gold hook and put the bracelet around my wrist for me. 'Fitting.'

John opened a smaller box and held it out. 'Earrings.'

'It's good your ears are pierced,' Jade said. 'You can choose something nice.'

I pulled a pair of black jade earrings out of the box. 'I like these.' They were flat jade disks with a square hole in the centre, like traditional coins. A large diamond filled each hole. But the jade itself was unusual: it was jet black. I passed them to Jade. 'They'll go well with the general colour scheme.'

'These diamonds are very fine,' Jade said, turning the earrings over in her fingers. 'But the jade is spectacular. Black jade is extremely rare, and these are exceptional pieces. But I am not sure that Lady Emma should wear black jade, my Lord. It has many unpleasant connotations. I hate to think that she might share the same fate as its namesake.'

'I have sworn. It will be,' John said, and Jade nodded, satisfied.

'What?' I said. 'What unpleasant connotations?'

'I think it is better that you do not know for now,' Jade said, 'but we must arrange a tutor for you. You will require a Classical education, my Lady.'

'I forbid it,' John said.

Jade glanced sharply at him. 'My Lord?'

He didn't say anything else, so she returned to the earrings. 'The shape is not entirely suitable, but if it is your wish then there will be no dispute. Where did these come from, my Lord?'

'Hell.'

Jade gasped and dropped the earrings.

I picked them up and opened my mouth to ask.

'It is a long story. I might tell you about it later.' He pulled a small black silk purse out of the bottom of the box. 'I forgot I had this. Gold would be very upset if he knew.'

'Gold?' Jade said.

Mr Chen nodded. He opened the purse and tipped a ring into his hand: a small square piece of green jade set onto a simple gold band. Three gold studs on either side of the stone were the only decoration. The jade was so old that most of the polish had worn away and the stone didn't shine at all.

'This is very plain,' Jade said. 'Quite unsuitable really. The stone is very good, but it is badly in need of a polish.'

He passed it to her and she turned it over in her hands. 'Very, very old.'

'Study the stone,' Mr Chen said.

Jade touched the stone with her finger and concentrated. She snapped back and her eyes widened. 'My Lord!'

'Don't drop it,' he said. 'I don't think the stone would like it.'

She returned the ring to him, her face full of awe.

He took a deep breath, then let it out. He shook out his shoulders. 'Give me your hand, Emma.'

I held my hand out.

'No, left hand.'

'Oh.' I held my left hand out for him. His own hand hovered over it, holding the ring, without touching me.

He gazed into my eyes. 'Will you marry me when I return, Emma Donahoe?'

I returned his gaze. 'Yes I will, Xuan Wu.'

He quickly took my hand and slipped the jade ring onto my ring finger. 'Thank you.' He pulled his hands away and grinned. 'It would be ironic if I killed you by asking you to marry me.'

'You're a complete moron sometimes, John,' I said. 'You should have just given it to me.'

'I wanted to do it myself,' he huffed. 'Traditional. Oh.' He smiled slightly. 'A diamond is traditional in the West. Do you want one?'

'I don't need anything,' I said, leaning across the table to gaze intently at him. 'Your promise is more than enough for me. You didn't even need to ask me out loud; you know we don't need words.'

Jade sobbed loudly, leapt to her feet and ran into the house, tears streaming down her face. We watched her indulgently.

'Now that you wear my ring, all will accept you as my equal,' he said. 'Jade will ensure that everyone in the Heavens is aware of our pact by nightfall. She is absolutely the worst gossip on the Celestial Plane.'

I studied the ring on my finger. 'What's so special about it, John?'

'This ring was made for the Yellow Emperor himself; his Empress wore it. It is as old as history; it is a Building Block of the World. It is sentient, and its size and shape are dependent on its use. It has been sleeping for nearly five hundred years, but it may wake for you if you wear it constantly. The setting is at least two thousand years old. Don't lose it.' He raised his hand. 'Don't worry; if it wakes you won't be able to lose it. It will find you.'

'What about training?'

'Remove it for physical training; it will not mind.'

'How about I wear it on a chain around my neck for training?'

'I think you are smarter than me, Emma.'

'Maybe it's just that you're cold-blooded — your brain is slower.'

He laughed quietly at that.

'What about energy work?'

'Leave it on for energy work. If it doesn't like the sensation, it will wake and tell you.'

I studied the ring. 'It can talk? Does it have a name?'

'It has not spoken in more than five hundred years,' he said. 'It once said that it was above such banalities as names; it was much too important to need one.'

'So I have an engagement ring with attitude.'

'Yep. You're a matched set.'

I raised my hand to shove him and changed my mind. He grinned.

Before we returned the rest of the jewellery to the casket, I selected a light plain gold chain, in eighteen carats. It had a traditional spring clasp rather than the bendable hook for pure gold that would break with too much use. I popped it over my head to hold the ring when I was training.

John closed the casket and placed his hand on top of it. 'Keep it all. You might as well.'

I put my hand on the casket next to his. 'I'll keep this for Simone until you come back.'

'Keep it as my Lady until I come back, and when I return, I will fill it full for you.'

'No need,' I said. 'Having you back would be all that I would need in the world.'

'Enough.' He pulled his hand away. 'You'll make me rush inside like Jade.'

I raised both hands in surrender. We sat silently together and shared the tea.

CHAPTER FORTY-TWO

I swung my sword at Leo's head and he blocked me. We moved closer, our swords locked at the hilts, and he grinned. He threw his arms out into a massive push and flung me almost to the other side of the room. I landed smack on my behind and we both laughed.

John had come in without us noticing. 'Come on, Emma, you can do better than that.' He closed the door behind him and leaned against the wall with his arms crossed over his chest, watching us. 'That was absolutely pathetic. Stop trying to match Leo's strength, you know he is much stronger than you. Match him with skill.'

Leo lowered his sword, came to me and put one hand out to help me up.

When I was on my feet I readied myself again. 'Can you look after Simone while we're at the ceremony tonight?' I asked him. 'I don't think she should go along.'

Leo lowered his sword. 'Why not? They'll all take True Form. She loves it when they do that.'

'She'd really enjoy it, Emma,' John said.

'John, they'll be discussing your oath. They'll be talking about you going and about you coming back.

465

Do you want to have to explain that to her right in the middle of the ceremony?'

John and Leo shared a look. 'She's not completely aware that you'll be leaving her, my Lord,' Leo said.

'You're probably right, Emma,' John said. 'Leo?'

'I'll mind her. She'll be fine here.'

'We'll have to tell her eventually, Emma.'

I sighed. 'I know.'

'But you should be the one to choose the time. I trust you.'

'Good idea, my Lord.' Leo readied himself. 'Try again.'

I raised my sword and threw myself at him. Leo flattened me before I was even close.

'Pathetic,' John said, and went out.

Leo grinned at the door. 'He is so damn impressed with you.'

I pulled myself to my feet. 'How about we give him something to be impressed about?'

Jade nodded when she was finished preparing me for the ceremony. I rose and checked myself in the changing room's mirror. I did look like a princess. It didn't feel like me at all.

'He's waiting outside, my Lady,' Jade said. 'I'll be along shortly, just let me fix my make-up.'

John was leaning against the wall outside the changing room. He pulled himself upright when he saw me and his eyes shone. He wore a black silk robe, trimmed with gold on the toggles and loops, the ends of the full-length sleeves and the edge of the mandarin collar.

'I've never seen you in this one before; it's always been plain black,' I said. 'I like the gold edgings.'

'You like it? Mr Li made it to match your dress.'

'It's wonderful, but your hair's already coming out. Turn around and let me braid it for you; it might stay put longer.'

He obligingly turned. I raised my hands to take out the tie and stopped. 'Can I do this?'

'Yes, but only my hair. Nowhere else.' He grinned over his shoulder. 'Especially while you look like that.'

'I'll take that as a compliment.'

I pulled his hair from its tie, carefully smoothed it and braided it for him. I raised it to my face; it really did smell of the sea. I lingered, enjoying the silken feeling.

'You'd better stop now, Emma. That feels ...' He hesitated. 'A little *too* good.'

I tied the end of the braid and moved my hands away. 'Done.'

He turned and smiled down at me. 'Now you turn around, let me see.'

I did a quick twirl and he watched with admiration. He moved closer to see the detail of the work Jade had put into my hair and froze.

'*Jade*!'

Jade came out of the changing room in a plain black cheongsam. She saw his face and stopped dead.

John roared with fury and pointed. 'What is Lady Emma wearing in her hair?'

'Just some lovely old pieces that I lent her ...' Jade's eyes widened. She collapsed onto the floor and fell over her knees. 'My Lord, forgive me, I will remove them immediately ...' She gasped a huge sob. 'This affront was not intended. I cannot believe I have insulted you like this. Please permit me to hang myself when the ceremony is completed.' She moaned softly, shaking her head through the tears. 'Apologies, apologies.'

'John —'

He raised his hand to stop me. 'Please, Emma.'

His voice changed as he spoke to Jade; it was as cold as ice. I had never seen him so angry. 'I do not give you permission. You will remove these items and give them to me, together with any others you hold in your possession, directly after the ceremony. They must be cared for properly. You have obviously had these items in your possession for a long time ...' He took a deep breath. '... *while in my service*, without thinking of the ramifications. I will consider appropriate punishment for you later. Sometimes I wonder where your brain is, Jade.'

He turned to me and spoke more warmly, ignoring Jade quivering at his feet. 'You couldn't have known, Emma. You'll probably be as upset as I am when you find out what they are. Go inside with Jade and have her put something else in your hair. Hurry, most of the dignitaries are already here.'

Jade rose, brushed down her cheongsam and led me back into the changing room without looking at me. As soon as we were inside she closed the door, raced to the table and grabbed some tissues to wipe her face. Her make-up was ruined; she concentrated and it all disappeared.

She sat me in front of the mirror and quickly plucked the ornaments from my hair. I lifted one from the table; it was stiff and transparent, with bands through it of darker and lighter shades of brown. The end was gilded with twenty-four carat gold and had small bells hanging off to make a musical sound as I moved my head.

I realised what it was. I shot to my feet in horror and flung the comb onto the desk. 'Oh dear Lord, that's *tortoiseshell*!' A wave of nausea hit me and I bent to take deep breaths. 'Jade, that could have been *him*! Left on a beach to die, chopped into pieces and used to make *this*! He wouldn't have been able to defend himself in True Form if he was in front of humans.'

Jade grabbed some more tissues and wailed into them. 'I *know*! I deserve to die.'

I sat down again. 'Put something else in, quickly. Why the hell do you have these?'

'Like I said, my grandmother gave them to me. I've had them for a long time. Most hair combs and ornaments are made of tortoiseshell — it's the best for combs, it never breaks your hair.' She gasped and stared at me in the mirror. 'I have snakeskin shoes in my apartment in Happy Valley. Please don't tell him. I'll remove them immediately.'

'My God, Jade, you're a dragon, you're a serpent yourself! How could you have snakeskin shoes?'

'I just thought of them as nice clothes.' Her voice dropped to a whisper. 'Please don't tell him, my Lady.'

'Don't worry, I won't, but you are in *serious trouble*.'

'I know,' she moaned. 'I hope the punishment is something fitting. I deserve to suffer most mightily for this offence.'

'I'll think of something,' I growled softly.

'Thank you, my Lady,' she whispered. 'There. These are only sterling silver, and do not match the dress, but they are better than nothing. You'd better run.'

John tapped on the door. 'Sorry, Emma, you have to come, it's starting.'

'I'm coming.'

John led me to the entrance of the ballroom and stopped. He smiled down at me. 'You will be fine, Emma.'

I took a deep breath. 'I can do this.'

We walked into the room together.

A long black carpet stretched before us, through the middle of the ballroom to the throne at the end. All the dignitaries knelt in orderly ranks on both sides of the carpet, facing the throne, silent.

The throne was raised on a dais above the floor and was an old-fashioned Chinese Imperial style, made of jet-black ebony. The back was elaborately carved, but not with the usual dragons; instead it was an elaborate pattern of twining snakes and fierce-looking dragon-headed turtles.

John and I walked side by side along the aisle to the throne. It was eerie to pass through that silent space with so many people kneeling on either side of us. I desperately wished I could hold his hand.

Jade and Gold followed behind us; both had changed their clothes. Jade's cheongsam was plain black; Gold's long robe was also black, without any decoration.

When we reached the throne John gestured for me to sit first, his eyes glowing with amusement. I sat, and he sat next to me. 'You're doing fine,' he whispered.

Jade and Gold both knelt in front of the throne, then took their places as Retainers standing behind us. Jade still sniffled occasionally and her eyes were red. She hadn't bothered to replace the make-up and she looked pale and drawn.

'Am I on the right side?' I said under my breath.

'Doesn't matter at all,' he replied in the same low tones. 'This will dissolve into anarchy the minute all the oaths are sworn anyway.'

Everybody in the hall chanted the Imperial greeting 'Ten thousand years' without looking up. 'Wan sui, wan sui, wan wan sui.'

The rustling of their robes echoed through the ballroom as they rose and silently moved to the sides of the hall.

Many round twelve-seater tables appeared, together with elegantly dressed waiters. Everybody sat and the drinks were served.

'We don't get anything to eat or drink until this whole insufferable charade is over,' John said. He smiled sideways at me. 'But it's worth it to see the look on your face.'

'You really are enjoying this far too much,' I growled.

'Oh, the fun is just beginning,' John said, and rose.

Everybody in the hall stood also. There was complete silence.

'I have chosen Emma Donahoe to be Guardian and Regent after I have lost this form,' John said. 'You will serve her as you serve me. Her orders are to be obeyed as mine. And I swear . . .' He took a deep breath and the silence became even thicker. 'I swear that when I return, I will find Emma, and Raise her, and marry her, and take her to live on my Mountain. This I swear as Xuan Tian Shang Di.' His voice became fierce. 'She is my chosen, my promised, my Lady. Is there any dispute?'

Nobody made a sound.

'Good. Swear allegiance to my Lady,' John said, and sat.

'Way to go, Ah Wu!' Bai Hu shouted from one of the front tables, and everybody dissolved into loud applause. I even heard a couple of cheers: there appeared to be some Westerners towards the back. The guests relaxed, talking and laughing.

'Close your mouth, Emma,' John said without looking at me.

'How come they're all so thrilled?' I said. 'They should be horrified. I'm just a nanny.'

'Word gets around fast,' John said. 'Jade's told everybody all about you. She told her grandchildren, just like she said she would.'

'I didn't know she was married and had children and grandchildren,' I said. 'But I suppose I shouldn't be surprised.'

'Dragons don't usually marry,' he said with amusement. 'They are too fickle. We reptiles are a degenerate bunch. Often the Jade Emperor is at his wits' end at our behaviour.'

'He's not the only one,' I growled softly.

He made a soft sound of amusement. 'They're all quite impressed, particularly that you stayed with Leo and Simone when the demons attacked the Peak apartment. They agree with Bai Hu. You really are exceptional.'

'I don't want them to kneel to me.' I sighed with exasperation. 'They're gods, John, and I'm just an ordinary human, nothing special at all. It will kill them if they have to bow down to me.'

Bai Hu rose and came to the base of the dais. He fell to one knee and saluted us. 'I swear allegiance to you, Lady Emma, as Regent in the absence of Lord Xuan and the minority of Princess Simone. I vow to obey you for as long as you live.'

He rose and raised his arms. 'Look, my Lady, it didn't kill me at all.'

Tiger hearing. I should have known.

He became more serious. 'You're the best one for the job, Lady Emma. Lord Xuan has chosen well. I look forward to the wedding. You will make a fine Empress of the North.'

He changed to an enormous white tiger, at least three metres long. He bowed to me in True Form, then changed back to human form.

John and I nodded back.

Bai Hu grinned, winked and returned to his table.

Qing Long rose. He wore his old-fashioned robe of turquoise silk embossed with silver scales. His long turquoise hair floated behind him as he moved.

He fell to one knee at the base of the throne without saying a word.

'Words are not necessary from one such as he,' John said as we both nodded back.

Qing Long took True Form and I jumped.

'Steady, Emma,' John said.

I gathered myself and let him know I was okay with a very slight nod.

Jade was about two metres long in dragon form. Qing Long nearly filled the hall. He was close to twenty metres long, all glittering silver and blue. His scales shifted from pure turquoise to shining silver as he moved. He raised his head and the scales rattled like steel knives. His head was the size of a pony; it nearly brushed the high ceiling. He lowered his head to see us and his eyes came to the same level as ours on the dais, still an astonishing shade of blue. His fearsome teeth were only about two metres from my head.

He bowed gracefully as a dragon as we both nodded back.

He changed back to human form and stood for a while without moving. Then he fell to one knee again, saluted us, and spoke loudly and clearly. 'My Lady Emma. I am your servant.'

John and I nodded to him again. He backed away, then returned to the table he shared with the other two Winds.

'He does you great honour, my Lady, and I am very pleased,' John said.

'I'm just scared to death,' I whispered. 'But you were right. Truly exquisite.'

Zhu Que rose from the table and came to the bottom of the dais. She fell to one knee and saluted. 'I vow to serve you, my Lady.'

She rose, and took True Form. She was a huge phoenix, at least three metres tall. Her feathers were mostly red, with a rainbow of iridescent colours shimmering through them. Her tail spread behind her, similar to a peacock's, but red shot through with shining colours.

She bowed, then reached around with her beak and

pulled out one of her tail feathers. A few people in the hall gasped.

She changed back to human form and walked gracefully up the stairs to the top of the dais, her red robe flowing around her. She held the feather out to me with both hands and I rose to take it. It was nearly a metre and a half long, but hardly weighed anything.

'Thank you,' I whispered. 'You are incredibly beautiful.'

'My Lady.' She bowed, smiling, then turned and walked back down the stairs. She turned to us and bowed again, then returned to the table. She glowered at the Tiger before smiling at me.

I admired the gorgeous feather in my hand.

'She also greatly honours you,' John said. 'A gift of one of her feathers is a rare thing indeed. It has miraculous powers. Look after it carefully, it is very precious.'

'They're showing the Tiger up,' I whispered. 'They're doing their best to put his nose out of joint by outdoing him.'

'You are very perceptive sometimes.'

Most of the remaining dignitaries that saluted me and swore allegiance were people I hardly knew. All of the Generals were there; others were staff from the Mountain. A couple were Westerners and were particularly sympathetic when they swore allegiance.

They all bowed to me in human form and in True Form, if their True Form was different.

It was appalling.

What would I tell my father and mother if they came to visit? The ring John had given me was obviously an engagement ring, even though it wasn't a diamond. And they'd hear everybody call me Lady Emma. I was in *so* much trouble.

* * *

About two hours later, when everybody had sworn allegiance, John led me down off the throne and we sat at the table with the other three Winds. Everybody rose and congratulated us. Bai Hu embraced me, kissed me on the cheek, and shook John's hand before sitting next to me.

'Thanks for the ballroom,' I said.

'My pleasure. Most of the staff are tame demons. Running costs are really low.'

'I thought that must be the case,' I said. 'They don't seem at all bothered by anything.'

Bau Hu grinned. 'I'll trade you fifty of mine for this one,' he said to John.

'No deal,' John responded, lightning-fast.

'You don't give up, do you?' I said.

'It's not fair. I have hundreds of women, and not a single one could possibly hold a candle to you.'

'She can do level five energy work. She can destroy level fifteen demons with her bare hands. She has nearly completed a part-time MBA, with a High Distinction in Accounting,' John said.

'It's not fair,' Bai Hu said. 'None of *my* women has anything beyond a diploma.'

'Women like me just have too much sense to be carried away by something as despicable as you,' I said.

'She has a point, Ah Bai.'

'A hundred. A hundred of mine. And ten fine Arab stallions.'

'Still no deal,' John said. 'She's *mine*.'

'The hell I am,' I said. 'I don't belong to you.'

John's smile widened.

'Twenty Arab stallions and fifteen war-trained Arab mares, some with foal at foot.'

'You have Arab horses?' I said.

'Don't tell me she rides as well,' Bai Hu said. 'It's really not fair.'

'Lady Emma is quite a passable equestrian,' John said.

Bai Hu looked at me with admiration. 'I would be honoured if you would permit me to give you an outstanding war-trained Arab mare, my Lady.'

I glanced at John, thrilled. He smiled indulgently at me. 'If it pleases you, my Lady, I could think of no better gift.'

'I will bring a selection with me,' Bai Hu said. 'I will bring some to your house on the hill, and you can choose one, then we'll arrange for it to be stabled with Dark Star.'

'Will the Jockey Club let me do that?' I said. 'Those stables are only for ex-racehorses.'

'They'll do what I tell them,' John said evenly.

I had a sudden wonderful idea. 'Could you bring a pony for Simone? I know she'd love a well-trained pony of her own. In fact, you don't need to worry about a horse for me, just bring a sweet pony for Simone.'

'Two hundred women, twenty-five fine war-trained Arab mares, twenty warm-blood warhorses, and my best thoroughbred racing stallion.'

'That's a good deal, John, you should think about it.'

'It'll be an anticlimax returning to training after that,' I said as John drove us back up the hill.

'Things have changed now, Emma,' he said.

I sighed and sagged into my seat. 'I just want to sleep.' I checked my watch: 3 a.m.

'Me too.'

We drove in companionable silence for a while. It felt good.

'Bai Hu will bring the horses in three days.' He winced. 'No, that's the day after tomorrow now. In the afternoon.'

'That was all for real?'

'Of course it was. I think it's a terrific idea.'

'I don't really have time to go out riding, John. I'm flat out caring for Simone.'

'If you can't ride the horse then Bai Hu can provide someone to ride it for you. And we can hire someone to care for Simone if you like. You are no longer the nanny; you are Lady of the House of Chen.'

'No way I am! Not until I have that shell of yours safely tied up and nailed down, and a wedding band on your scaly little claw.'

He roared with laughter.

'What?'

'It's not that little. And sometimes it's a flipper.'

'Whatever. Nobody else cares for Simone. It's either you, me or Leo. I wouldn't trust anybody else with her.'

'As you please. But you are my partner now.'

'I wish.'

Some of my feelings came out in my voice, and he changed the subject; probably a good idea in such a small space.

'Any suggestions on punishment for Jade?'

'Yeah. I've been thinking about that. She feels tremendously guilty, John, she really didn't think. Don't be too hard on her.'

'I won't be. Because you will be the one to punish her.'

'Oh, *thank you very much*. What is this: good god, bad god?'

'Precisely. You want to send her back to the Jade Emperor?'

'*Back* to the Jade Emperor?'

'The Celestial has been exceptionally generous in providing her and Gold to help me in my current situation.'

'Don't throw her out,' I said. 'She loves us both. She's a dear friend.'

'Okay, then you'll need to think of something suitable to allow her to work off the guilt. Shame her slightly, Emma, but not too much. Probably something along the lines of unpleasant physical labour — she's not used to that, she regards it as beneath her.'

'Washing windows?'

'Perfect.' He smiled slightly. 'In True Form.'

'Oh, now that's *mean*. She can clean out the gutters as well.'

'Perfect! She'll have to get her precious golden claws dirty.'

We laughed together.

'And no conjuring rain to make the job easier,' I said, still laughing.

'By the Heavens, you are wonderful, Emma. I do love you,' he said, and froze.

He quickly pulled the car to the side of the road, opened the door and threw himself out.

I rested my head on the dashboard, full of joy and anguish. 'We are both such idiots!'

It took him a long time to regain control. I moved to the back seat of the car. We didn't speak to each other at all the rest of the way back up the hill.

Dawn was painting the sky a dusky pink as we arrived at the front of the house.

CHAPTER FORTY-THREE

Both of us wandered out very late the next morning and met in the kitchen. He looked as exhausted as I felt. We both wore ratty clothes and *both* stopped to tie our hair back.

Ah Yat had made some vegetarian noodles and presented them to us triumphantly, pushing us into the dining room out of the way. She could see that we'd had a great time.

'Where's Leo?' John said.

'Outside with Simone, sir. They have spent the whole morning together.'

'Good.'

We tucked into the noodles without needing to say a word to each other.

Ms Kwan appeared on the other side of the table.

'Ah Yat!' John shouted. 'Another teacup!'

His voice became softer as he spoke to Ms Kwan. He used his chopsticks to point at the noodles. 'Would you like some, Mercy?'

'No, thank you, Ah Wu. But you two eat. I can see you had a tiring evening.'

Ah Yat brought another teacup and John filled it for

Kwan Yin. She smiled sadly. 'Have you spoken to the Jade Emperor recently, Ah Wu?'

John shook his head. Then he put his chopsticks down and placed his hands on either side of the bowl of noodles. 'Oh, shit.'

'Ah Wu, really! You have been around that Tiger altogether too much!'

He picked his chopsticks up again. 'Tell us the worst.'

'What, John?'

'Emma. Dear Emma.' Ms Kwan sighed. 'Let me tell you a story.'

John opened his mouth but she waved him down. 'Let me, Ah Wu.

'Once there was a very foolish Shen who fell in love with a human woman. He married her, and had a child with her. He gave up his duties and dominion to be with her. It was a scandal throughout the Celestial. He was warned by the mighty Jade Emperor that such a dereliction of his duty was not acceptable.'

'I told the Jade Emperor where to go.' John's eyes sparkled over the noodles. 'You should have seen his face. He nearly had me executed on the spot.'

'The Jade Emperor decided that if the Shen was in love to such a degree — if it made him insane enough to show such open defiance — then Heaven should not stand in the way.'

'I still can't believe I got away with it. Nobody in the history of the world has ever done such a thing. Nobody, I think, ever will.'

'His Celestial Majesty gave the Shen permission to spend a human lifetime with the woman.'

John dug his chopsticks into the noodles. 'And there were quite a few noses out of joint.'

'A great many of his advisors wanted the Shen thrown from Heaven.'

'There are always people who want me thrown from Heaven. I am what I am. But I am also a good General and the best Heavenly Administrator. No one can fault my performance. The Northern Heavens are the best run of all.'

'The Shen returned to his wife and child. The wife was killed by a demon. The Shen was given permission to stay with the child.'

'Good thing, too,' he said through the noodles. 'I would have stayed with her anyway, regardless of orders.'

'You are absolutely incorrigible,' she said.

'That's why you like me.'

'And that's why I love him.'

'You, Emma, are just as bad.' Her voice softened. 'And now he has done this.'

I understood. My Regency. His oath to me.

'You are in very serious trouble, aren't you?' I said to him.

'I don't think even he realises the depth of the trouble he's in,' Ms Kwan said.

'Tell me the worst.'

'You are in danger of being demoted, Ah Wu. You may lose the Northern Heavens.'

'Good,' he said crisply. 'The Northern Heavens are a hell of a lot of work and take up far too much of my time. If I didn't have to do that, I could spend more time with my family.' He smiled at me.

'You may lose your Mountain, dear heart.'

His smile disappeared.

I knew how much his Mountain meant to him. It was a part of him. The damage caused by the demons still tortured him.

'Can he take it all back, Ms Kwan?'

They both stared at me.

'Don't you want to marry me and live on my Mountain, Emma? Why didn't you say so?'

I tapped his arm with the ends of my chopsticks. 'Of course I do, don't be ridiculous. But I don't want you to lose your Mountain for me.'

John and Ms Kwan looked at each other, then back to me.

'Don't sacrifice your Mountain for me. I can't bear the thought of you losing what you love. If you can take your oath back, then you should.'

I turned to Ms Kwan. 'Please, tell the Jade Emperor that this was all a big mistake. He'll forget about me and return to his duties. If it costs him this much suffering, then it's not worth it.'

John looked away, his face full of pain.

'You are truly worthy,' Ms Kwan whispered.

He slammed his chopsticks onto the table and rose.

I put my head in my hands. 'Oh no, here we go again.' I slapped him lightly on the behind. 'Sit down, Xuan Wu, there's no need for theatrics. Let's just talk about this.'

John sat back down with a bump. 'I stand by my oath.' He picked up his chopsticks. 'Theatrics or no. She is mightily worthy, as you have seen. I want her by my side. If it means losing my Mountain, then so be it.'

'If you lose it, then how can we go live on it?' I said. 'Maybe we should just let our relationship go.'

'No. The Jade Emperor can go to hell,' John said. 'I stand by my oath. Emma deserves nothing less.'

'You are a tremendous fool,' Ms Kwan said. 'But I'll do my best for you.'

'I'm an even bigger fool,' I said. 'You warned me what I was getting into, and I walked into it with both eyes open.'

'We're a pair of fools together,' John said.

'You forgot happy,' I said.

'Eat your noodles,' Ms Kwan said, sounding like a long-suffering mother. She disappeared.

We ate in silence. Words weren't necessary.

The next day Gold returned and we resumed training. We only had a few more days in the house on the hill and there were still things we needed to learn.

'Only Emma can do the first exercise — it's energy weapons,' John said. 'You're not big enough to do this sort of weapons training yet, Simone. You can stay back here with Leo if you like.'

'Can we come and watch?' Simone said.

'No need, guys,' I said.

John shrugged. 'If you want.'

'Oh no, please.' I ran my hands through my hair. 'Do you have to watch?'

'Yep,' Leo said.

We went to the top of the hill. Gold stood me about twenty metres from a straw dummy and passed me my sword.

'Stand well clear,' John said, moving Leo and Simone away from me. 'This could backfire. Emma, please be very careful.'

I glanced at him, concerned.

'You'll be fine, just take it slowly.'

I shrugged and turned back to the dummy.

'Take the sword out, Lady Emma,' Gold said, 'and hold it in front of you.'

I did as he said. He took the scabbard and put it on the grass away from us.

'Now. Move some chi into the sword. Do it slowly, feel the sensation. Hold the sword with both hands and move the chi in. It will feel strange, be ready for it.'

I held the sword in front of me and concentrated.

'Only a small amount, Emma,' John called.

Gold raised his hand. 'The Dark Lord is quite correct, my Lady, only a very small amount.' He bobbed his head. 'My apologies.'

I held the sword out, concentrated, and moved about a golf ball's worth of chi into it.

The recoil knocked me backwards off my feet and sent the sword spinning out of my hands. I landed smack on my behind. Simone giggled. Leo guffawed. Even John laughed.

'Do that again, Emma, that was funny!' Simone squealed.

'Wish I had a camera,' John said. 'The look on your face is priceless.'

Leo didn't say anything. He was bent double, speechless with laughter.

I pulled myself to my feet. 'You will all keep!'

Gold had difficulty controlling his face. 'Less than that, I think, to start.' He fetched my sword for me. 'Try again. Hold it tight. You'll have less recoil as the sword becomes used to it.'

'The *sword* has to get used to it?'

'Just try it and feel it,' John said. 'I could explain about the sword, but it might be better if you just practise first.'

I took a firm hold of the sword, held it in front of me and gingerly moved a minuscule amount of energy into it. The sword vibrated, but I could hold it. I moved more in, and the vibration intensified, but I could still hold it easily.

I eased more chi into it until I reached a normal working level. The vibration intensified, then the sword stopped shaking and sang with a pinging crystalline whine that ran straight through my head like a glass blade.

I pulled the energy out of the sword and it went silent.

'All the demons for miles will run when they hear that,' I said. 'What an annoying sound.'

'It will do more than annoy them,' John said. 'It will destroy any small ones that are close, and disable them if they are within earshot.'

'How small?' I said.

'That depends entirely upon your own level of skill. The more you practise, the larger the demons you can destroy with it.'

'I hope I didn't hurt the house staff,' I said, concerned.

'I sent them down to the city,' John said. 'And they're your staff too, now.'

Leo snorted with amusement.

'Give it a rest. That's a really useful technique, Gold, thanks.'

'That is not the technique. That is just an interesting side effect of the particular nature of this sword.'

'What's the technique then?'

'Put the sword down and I'll show you.'

I placed the sword on the grass.

'Using a standard chi blast of about so big,' he said, indicating a ball about the size of a basketball, 'hit the target.'

I generated the chi and threw it at the dummy. I wasn't accurate; the chi hit the dummy slightly to one side and it burst into flames.

'Pathetic,' John said.

'Leave her alone, Daddy, that was really good,' Simone said, shoving him.

Gold concentrated and the fire went out. 'Now, load the sword with chi and use it like a slingshot to throw the energy. Only use about this much.' He indicated a ball about the size of a tennis ball.

I picked up the sword, held it front of me and filled it with energy. It sang. 'That's really annoying. How do I shut it up?'

The sword went silent.

'Okay, obviously I just ask it.'

'Just tell it what to do,' John called. 'Tell it to sing again.'

The sword sounded without me saying anything. I ordered it to shut up and it went silent. 'Is it sentient?'

'No,' John said. 'Has the stone in the ring said anything yet?'

'No.'

'Stone in the ring?' Gold said. I held the ring up for him to see. 'Are you sure that was a good idea, my Lord? It will waken eventually.'

'Emma can handle it,' John said.

'If anyone can, she can,' Gold agreed. 'I look forward to it waking. It's been a long time.'

I tried something. I ordered the sword to sing, and it sounded. I ordered it to make the sound lower, and it obliged. I ran it through some excruciatingly painful scales.

A dog barked some distance away and others picked up the refrain. The hillside echoed with their howls of distress.

'Enough! Enough!' John called, laughing. 'I didn't know it could do that!'

I ordered the sword to shut up and my ears rang in the sudden silence.

'Don't do that again, please, Emma!' Simone said. 'That was awful!'

I bowed to them, then turned to face the dummy. This time I used the sword as a slingshot to throw the energy. The dummy exploded into a million pieces. The force of the blast showered us with straw. John had to shield Simone from the flying debris.

The chi returned to the sword without my guidance.

'That was only about one-fifth of what I used the first time,' I said.

'That is correct,' Gold said. 'You will achieve five times the power, combined with five times the distance, by using the sword to throw the chi. You also do not need to guide the energy back.'

'Sweet! Hey, John, do you have any demons I can practise on?'

'Sure. I have a jar in the basement. Just hold on, I'll get it for you.'

'I may play them some tunes as well,' I mused aloud.

'Leo, I want to go inside *right now*, please,' Simone said.

'Yeah, we're out of here,' Leo said. 'Come and get us when you're finished.'

John followed Leo and Simone back to the house. Then he stopped, stiffened, and walked swiftly back.

'Looks like we won't need the jar,' he said, studying the sky.

Gold looked up as well. 'You have sky seals?'

'Yes,' John said. 'Let's see what happens. Emma, fill the sword with chi. You may have your chance right now.'

I filled the sword with energy and ordered it to be silent. 'What's coming?'

'Flyers,' Gold said.

'How big?'

'Oh, about twenty,' John said casually, still studying the sky. 'About twelve of them. Second wave.'

The flyers appeared as black spots in the cloudy sky. They looked like ravens.

'Are they like crows?'

'Nope,' Gold said. 'Completely different. And much bigger.'

The flyers came closer and I suddenly saw that they weren't the size of ravens, they were much, much bigger. Their altitude had hidden their true size. Each had a wingspan of probably about two metres.

'Can we handle them?'

'Oh, yes,' John said. 'This should be good. They don't know I've given you the sword. They will find out in a hurry. When I tell you, make the sword sing.'

The flyers were like large flying lizards, or small black dragons. They had scales, four legs, and wings. Their eyes glowed red as they approached us.

When they were about fifty metres away, I hefted my sword.

'Wait,' John said without moving.

'They're awfully close, John,' I said, concerned. The flyers sped towards us.

'Trust me, Emma.'

The flyers opened their mouths when they were about twenty metres away; around twelve of them. They flew together in a mass of black scaly legs and wings.

'Will they blow fire like the dog?' I said, clutching my sword.

'No,' John said. 'They're just smiling.'

The flyers were only ten metres away, and my heart raced.

'Now,' John said.

I held the sword in front of me and made it sing.

Every single one of the demons exploded, dissipating into feathery black streamers.

'Well done, my Lady,' Gold said with admiration.

'Good. I don't need to waste any demons out of the jar.' John grinned. 'Come inside and we'll take a break. You have that skill mastered.'

I lowered my sword and shook my head.

'What?'

'We were just attacked and you're acting like it was nothing.'

'It *was* nothing,' John said with a shrug. 'The next wave will be the one we need to worry about. But we know they're coming, so we are prepared. I'm not too concerned about losing my head, particularly when I have you here to defend me.' His grin widened. 'I thought I told you to read the Tao.'

'Oh, give it a rest.' I followed him back to the house.

CHAPTER FORTY-FOUR

Gold shared lunch with us. Ah Yat cleared the dishes when we'd finished.

'What's on for this afternoon?' I said.

'Demon-binding,' John said. 'Leo, this is another energy technique that you can't do, and it's not very interesting to watch. Want to do some wudang spear outside instead?'

Leo's face lit up. 'My Lord.'

'Hey, I want to do some spear too,' I said. 'There isn't space for full-on spear work back home.'

'You're not good enough yet,' John said. 'Wait a few more months.'

Leo grinned with triumph.

'You will both keep,' I growled.

'My Lady,' Leo said with delight.

'Oh, cut it out.'

John concentrated. Ah Sum and Ah Say came in. They looked like ordinary middle-aged Chinese men.

'We require a volunteer,' John said. 'The ladies need to learn binding. You know how dangerous this can be, so I will not order you to do it. Volunteers only, step forward.'

Both of them stepped forward.

'Ah Sum,' John said.

Ah Say's face fell.

'Ah Sum is larger, he will be more difficult to bind. You will have your chance tomorrow, Ah Say,' John said. 'We will be doing spotting tomorrow morning, and I will need you strong. Ah Sum, stay. Ah Say, dismissed.'

Ah Say bowed and went out.

I rose. 'Let's go.'

Gold took us to the lawn beside the tennis court. Ah Sum stood patiently as Gold explained the technique to me.

'I'll show you the simplest way to bind demons,' Gold said. 'It's a two-step process. First, you check how much chi the demon has. Then you take out the chi; just over half. Less than that, the demon won't be bound; more than that and the demon will be destroyed. If you take out the right amount of chi then the demon is so weak that you can control it. To release the demon, return the chi.'

'That's not what John does,' I said. 'I've seen him release the demons that are bound in the jar, and he doesn't give them chi.'

'There are a number of different ways to bind demons,' Gold said. 'The Dark Lord can't give them chi; he doesn't have enough.' He smiled and shook his head.

'What?'

'It will take me a while to become accustomed to the idea of anybody calling him "John".'

I opened my mouth to ask what Michelle had called him, but changed my mind. Simone was next to me.

'Does that mean that Daddy can draw energy out of demons?' Simone said. 'Why doesn't he do that when he's so drained?'

'To him, the amount of chi in most demons is like a grain of rice to a starving man,' Gold said. 'If he were to drain a demon, he could drain all those around him as well. He is so weak that if he were to start the drain, there is a good chance he could not control it.'

'Oh,' Simone said.

I put my arm around her shoulders. 'Don't worry, Simone, he could never drain you. He loves you far too much.'

Simone stood silently.

'Is the chi inside demons the same as ours?' I said. 'It looks different.'

'It is different. Well done. Demons have dark energy, dark chi. It is similar to ours; we can absorb it and manipulate it once we have taken it.'

'So the black goo isn't their essence?'

'No, their essence is the breath of life, same as ours. But most demons are not really alive.'

'Do you have the same sort of chi, Master Gold?' Ah Sum said.

'Similar in many aspects, Ah Sum,' Gold said, grinning. He raised one hand. 'We'll never get there if we keep talking like this. Let's try binding. Hold my hand, Lady Simone, and I'll demonstrate.'

Simone moved forward and took his hand.

Ah Sum took a deep breath and closed his eyes.

'Don't worry, Ah Sum, I won't let them hurt you,' Gold said.

'I thank you, my Lord, but I am deeply honoured anyway,' Ah Sum said.

Simone concentrated as Gold did something. Ah Sum's eyes widened, then he went rigid and his eyes glazed over.

'Returning,' Gold said.

Ah Sum relaxed and smiled.

'Now you,' Gold said, still holding Simone's hand.

Simone dropped her head slightly and stared at Ah Sum. Ah Sum's smile froze. Then he relaxed.

'Oh, very good, my Lady, right first time,' Gold said. 'Try again.'

Ah Sum froze and unfroze again.

'Do it three or four times,' Gold said, releasing Simone's hand, 'then you can rest. Well done.'

Simone practised the skill a few times on Ah Sum.

'That is very impressive, my Lady,' Ah Sum said.

'Thanks, Ah Sum, but it's easy.' Simone stepped back. 'Your go, Emma.'

I moved forward and took Gold's hand.

He blushed furiously. Chinese tradition for a long time held that men and women didn't touch unless they were married. He was being ridiculously old-fashioned.

'Give it a rest, Gold,' I said. 'You're far too young for me anyway.'

'I am one thousand, three hundred and fifty-eight years old,' he said stiffly.

'See? Far too young,' I said, and he laughed softly. 'Show me what to do.'

I concentrated as I held his hand and watched what he did. He seemed to size up Ah Sum, then drain the energy out of him, but I wasn't sure how he did it.

'Again.'

He demonstrated for me again.

'A couple more times, Gold, I want to see.'

He bound and unbound Ah Sum.

'Stop.' He continued holding my hand. 'Tell me if this is right.' I concentrated on Ah Sum and gauged the amount of chi that he contained. Gold nodded; I had it right.

I drained the energy out of Ah Sum and found to my horror that I couldn't stop. I lost control of the drain; I was killing Ah Sum. Ah Sum's eyes widened, then he smiled, nodded, and closed his eyes, ready to die.

'Help, Gold!' I hissed.

Gold cut in, stopped the drain and returned the energy to Ah Sum. Ah Sum snapped back and grinned broadly.

I tried to pull my hand free from Gold's but he wouldn't release me.

'Let me go.'

He released my hand.

I turned and walked back to the house.

John appeared around the corner of the house from the other side. 'Emma!'

I ignored him, went inside and stomped up the stairs to my room. John followed me. I tried to close the bedroom door in his face, but he wouldn't let me. He shoved his foot into the gap.

'Stop it!' I shouted.

'No,' he said, very calm. 'Let me in. We need to talk.'

I turned away and he came in. He sat in one of the chairs next to the wall. I sat at the desk where I could see him in the mirror.

'You have to learn to bind demons, Emma.'

'I nearly *killed* him.'

'Ah Sum understands that you need to learn, Emma. He volunteered; he knew the danger. Gold is skilled enough to keep him safe anyway.'

I crossed my arms on the desk and buried my head in them. 'I suppose you're right, but I don't want to hurt anybody. Particularly wonderful people like Ah Sum. He shouldn't have to suffer for me. I scared him to death.'

'How much do we suffer for each other, Emma? You and me?'

I raised my head so that I could look at him in the mirror. He wasn't looking at me; he was gazing out the window.

'That's different, we ...' I couldn't finish.

He turned his head to see me. 'It is an honour to suffer for those you love, isn't it?'

I rested my chin on my arms and watched him.

'My demons love me dearly. And so they love you, as my Lady. Ah Sum was delighted to die for you. He was honoured.'

'That is so wrong.'

'That's the way it is. You need to learn to bind demons, Emma. Please.' He looked out the window again. 'Go back to Gold and complete the training. The fact that you nearly drained Ah Sum is a very good sign. You should have the skill mastered next time you try.'

'Wouldn't it be nice if we could just go to your Mountain with Leo and Simone, and stay there, just the four of us? Not have to worry about demons, or energy drains, or Simone's safety, or anything? Just live a peaceful life together, as a family. Free to share our joy, our feelings, our love, everything.'

'That would be the most wonderful thing in all the world,' he said, full of pain. 'I would give anything to be able to Raise all three of you and take you to live on my Mountain with me. But remember . . .' He looked at me in the mirror and smiled sadly. 'Most of the Mountain is gone.'

He rose. 'Go and learn the skill, Emma. It is the last skill you will learn here. We'll stay a couple more days to teach Simone the rest of the skills, then we will go home and you can help me to rebuild.'

He opened the door for me and we went back downstairs together. Gold and Ah Sum waited patiently for me on the lawn.

I had it exactly right next time I tried.

The next morning Simone ran through the field with us trailing.

She stopped and pointed towards the trees that lined the field. 'Ah Yee! There.'

Ah Yee emerged from a thicket and bowed. 'Well done, my Lady.'

'Stop here, you're about in the middle,' John said. 'See if you can spot the rest of them.'

Simone dropped her head and concentrated. She turned slowly on the spot. Then she stopped and grinned, pointing. 'Ah Sum!'

Ah Sum came out of the trees a good fifty metres away at the end of the field. He waved his arms and grinned.

Simone pointed right. 'Ah Say!'

Ah Say was about twenty metres away at the side of the field.

Simone concentrated again. 'And Ah Yat's on her way back from the city.'

'What?' John stopped and concentrated too. 'Well done, Simone, she's a good two kilometres away. Can you sense any others?'

Simone turned, looking. She pointed. 'There's about five dog demons over there, and a big lizard thing.'

John concentrated as well. His face went rigid. 'I can't see them, Simone. Wait.' He concentrated again, and Jade flew down to us in dragon form, with a bucket in one claw and a rag in the other. 'How far away, Simone?' John said.

'Twice as far as Ah Yat.'

John indicated the direction Simone had pointed. 'She says there are about five dogs and a reptile that way. Should be four, five kilometres. Fly up and have a look.'

'My Lord,' Jade said. She dropped the bucket and cloth, raised her head, her green eyes flashed, and she flew into the air.

'Why's she holding a bucket?' Simone said.

'She's in trouble and she has to wash the windows in her True Form,' John said.

'Oh, that's *mean*, Daddy.'

'It was Emma's idea.'

Simone giggled. 'You're mean, Emma.'

'She did something really, really naughty, Simone.'

Jade landed lightly on the grass. She bowed, still as a dragon. 'Princess Simone was quite correct. Five dogs and a reptile. They sensed me coming and fled.'

We all shared a look. Simon Wong's little friends.

John shrugged. 'You can sense them coming from a long way off, Simone. You'll be fine at school.'

Simone jiggled with delight. 'Cool!'

'Return to the windows, Jade. You should be onto the gutters by now.'

Jade picked up the bucket and cloth and grinned, revealing gleaming white dragon teeth. 'Yes, my Lord.' She flew back to the house.

'Why could Simone sense them and you couldn't, John?' I said.

'Right now I think Simone is slightly more powerful than me,' John said. 'Now.' He dropped to one knee to talk to Simone. 'Have you noticed how I summon Jade and Gold sometimes?'

'You mean when you call them?' Simone said.

'Exactly,' he said. 'I can call them to come to me. It doesn't matter how far away they are, I can tell them I need them.' He paused and selected his words. 'It would be good if you could call us when you're at school, if you see a demon. That way we can come and get it for you.'

'That's a good idea, Daddy,' Simone said, her little face serious. 'That way I can study hard and not worry about demons.'

'Okay,' he said, rising. 'Let's try it.'

'How do I do it?' she said.

'Hold my hand and I'll show you. I'll call Emma. It's about time I showed her how this works.'

He smiled into my eyes. 'The first time this happens it can be quite disconcerting, and I've been waiting for a chance to show you ...' His voice trailed off.

'Without freaking me out?' I said.

Yes, he said, and I jumped. It sounded as if he'd spoken right into my ear.

Are you okay?

'That's a very strange sensation.'

'Did you see what I did, Simone?' he said.

'I don't know, Daddy. Could you do it again?'

Lady Emma, please remain right where you are.

Hello, Emma, Simone said. 'Did you hear that?'

'Yes I did, Simone, well done.'

She jumped up and down and clapped her hands with delight. Then she hugged her father around his legs. He hoisted her and kissed her, and she wrapped her arms around his neck. They shared a moment of triumph.

'Call Leo,' John said, still holding Simone in his arms.

Simone went still.

Leo came charging out the front door, across the lawn and skidded to a halt in front of them.

'Try calling Gold,' John said. 'This will be harder. Let me see where he is.' He paused. 'He is on the Mountain. The Shadow one, on the Earthly Plane. It may be too hard for you.'

Both of them stilled, and a minute later Gold appeared. 'Yes, my Lady Simone?'

Simone threw her arms above her head with triumph. 'Yay!' she yelled. 'I'm really good!'

John twirled her and she shrieked with delight.

'Try it, Emma!' Simone shouted. 'It's really easy!'

'Emma can't do it, Simone. She's not half Shen like you are,' John said.

'Don't be silly, Daddy, I'm not half Shen. Shen are the gods that you see in the temples back in Hong Kong. I can't be half one of them.'

John lowered her and went down on one knee to speak at her level. 'I'm a Shen, Simone.'

'No, you're not, silly Daddy, you're just a special man,' she said, explaining patiently.

'I'm a Shen.'

She put her little hands on her hips, disbelieving. 'Okay then, which Shen are you?'

'Remember the temple on Cheung Chau? The one for Pak Tai?' he said, using his Cantonese name.

'I remember that temple.' She wrinkled her nose. 'It was really yucky. Too much incense.'

'I am Pak Tai. I am Xuan Wu.'

She didn't say anything, she just glared at him, hands on hips.

'Which Shen is in charge of the West?' he said.

'The White Tiger God, everybody knows that.'

'Yes,' he said. 'Bai Hu.'

Her hands fell from her hips and her eyes went wide. She flopped to sit on the grass.

'She's just realised,' I said quietly.

'I wondered when she would,' he said just as softly. He sat next to her. I sat on the other side.

John waved Leo and Gold away. Leo walked back to the house; Gold just disappeared.

'Kwan Yin,' she said softly.

He nodded.

'Xuan Wu.'

He nodded again. 'That's me.'

'You're a *snake turtle*?' she said with disbelief. 'My daddy's a *snake and a turtle*?'

'I'm the turtle,' he said gently. 'I don't know where the snake is. I'll find it again soon.'

Simone looked at me.

'I'm just an ordinary person.'

'Did you know he's a turtle, Emma?'

'Yes, I did, Simone. I've known for a long time.'

'Did you know he was a Shen?'

I nodded.

She looked down, digesting this for a moment. Then she quickly glanced up at her father. 'Mummy?'

'Mummy was a normal person too. She was very beautiful, and very wonderful.'

'I think I should go now,' I said, moving to rise.

'Please stay, Emma,' Simone begged me, putting her hand on my arm. 'Don't go away right now.'

'Okay.' I sat next to her and held her hand. 'I'm here.'

Simone watched her feet for a while. Both of us waited patiently to see what would come out next.

'Can you show me the turtle, Daddy?' she said. 'Bai Hu is always giving me tiger rides.'

'I can't change into the turtle right now.'

'Why not?'

'Because if I change into the turtle, I can't change back again,' he said, very sad. 'I'd be stuck like that for a long time.'

'Why?'

'You know how I'm low in energy?'

She nodded, her little face serious.

'If I lose human form and turn into a turtle, I don't have the energy to change back again.'

'You have to stay in human form?' She studied him carefully. 'That must be really hard. Uncle Bai has to change back into a tiger all the time.'

'Kwan Yin is helping me.'

'So that's why we go to Paris,' she said, wide-eyed.

'You are very clever, you know that?'

'You need to look after yourself, Daddy, so you don't change into a turtle,' she said. 'If you change into a turtle then you can't fight the demons for me. Leo will have to do it all.'

'Should I, Emma?' John glanced desperately at me; he wasn't sure if he should tell her he was leaving. His voice was thick with emotion. 'Help me, Emma, I don't know what to do.'

I wanted so much to hold him and comfort him. He needed me; his face was full of pain. I remembered what Simone had said in London. She didn't understand, she was still too young. Soon, though. Something I wasn't looking forward to.

'I think that's enough for now, John. The rest can wait until later.'

He nodded and rose, taking Simone's hand and helping her up. I rose as well.

'Are you and Emma going to get married?' Simone said. 'Don't worry, I won't be mad, I'd be happy. I want you to.'

I nearly fell to sit again. She'd seen the ring. She'd heard me call him John. She'd heard me called Lady Emma. She wasn't stupid.

'Right now I can't even touch Emma,' he said sadly. 'I'm too drained. I'd hurt her.'

'You'd just suck all the energy out of her,' Simone said. Her voice became breathless as she understood. 'Goodness, Daddy, make sure you don't touch Emma, you could kill her.'

'Don't worry, we're very careful,' I said.

'But that means you can't get married, 'cause you can't kiss each other,' she said with a child's logic. 'That's really sad.'

'I'm happy to be with your daddy and I'm happy to be with you,' I said. 'That's what's important.'

'I've promised Emma that one day I *will* marry her, Simone.' John moved slightly away from me. 'So she's

500

not the nanny any more. She's my Lady, the one who'll marry me one day.'

'Good,' Simone said, very serious. 'I'll be a flower girl.' She screwed up her face. 'I'm *hungry*.'

'Why don't you call Ah Yat and tell her to have something ready for you back at the house?' John said.

Simone concentrated. 'I asked her to make some tea for you too, Daddy.'

Come on, Emma, she said straight into my ear, and I jumped. *Let's go.*

'I can see that in the very near future I will really regret that you've learned this,' I said.

CHAPTER FORTY-FIVE

Jade's face spoke volumes when she returned with Simone's and my riding gear. She'd done well to find mine in the disaster area that passed for my wardrobe.

'It's mine,' I said.

'I'm not saying anything, ma'am,' she said with a small smile.

About mid-morning Bai Hu turned up with three horses, two ponies and five grooms to help. The horses were superb: pure-bred Arabs, two steel grey and one black, all small and solid with gorgeous dish-shaped faces. Simone grinned in delight when she saw the ponies and raced to try them. The smiling grooms helped her to mount.

'She'll be fine. Those ponies are completely bomb-proof,' Bai Hu said. He waved a hand and one of the grooms brought the black Arab mare to us. She stood just over fifteen hands, and when the groom stopped with her she remained completely still, watching us with huge, intelligent eyes.

'I have chosen this one particularly because she is the Dark Lord's colour,' Bai Hu said. 'She's slightly small for you, my Lady, but she can carry you easily. She is well-trained, sound and has a very even temperament.'

'She's gorgeous.'

Bai Hu vaulted onto her. He pushed her into a trot and she stepped out beautifully. He flung her into a full-out gallop. She was magnificent; her tail went up and her long silken mane flowed as she ran. He stopped her about thirty metres away, spun her around and galloped back; going direct from gallop to halt in front of us. The horse stopped dead and didn't move a muscle.

Bai Hu saw my face. He rode like a Mongolian — all arms and legs and loose reins flying. My pony club instructors went berserk at him in my head.

He turned the horse and galloped her away again, arms and legs flying. He stopped about fifty metres away and spun her on her haunches.

He straightened in the saddle, took up the reins and pushed her into one of the nicest collected canters I had ever seen. He performed two turns on the haunches at the canter, then dropped her into a trot. He trotted her sideways in a near-perfect half-pass. He half-passed both ways, then brought her, still trotting, to a near standstill: a flawless piaffe. He cantered her forward and changed legs every stride, showing off.

He stopped her. She stood perfectly still in a square halt. He made her leap straight up into the air and kick out behind her in mid-air, all in faultless control: a perfect capriole.

'War-trained, as he said,' John said. 'I love the colour.'

'No way am I good enough to ride that,' I said. 'That was Grand Prix stuff. That last bit was Spanish Riding School stuff.'

'Don't worry about that, all the Tiger's horses are like that. You can do what you like with her; just ride her out on the trail with us if you want.'

The Tiger threw himself off the horse and brought her over. 'I think this one is the pick of the bunch. Have a try.'

I touched the horse's head and she didn't move. 'Isn't she scared of you? Doesn't she know that you're a tiger?'

'These horses have been trained not to be scared of anything, not even a tiger. Most untrained horses are terrified of me.'

I scratched the horse between the eyes and she sighed with pleasure. 'Is she really just an ordinary horse? She's not some sort of supernatural creature?'

'Perfectly ordinary Arab mare, just trained by the best in the world.'

'What's her name?' The horse dropped her head and nudged me affectionately.

'Black Jade.' Bai Hu's head shot up and he glanced at John. 'What?'

'That's the second encounter Lady Emma has had with black jade in three days,' John said. 'The earrings she chose for the ceremony were also black jade.'

The Tiger stood very still for a moment. 'I don't like the implications of Lady Emma being presented with so much black jade. Let's look at the other horses instead.'

'You will tell me what all this is about later, John,' I said.

'Is that an order?' His eyes were alive with amusement.

'Damn straight it is.'

The Tiger burst out laughing. 'I would never have believed it. The Dark Lord has met his match, and she is an ordinary human a good head shorter than him.'

'Nothing ordinary about her,' John said, smiling into my eyes.

'Give it a rest.' I checked the length of the stirrup leathers and pulled them up to suit me. 'I'm not superstitious, whatever this black jade thing is. Let me have a sit on her.' I stopped when I saw the saddle. 'This is an Australian synthetic saddle.'

'Very useful,' the Tiger said. 'Washes clean, adjusts to size, a good fit on most horses, even these round Arabs. Saves a tremendous amount of work for the grooms.'

'How many horses do you have?'

'I have no idea. Two five nine! How many horses we got right now?'

'Nine hundred and forty-eight altogether, my Lord, in the Palace,' the groom called back. 'Another couple of hundred on the Earthly Plane in the racing stables, and some of this season's mares have yet to drop.'

'The answer is: I have an awful lot of horses, my Lady. Try the mare.' Bai Hu nodded towards Simone, who was gleefully charging around on a cute skewbald pony. 'I think Princess Simone has already chosen. I knew she'd pick the coloured one.'

I couldn't ride well enough to get nearly as good a performance out of Black Jade, but nobody seemed to care. I tried the other two, but couldn't wait to get back on the first mare.

'You want her?' John said.

I nodded as I trotted past.

'You'll have to get off her eventually, Emma.'

'Can the Tiger teach me how to capriole?'

'Certainly, my Lady, that is a very useful skill in battle. You handle the demons to the front and side, the horse can handle those behind. We've bred some heavier blood into the Arabs to give them the bone to handle Airs Above, but you will have to be careful not to stress her bones too much.' He nodded with satisfaction. 'It's a good fit. You will make a striking couple riding together at the country club, my Lord. Send me a photo, I'll put it up above my desk.'

'You'll never see it then,' John said. 'You never do your own paperwork.'

'Then I'll put it up above my bed.'

I cantered to the Tiger, stopped behind him and rapped him sharply on the top of his white hair with the butt of my whip. 'Don't you dare.' I galloped away again.

I didn't hear what John said, but both of them laughed.

Then they went quiet. There was a silent rush of sound and a huge vibration through the ground.

'Emma! Come back!' John shouted, but I was already galloping towards him. I stopped in front of them and threw myself off Black Jade. One of the grooms grabbed her.

Leo charged out of the house, pulled Simone off her pony and carried her over to us.

The Tiger and John were both rigid, concentrating.

'This is it,' John said, eyes unseeing. 'Take Simone into the house, get the demons to lock it up, and send them down to the city.' He snapped back. 'Leo, take Dark Heavens. Emma, use your own sword. Prepare for battle on the top-floor hallway.' His eyes turned unseeing again. 'This is a big one.'

The Tiger vaulted onto Black Jade without bothering to put his feet in the stirrups. 'You want a horse, Ah Wu?'

'I'll be better on the ground. But do me a favour, fetch me my sword?'

'Seven Stars?'

'Yep.'

The Tiger dropped his head and concentrated, then threw the large sword to John who caught it easily.

The other grooms mounted the remaining horses and weapons appeared in their hands. The ponies disappeared.

'Go,' John said. 'Upstairs hallway.'

'So, is this it?' I whispered.

'It could be, love.' He smiled at me. 'We don't have time for goodbyes, Emma. Go.'

'We don't need words anyway.'

I turned and followed Leo towards the house. Ah Yat waited for us next to the front door, her face ashen.

Just as we reached the door the Tiger roared with fury. 'That fucking bastard is *mine*! He broke into my stables in Ireland, killed all my horses, and raped and mutilated two of my women. Nobody is to touch him but *me*!'

'Don't kill him, I want him alive!' John shouted back. 'That one threatened my *family*!'

'First to get him can have him, Ah Wu!'

'You're on,' John said, but his voice was icy.

Leo and I shared a look. Only one demon could stir such emotion.

We made a stop in the training room to collect the weapons, then raced up the stairs to the hallway, Ah Yat trailing behind.

'You know what's happening, Simone?' I said.

'I know, Emma.' She sounded unsure. 'There's an awful lot of them.'

At the top of the stairs I turned to Ah Yat. 'Lock up the house, and then all four of you head down to the city.'

'We will stay and help you defend, my Lady.'

'Do as you're told!' I shouted. 'That's an order!'

She bowed and disappeared.

The upstairs hallway was the perfect place for a defensive stand. It was more like a room than a hall; it had a comfortable couch, a television, and many of Simone's toys strewn around on the floor. Simone used it as a playroom during the day. Leo and I kicked the toys to the side, clearing a space. The hall had a large picture window overlooking the lawn. We could see the Tiger, John and the grooms standing there, waiting.

A flurry of bangs and crashes echoed through the house as the demons locked up.

'Only our demons so far, Simone?'

'Yes, Emma.'

Ah Sum came out of one of the upstairs bedrooms and bowed. 'All secure, my Lady.'

'Good. Go.'

He hesitated, then came to me and quickly embraced me; then Simone, kissing her on the cheek. 'Defend them, Lion.'

'I will,' Leo said gruffly.

Ah Sum disappeared. The other three demons appeared at the bottom of the stairs, bowed to us, and disappeared as well.

'All our demons are gone now, Emma,' Simone said.

'How far away are the other ones?'

'They'll be here soon. Daddy shouldn't be fighting them, he's too weak.'

'That's why they're here, sweetheart,' Leo said. 'They want to get him while he's weak. If he was strong, they wouldn't have a hope.'

'They don't have a hope anyway, Simone.' A rush of cold fury went through me. 'Your dad is the best there is. He has the Tiger with him. The demons don't have a hope.'

Simone nodded, her little face serious.

'Same formation as before, Emma?' Leo said.

'Yeah, I think so. You're still much better than me at hand-to-hand.'

'If you're going to throw energy, for God's sake let me know and I'll get out of the way,' he said with grim humour.

'Me too,' Simone said. 'I can do it too. I want to help.'

'I don't know if that's such a good idea, Simone.'

Simone hesitated and watched me.

Let her, John said. *Let her help if she wants. Keep her to the rear, she can be a last resort.* His voice changed slightly. *Lion. If it comes to that, you know what to do.*

'My Lord,' Leo whispered.

'What?'

'I don't know, Emma,' Simone said. 'It's something with Daddy and Leo.'

'Tell your dad to tell Emma,' Leo said.

Sorry, Emma. If it comes to that, if Leo goes down and it looks like Simone is in danger, tell them they can have my head.

'No!' I shouted.

Oh. And if you destroy them with chi, *be careful. If you kill too many demons with* chi, *you could overload yourself with their energy and explode. Take care, love.*

'Simone, could you pass this on to your dad? Thank you. You will definitely keep for that one.'

His voice chuckled in my ear. *Sorry. I hope you have the chance to tell me off.*

'Here they come,' Simone said.

There are about twenty-four dogs, twelve worms, ten or so humanoids, and a Demon Prince that I would very much like to see the back of.

We moved into position, Leo in front of me and Simone behind me. We stood silently and waited.

'I love you, Daddy,' Simone whispered.

I love you too. All of you. My family. We can do this.

Bring it on, the Tiger growled in my ear. *I want that bastard.*

Leo made a soft sound, readied himself, and then went still.

'They're here,' Simone whispered a few minutes later.

I checked through the window. It was a carnival of horrors.

The dog demons looked like ordinary brown farm dogs, but their faces were split into huge unnatural grins. They shot fire out of their mouths. The warriors on the lawn seemed to be able to deflect the fire, except John. He had to dodge the blasts; he was very weak compared to even the grooms.

The giant worms were shining black with a coating of slime, which they left in a revolting toxic trail. They were slower than the dogs. I'd faced these before, from the demon jar: I had to cut them into many tiny pieces to kill them. If I left them in large bits, they would continue to come at me, still spitting poison. The best way to deal with them was to blow them up with chi.

The ten-foot-tall humanoids wore armour and carried weapons. They had two legs and two arms, but their faces were grotesque and twisted, with huge bulging eyes and gaping mouths with tusks. Some had hair sticking out from their heads in tufts; others were bald with horns. Some were scaly. Some were slimy. Most were shiny black, but two were blood-red. I'd faced these in training as well. Nasty demons, difficult to destroy. Sometimes they could block chi blasts, and when they did, the chi would backfire and knock its sender over. Better to attack physically.

Simon Wong brought up the rear. He was carrying the Wudang sword and rode some sort of two-legged purple lizard. He saw me watching through the window, and waved and blew me a kiss.

The men on the lawn charged to meet the demons. I turned away and concentrated on the stairs. I had an incongruous thought: Simone and I were the only females there. I hefted my sword. Time to show them just what we chicks could do.

Glass shattered downstairs.

'What've we got, Simone?' Leo said.

'Dogs. A lot of them.'

The dogs raced out of the dining room into the downstairs hallway in a rippling brown pack. There appeared to be about fifteen of them. They turned together, charged up the stairs and opened their mouths to blow fire at us.

I made my sword sing and they froze.

Leo dashed down the stairs and made short work of them, tearing through them with Dark Heavens. He swung the sword so fast it whistled. They shredded where he touched them.

When they were all gone he turned to come back up the stairs, his face full of grim triumph. I pulled the chi out of my sword and it went silent.

'No, Emma!' Simone cried, but it was too late.

A ball of flame hit the back of Leo's head and knocked him off his feet. He hit the floor at the bottom of the stairs, face down, with a sickening thump. The dog that had hit him ran from under the stairs and turned, scrabbling for purchase on the tiles.

I hit the demon with a ball of chi and it exploded all over Leo.

I didn't move. Neither did Simone. Leo lay scorched, blackened and unmoving at the base of the stairs.

'Any more demons down there?' I said.

'One more, hiding,' Simone said. 'It's around the corner, under the stairs.'

'Any more apart from that?'

'No.'

'Any demons close enough to come into the house in the next two minutes?'

Simone concentrated, then, 'No.'

'Okay. This is what we'll do. I'll make the sword sing. If the demon is frozen, we'll go down and you destroy it with chi. Then we can help Leo.'

'Okay,' she whispered.

I made the sword sing. Simone nodded: the demon was frozen.

We carefully eased down the stairs. The dog demon stood unmoving next to the base of the stairs. Simone threw a ball of energy at it and it exploded.

'Any more?' I whispered.

Simone didn't answer. She raced to Leo and fell to her knees next to his head. She turned to me to say something, then her eyes went wide.

Simon Wong appeared, crouching behind her. He grabbed her around the waist. He grinned at me over the top of her head and winked.

'Don't move, Simone,' I said.

'Help, Emma,' she said softly.

I made the sword sing. Wong froze. I gingerly eased myself towards him, trying to find the distance I needed to blow him up.

Simone yelled: he'd squeezed her. He wasn't frozen at all.

'Don't come any closer or I'll squeeze her so hard I'll break her.'

I concentrated, gathered myself, and threw a huge ball of chi straight at his head, using the sword as a slingshot.

He raised one hand and the energy was deflected. It returned to the sword. If I'd lost that much chi, it would have killed me.

'Try anything stupid like that again and I'll rip one of her arms off,' he said as if he was passing the time of day.

I remained still with my sword in front of me. I checked Leo: he looked dead. If the demon was past John and the Tiger, then they were dead too. And if Jade and Gold were any example, it would be a long time before they were back. Maybe more than a lifetime for John.

If I attacked the demon with anything physical he'd hurt Simone.

I was out of options.

He saw me hesitate. 'Why don't you come with us and care for her? Wouldn't you like that, dear one? You can keep an eye on her for me.'

I lowered my sword. It didn't matter where Simone went, I would follow her to the depths of Hell if I had to.

He grinned with triumph. 'Put your sword down and come a little closer, my darling. Let's go and have some *real* fun. And then when your boyfriend turns up, you can help me take his head off.'

I put my sword back into its scabbard and placed it carefully on the floor. I walked slowly to him with my hands raised.

He grinned with menace. 'Let's go.'

The room changed around us. We were in some sort of large apartment — a single room with no windows. It had been expensively furnished with low sleek European furniture. A pair of cream couches flanked one wall; a dining table with four chairs sat on the other side of the room. A double bed was set against another wall, about five metres away.

Wong still held Simone, crouched behind her. He moved his hands over her little body and buried his face in her neck.

I went to rush towards them and he grinned up at me. I couldn't move. He'd bound me.

Simone squealed and tried to wriggle out of his grasp, but he gripped her tighter.

He slipped his hand under her little dress and she shrieked.

I tried to yell but I couldn't make a sound. My body was made of lead; it was like a bad dream. I couldn't move. I struggled against the heaviness.

Simone stopped shrieking and sobbed as he ran his hand under her dress. He nuzzled her hair.

I tried to release my fury and relax. I gathered my chi into my dan tian. I could move my chi; so I concentrated. I didn't need my hands to throw chi.

Simone lowered her head and screwed up her face.

Wong flew backwards with his arms outstretched as if he'd been struck. He pulled himself to his feet, wide-eyed with fear.

He grimaced. 'It doesn't matter. I have you. You can't get out.'

He disappeared.

Simone fell to her knees on the floor and curled up in a little ball.

I could move. I ran to her, knelt and bundled her into my arms. I held her close and stroked her hair. 'He can't hurt you, sweetheart, you're too strong. He can't hurt you.'

'He can hurt *you*, Emma.' She gasped, a huge breath. 'He's a *bad* one.'

'Call Daddy,' I whispered.

She concentrated. 'Daddy's not answering.' She pushed her face into my shoulder. 'What if he's dead?'

'He can't die, he's a Shen,' I said. 'How about Uncle Bai?'

She shook her head into my shoulder.

'Jade? Gold? Aunty Kwan?'

She hesitated, then shook her head again.

'Okay.' I gently pulled her head around to me so that I could see into her tear-stained face. 'We just have to find a way out of here.'

She dropped her head onto my shoulder. I looked around. No windows; no doors; no nothing. No way out.

'Do you have any idea where we are, sweetheart?'

She shook her head again.

I sat on the floor, still holding her in my arms. We were trapped.

CHAPTER FORTY-SIX

I checked my watch: 6 p.m. Two hours had passed. Simone lay asleep on the bed, exhausted. I sat on the other side of the bed and put my head in my hands.

The demon hadn't returned. I'd checked the room thoroughly; there was no way out. There was a small bathroom in one corner of the room with running water, so at least we wouldn't die of thirst. But if we were in China the water wasn't drinkable anyway.

I glanced at Simone's peaceful face. Simon Wong was probably holding us to swap for John's head. It was quite likely that the negotiations were happening right now.

If John wasn't dead.

I shivered. Simone was strong enough to hold him off if he tried anything.

I wasn't.

I woke and shot upright to sitting. Simon Wong stood over me, grinning.

Up close, he looked like a perfectly ordinary Chinese. About thirty, good-looking; only his eyes betrayed his true nature.

He sat on the bed next to me and stroked my arm, smiling into my eyes. 'Hello.'

I wrenched my arm away and he bound me again. I couldn't hold myself upright; I fell back. I lay helpless as he leaned over me.

He ran his hand down the side of my face and over my throat. I wanted to scream but I couldn't make a sound.

His hand traced lower, between my breasts. I desperately struggled to free myself.

The hand circled my stomach. He lowered his face and kissed me on the side of the throat, then ran his tongue over the edge of my jaw. He licked up the side of my face.

I relaxed, tried to phase out. I released all of the tension and gathered my chi.

He slipped his hand under the hem of my shirt, above my riding pants, and I blasted the chi straight out of my dan tian into his hand. He snatched his hand away, tearing my shirt, and leapt back, clutching his arm to his side. I'd burnt him.

He lunged towards me again. I scrambled to sit upright against the bedhead, generated a ball of chi and held it in front of me.

He hung back, his face rigid with menace. I raised the chi slightly and floated it between us.

'I'll be back,' he growled, and disappeared.

Simone whimpered and rolled over. She'd slept through the whole thing.

'Emma.' A soft voice in my ear. 'Emma.'

I woke up and cast around. I saw a pair of blood-red eyes and scrambled away, knocking into Simone and waking her.

I grabbed Simone and leapt off the bed, moving as far away from this strange person as I could. He smiled.

It wasn't Wong; it was somebody else. He was Chinese, about twenty-five, with a boyish, cheeky face. He had black hair tied in a short ponytail, but his eyes were the colour of dried blood. He wore a pair of maroon stonewashed jeans and a maroon T-shirt.

He held his hands out. 'I'm not here to hurt you.'

'This is a really big demon,' Simone whispered.

'Bigger than the bad one?'

Simone nodded.

'I swear,' the demon said. 'I can get you out. Would you like to come with me?'

I lowered Simone to the floor and she held onto my leg. 'Why do you want to help us?'

He shrugged. 'Maybe I think One Two Two is a creepy bastard.'

'So?'

'Maybe I don't want him to be Number One.'

'You'll just take us to swap for the Dark Lord's head,' I said. 'You want to be Number One yourself.'

He chuckled. 'I have absolutely no desire to be Number One. None at all.'

The scene around us shifted and we were in a street in Guangzhou; the sounds of voices and traffic blasted around us. Simone clutched my leg.

Silence. We were back in the prison.

'I can take you out,' he said. 'All you have to do is come with me.'

'Promise you won't hurt Simone.'

He smiled gently at Simone. 'I give you my word I will not harm Simone.' He glanced at me. 'I promise I will not harm either of you. I am here to get you out.'

I moved closer to him. 'Which one are you? Are you one of the other princes?'

'You can call me George.'

'*George?*'

He shrugged. 'You want me to take you out? You want to come with me?'

'Yes, please,' Simone said, her voice very small.

'Okay,' I said.

'I want something in return.'

I sagged. 'Why am I not surprised?'

He gestured towards me. 'Leave Simone there, I want to talk to you in private. Come over here. I'll tell you what I want.'

Simone released me and gave me a push. 'I'll be okay, Emma, talk to him.' Her eyes were wide with hope. 'I want to go home to Daddy.'

I nodded and went to the demon. He led me to the other side of the room and leaned against the wall.

'Well, what do you want?' I said.

'Here's the deal,' he said, businesslike. 'Agree to come with me and I'll take you out of here.' He nodded towards Simone. 'I'll put her under for a while and we can do it.'

'You want to have sex with me?'

He nodded.

I raised my arms. 'Why the hell me? I'm nothing special, I'm just an ordinary human female. I'm not even particularly good-looking. Why?'

He smiled slightly. 'The Dark Lord seems to think that you're something special.'

I stared at him.

'Regent of the Northern Heavens, eh?' he said. 'You must be something *extremely* special.'

'You know about that?'

'Everybody knows about it. Heaven and Hell are both abuzz.' He moved his face closer to mine and studied me carefully, still smiling. 'I'd really like to see what all the fuss is about.'

I stood watching him as I thought about it. Then, 'No. I'll take my chances with Wong.'

'How about a bit of oral? No penetration.'

'Shit!' I cried softly. 'This isn't a market stall!'

He moved closer and gazed at me with his blood-red eyes. 'I'll take you out of here for a kiss.'

I looked at him. 'One kiss?'

'You would do that for Simone, wouldn't you?' He moved even closer and touched my arm. 'One kiss won't hurt you. It's not being unfaithful to your Dark Lord; he would understand.' He glanced at Simone. 'I'll get her out of here for you. All you have to do is kiss me, and agree to come along.'

'Okay. One kiss. You take Simone and me out of here, you don't hurt either of us, and then you let us go.'

He jerked with surprise, then smiled. 'You drive a hard bargain.'

'Do we have a deal?'

'Tell Simone to stay put and not interfere, and we have a deal.'

I turned to Simone. 'Stay right there and don't do anything, Simone. He wants to kiss me before he takes us out. Don't look, okay?'

'Daddy won't like that.'

'I hope he has the chance to be jealous.' I turned back to the demon. 'Do it.'

His eyes were very intense. 'You have to kiss me like you mean it.'

'Whatever. Get us out, let us go. Okay?'

He moved his face right into mine. 'Okay,' he breathed against my mouth, then closed the gap.

His hands slipped down my back and pulled me into him. He opened his mouth and his tongue flicked against my lips.

My hands were limp by my sides; he took them and put them onto his back.

'Relax into it, Emma,' he whispered into my mouth. 'Do it right, or I won't take you anywhere. Do it like you mean it.'

I wanted Simone out of there. I pulled him into me, opened my mouth and put everything I had into it.

He moaned and thrust gently against me, then pulled away slightly to speak. 'Sure you don't want more?'

'I'm sure.'

'Shame,' he said. 'Every human woman I've ever had has said I'm absolutely the best.'

'You going to take us out now?' I whispered.

'One more,' he said, and closed his mouth on mine again.

He stopped kissing me and went still. Then he thrust his consciousness into me, like a black dagger between my eyes. He held me, his mouth on mine, and raided my brain. What John had done gently he did with brutal force. He wrenched my soul open and examined it.

I struggled to fight him, but my body and my mind were in a vice; I couldn't move anything.

Something huge, dark and fierce erupted from the base of my skull. It coiled through my brain, surrounded him and thrust him out roughly. It slammed the door in his face.

He released me and staggered back, stricken. 'What the hell was that?'

I was three times bigger, three times darker and three times more ready to kill. I grinned at him. 'Me.'

He flopped to sit on the floor and stared up at me.

I leaned over him. 'Now you have to take us out.'

'Sure, Emma, whatever you say.' He shook his head. 'Give me a moment. Whatever that was, it was powerful.'

The dark thing receded and I sank to the floor as well. I put my head in my hands as I felt a moment of dizziness; then my vision cleared. 'What was that?'

'That was the first time that thing has come out?'

I shook my head, trying to clear it. 'Yes.'

'Hm,' he said, studying me. 'Maybe it was me.'

I didn't have time to worry about it. 'Just take us out of here.'

He rose and held out his hand.

I pulled myself up without his help, and leaned against the wall.

'You *are* something extremely special,' he said.

He turned to Simone. 'Come on, sweetheart, I'll take you out.'

Simone sidled towards us. 'Are you okay, Emma?'

'I'm okay,' I said, and we were in the street again.

It was the wild animal market in Guangzhou. We were in front of the frog stall. A man held a wriggling frog on a chopping board, sliced down the middle of its back, turned it inside out and ripped its legs off. He threw the wriggling front end into a bamboo waste basket and added the skinned hind legs to a pile at the side of the chopping board. An elderly Chinese woman watched carefully as he did it.

The demon eyed the basket of frog heads with fascination. Then he shook himself and grinned at me. 'Maybe later.'

'Doesn't that hurt them?' Simone said.

'No, sweetheart, they're only low animals, they don't feel anything,' the demon said.

'Don't lie to her,' I said. 'Of course it hurts them, Simone.'

'Is that why you wouldn't eat frogs' legs?'

'Yes.'

'It's wrong,' Simone said. 'They should cut the poor frogs' heads off before they do it.'

'You are teaching her too much of your soft Western ways, Emma,' the demon said. He gestured. 'Come with me. I'll take you to your house demons.'

'Is Daddy okay?' Simone said.

'Everybody is just fine,' the demon said. 'Leo has been injured, but he'll live.' He smiled. 'It seems that

521

Leo is always putting himself in harm's way for you. All of you.'

The pavement was slick with blood and water as the stall holders hosed it down. We passed stalls selling meat from animals of all types. Regular poultry stalls killed chickens, ducks, geese, pigeons and quails to order; more exotic shops sold mammals like cats, dogs and wildlife like monkeys and civets. A reptile stall had aquariums full of snakes and tortoises.

'Daddy would be very cross,' Simone said.

'I know.'

A small crowd had gathered outside one cage. As we neared, the people stopped looking at the animal in the cage and stared at me. Foreigners weren't terribly common in Guangzhou, particularly in this part of town.

The cage held a dark brown animal about the size of a corgi, with short fur and long ears. It looked like a giant rabbit.

'What's that?' Simone said.

The animal shifted slightly and I saw its tiny hooves.

'It's a baby donkey,' I said.

Simone raced to it and crouched in front of the cage on the wet concrete. The people who had been looking at the donkey watched her with broad, artless grins.

The demon stood behind Simone. 'Baby donkey is the latest fad here right now. It's called "exotic beef". Supposed to be really good.' He shrugged. 'I haven't tried it yet.'

Simone looked up at me, eyes wide. 'I want to take it home. Can I take it?'

'I'm sorry, Simone. Remember, we can't even have a dog. We don't have room.'

'The house on the hill has room.' Simone rose and took my hand. 'Ah Yee can look after it. Please buy it. I don't want anybody to eat it. It's so tiny!'

'How about I buy it for you?' the demon said. 'A show of good faith. I'll even take it up to the house for you, but you'll have to meet me at the front gate. I can't go in.'

Simone gazed imploringly at me. 'Please, Emma.'

I looked from Simone to the demon. He smiled slightly and raised his eyebrows.

I sagged. 'Okay.'

Simone jumped up and down and nearly fell over on the slippery concrete. She hugged me tight, then turned to hug the demon.

He quickly stepped away, raising his hands. 'Don't touch me, please, dear. I don't know how much damage you would do to me.'

Simone dropped her arms and stood very still, watching him. Then she nodded, more restrained. 'Thank you.'

'My pleasure.' He gestured towards the end of the street. 'Your city house is about two li that way. I'll take you there, then come back and collect this little fellow for you.'

He shouted into the shop, and a few of the people who had been watching us laughed. The shopkeeper came out. He wore a pair of jeans and a T-shirt underneath an enormous white apron stained with blood. The demon negotiated quickly for the donkey, then pulled his wallet out of his hip pocket and handed over a few hundred Chinese yuan.

'Daddy will pay you back,' Simone said.

'Your father won't give me money,' the demon said. 'I've tried to sell him a few things in the past, but he won't deal.'

I took Simone's hand. 'Let's go home.'

We walked further and eventually stopped at an apartment building with a single door facing onto the street. The demon held his hand over the handle of the metal gate, and it unlocked and fell open. He led us up the narrow stairs to the landing.

'Have you been here before, Simone?' I said.

'No. I only go to the house on the hill. This place is just for the demons.'

The demon stopped in front of the apartment's metal gate and concentrated.

The door flew open; Ah Yat stood there. She saw us and smiled broadly, then saw the demon and her smile froze.

'Hello, little one,' the demon said. 'I've brought your mistresses home.'

Ah Yat didn't move or speak. She watched the demon like a rabbit caught in headlights.

'Let us all in, Ah Yat,' Simone said.

Ah Yat carefully opened the metal gate and it swung outwards. Simone threw herself at Ah Yat and buried her face in her stomach. Ah Yat didn't stop watching the demon.

'I've brought them back unharmed,' the demon said. 'Take them home.'

Ah Yat glanced at me. 'You have not been harmed, my Lady?'

'We're fine,' I said. 'I hope you have something to drink in here, I'm dying of thirst.'

'Me too,' Simone said.

'Me three,' the demon said, and Simone giggled. 'Can I come in and have a drink too? Buying your donkey was hot work.'

'Yeah, sure!' Simone said. 'Let us in, Ah Yat.'

Ah Yat moved back and gestured for us to enter. The demon followed, closing the door behind us.

The living room had a high ceiling and bare concrete walls. The only furniture was a rosewood sofa and coffee table.

The demon strolled in and sat on the sofa.

'I'm really thirsty, Ah Yat,' Simone said. 'Do you have any lemon tea?'

Ah Yat dropped to hug Simone and held her close. Her voice trembled. 'Yes, my darling.' She glanced at me. 'My Lady?'

'Cold filtered water, please, Ah Yat.'

'Me too,' the demon said.

'Wait here.' Ah Yat released Simone and went out of the room.

Ah Yee, Ah Sum and Ah Say sidled into the room. They saw the demon and froze.

The demon gestured. 'Come in.'

They crept further into the room.

The demon leaned his arms on the back of the seat. 'Tamed, eh?'

The three house demons didn't move or speak.

'How many of them do you need to escort you home, Simone?' the demon said.

'Ah Yat can take me home,' Simone said.

'Good.' The demon waved one hand. The three house demons exploded into black streamers and disappeared.

'Bye, girls, see you later.' The demon disappeared too.

Simone flopped to her knees and put her head in her hands. I went to her, wrapped my arms around her and rocked her as she cried with huge gasping sobs. We stayed like that until Ah Yat returned with the drinks on a tray.

When Ah Yat realised what had happened, she fell onto the sofa and wept as well.

CHAPTER FORTY-SEVEN

The taxi driver tried to rip us off when we reached the gates to the house. Ah Yat had a protracted argument with him, but eventually I couldn't wait any longer and gave him a hundred yuan extra to shut him up and send him away.

The gates hung open. It was a long walk up the hill to the house. The sun was setting behind us, casting an eerie red glow over everything. The blood on the grass was black and shining. It was like a scene from an old war movie. There were bodies everywhere.

'*Daddy*!' Simone shrieked and raced to John. He lay face down on the grass. Bai Hu lay next to him in True Form, his white fur stained with blood.

Black Jade lay near them. She had been disembowelled and her white and blue entrails glistened on the grass. Her mane was matted with blood, her eyes wide and unseeing. One of the grooms lay dead next to her, his arm thrown over her neck.

I fell onto my knees next to Simone and John. The grass was slick with blood.

The Tiger moved slightly and I grabbed his shaggy head and raised it. 'Bai Hu! Bai Hu!'

'What the fuck happened?' he growled.

'Quickly. Some of them may still be alive.'

He pulled himself to his feet, groggy, and shook his head. When he saw John next to him he quickly changed to human form. 'Ah Wu! Ah Wu!' He shook John's shoulder. 'Wake up!' He dropped his voice. 'Stupid goddamn Turtle.'

'I should call you out for that,' John said into the grass.

Both Simone and I sighed with relief. 'Can I help anyone else?' I said.

Bai Hu turned John onto his back and knelt next to him. 'Let me see. Nope. Leo.' He shook his head, his white hair stained with blood. 'Leo's alive. Nobody else but Ah Wu made it. That was a strong one.' His eyes unfocused and he took both of John's hands in his. 'Shen or chi?'

'Anything but ching. I have enough of that as it is,' John said without moving. 'Simone?'

'I'm okay, Daddy.'

'Emma?'

'I'm here, John. Will he be okay, Tiger?'

'He'll be fine.' Bai Hu raised his hands, still holding John's, and a silver glow appeared around both of them.

'What about Leo?' I asked. 'He took a demon fireball to the back of the head.'

'How long has he had that demon stuff on him?'

I checked my watch. 'Oh dear Lord, nearly three hours.'

Bai Hu lowered his head, still holding John's hands. 'I've put him in the upstairs bathroom. Strip him down, wash him off and then we'll deal with the burns.'

'Show-off,' John growled. 'Two at once.'

'Always,' the Tiger said, his eyes unseeing. 'Go, Emma. Take Simone with you.'

'I'm staying here with my daddy!' Simone said.

'Go inside, sweetheart,' John said without moving. 'Take Ah Yat too, please.'

'Okay, Daddy.' Simone rose and took Ah Yat's hand. 'Come on, Emma, you need to give Leo a bath. He's going to be really embarrassed.'

'You okay to do that, Emma?' John said, concerned.

'I don't think he'll care too much,' I said.

We went inside, leaving John and Bai Hu with their grim companions on the grass.

Simone stopped at the bottom of the stairs and put her hand over her mouth. 'I need to use the toilet,' she gasped. 'In *a hurry*!' She ran into the downstairs bathroom, Ah Yat racing to follow her.

I went upstairs and left them to it. Leo was in the upstairs bathroom; the Tiger had landed him in the bath. His eyes were open but he didn't seem to be focusing on anything. I fell to my knees next to him and took his hand. It was ice-cold.

Simone started to wail downstairs. It had caught up with her. I was still completely calm; in fact so calm I was surprised at myself.

Leo cast around, unseeing. 'Emma? Simone?'

'It's me, Leo. Everything's okay.'

I pulled at his polo shirt; the demon stuff had soaked through onto his skin. 'Lean forward, you're covered in demon stuff. I need to wash you off.'

He tried to do as I asked, but he could hardly move. 'Hurry, Emma, it's burning.'

'You'll need to help me, you're too big. Raise your arms.' I carefully removed the shirt, trying not to touch the burn on the back of his head.

He grimaced. 'What happened to my head?'

I turned on the water and checked the temperature; he didn't need to be scalded on top of everything else. 'Don't worry about that, let's just get this demon stuff off you.'

I washed his chest down; fortunately the demon stuff came free under the water and rinsed away. 'Lean back, let's get these pants off.'

After all the demon stuff was gone, I pushed him forward to check his head. He seemed to be focusing better and able to see me, but his face was rigid with pain. The demon had hit him slightly to one side. It looked bad. The wound was scorched around the edges, and there appeared to be bone shining through in the middle. I hissed under my breath.

I dried him off with a towel. He made an effort to help me, but could still barely move.

'Are you ready in there?' the Tiger called from outside.

'All done,' I said.

'Hey, put a towel around me first,' Leo said.

I threw a towel to cover him just as he disappeared. I rushed out of the bathroom and nearly ran into Bai Hu. He caught me before I fell.

'How's John?' I asked.

'I've put him in his room. I managed to restore some of his energy, so he'll be okay until you see the Lady next. He should see her within the next three to four months though. That was the best I could do. I'll be out of action for a while — my women will be very upset.'

'A little restraint never hurt anyone,' I shot back.

We went into Leo's room together. Leo was lying on the bed, staring grimly at the ceiling. I quickly pulled the covers over him and removed the damp towel.

'Thanks, Emma.'

The Tiger levered Leo onto his side to examine the burn. 'He should go to Hong Kong for treatment.'

'John's too weak to provide blood to heal him, isn't he?' I said.

The Tiger glanced at me. 'He's done that before?'

I nodded.

'And it worked?'

I nodded again.

The Tiger studied Leo appraisingly. 'Interesting. Not a good idea, though, unless he's near death. If you gave him the Turtle's blood when the injuries are not mortal, the blood itself could kill him. Do you still have that feather the Phoenix gave you?'

'Yes,' I said. 'It's in my room.'

'Run and get it,' Bai Hu said.

He didn't move to take the feather when I returned. 'I'm not capable, I'm too drained. You will have to do it.'

'What do I do?'

'Fill the feather with chi and run it over the wound.' He raised Leo to sit upright and held him around the shoulders. 'All right, my friend?'

Leo grunted but his face was taut with agony. He grimaced. 'Is Simone okay? She's crying her lungs out downstairs.'

'Nervous exhaustion,' the Tiger said. 'She needs to have a really good cry, then she'll feel better. It's a shame she had to see the bodies. That must have been a shock for her.'

Leo turned his head slightly. 'Bodies?'

'Don't worry, my friend.'

'Is Mr Chen okay, Emma?'

'Mr Chen is fine.'

I held the feather about halfway along and loaded it with chi. It seemed to hold the energy the same way my sword did, and glowed with a rainbow radiance just at the edge of vision. I touched the end of the feather to the edge of the burn. I expected Leo to flinch, but he relaxed and smiled instead. 'That feels really good.'

I moved with more confidence and watched in amazement as the feather healed the burn. Fresh new skin of a slightly lighter colour grew where the burn had been. I ran the feather completely over the wound, and it was as if the burn had never been there. Leo closed his eyes and relaxed into the Tiger's arms, smiling.

I withdrew the energy from the feather. Less chi came out of it than went in, and the colours had faded. This was obviously a destructive process for the feather.

'Are you drained, my Lady?' Bai Hu said. 'You seem fine.'

'It's used about a third of my chi, but I'll live.'

Bai Hu ran his hands down Leo's arms and took his hands. He closed his eyes and concentrated, then snapped back. 'You should have told us how bad it was, my friend.'

Leo didn't say anything.

'Move forward, I need to sit behind you,' the Tiger said. 'The poison is in your blood. We'll need to force it out.'

He crawled onto the bed to sit cross-legged behind Leo. 'Look, you have me where you wanted me.'

Leo didn't smile at the quip. He leaned heavily against me as I held him upright. He was obviously having trouble staying conscious.

The Tiger dropped his head and concentrated. Ah Yat came in with a large bowl, passed it to me, then quickly went out.

'Hold it in front. To catch it when he spits,' the Tiger said. He put his hands on Leo's bare back. His face went rigid. Then he pulled his hands slightly away and performed a lightning-fast set of chi gong moves. I recognised them: internal energy manipulation. The final move was to hit Leo hard on the back with both hands.

Leo's head snapped back and then forward, and he spat a cupful of blackened blood into the bowl.

The Tiger lowered his head. 'More.'

He hit Leo again, and again Leo spat blood. This time it was redder.

The Tiger levered himself off the bed and gently lowered Leo. 'That should do it.'

I put the bowl to one side and pulled the covers back over Leo. He'd already fallen asleep, his face childlike and innocent. I touched his forehead and kissed him on the cheek.

I turned to Bai Hu and clasped his hands. 'Thank you so much, Tiger. For everything. Let's go and check on Xuan Wu.'

'You go,' the Tiger said. 'Ah Wu will be fine. I need to fix up my horsemen downstairs. Tell everybody to stay inside until I've finished. It's a big mess out there.'

'I know,' I said. 'I'm sorry about your men.'

'You are quite remarkable, you know that?' he said. 'You've remained perfectly calm through all of this.'

I shook my head. 'I know. I don't know what's wrong with me. I should be freaking out. I walked right past all those bodies and didn't even flinch.'

'How did you get away from the demon?'

'A bigger demon helped us escape,' I said. 'Looks like we were pawns in demon politics.'

Bai Hu left me at the door of John's room.

'Emma, he can't drain you while he's asleep. You'll be able to touch him. Take care if he wakes, though.'

My heart twisted.

His face was peaceful as he slept. I quietly pulled a chair over to sit next to him.

His hand was resting on the covers. I touched it. He didn't move, so I took it, and held it in mine. His skin was smooth and cool. I ran my finger along the prominent veins and rubbed my calluses against his. I took a deep breath and let it out slowly. Maybe one day we really would be a matched set.

I held my breath and touched his face. He grimaced, but didn't wake. I ran my fingers down the side of his face and he smiled slightly.

I raised his hand and put it on my cheek.

I wondered where the Serpent was, and why it had disappeared. Was it jealous of Michelle? How could it be? They were the same creature. A snake and a turtle combined. He was so weird. The other three were nearly *normal* compared to him.

And what had happened when the demon pushed into my head? Something huge and dark had thrust it out. John hadn't seen it when he'd looked inside me. What was it? It had been a frightening feeling; as if I could have destroyed everything around me, and worse, *enjoyed* it.

I would talk to him about it later. He would know what to do.

His hand squeezed mine and drew away. I looked down into his dark eyes. 'Go, Emma. You are very precious to me and I hate the thought of hurting you. Let me rest, then we'll go home.'

I went out without saying a word. Words weren't necessary.

Simone and Ah Yat were sitting on the couch in the upstairs hallway. Ah Yat had showered Simone and changed her bloodied clothes. Simone was in Ah Yat's lap, her head on the demon's chest, her eyes wide and glittering. When she saw me, she climbed down carefully and came to me.

I sat on the couch and pulled her into my lap. Ah Yat nodded and went downstairs.

'Is Daddy okay?'

'Daddy's fine, he just needs to rest.'

'Is Leo okay? He was hurt.'

'Leo's fine too. The Tiger fixed him up.'

'What about his head?'

'The Phoenix gave me a feather from her tail when I went out with your dad the other night. It fixed it right up.'

'That demon is really horrible,' she whispered. 'I hate it. It killed all the men downstairs, nearly killed my daddy and my Uncle Bai, and hurt my Leo.'

'We will get that demon one day soon, darling, and then you won't have to worry about it any more.'

'It was going to do bad things to me.'

I held her silently.

She clutched my shirt and turned her head to see me. 'You went with me.'

I pulled her tight. 'Anywhere you go, I'll go too. I love you more than anything in the world.'

Her little hand brushed my cheek. 'I love you too, Emma.'

'Your dad will wake up soon, and then we can go home,' I whispered into her hair.

CHAPTER FORTY-EIGHT

John was able to join us for dinner, but Leo slept on.
'Wong took us to some sort of prison,' I said. 'An apartment with no doors, no windows. He didn't hurt us. He tried, but Simone was too strong.'

'Then the other demon came and took us out,' Simone said.

'Tell me about the other demon,' John said.

Ah Yat poked her head in the room. 'The King is here with the donkey, sir.'

'Oh my God,' I said. 'Calls himself George. Eyes the colour of dried blood, clothes the same colour. Looked about twenty-five. That's the King?'

'That's him,' John said. He hesitated, thinking. 'No, I won't leave either of you here, you're safer with me. Come with me and we'll talk to him. What donkey?'

'He bought me a baby donkey in the animal market,' Simone said. 'I thought he was nice. Then he killed everybody in our house in the city.'

'He should not have been able to get into that apartment,' John said. 'It's sealed. Not even the King himself should be able to enter.'

'I told Ah Yat to open the door and let us in,' Simone

said. 'I forgot, Daddy.' Her little shoulders shook with sobs. 'It was my fault!'

I wrapped my arm around her shoulder and held her as she cried. We all walked together down to the gates.

'So the King came into Wong's nest and took you out,' John said. 'Only he would be able to do that, and only if you agreed to go with him.'

'We did agree to go with him,' I said.

'That's interesting,' John said as we neared the gates. 'He was within his rights to keep you in his own nest, once you'd agreed to go with him. That's the way it works.'

'I made him promise to let us go,' I said.

John stopped and stared at me. Then he grinned and shook his head. 'Well done!'

The King was waiting on the other side of the huge metal gates. The tiny donkey stood beside him with a piece of string around its neck, its little tail swishing furiously. John raised his hand and the gates swung open.

Simone moved towards the donkey, then stopped. She shifted to stand behind her father.

The King saluted John. 'Xuan Tian.'

John saluted back. 'Mo Wang.'

The King waved and smiled. 'Hi, Emma.'

I didn't respond.

'Why did you release my wife and daughter?' John said. 'If you'd let One Two Two keep them, you could have had my head by now.'

The King grinned broadly. 'If you went off and married her on the sly, you are in even bigger trouble than everybody says you are. I didn't think even *you* would disobey the Jade Emperor that much.'

John waved it away. 'To me, Emma is my wife, and she will be for as long as she lives.'

The King bent over with mirth, his hands on his knees. 'Oh my God, that is just so goddamn *cute*!'

'That's the way I feel too,' I said. 'The fact that we can't formally marry right now is beside the point.'

The King pulled himself upright and shook his head. 'What a pair of idiots.'

'Why did you release Emma and Simone?' John said.

The King shrugged. 'Maybe I just wanted to piss off that little bastard. Somebody else will bring me your head. It's just a matter of time.'

Simone squeaked and grabbed her father's leg.

'Sorry, pet,' the King said with genuine remorse. 'I didn't mean to say it like that.'

'Why did you kill my demons?' Simone snapped from behind John. 'They didn't do anything to you!'

The King bent to speak kindly to her. 'If a demon defects, they know the penalty. If I find one of mine that has been tamed by a Celestial, I destroy it. That's the way it works, Simone. They knew they were dead the minute they saw me.'

'And I *let you in*!' Simone wailed.

The King gestured towards Simone. 'You're a fool, Xuan Tian. She's a delightful child. And every single one of my demons wants her.' He shook his head. 'You should never have done this. Creatures such as yourself should never attempt to have human children.'

'I know,' John said.

The King sighed. 'Love makes fools of us all.'

'I know,' John said again, softly.

'Come and get your little donkey, sweetheart,' the King said. 'I won't hurt you, I promise. You'll need to give it a name. It's a girl donkey.'

Simone buried her face in her father's leg and didn't move.

'Emma,' the King said, and raised the piece of string.

I glanced at John, who nodded.

I sidled forward and took the string. The King smiled into my eyes and whispered to me, 'I know he can't touch you, but I can. Any time you want a really nice touch, just give me a call.'

'Go to hell,' I whispered back, and led the donkey to Simone. She wrapped her little arms around its neck.

'Have you told him about that dark thing?' the King said.

John glanced at me.

'Obviously not,' the King said. He saluted John. 'Xuan Tian. See ya.' And disappeared.

'What dark thing?' John said.

'Let's go back and finish our dinner, and I'll tell you all about it,' I said.

'I negotiated him down to a kiss. He kissed me, and pushed his way into my head, and then the dark thing came out.' I dropped my head into my hands. 'I am so sorry.'

He poured me some tea. 'Why?'

I stared at him.

He leaned back and glared at me. 'Don't for one minute think that I am jealous. Of course I'm not. What we have is greater than any jealousy, and you know it.'

'Oh my God,' I whispered. 'You're an Emperor.'

His face went rigid and he watched me.

'I know the tradition: it's the Emperor's duty to have as many children with as many wives as possible.'

He didn't say a word.

'How many wives do you have? In the Northern Heavens? On the Mountain?' I raised my hands. 'No. Don't tell me. I don't want to know. I don't want to know anything about it. Just please make sure that I never meet any of them.'

'Any of my other wives?'

'Yes.'

'Not going to happen, Emma,' he said with a small smile. 'My number is one.'

'Only one wife?'

'Right now, you are my only one,' he said. He leaned forward and gazed into my eyes. 'You were prepared to share me?'

'Women do incredibly stupid things for the love of a man,' I said.

'And vice versa.'

I smiled. 'Yeah.'

'So this dark thing was powerful enough to push the King away?'

'Yes. It was pretty scary.'

'What was scary?' Leo said from the doorway. He saluted John and me. 'My Lord. My Lady.'

'Cut it out and come and have some tea,' I said. 'How do you feel? Up to eating something?'

Leo sat at the table. 'I have the biggest migraine in the whole world. Right now, all I want is coffee.' He glanced around. 'Where's Simone?'

'Asleep,' I said. 'Ran around with the donkey so much she wore herself out.'

'Donkey?'

'I'll tell you later.'

'But you'll tell me more about this dark thing right now,' John said. 'He kissed you and invaded your mind. Something dark rose within you and pushed him out. Yes?'

'Yes.'

He leaned his chin on his hand. 'I didn't see anything like that when I looked inside you.'

'He said maybe it was just him,' I said. 'What did he mean?'

'Maybe it only comes out for someone with a demonic nature.'

'Damn,' I whispered.

'Don't worry about it.' He poured some more tea. 'If it's important, it will emerge. If it doesn't emerge then

539

it's not important. It didn't welcome the King; it forced him out. That's good enough for me.'

Ah Yat came in with Leo's coffee and he nodded his thanks to her, then turned his attention back to us. 'King?'

'The King of the Demons has taken a shine to my Emma,' John said. 'He rescued her and Simone from One Two Two and bought Simone a baby donkey for good measure.'

'Just when I thought our lives couldn't be any more complicated,' Leo growled.

The next morning Leo was fine but John was still very weak. He put on his navy suit and changed to his older form, ready for the border crossing. Leo drove.

John kept falling asleep in the car. I had to constantly remind him to change his hair; he seemed to have trouble keeping it short.

When we reached the stables, John pulled his bag out of the boot and went inside to change. Simone lay on the seat next to me.

Leo stiffened, then quickly pulled himself out of the car. Five armed demons approached us in the car park; level twenty or thirty. They looked like triads; their hair was dyed blond and red. They wore filthy jeans and T-shirts, and carried Chinese cleavers, the weapon of choice for Hong Kong gangsters.

I hopped out of the car, leaving Simone sleeping on the seat. I went around and stood next to Leo.

'There're some swords in the boot.' Leo moved his hand and the boot popped open. 'Pull out Dark Heavens for me, will you?'

I went and pulled out Dark Heavens, the sword that usually resided on clips in the hallway back at the Peak. My sword was there, and I took it as well, then slammed the boot shut.

I passed Dark Heavens to Leo.

'Thanks,' he said. 'Go and get Mr Chen.'

'No need,' I said. 'We can handle this.'

He glanced down at me.

'I'll take the two on the right. You take the three on the left.' I pulled my sword from its scabbard. 'Ready?'

Leo turned back to the demons. 'Hell, yeah.'

They ran towards us and we moved to give each other room.

I pushed some chi into the sword and made it sing; it didn't affect them at all. They continued to run at us. I threw the chi at the demon on the far right and it exploded. The demon next to it was too close to hit with chi. It came at me with weapon raised and its face a grimace of anger.

It attacked me with the cleaver. I felt perfectly calm as I watched it coming at me, then sidestepped.

The demon was fast; it followed my movement, and turned to hit me horizontally.

I blocked the cleaver with my left hand on the demon's elbow, then pushed its arm in the direction it was already going. As the demon unbalanced with the push, I raised my own sword, spun, and sliced it in half.

I didn't have time to get out of the way, and the demon exploded all over me.

I checked Leo; he had already destroyed one and faced the other two. He sliced one demon's head off with a swinging arc of the sword, then swept down, moved back, and took another demon through the abdomen with an upward backhand slice. Both demons exploded on him.

I saw movement and glanced up. Simon Wong stood at the end of the car park, arms crossed, watching. I filled with ice-cold fury, hefted my sword, and ran towards him.

'Leo, there he is,' I cried. 'Let's *get* him!'

Leo looked up and saw Wong. He leapt to run towards the demon as well.

Wong uncrossed his arms, put his hands on his hips and disappeared.

Leo and I skidded to a halt.

'That freaking *coward*!' I shouted. I nearly threw my sword on the ground with frustration, but I'd put a great deal of work into its edge. 'I am going to *get* him!'

'Scary,' Leo said.

'You have no idea,' I growled.

We turned back to the car. John stood at the entrance to the country club, holding his bag, waiting for us.

'I am going to *get* that ugly little freak if it is the last thing I ever do,' I said.

'You know what?' Leo grinned down at me. 'I believe you.' He wrapped his arm around my shoulders and gave me an affectionate squeeze, nearly knocking me off my feet. 'We'd better go into the change rooms and have a shower, my Lady.'

'Call me "my Lady" one more time and you'll feel my sword as well,' I said.

'Yes, my Lady,' Leo said, saluting me with Dark Heavens still in his hand.

'Shit,' I said under my breath. I tried to shake the black stuff off my hands but it stuck. Leo was right; we both needed a shower.

Simone had woken and hopped out of the car as we approached. 'You were terrific, Emma!' she squealed, jiggling with delight. 'You were as good as *Leo*! Isn't she, Daddy?'

John smiled with admiration. 'Absolutely.'

'Let me get a change of clothes. I need to have a shower.' Leo popped the boot again and I threw my sword in, found a towel, and wiped my arms and face. Leo put Dark Heavens into the car. I handed the towel to him and he wiped the demon stuff off as well.

I scrabbled through my duffel bag for a change of clothes. Leo opened his bag as well.

I stopped dead as I saw the contents of Leo's bag.

'What?' Leo said.

Leo's bag was immaculately packed. Everything was neatly folded and arranged.

'Geez. You can pack *my* bag next time,' I said.

'It would be an honour and a pleasure, my Lady,' Leo said. 'Your bag looks like it's full of dirty laundry.'

I found a pair of jeans and a shirt. 'You are so going to keep, Leo.'

Leo saluted me. 'My Lady.'

'We'll have something to eat on the terrace while you change,' John said. 'Simone says she's hungry.'

'Okay.' I shoved Leo as I walked past him. 'Bastard.'

'I heard that, *my Lady*.'

When we arrived home, Leo parked the car under the Peak apartment building and we all piled out. He went to the boot and grabbed John's and my bags.

'I'll take my own bag,' I said.

'It is my duty as Retainer to serve you, my Lady,' Leo said with a broad grin. 'I'll return to the car later and collect the other luggage.'

I tried to grab my bag from Leo but he wouldn't let me. He moved it out of the way every time I tried to take it, and eventually just raised it out of my reach.

John took Simone's hand and led her to the front door. 'Watching you two is the most amusing thing I've seen in centuries.' He glanced down at Simone. 'What do you think?'

Simone giggled. 'Yeah, they're *funny*. They're *stupid*.'

Jade and Gold were waiting for us inside. They both fell to one knee and saluted us. 'My Lord. My Lady.'

Leo took the bags down the hall, grinning broadly. I wanted to thump *him*.

'We have an urgent problem that must be dealt with immediately,' Gold said. 'The engineers have discovered that the student dormitories on the Mountain are so badly damaged they must be demolished. We need to find somewhere for the students to live while we rebuild.'

'I need to rest,' John said. 'Emma can handle it.'

My mouth dropped open and I looked from John to the Retainers.

'You can do it, Emma, I have complete faith in you,' John said. 'Could you come with me for a minute first? I need to talk to you.'

I sighed with resignation and indicated for Jade and Gold to go into the dining room. 'Wait for me in there.'

Leo came down the hallway from the bedrooms, saw me and fell to one knee, saluting.

'Cut it out,' I said.

He rose and grinned. 'Face it, Emma, your life is about to become a hell of a lot more interesting.' He saluted me again. 'My Lady. I'll take Simone while you meet with your staff.'

I ran my hands through my hair in exasperation and followed John into his room.

He turned away from me and pulled off his T-shirt. The muscles flexed over his back, golden and glowing. He undid his black jeans and pulled them off. He had black silk boxers underneath. He turned to me as he retied his hair and the skin rippled over his abdomen.

I swallowed hard. 'I think I'd better go.'

'Oh, come on, Emma. I've seen inside your head, remember? I know what you want. I'd like to let you see all of me, but it wouldn't be a good idea. I don't think I could control it.'

He sat cross-legged on the bed and gestured for me to come closer. 'Sit. I need to talk to you.'

'Isn't there any way at all that we can ...' My voice trailed off as I sat on the bed, as near to him as possible without touching.

'None that I can think of.' He shrugged. 'We'll find a way. There has to be a way.'

'*Look but don't touch*. It'll kill me. Next time you're going to undress in front of me, let me get a video camera.'

'If you like. Don't reciprocate though; much as I'd like you to, I'd definitely lose control.' He saw my face. 'What?'

'I was expecting you to be more old-fashioned Chinese about this. We're not even married.'

He smiled gently. 'I'm an animal Shen. You've seen the Tiger. I'm a Turtle. A reptile. Many human attitudes don't make much sense to us. As I said, the Jade Emperor often doesn't know what to do with us. Particularly me. There are many people on the Celestial Plane who firmly believe that I don't belong there.'

'John Chen Wu, you never cease to amaze me.'

He looked me right in the eyes. 'Good.' I sat on the bed next to him. 'Too close.'

I edged slightly away.

He sighed. 'Emma, the demons all know about you now. If you want, I can move you somewhere safe where they can't get you.'

'No. We won't have much time together before you go. I know you promised to come back for me, but there are no guarantees in life. I want to spend as much time as I can with you now. Besides, I'm here to look after Simone.'

He pulled his knees up and wrapped his arms around them. 'We really are a pair of fools.'

'I know. Lie down.'

He stretched his long legs under the covers and I pulled the blankets over him, careful not to touch him. 'Now get some rest.'

'Is that an order?' he growled. He wriggled under the covers and banged his head on the pillow.

'Damn straight it is.' I turned to go out.

'Emma.'

I turned back to him.

'I love you.'

'I love you too, Xuan Wu.' I had a sudden inspiration. 'How about later this evening I go into my room and call you on your mobile?'

He shot upright to stare at me. He opened his mouth to speak, then closed it. His gaze was very intense as he shook his head.

'Is that a no?'

He fell back onto his pillow and his voice floated to me, soft and deep. 'No, my love, that is very much a yes.'

I went out to talk to Jade and Gold. Leo was right. My life *was* about to become a hell of a lot more interesting.

The Serpent sleeps buried in
the silken mud at the bottom
of the sea. The water is freezing
and dark and suffocating.
The Serpent awakes and shifts,
raising the mud in a floating cloud.
The Serpent cries.
There is no answer.

GLOSSARY

The Chinese language is divided by a number of different dialects and this has been reflected throughout my story. The main dialect spoken in Hong Kong is Cantonese, and many of the terms I've used are in Cantonese. The main method for transcribing Cantonese into English is the Yale system, which I have hardly used at all in this book, preferring to use a simpler phonetic method for spelling the Cantonese. Apologies to purists, but I've chosen ease of readability over phonetic correctness.

The dialect mainly spoken on the Mainland of China is Putonghua (also called Mandarin Chinese), which was originally the dialect used in the north of China but has spread to become the standard tongue. Putonghua has a strict and useful set of transcription rules called pinyin, which I've used throughout for Putonghua terms. As a rough guide to pronunciation, the 'Q' in pinyin is pronounced 'ch', the 'X' is 'sh' and the 'Zh' is a softer 'ch' than the 'Q' sound. Xuan Wu is therefore pronounced 'Shwan Wu'.

I've spelt chi with the 'ch' throughout the book, even though in pinyin it is qi, purely to aid in readability.

Qing Long and Zhu Que I have spelt in pinyin to assist anybody who'd like to look into these interesting deities further.

Aberdeen Typhoon Shelter: A harbour on the south side of Hong Kong Island that is home to a large number of small and large fishing boats. Some of the boats are permanently moored there and are residences.

Admiralty: The first station after the MTR train has come through the tunnel onto Hong Kong Island from Kowloon, and a major traffic interchange.

Ancestral tablet: A tablet inscribed with the name of the deceased, which is kept in a temple or at the residence of the person's descendants and occasionally provided with incense and offerings to appease the spirit.

Anime (Japanese): Animation; can vary from cute children's shows to violent horror stories for adults, and everything in between.

Bai Hu (Putonghua): The White Tiger of the West.

Bo: Weapon — staff.

Bo lei: A very dark and pungent Chinese tea, often drunk with yum cha to help digest the sometimes heavy and rich food served there.

Bu keqi (Putonghua, pronounced [roughly] 'bu kerchi'): 'You're welcome.'

Buddhism: The system of beliefs that life is an endless journey through reincarnation until a state of perfect detachment or Nirvana is reached.

Cantonese: The dialect of Chinese spoken mainly in the south of China and used extensively in Hong Kong. Although in written form it is nearly identical to Putonghua, when spoken it is almost unintelligible to Putonghua speakers.

Causeway Bay: Large shopping and office district on Hong Kong Island. Most of the Island's residents seem to head there on Sunday for shopping.

Central: The main business district in Hong Kong, on the waterfront on Hong Kong Island.

Central Committee: Main governing body of Mainland China.

Cha siu bow: Dim sum served at yum cha; a steamed bread bun containing barbecued pork and gravy in the centre.

Chek Lap Kok: Hong Kong's new airport on a large swathe of reclaimed land north of Lantau Island.

Cheongsam (Cantonese): Traditional Chinese dress, with a mandarin collar, usually closed with toggles and loops, and with splits up the sides.

Cheung Chau: Small dumbbell-shaped island off the coast of Hong Kong Island, about an hour away by ferry.

Chi: Energy. The literal meaning is 'gas' or 'breath' but in martial arts terms it describes the energy (or breath) of life that exists in all living things.

Chi gong (Cantonese): Literally, 'energy work'. A series of movements expressly designed for manipulation of chi.

Chinese New Year: The Chinese calendar is lunar, and New Year falls at a different time each Western calendar. Chinese New Year usually falls in either January or February.

Ching: A type of life energy, ching is the energy of sex and reproduction, the Essence of Life. Every person is born with a limited amount of ching and as this energy is drained they grow old and die.

Chiu Chow: A southeastern province of China.

Choy sum (Cantonese): A leafy green Chinese vegetable vaguely resembling English spinach.

City Hall: Hall on the waterfront in Central on Hong Kong Island containing theatres and a large restaurant.

Confucianism: A set of rules for social behaviour designed to ensure that all of society runs smoothly.

Congee: A gruel made by boiling rice with savoury ingredients such as pork or thousand-year egg. Usually eaten for breakfast but can be eaten as a meal or snack any time of the day.

Connaught Road: Main thoroughfare through the middle of Central District in Hong Kong, running parallel to the waterfront and with five lanes each side.

Cross-Harbour Tunnel: Tunnel that carries both cars and MTR trains from Hong Kong Island to Kowloon under the Harbour.

Cultural Revolution: A turbulent period of recent Chinese history (1966–75) during which gangs of young people called Red Guards overthrew 'old ways of thinking' and destroyed many ancient cultural icons.

Dai pai dong (Cantonese): Small open-air restaurant.

Dan tian: Energy centre, a source of energy within the body. The central dan tian is roughly located in the solar plexus.

Daujie (Cantonese): 'Thank you', used exclusively when a gift is given.

Dim sum (Cantonese): Small dumplings in bamboo steamers served at yum cha. Usually each dumpling is less than an inch across and four are found in each steamer. There are a number of different types, and standard types of dim sum are served at every yum cha.

Discovery Bay: Residential enclave on Lantau Island, quite some distance from the rush of Hong Kong Island and only reachable by ferry.

Dojo (Japanese): Martial arts training school.

Eight Immortals: A group of iconic Immortals from Taoist mythology, each one representing a human condition. Stories of their exploits are part of popular Chinese culture.

Er Lang: The Second Heavenly General, second in charge of the running of Heavenly affairs. Usually depicted as a young man with three eyes and accompanied by his faithful dog.

Fortune sticks: A set of bamboo sticks in a bamboo holder. The questioner kneels in front of the altar and shakes the holder until one stick rises above the rest and falls out. This stick has a number that is translated into the fortune by temple staff.

Fung shui (or feng shui): The Chinese system of geomancy that links the environment to the fate of those living in it. A house with good internal and external fung shui assures its residents of good luck in their life.

Guangdong: The province of China directly across the border from Hong Kong.

Guangzhou: The capital city of Guangdong Province, about an hour away by road from Hong Kong. A large bustling commercial city rivalling Hong Kong in size and activity.

Gundam (Japanese): Large humanoid robot armour popular in Japanese cartoons.

Gung hei fat choy (Cantonese): Happy New Year.

Gwun Gong (or Guan Gong): A southern Chinese Taoist deity; a local General who attained Immortality and is venerated for his strengths of loyalty and justice and his ability to destroy demons.

H'suantian Shangdi (Cantonese): Xuan Tian Shang Di in the Wade-Giles method of writing Cantonese words.

Har gow: Dim sum served at yum cha; a steamed dumpling with a thin skin of rice flour dough containing prawns.

Hei sun (Cantonese): Arise.

Ho ak (Cantonese): Okay.

Ho fan (Cantonese): Flat white noodles made from rice; can be either boiled in soup or stir-fried.

Hong Kong Jockey Club: Hong Kong private institution that runs and handles all of the horseracing and legal gambling in Hong Kong. There can be billions of Hong Kong dollars in bets on a single race meeting.

Hutong (Putonghua): Traditional Chinese house, square and built around a central courtyard.

ICAC: Independent Commission Against Corruption; an independent government agency focused on tracking down corruption in Hong Kong.

Jade Emperor: The supreme ruler of the Taoist Celestial Government.

Journey to the West: A classic of Chinese literature written during the Ming Dynasty by Wu Cheng'En. The story of the Monkey King's journey to India with a Buddhist priest to collect scriptures and return them to China.

Kata (Japanese): A martial arts 'set'; a series of moves to practise the use of the weapon or hand-to-hand skills.

KCR: A separate above-ground train network that connects with the MTR and travels to the border with Mainland China. Used to travel to towns in the New Territories.

Kitchen God: A domestic deity who watches over the activities of the family and reports annually to the Jade Emperor.

Koi (Japanese): Coloured ornamental carp.

Kowloon: Peninsula opposite the Harbour from Hong Kong Island, a densely packed area of highrise buildings. Actually on the Chinese Mainland, but separated by a strict border dividing Hong Kong from China.

Kowloon City: District in Kowloon just before the entrance to the Cross-Harbour Tunnel.

Kwan Yin: Buddhist icon; a woman who attained Nirvana and became a Buddha but returned to Earth to help others achieve Nirvana as well. Often represented as a goddess of Mercy.

Lai see (Cantonese): A red paper envelope used to give cash as a gift for birthdays and at New Year. It's believed that for every dollar given ten will return during the year.

Lai see dao loy (Cantonese): 'Lai see, please!'

Lantau Island: One of Hong Kong's outlying islands, larger than Hong Kong Island but not as densely inhabited.

Li: Chinese unit of measure, approximately half a kilometre.

Lo Wu: The area of Hong Kong that contains the border crossing. Lo Wu is an area that covers both sides of the border; it is in both Hong Kong and China.

Lo Wu Shopping Centre: A large shopping centre directly across the Hong Kong/Chinese border on the Chinese side. A shopping destination for Hong Kong residents in search of a bargain.

Love hotel: Hotel with rooms that are rented by the hour by young people who live with their parents (and therefore have no privacy) or businessmen meeting their mistresses for sex.

M'goi sai (Cantonese): 'Thank you very much.'

M'hai (Cantonese): Literally, 'no need', but it generally means 'you're welcome'.

Macau: One-time Portuguese colony to the west of Hong Kong in the Pearl River Delta, about an hour away by jet hydrofoil; now another Special Administrative Region of China. Macau's port is not as deep and sheltered as Hong Kong's so it has never been the busy trade port that Hong Kong is.

Mah jong: Chinese game played with tiles. The Chinese play it differently from the polite game played by many Westerners; it is played for money and can often be a cut-throat competition between skilled players, rather like poker.

manga: Japanese illustrated novel or comic book.

MTR: Fast, cheap, efficient and spotlessly clean subway train system in Hong Kong. Mostly standing room, and during rush hour so packed that it is often impossible to get onto a carriage.

New Territories: A large area of land between Kowloon and Mainland China that was granted to extend Hong Kong. Less crowded than Hong Kong and Kowloon, the New Territories are green and hilly with highrise New Towns scattered through them.

Nunchucks: Short wooden sticks held together with chains; a martial arts weapon.

Opium Wars: (1839–60) A series of clashes between the then British Empire and the Imperial Chinese Government over Britain's right to trade opium to

China. It led to a number of humiliating defeats and surrenders by China as they were massively outclassed by modern Western military technology.

Pa Kua (Cantonese): The Eight Symbols, a central part of Taoist mysticism. Four of these Eight Symbols flank the circle in the centre of the Korean flag.

Pak Tai: One of Xuan Wu's many names; this one is used in Southern China.

Peak Tower: Tourist sightseeing spot at the top of the Peak Tram. Nestled between the two highest peaks on the Island and therefore not the highest point in Hong Kong, but providing a good view for tourist photographs.

Peak Tram: Tram that has been running for many years between Central and the Peak. Now mostly a tourist attraction because of the steepness of the ride and the view.

Peak, the: Prestigious residential area of Hong Kong, on top of the highest point of the centre of Hong Kong Island. The view over the Harbour and highrises is spectacular, and the property prices there are some of the highest in the world.

Pokfulam: Area of Hong Kong west of the main business districts, facing the open ocean rather than the harbour. Contains large residential apartment blocks and a very large hillside cemetery.

Putonghua: Also called Mandarin, the dialect of Chinese spoken throughout China as a standard language. Individual provinces have their own dialects but Putonghua is spoken as a common tongue.

Qing Long (Putonghua): (pronounced, roughly, Ching Long): The Azure Dragon of the East.

Ramen (Japanese): Instant two-minute noodles.

Repulse Bay: A small swimming beach surrounded by an expensive residential enclave of high- and low-rise apartment blocks on the south side of Hong Kong Island.

Salute, Chinese: The left hand is closed into a fist and the right hand is wrapped around it. Then the two hands are held in front of the chest and sometimes shaken.

Sashimi (Japanese): Raw fish.

Sensei (Japanese): Master.

Sha Tin: A New Territories 'New Town', consisting of a large shopping centre surrounded by a massive number of highrise developments on the banks of the Shing Mun River.

Shaolin: Famous temple, monastery and school of martial arts, as well as a style of martial arts.

Shen: Shen has two meanings, in the same sense that the English word spirit has two meanings ('ghost' and 'energy'). Shen can mean an Immortal being, something like a god in Chinese mythology. It is also the spirit that dwells within a person, the energy of their soul.

Shenzhen: The city at the border between Hong Kong and China, a 'special economic zone' where capitalism has been allowed to flourish. Most of the goods manufactured in China for export to the West are made in Shenzhen.

Sheung Wan: The western end of the Hong Kong Island MTR line; most people get off the train before reaching this station.

Shoji (Japanese): Screen of paper stretched over a wooden frame.

Shui (Cantonese): 'Water'.

Shui gow: Chinese dumplings made of pork and prawn meat inside a dough wrapping, boiled in soup stock.

Shroff Office: A counter in a car park where you pay the parking fee before returning to your car.

Sifu (Cantonese): Master.

Siu mai: Dim sum served at yum cha; a steamed dumpling with a skin of wheat flour containing prawn and pork.

Sow mei (Cantonese): A type of Chinese tea, with a greenish colour and a light, fragrant flavour.

Star Ferry: Small oval green and white ferries that run a cheap service between Hong Kong Island and Kowloon.

Sticky rice: Dim sum served at yum cha; glutinous rice filled with savouries such as pork and thousand-year egg, wrapped in a green leaf and steamed.

Tae kwon do: Korean martial art.

Tai chi: A martial art that consists of a slow series of movements, used mainly as a form of exercise and chi manipulation to enhance health and extend life. Usable as a lethal martial art by advanced practitioners. There are several different styles of tai chi, including Chen, Yang and Wu, named after the people who invented them.

Tai chi chuan: Full correct name for tai chi.

Tai Koo Shing: large enclosed shopping mall on the north side of Hong Kong.

Tao Teh Ching: A collection of writings by Lao Tzu on the elemental nature of Taoist philosophy.

Tao, the: The 'Way'. A perfect state of consciousness equivalent to Buddhist Nirvana, in which a person becomes completely attuned with the Universe and achieves Immortality. Also the shortened name of a collection of writings (the *Tao Teh Ching*) on Taoist philosophy written by Lao Tzu.

Taoism: Similar to Buddhism, but the state of perfection can be reached by a number of different methods, including alchemy and internal energy manipulation as well as meditation and spirituality.

Tatami (Japanese): Rice-fibre matting.

Teppan (Japanese): Hotplate used for cooking food at teppanyaki.

Teppanyaki (Japanese): Meal where the food is cooked on the teppan in front of the diners and served when done.

Thousand-year egg: A duck egg that's been preserved in a mixture of lime, ash, tea and salt for one hundred days, making the flesh of the egg black and strong in flavour.

Tikuanyin (Cantonese; or Tikuanyum): Iron Buddha Tea. A dark, strong and flavourful black Chinese tea. Named because, according to legend, the first tea bush of this type was found behind a roadside altar containing an iron statue of Kwan Yin.

Tin Hau (Cantonese): Taoist deity, worshipped by seafarers.

Triad: Hong Kong organised-crime syndicate. Members of the syndicates are also called triads.

Tsim Sha Tsui: Main tourist and entertainment district on Kowloon side, next to the Harbour.

Tsing Ma Bridge: Large suspension bridge connecting Kowloon with Lantau Island, used to connect to the Airport Expressway.

Typhoon: A hurricane that occurs in Asia. Equivalent to a hurricane in the US or a cyclone in Australia.

Wan Chai: Commercial district on Hong Kong Island, between the offices and designer stores of Central and the shopping area of Causeway Bay. Contains office buildings and restaurants, and is famous for its nightclubs and girlie bars.

Wan sui (Putonghua): 'Ten thousand years'; traditional greeting for the Emperor, wishing him ten thousand times ten thousand years of life.

Wei? (Cantonese): 'Hello?' when answering the phone.

Wing chun: Southern style of Chinese kung fu. Made famous by Bruce Lee, this style is fast, close in ('short') and lethal. It's also a 'soft' style where the defender uses the attacker's weight and strength against him or her, rather than relying on brute force to hit hard.

Won ton (Cantonese): Chinese dumplings made mostly of pork with a dough wrapping and boiled in soup stock. Often called 'short soup' in the West.

Won ton mien (Cantonese): 'won ton noodles'; won ton boiled in stock with noodles added to the soup.

Wu shu (Putonghua): A general term to mean all martial arts.

Wudang (Putonghua): A rough translation could be 'true martial arts'. The name of the mountain in Hubei Province; also the name of the martial arts academy and the style of martial arts taught there. Xuan Wu was a Celestial 'sponsor' of the Ming Dynasty and the entire mountain complex of temples and monasteries was built by the government of the time in his honour.

Wudangshan (Putonghua): 'Shan' means 'mountain'; Wudang Mountain.

Xie xie (Putonghua): 'Thank you.'

Xuan Wu (Putonghua), pronounced [roughly] 'Shwan Wu': Means 'Dark Martial Arts'; the Black Turtle of the North, Mr Chen.

Yang: One of the two prime forces of the Universe in Taoist philosophy. Yang is the Light: masculine, bright, hot and hard.

Yang and yin: The two prime forces of the universe, when joined together form the One, the essence of everything. The symbol of yang and yin shows each essence containing a small part of the other.

Yellow Emperor: An ancient mythological figure, the Yellow Emperor is credited with founding civilisation and inventing clothing and agriculture.

Yin: One of the two prime forces of the Universe in Taoist philosophy. Yin is Darkness: feminine, dark, cold and soft.

Yuexia Loaren (Putonghua): 'Old Man Under the Moon'; a Taoist deity responsible for matchmaking.

Yum cha (Cantonese): Literally 'drink tea'. Most restaurants hold *yum cha* between breakfast and mid-afternoon. Tea is served, and waitresses wheel around trolleys containing varieties of dim sum.

Yuzhengong (Putonghua): 'Find the True Spirit'; the name of the palace complex on Wudang Mountain.

Zhu Que (Putonghua), pronounced [roughly] Joo Chway: The Red Phoenix of the South.

About the Mythology

In undertaking to write this story I had to do a tremendous amount of research on the nature of Taoism and the deities that appear in the book. I'm by no means an expert, but I thought the reader would like a small amount of further information on how Chinese beliefs fit together.

Chinese folk beliefs are a mixture of animism, Buddhism and Taoism, which all seem to fit seamlessly together with a liberal dose of Confucian philosophy. Buddhism and Taoism both teach that a person who transcends the barriers inherent in our physical world will attain Immortality. Therefore, many famous historical figures are considered to be still around today and can be called upon to intervene when times are tough.

Chinese believe that the spirits of their ancestors continue to guide and protect them, and therefore must be cared for and regularly visited. There are two festivals a year when families visit the graves of dead relatives to clean the graves and provide food and offerings of paper money and consumer goods. The paper offerings are burned and help the dead relatives live a life of ease in the Afterlife.

Buddhism, with its philosophy of reincarnation, is also prevalent, with the belief that a person who casts off worldly needs can attain a perfect state of alignment with the Universe, or Nirvana. People who have attained this state are called Buddhas (there is more than one) and may return to Earth in human or animal form to help those in need. Kwan Yin is one of the most famous of these Bodhisattvas and the image of a Buddha on a car dashboard or in a roadside altar is often that of Kwan Yin.

Taoism is a complex and fascinating spiritual philosophy. Through internal and external energy manipulation, alchemy and spiritual enlightenment, a person may achieve perfect alignment with the basic nature of the universe, the Tao. To talk about the Tao is to escape its meaning because it is wordless. The essence of the Universe is formless, without structure or striving, and nameless; therefore, to achieve the Tao many practitioners cast off all physical pursuits and pursue a simple ascetic life of solitude and meditation. Once having reached the divine state of Taoist Immortality, these Immortals ascend to Heaven to join the Heavenly Bureaucracy, with the Jade Emperor presiding over a vast court of fascinating mythological personalities.

Both Taoist and Buddhist deities exist side by side in Chinese mythology; in the legend of the Monkey King (*Journey to the West*), the Monkey creates havoc in Heaven and the Celestial Taoist Bureaucracy is unable to stop him. The Buddha himself intervenes and subdues the Monkey, giving him the task of travelling to India to collect Buddhist scriptures to return to the people of China.

All of the spirits of those who are Immortal — be they Buddhist icons who have achieved enlightenment, spirits who represent forces of nature, or historical figures who are regarded as having attained Immortality — are collectively called Shen. All Shen are believed to exist on a higher plane, but are able to come to Earth either through incarnation as an ordinary person or by taking the form of an ordinary person. The world is therefore believed by many to be full of Shen who live among us as humans.

The ideas of life after death and reincarnation are seamlessly joined together into the concept of Hell. After someone dies, their soul is judged and if it is found to be Worthy, it is escorted directly to the lowest level of Hell and released to Heaven to join the ranks of the Immortals. Those who are not Worthy are judged by the ten ranks of Courts in Hell. If found guilty, they are punished by demons for each set of crimes they have committed during their lifetime. When they have completed their punishment they are given a Soup of Forgetfulness and released back into the world to be reincarnated. Thus existence is an endless series of births, deaths and punishments, which continues until one is judged Worthy of Immortality.

The Four Winds (the White Tiger, Black Turtle, Red Phoenix and Blue Dragon) are slightly different from the Raised Immortals. They are more like signs of the zodiac than actual gods. They represent the four points of the compass and four of the five elements or essences of the universe: the Tiger is Metal; the Phoenix is Fire; the Dragon is Wood; and the Turtle is Water. The fifth essence of Stone or Earth is the Centre and represented by the Jade Emperor himself. The five essences are used throughout the practice of *fung shui* to provide symbolic references to both the compass points and the relevant essences; for example, turtle figurines will be placed on the northern side of a house to increase its water influence.

Xuan Wu himself is a fascinating and paradoxical god. He developed from the Black Turtle of the North, which sometime in its history was combined with a snake to become a combined serpent/turtle icon. The ancient Chinese believed that male turtles had no sex organs and that female turtles mated with snakes to produce eggs. Xuan Wu symbolises this union. Calling a man a 'turtle' also refers to this legend; it's calling him a cuckold whose wife is finding her satisfaction elsewhere. Chinese place a great deal of importance on family history and ancestry, so the idea that a female turtle mates with multiple males to produce clutches of eggs with mixed parentage is abhorrent. To call someone a 'turtle egg' is to call their parentage into question and is a very powerful insult.

Xuan Wu has changed over the centuries to become a human deity as well as the symbolic representation of the North; he has become the Dark Emperor Zhen Wu, the symbol of ultimate martial arts, the quintessential warrior. He was taken by the Ming Dynasty emperors as a patron and the Wudangshan Mountain complex was built in his honour. He is worshipped for his connection with water (thus the temple on Cheung Chau Island for Pak Tai) as well as his connection with martial arts.

One of the Chinese classics, *Journey to the North*, is the story of Xuan Wu and how he overcame two demons, a snake and a turtle, and through many incarnations in pursuit of the Tao attained Immortality. In another classic, the *Creation of the Gods*, he is incarnated as a great human general, and at the end of the battle is rewarded for his valour by being granted Immortality and the title of Celestial General.

The Chinese gods are more than static deities with fixed features. They are constantly evolving as stories are woven about them; they are considered to be alive and present in everyday affairs, involved in the running of the Universe and intervening whenever necessary. I hope that my novels will remain true to the storytelling tradition of this mythology, because I have nothing but the greatest respect for this wealth of wonderful beliefs, myths and legends.

Kylie Chan, Brisbane, 2006

Suggested Further Reading

Before I list some of the many sources that I waded through trying to find further information about the gods I used in my story, I should acknowledge one particularly useful resource that provided a great deal of my inspiration. It is a book called *Chinese Gods, the Unseen World of Spirits and Demons* by Keith Stevens. This huge glossy coffee-table type book is a meticulous cataloguing of the many gods the author encountered during his explorations through the temples of China and South East Asia. Although *Chinese Gods* is no longer in print, a more compact version called *Chinese Mythological Gods* by the same author is currently available from Oxford University Press and is listed in the suggested readings below.

Another source that merits particular mention is the Washington State University website on Chinese History and Philosophy:

www.wsu.edu:8080/~dee/CHPHIL/CHPHIL.HTM

These brilliant, tautly written and deeply researched pages are a treasure-trove for those interested in either the history of China or the different religions practised in this part of Asia.

Following is a (not exhaustive) list of some of the resources I referred to when creating this story.

General Reference

A Chinese-English Dictionary, Beijing Foreign
Language Institute, Beijing 1986.

The Art of War, A New Translation, Sun Tzu,
(translated by the Denma Translation Group),
5th ed, Shambhala Publications Inc, Boston 2001.

Lillian Too's Basic Feng Shui, Lillian Too, Konsep
Books, Kuala Lumpur, 1997.

The Right Word in Cantonese, Kwan Choi Wah,
The Commercial Press, Hong Kong, 1996.

The Mythology

*Chinese Gods, the Unseen World of Spirits and
Demons,* Keith Stevens, Collins & Brown, London,
1997 (out of print).

Chinese Mythological Gods, Keith G Stevens, 2nd ed,
Oxford University Press, London, 2001.

Dragon, compiled by Wang Congren, Hai Feng
Publishing Co, Hong Kong, 1996.

Discovering Kwan Yin, Sandy Boucher, 4th ed,
Beacon Press, Boston, 1999.

Phoenix, compiled by Wang Congren, Hai Feng
Publishing Co, Hong Kong, 1996.

White Tiger, compiled by Wang Congren, Hai Feng
Publishing Co, Hong Kong, 1996.

Xuan Wu, compiled by Wang Congren, Hai Feng
Publishing Co, Hong Kong, 1996.

Taoism

Daoism, A Short Introduction, James Miller, One
World Publications, Oxford, 2003.

Seven Taoist Masters, a Folk Novel of China,
(translated by Eva Wong), 11th ed, Shambhala
Publications Inc, Boston, 1990.

Tales of the Taoist Immortals, Eva Wong, Shambhala
  Publications Inc, Boston, 2001.
Tao Teh Ching, Lao Tzu (translated by John C. H. Wu),
  8th ed, Shambhala Publications Inc, Boston, 1990.
Taoism, Paul Wildish, Thorsons, London, 2000.
The Shambhala Guide to Taoism, Eva Wong, 5th ed,
  Shambhala Publications Inc, Boston, 1997.
The Spiritual Teachings of the Tao, Mark Forstater,
  Hodder & Stoughton, 2001.
The Way of Chuang Tzu, Thomas Merton, New
  Directions, New York, 1965.